Don't miss the first two adventures of the series!

Sierra Nevada Trail of Murder:

When Rachel Winters looked into the man's lifeless eyes, little did she know that her dog's discovery would change their lives forever.

On the run from a killer, Rachel, Bella, and Private Investigator Luke Reed must unravel a deep-rooted environmental conspiracy stretching from California to Colorado.

Sierra Nevada River of Lies:

A gruesome murder, a missing professor, and an attempted carjacking. Or was it?

An offer to help a friend leaves Rachel Winters in a killer's sights. As Luke Reed's family ties threaten them both, Rachel, Bella, and Luke become entangled in a dangerous scheme spanning across the northern Sierra Nevada.

Also by Jennifer Quashnick

Sierra Nevada Trail of Murder

Sierra Nevada River of Lies

Sierra Nevada Dangerous Developments

[signature] + Bella + Ari

JENNIFER QUASHNICK

South Lake Tahoe, CA
mountaingirlmysteries.com

ISBN: 978-0-9906750-5-1

Library of Congress Control Number: 2017915983
Copy Editor: Mary Cook
Cover Design and Interior: Kristen Schwartz
Cover Photo: Jennifer Quashnick

Orders, inquiries, and correspondence should be addressed to:

Mountaingirl Mysteries
PO Box 550145
South Lake Tahoe, CA 96155
mountaingirl@mountaingirlmysteries.com
mountaingirlmysteries.com

To powder days.

In every walk with nature one receives far more than he seeks.

—John Muir

Prologue

Rachel had barely completed just two turns with her skis in the thick snow when the first gunshot echoed through the trees. Cold wind slapped her cheeks and tears streaked her face. What had been a beautiful winter scene a moment before had now become a lethal obstacle course. To her right side, a familiar blur of black indicated her dog, Bella, had followed her when she launched her skis off the frozen cornice moments ago.

Speed was imperative. Rachel aimed her skis straight down the mountain, accelerating rapidly—a little too fast, even for her adrenaline-craving self. Out-of-focus images of intermittent pine and fir trees brushed past her on either side. Just twenty more feet and she'd be sheltered within dense tree cover. Her eyes darted back and forth, scanning the scene in front of her to assess the safest path.

"This way, girl!" she called out to Bella as she entered the thick patch of forest. Once shielded from view of the two men she was trying to escape, she slid into a parallel stop and whipped her head around, listening. Rachel's heartbeat was so loud she could barely hear anything else. She sighed with relief when she saw Bella come running up behind her.

Again, Rachel propelled her skis forward, regaining velocity as she weaved in and out of the evergreens. She suspected it wouldn't take long for the men to unload their skis from their stalled snowmobile and click into their bindings to follow her. And it was impossible to disguise her tracks in the snow. All she could do was zip down to safety as fast as possible.

Rachel wasn't sure how much time had passed. Thankfully she had just one more short line through the forest and they'd be minutes away from the safety of her pickup. Then, she heard it: a second gunshot. How close was the shooter? She dared a quick look behind her while gliding into another turn. No movement in sight. Rachel whipped her head back around to watch her path. The quick maneuver caused her body weight to shift, and her right ski tip slipped too deep under the surface of the snow. Her ski caught on something, and Rachel peered down as she reacted to correct her balance. At first, she thought she'd avoided crashing. But she looked up and her brain barely had time to register the brown solid bark structure in front of her. Instinct caused her to reach out her arms against the tree. They took the force of the first blow but didn't stop her body's forward movement. Rachel's face bounced off the tree, her neck wrenched backward, and her whole body collapsed sideways.

She was partially propped up against the sloped bowl of snow encircling the wide trunk. Rachel didn't move. How bad was it? She focused inward. Her head was intact. *Check*. Neck turned in each direction. It felt tight, but there was no shocking pain or loss of range of motion. *Check*. Arms still worked. *Check*. Then it hit her. An intense shockwave roared through her brain. She clenched her jaw and squeezed her eyes shut as something immense seemed to swim around in her skull for a minute. Or maybe less—it was hard to tell. As quick as it had attacked her, the pain began to wane. Soon, only a dull, distant ache remained. She was afraid to open her eyes. Would it hurt more?

Something wet swiped against her cheek, and she risked looking. Bella stood nearby. If a dog could be concerned, it would look just like Bella did right now. And that was probably exactly what was going on. Border collies were smart.

She smiled, ready to reach up to pet Bella's ears, when her mind seemed to suddenly recall why she'd been racing through the trees in the first place. Men were shooting at her. Real, actual bullets. The kind that could kill.

Rachel placed her poles on either side of her body and pushed up. She noticed an odd sensation in her left cheek and around her eye. *It's swelling up*, she thought. *Oh, girl, what did you just do?* There was no time to ponder that now. She peered down to make sure her skis weren't stuck under anything. As she bent over, several drops of red appeared in the snow. *Uh-oh.* That had to be coming from her face. She turned around, scanning the scene behind her. No movement. Yet they were out there, somewhere.

"Bella, run!" She kept her voice low enough so as to not to give away their position yet excited enough to prompt the canine into immediate action. Rachel poled and skated forward until she was once again coasting down the rest of the mountain. When she glided out of the dense thicket of trees, she let out the breath she hadn't realized she'd been holding. Parked less than ten feet in front of them was the glorious site of her blue dirt-covered Toyota Tacoma.

Chapter 1

Two Hours Earlier

It was one of those crisp, clear February days in the Sierra Nevada. Rachel couldn't help but look around and smile. The mountain sky was a deep, uninterrupted blue; the ridgelines of the rough-edged mountains between Carson Pass and Ebbetts Pass jutted out from sparkling blankets of white. The frosted crests of Freel and Job's Sister Peaks, which lined the southeastern rim of the Lake Tahoe Basin, shimmered in the sunlight. The top layer of snow was, at most, a few days old; thanks to cool temperatures and relatively mild breezes, fluffy pockets of white still clung to the evergreen trees. Albeit slightly compacted, snow conditions for backcountry skiing remained favorable. The forecast called for an intense storm to arrive later that night, but for the moment, the air was relatively warm. No smoke from fireplaces polluted the air out here. Despite the close location of State Route 88, the topography helped to shield the noise. Rachel knew that could change if snowmobiles arrived on the popular off-road route nearby. For now, she'd just enjoy the serenity. All she could hear were chirping birds, the soft echoes of intermittent wind gusts rustling the tops of the scattered pines, and a swooshing sound coming from the direction of Bella, who had proceeded to dig in the snow moments after jumping down from the passenger side of Rachel's pickup.

"I can't believe I'm getting paid to do this, Bella!" Laughing to herself, Rachel recalled telling her boyfriend, Luke, that she didn't talk to herself; she just kept Bella well-informed. While they spent time outdoors almost every day, often their treks were more of an extended lunch break and she'd have to come back home and finish her work on her computer. There were benefits to self-employment, and she was thankful that her job as an environmental scientist involved protecting the Lake Tahoe Basin. But contracts had waned lately, so when this opportunity came up to earn a few hundred dollars for a day taking pictures with a borrowed high-quality camera, Rachel couldn't say no. Today was the only bright sunny day expected this week, and the bluebird skies created the perfect backdrop for natural photos that would be used in advertisements by local resorts.

Excited, Rachel adjusted her pack, turned to face the mountain, and started the trek up. The snow was firm enough to provide good traction for her skis, wrapped with climbing skins for traction, yet soft enough that she expected to make easy turns on her way down. Nearby, Bella bounced around like a rabbit in the frosted wonderland, her tail wagging and her nose occasionally dipping underneath the powdery surface. The dog's ability to locate and retrieve buried pinecones and branches in deep snow never ceased to amaze Rachel.

After reaching the top of a small knoll, she stopped and turned. Red Lake Peak, a dominating volcanic mountaintop comprised of sunset-like colors when not covered in snow, rose above the southwestern edge of Hope Valley. Though located a mere fifteen minutes outside of the Lake Tahoe Basin, Hope Valley and her sisters, Faith and Charity Valleys, did not receive the attention, nor the visitation, that often overwhelmed Tahoe. Rachel snapped several shots, then turned and continued on a southern route along the small crest. Several more vistas presented themselves, and she clicked away as Bella altered between rolling and digging in the snow. With the camera safely attached around her neck, Rachel dropped down in elevation to find safe passage to another viewing spot she knew of farther along the ridge. When she came around a corner, she was startled by the unexpected image of two people standing in a tight embrace next to a bright orange and yellow snowmobile.

~

"It won't start!" Bob muttered as he stood up and kicked at the large machine following another failed attempt. The engine sputtered but would not turn over and engage.

"That's not going to fix it, man," Conway chuckled.

"I know. Just . . . well, it's not like we can call for help. You know damn well no one can see us together." Bob sighed, plopped down on the seat, and gazed into the distance, mostly as a means to avoid Conway's penetrating stare. He knew they were both worried. Each man had something to lose, although Bob felt his partner's situation was far less dire than his own. He didn't have a wife and two kids who would leave him if they found out his secret. Nor was he running for an elected position in public service. So much for taking his friend's new snowmobile for a "quick little spin to do something fun for a change."

"I agree. Look, we aren't exactly out in the middle of nowhere. Let's throw on our skis and get back to the parking lot. Or you can stay here and I'll ski down since, as you said, I'm faster." Conway paused. Bob knew he was waiting for a mock glare or some kind of response to his joke. Bob looked his way but wasn't about to laugh. This was serious. Conway sighed and then continued, annoyed. "You hang here, and I'll head down. It's not that far, shouldn't take me long to—"

"And then what?" Bob interrupted.

"I, well, I don't know. I'm trying to throw out some ideas here." Conway took a step toward him, reaching out. Bob paused, trying to reign in his irritation.

"I know you are." Bob craned his head upward and met the other man's gaze with his own. He took the outstretched hand and let himself be pulled off the snowmobile's hard seat into the other man's arms. Bob relaxed as they kissed. Who knew when their next opportunity to spend time together would be? Sneaking away was becoming more difficult; his political ambitions meant he was more often surrounded by other people.

"Oh gosh, I'm sorry," interrupted a female voice. Bob's gut sank as he swiftly withdrew from Conway's embrace and peered around them. A woman stood on a nearby ledge. He couldn't see her face under her gear; a black helmet, pink goggles, and loose winter clothing hid any distinguishing features, other than two long brown braids sticking out from underneath her helmet. Bob glanced behind her. Tracks in the snow indicated she'd been skiing downward at an angle, straight toward them. *How long has she been standing there?*

"What the hell?" he uttered without thinking.

"I . . . I didn't hear anyone," she stuttered. "My apologies. I'll be on my way," she stated, clearly uncomfortable. Bob watched her eyes move, her gaze sweeping to his side, pausing presumably on the snowmobile. *Perfect.* He knew they'd crossed the boundary into the wilderness area where they weren't supposed to ride. He simply hadn't cared. No one was patrolling the area; they had it to themselves. What would one track hurt? Or so he'd thought hours ago when they first started riding. His initial concern that she might report them for snowmobiling in a prohibited area immediately shifted when he noticed the camera dangling from a strap around her neck. *Son of a bitch!* She was following them on purpose. Taking pictures. For his opponent?

Conway's tone was friendly. "Our engine died—"

"Who hired you!" Bob interjected, stepping away from Conway and toward the woman. She inched backward, retracing her tracks, her eyes darting between him and his friend.

"Whoa. I'm just taking some nature pictures. That's all," she said, her poles dangling in the air from the straps looped around her raised hands. Bob took another step forward. Silence fell over the trio. A loud bark interrupted the quiet scene. A black dog came running up behind the woman. Its tail hung in midair, and its eyes fixed directly on him. The canine started to growl, baring its teeth as it took homage next to the woman.

"Relax." Conway's hand gently grabbed Bob's shoulder. Bob jerked away and took a step toward the photographer, sinking about half a foot in the snow. He didn't know who had found out about his "meeting" today, but someone obviously had and aimed to use pictures against him. That couldn't happen.

As he took another step closer to her, he reached into his inner coat pocket where he'd taken to stowing his small sidearm. He removed the weapon, his thick gloves making his grip clumsy. Though it slid from his right hand, he managed to catch it in his left palm. Silence followed. He stood for a moment, just staring at it. *What was he doing? Grab it and aim!* he thought. Bob's eyes shifted from the weapon to the female as he grasped the handle and lifted his arm. While her facial expression was difficult to see under her goggles, her body language was clear. She was going to bolt. As his finger slipped on to the trigger, the skier whipped sideways and pushed herself from the ledge. She yelled something and the mutt disappeared, sprinting down after her.

7

"Damn!" Bob turned around and reached for his skis. There was no way could he run after her given how much he was sinking in the snow.

"What are you doing?" Conway demanded.

"I can't let her give photos of us to whoever hired her!" he yelled as he tossed his skis onto the snow and lined up the bindings.

"I don't think she was—"

"Why else would someone be out here? Today? With a camera?" Bob couldn't believe how trusting Conway could be. He clicked into the bindings.

"The mountains. Like she said."

Bob barely heard the last few words. He was already in a mad dash, hammering his poles into the soft surface in order to propel himself in her direction.

"Aw, crap!" Bob heard Conway's resigned voice behind him. It wouldn't take him long to catch up. Bob continued to follow the two narrow grooves left by the woman. She was fast; however, following in the tracks she'd left behind would reduce any resistance that might otherwise slow him down. And that one advantage was all he needed.

Chapter 2

Rachel slashed the tire on the only other pickup in the small parking area with the folded knife she carried in her pack. She was confident the truck belonged to her pursuers because of the matching orange and yellow cargo trailer it towed. Rachel let out a breath as she hopped into her driver's seat. She briefly eyed the compact car parked several hundred feet away, threw her truck into gear, and pressed down on the accelerator, rushing up to the other vehicle. As she plunged the knife into the tread, she internally apologized to the owner in the event they were an innocent bystander. She just couldn't afford the risk. Her hands shook as she retrieved the sharp weapon and dove back into her truck. *Stay calm. Get out of here now. Your mind can break down later.* She noticed the left side of her face felt strange. An odd pressure had built up around her eye. Bella's standing form blocked her view of the main highway to her right. Her nose was tucked between the window and dash—a common position she took that always left "nose art" smudges along the windshield.

"Bella, sit," she instructed. The dog obeyed, her back now resting against the passenger seat.

Rachel glanced into her rearview mirror one more time before turning east on Highway 88. There he was. The man with the gun. When she'd first stumbled upon the couple, this man—who stood out by virtue of his bright red coat—had looked familiar to her. At least she remembered that sudden feeling of recognition. Yet now it was as if the details of his face had been washed from her mind. She couldn't visualize him at all and could make out no features from this distance.

The stranger stood where she'd just been parked, his gun raised in her direction. *Shit!* Suddenly his arm was yanked down. She saw him turn to look at the other man now standing behind him. The shooter peered back in her direction, but his arms remained at his side. It occurred to her he was probably trying to read her license plate. She only hoped that the snow packed on her bumper from the last winter storm was still there covering the numbers.

Once on the highway, her pickup swiftly gained speed. Her nerves settled, and she leaned her head against the back of the seat. Tingles and half-sensations indicated the left side of her face was probably swollen. Looking down, she saw that her coat was covered in blood. Rachel flipped down the sun visor and peered into the small mirror to assess the damage.

"Not good," she sighed as she looked at the elevated and broken skin around her cheek and eye socket. "I think I need to get to the ER. Let's hope CiCi can meet us there," she muttered as she tapped her phone to search for CiCi's number. Bella glanced her way before promptly inserting her snout back into the crevice below the windshield. The nearest emergency room was at Barton Hospital in South Lake Tahoe, about thirty minutes away.

Rachel noticed a queasy feeling taking root in her stomach. She'd never had a concussion before. She'd heard nausea was one side effect. She retrieved a handkerchief from her side pocket and placed it against her face, wincing. It was going to be a long, miserable drive.

~

"Why did you do that? She got away!" Bob yelled after Conway had slapped his arm down.

"Were you seriously going to shoot her?" Conway's stare was penetrating. Bob sagged.

"No, I would have aimed for a wheel or something," he lied. He hadn't been thinking; he'd been reacting. Bob wanted to steer the conversation away from his gun. "I couldn't fully make out her license plate; it was partially covered by snow," he complained. "Between the two digits and those bumper stickers on the camper shell, I bet we can track her down. She's got some stickers that are typical for Tahoe locals." Bob massaged his left hand and then mumbled, "I smacked my knuckle against something on the way down. Think I broke a finger." He carefully started to remove his glove.

"Look, man, I think you're overreacting. She looked genuinely surprised when—"

"This is why I'm the politician and you're the support staff. You have no concept of what really goes on in these campaigns. I ran on a family values platform, for God's sake! And then there's that damn prenup with Barbara." Bob swore as he examined his bones. Then he clicked out of his skis. Conway remained in place, silent. Never a good sign. Bob looked up. "Oh, hell. I'm sorry," he said. His lover peered at the ground, avoiding eye contact. "I didn't mean that the way it sounded." He reached out to gently touch Conway's arm. The man stepped back.

"I'm sorry to be so much trouble for you," Conway said bitterly before bending down and releasing his boots from his skis.

"Look, that's not what I meant—"

"No, I think it's exactly what you meant." Conway's voice was raw. Almost emotionless. He had never spoken this way before. "You know what, Bob? I'm done. Sure, neither of us wants this to get out, but the extremes you are willing to go to cover up our love . . . well, it makes me wonder about a lot of things. And look, I understood your need to arm yourself after getting attacked by that mugger last year, but you just took it way too far. Hell, you *shot* at that woman! You could have killed her. What the hell is wrong with you?" Conway picked up his skis and walked along the short road, calling out over his shoulder, "I'll stay and deal with the snowmobile myself. And don't worry, I'll pretend I was alone. If anyone notices extra tracks, I'll make something up. So go ahead and leave. You don't need to worry about me anymore." A beep rang out as Conway pressed the button to disarm the truck alarm.

Bob remained in place, stunned and speechless. Sure, they'd had some disagreements stemming from his temper once or twice. But nothing like this. So direct and unyielding. Bob watched as Conway opened the tailgate and tossed his backpack in the truck bed. As he lifted his skis, Bob's gaze caught on something below him.

"Son of a—"

"What now?" Conway yelled impatiently.

"She slashed your tire!" he spat, his fury growing as he thought about the woman. Oh yes, he'd find that bitch.

~

"Rachel, I can barely hear you," Luke articulated.

"Tree . . . Barton. Can you—" The call dropped. Luke knew Rachel had gone out to the Red Lake area near Carson Pass today to take some pictures, yet he hadn't been paying full attention when she'd told him the details last night. The Barton reference worried him; she likely meant the emergency room in South Lake Tahoe. This couldn't be good news. It drove him nuts that she went off and did stuff alone. It had caused a few tense moments at the beginning of their relationship. Who was he kidding? Over a year later, it still resulted in some heated debates, although she had learned how to shut the conversation down quickly and effectively—she simply turned the tables and asked him if he felt he should be allowed to go do things solo. It made her point. While not raging about it on a regular basis, Rachel was surely a feminist who believed in gender equality. While he supported the concept, he hadn't necessarily been able to accept all of it in practice very easily.

Luke knew the cell service where she'd been was spotty at best. She could usually get a text message sent off, but as a rule she refused to use the verbal app or to text while driving. Usually she'd pull her truck over and type; that she wasn't doing so now made him worry even more; she was clearly in a hurry to get to Barton. The blinking red light on Luke's office phone caught his attention, reminding him he'd put a client on hold to take her call. He pressed the button to reopen the line.

"Hey, man, sorry about that. It looks like an emergency has come up that I need to deal with. Can I call you back later?" His request was half-hearted; he was too anxious about Rachel's situation to concentrate. Nevertheless, this particular client also referred several other well-paying customers to Luke's private investigation business, so he didn't want to annoy the guy.

"Sure. Hope everything's okay. Give me a buzz when you can." The called ended. Luke jumped up from his seat and headed toward the front door of his small office. He realized he'd left his cell phone on his desk, turned back around, grabbed the device, and then burst out the door.

Chapter 3

Rachel saw the small bright red car as she pulled into the emergency room lot of Barton Hospital and knew CiCi had been waiting for her. That was fast. It was just like her friend to drop everything when someone needed help. Rachel carefully tucked her vehicle into one of Lake Tahoe's infamously narrow parking spaces. She unlatched her seat belt, trying hard to focus in light of the nauseous feeling that had developed on her drive over. CiCi's face suddenly appeared outside her window, startling her. The strawberry-colored highlights in her friend's otherwise dark brown hair shone brightly in the sunlight. *What an odd thing to notice*, she thought.

CiCi knocked on the window and called out, "Rachel?" Her eyes were searching. The sun's glare on the outside of her window probably made it tough to see inside. However, Rachel could easily look out and see the worry lines etched on her friend's freckled face.

"I'm okay. I think," Rachel replied as she opened the window. Bella, in her usual spot on the passenger seat, attempted to lean across her upon seeing "Auntie CiCi," as they often joked. Cici didn't care what anyone called her with one exception—she never answered to her given name, Lucia. "Bella, sit," Rachel instructed, lightly pushing the canine's sixty-five-pound frame back toward the passenger seat. CiCi stared at Rachel, her eyes wide.

"Holy crap, girl! What did you do?" CiCi exclaimed, her Spanish accent growing stronger with each word as she studied Rachel's face from a foot away. She reached out as if to touch Rachel's cheek, then pulled back, apparently realizing that would likely hurt.

"I, uh, hugged a tree too hard." Rachel attempted to smile, although it felt as if only one side of her mouth moved. CiCi briefly continued her close examination before responding.

"Taking your passion for the environment a bit too far, huh?" she smirked. "Seriously, you've got to tell me what happened after we get you checked in."

"I was hoping you could watch Bella for me this afternoon, or at least drop her by my house," Rachel mumbled when CiCi stepped back to allow the truck's door to open. Once she'd stood up, she handed CiCi her phone. Her friend slowly walked her toward the emergency room's entrance.

"Of course. I'll take her to my place once we get you settled. I don't have anywhere I have to be today. I've got some boxes in the passenger seat I didn't get the chance to unload before coming over here, so I'll need to take your truck. I'll leave you the keys for my car. Then again, maybe you shouldn't be driving for a while." CiCi had a tiny two-seater car; it was fun to drive around and great on gas mileage, but it didn't provide much room.

"Thanks." Rachel sighed with relief. "Wow, I feel so sick," she whispered as they walked. The scene felt mildly surreal, as though she was not fully present in her body.

"I'm guessing you have a concussion. Hopefully nothing else. You look like hell." CiCi chuckled. "And here," she said as she dug into her pocket. "Replace that handkerchief. You're a bloody mess."

"Please, don't hold back on my account." Rachel tried to laugh as she took the proffered cloth, but it came out more like a croak. She suddenly remembered her cell. "Oh, my phone." Rachel paused and patted her pockets.

"I got it." Her friend held it up. "You don't remember handing it to me in the parking lot?" Her smile had dissipated; now CiCi looked even more concerned.

"I guess not." Rachel wondered how bad this injury was going to be. The idea that she'd forgotten something that had happened moments ago scared her. She tried to recall the scene involving her race down the mountain, worried that she might forget that, too. Already the image of the armed man seemed to have diminished. She remembered seeing him and feeling a sense of familiarity, yet when she tried to pull up his image in her mind, it was blurry. The memory of how things played out still seemed intact, though it was oddly exhausting trying to replay the scene in her mind. "I think I should record what happened out there before I forget anymore. Can you do that?" The electronic doors squeaked as they slid open to the ER. "Sure. There's an app for that," CiCi joked. Both women had been slow to warm up to smartphones, not understanding the app craze until years after it began.

"Rachel?" Luke's voice startled them both. Rachel turned to see him running toward them. Worry lines creased his brow as his eyes examined her face. "What happened?"

"I, well, I was—" Rachel stuttered. Luke wrapped his arm around her while they walked to the registration area.

"I don't know either," CiCi replied, giving Rachel a moment to breathe. "Hopefully they'll give her some antinausea meds right away. Then maybe we can both find out," she suggested. Despite the obvious worry in her expression, her voice was steady and calm. It was just what Rachel needed.

Luke nodded and then wondered aloud, "Where's Bella?"

"Outside in her truck. I'll take her to my place so you can stay here with Rachel for however long she needs." CiCi reached into her pocket. "In fact, here are my keys. I don't think she'll be driving anywhere else today, but I told her I'd leave them anyway."

"I'm right here," Rachel announced from beside them, trying to keep her voice playful, although she feared she'd sounded too serious.

"Sorry," Luke and CiCi said in unison.

"I was . . . oh, nothing," she responded, attempting to smile. Once again, it didn't feel right. Her face must be a mess.

~

As Bob placed the tire iron and jack into his trunk, his thoughts fell back to the woman. He was upset about Conway's reaction and needed to figure out how to win him back; the man hadn't spoken one word as they'd both replaced their damaged wheels. First, though, he needed to make sure the woman didn't share those photos. That was the priority. Bob thought about the scene he'd encountered toward the bottom of the mountain. The woman's tracks led straight into a large juniper, which is why he'd stopped long enough to see the red drops in the otherwise white snow. The pattern and extent of blood suggested she had spent at least a few minutes there, maybe more. *Makes sense after skiing into a tree*, he thought. Too bad it hadn't incapacitated her long enough for him to catch up to her. He smiled. *At least it probably hurt the bitch.* She'd been racing down pretty fast.

In fact, her misfortune could work in his favor. What were the chances she'd drive straight to the ER at Barton? It was the closest option. It couldn't hurt to try to locate her there. Her pickup would likely be easy to spot. That would sure save him the trouble of trying to figure out who she was from the partial information he'd glimpsed.

The red numbers on his dashboard clock read 2:27 p.m. The time he lost changing his tire meant the woman probably had a good half-hour head start on him.

Forty minutes later, with his anxiety level off the charts, Bob's eyes scanned the rows of parked vehicles at the ER. If only locating her could be this easy. He drove along the main row, seeing no trucks that even remotely resembled the woman's. He continued to drive up and down other rows, searching the nonemergency parking areas for the main hospital as well. Nothing. He smacked the steering wheel in frustration, which sent more pain through his wounded finger. *Idiot!* Where could she have gone? Now he'd have to track her down the hard way, and fast, before those pictures could forever ruin the career he'd so carefully crafted. Or his marriage and the wealth that came with it. The question was, should he wait here to see if anyone resembling her came out, or should he go check other medical facilities in the region? Bob examined his aching finger. It was too bad he couldn't get it treated here and now, as people knew him in town. It was probably safest to go down to Carson City at this point.

"This day just keeps getting better and better," he muttered to himself. Then again, maybe he'd get lucky and find the woman at that facility.

~

Luke sat in the small chair next to the empty spot that had held a hospital gurney minutes before, his nerves on edge. He started tapping his fingertips on a small table, only to have a nearby nurse ask him to stop. The shaking had relocated to his foot, but he caught himself before he annoyed more staff. He was visibly screened from the view of other patients by wide light-blue curtains, but nothing blocked the noise from machines and other voices. He thought about how banged up Rachel looked; seeing her swollen face in the bright lights as she was wheeled away for imaging scans had seriously shaken him.

He had to focus on something else. Luke thought back to what Rachel had told him and CiCi as she waited to be examined. He'd done his best to remain calm. He was thankful CiCi had recorded Rachel's story on her smartphone.

At the thought of those men attacking her, Luke's fists curled, and his insides twisted. Anger infused his entire body. He'd been clenching his jaw so tight his neck muscles hurt. It had taken effort for him to refrain from verbalizing any opinions about her having gone out there solo. It wouldn't change the situation and would only serve to upset them both. He still didn't understand what was wrong about caring for her safety—even more so lately since she'd been taking some risky adventures, both with and without other people around. He didn't know how to help her with whatever was driving the need inside of her. And he had his own demons to deal with as well; it was best not to be a hypocrite.

After they'd rolled Rachel out of the room for tests, CiCi departed, leaving Luke to bide his time in an uncomfortable chair until she returned. He debated on whether or not to contact his buddy Ted, a detective with the South Lake Tahoe Police Department, where Luke himself used to work, to enlist his help in finding the two snowmobilers. Chances were good that both the men, and their machine, were long gone by now. And while Ted had proven several times over that he could be trusted, Rachel still held an aversion to dealing with most cops, stemming from several bad experiences years ago. Of course, having been in danger last year after one of Ted's fellow officers had fed insider information to a killer had not helped improve her reception toward law enforcement.

Luke knew Ted couldn't follow up on his own. He'd need to follow the rules, to file reports that other officers would be privy to. Luke decided not to contact his friend—for now. For the moment, it was best to wait until after the tests were completed and they knew the extent of her injuries. Plus, he should leave it to her to decide how she wanted to proceed with reporting it. Unfortunately, in spite of having captured a whole slew of photos at the time, Rachel was confident that all of them were focused on the natural scenery. She didn't think she'd taken any that could have potentially captured the two men or their snowmobile. Yet Rachel also reminded him she'd forgotten a few things already, including details about what the men looked like, so Luke promised to review the camera's files in case anything helpful could be located. Unfortunately, the device she'd been using was in her pickup, which CiCi had already driven away. His mental musings were broken when the curtain moved and Rachel's bed was rolled back into the small space.

"We'll let you know when the radiologist has reviewed your scans," a nurse said to Rachel. The nurse then turned and closed the flap again.

"How did it go?" Luke asked.

"Ugh," Rachel said. One side of her mouth smiled, and the other side attempted but failed. "It's hard to concentrate. This is really freaking me out." The anxious expression on her face wasn't something he'd seen a lot; it broke his heart knowing she was so worried. He tried to stay optimistic for her as he reached for her hand.

"Seven to ten days. That's what I hear is standard for concussion recovery. You'll need to take it very easy, though," Luke said. Rachel sighed and squeezed his palm before laying back into the small pillow. "And don't forget, you're no spring chicken anymore," he teased.

"Thirty-two isn't that old. And who are you to talk? You're older."

"Right, but I didn't just slam my face into a big pine tree."

"As if it was on purpose."

Luke chuckled as he massaged her hand. Murmurs from patients and loved ones in nearby beds filled the silence between them. Rachel shifted so she lay on her side, facing him. "Go figure! Tomorrow's supposed to be one of the best powder days yet this year," she uttered in frustration. Now *that* was a typical Rachel comment, which made him feel much better. While Luke liked to snowboard, he didn't prioritize it as much as Rachel. She would bend her work schedule as much as possible to go skiing on days with fresh snow.

"Yes, you may need to sit this one out, Mountaingirl," he sympathized, using the nickname he'd assigned her when they first met.

~

Ted closed the large garage door after placing his cross-country skis inside what was more of a storage area than a garage, then rushed around his yard to his front door. Someday he would remodel this house and connect it directly to the garage. This detached stuff was the pits, especially in the winter. But he couldn't deal with the paperwork it would involve to get it permitted. Nor could he afford the expensive attorneys and consultants who knew how to navigate local regulations.

Light snowflakes had started falling on his drive home from cross-country skiing on Angora Ridge. He had been one of many locals out enjoying the views of Lake Tahoe while gliding along the packed snow surface of the old forest service road closed to vehicles for the winter. A chime alerted him to new messages on his cell. Spotty signals around the area often meant he'd get numerous messages all at once when he was in service range again. Ted used the speaker to play them as he peeled off his snow gear.

The first was from Madeline. *Uh-oh.* That was a fun "no-strings-attached" weekend gone bad; she apparently hadn't meant it when she suggested the original casual arrangement. After constantly calling and texting him, he'd politely asked her to leave him alone. It clearly wasn't working. As another rant about his "insensitivity" began, he pressed the delete option.

Ted's thoughts returned to the present as he listened to the second message. Luke's voice rambled. It wasn't like the man to talk so much. After he'd heard the entire recording, Ted understood why. He collapsed on his sofa and let out a long breath. So, Rachel was tangled up in another dangerous situation. *Shocker.* Despite being his good friend—and deep down Ted knew they certainly hadn't invited the people who'd harmed them over the past year and a half to do so—it was still frustrating. Those two attracted danger like yellow jackets to raw meat at a late August barbecue. He glanced at his watch. 5:56 p.m. Looks like his original plan to relax and watch a movie, a rare opportunity, was out the door. Luke's call, time-stamped roughly an hour ago, indicated they were leaving the ER and going back to Rachel's house, so Ted dialed Rachel's home line. Luke answered with a short "Hey."

"Dude," Ted greeted. "So, Rachel's dodging bullets again?"

"It's her new favorite pastime," Luke replied. Ted could imagine Rachel in the background, giving Luke one of her famous stares at this very moment. "Anyhow, Ted, I'm sorry to bother you. She's doing well enough, all things considered. No fractures, nothing's broken. Except her brain, apparently," he laughed. "Her eyes are closed. I think she's asleep now—"

"I heard that," chimed a female voice in the background.

"I stand corrected." Luke's voice grew distant as if the phone had slipped away.

"Guys, I'm still on the line," Ted cut in.

"Oh, sorry," Luke's voice blared as if a volume switch had suddenly been turned back up. "Hey, any chance you can come over here?" Luke asked.

Ted yawned and eyed his TV longingly. He sure saw that one coming.

Chapter 4

Twenty Years Earlier

Jason couldn't breathe. He tried to inhale, to suck in the oxygen his lungs desperately craved. Something else filled his airway. It was dry. Bitter. It coated the inside of his mouth. As he strained for precious air, his mind relived the last time he'd felt this scared—when he was trapped by an avalanche last winter. Snow everywhere. His body instinctively trying to draw breath while his mind acknowledged there was none to find.

Stay calm. Think. Although proper equipment and a good buddy system had saved him from the potential snow grave, he'd survived long enough to be rescued by keeping his wits about him. Remaining focused. Where was he now? How had he gotten here?

Jason coughed again, or rather choked. The jerking motion shifted whatever was coating his face. There it was. Renewed access to air. That's when he realized what was covering him. Dirt. He reached up to brush the grit from his skin. Oddly enough, his arm didn't move. In fact, he couldn't even feel it. Or his legs, for that matter.

This is a dream. That's it. I'll wake up and find Timber sleeping on my face again. Damn cat.

Thud. A distant sound interrupted his racing thoughts.

What was that? He wanted to open his eyes, yet deep down he knew it would do him no good. His eyes, nose, mouth—everything was covered. Something buzzed, and he recognized the hum of his pager. Strange—it was in his pocket, but he couldn't feel the vibration.

Thump. That noise was coming from somewhere above him. His brain struggled to piece together the images flashing through his mind, like a movie in fast-forward. Then, it all clicked into place. The memory felt old, faded, yet somehow he knew it had happened just minutes before.

Jason had been standing in the spot as instructed by the anonymous letter tucked under his windshield wiper—though he was pretty sure he knew who'd written it. She could try writing in all caps to throw him off; however, she'd already given herself away weeks ago. It had been obvious to him that she wanted to mess around with him without her boyfriend finding out. Apparently, she'd finally made a move and set up a special meeting, miles off the main highway where no one would be on a weeknight. He had to admire her style. Although, where was she? Rain pounded from the summertime thunderstorms gripping the night sky.

"Jason!" The voice scolded from somewhere behind him. It wasn't her; it was a man's voice. Instant pain blossomed across his back for just a split second. It was like a jolt of electricity had shot through him and then diminished as fast as it had started. He collapsed on the wet ground, his face angled to the side. He felt another blow, this time closer to his head. Was that crunching sound his neck?

It was cold. The wet blanket of pine needles cradled his cheek. There was nothing else. No longer did that blister from last Sunday's running spree remind him he needed a new pair of jogging shoes. The dull ache he'd felt from slamming his rib cage against the side of the rink at Ed's Roller Skate the other night had disappeared. There was no sensation of anything other than the shocking pain that flashed through his skull after the second assault.

"I'm glad you accepted my invitation," his attacker mocked.

So here Jason now lay, crippled by some madman. Jason recognized the voice, but he couldn't quite place it.

"Help me," begged a soft, distant voice. It took a second for Jason to realize it was his own. Or maybe it was just in his head. No response came.

"Help!" Jason whispered. He heard the crunch of footprints growing nearer from somewhere above him.

His body struggled to draw in the sweet cool night's air. Yet with each attempt, he sucked in more dirt. It lined his lips, his tongue, his throat. Jason couldn't move. He must be paralyzed. Like what happened

22

earlier in the year to the guy who played Superman. *Christopher Reeve. That was his name.*

Thwack.

One last synapse in his brain made the final connection. A shovel. He was being buried alive. In his last moment of awareness, he suddenly knew who was doing this to him. And why.

Chapter 5

"Rachel." The voice drifted from somewhere in the distance. At first, she couldn't tell who it was. It was like someone was speaking through a pillow. She opened her eyes to see shades of white and gray. Everything was bright. She strained to look around, but the glare was too much.

"Guess what? TRPA DENIED a massive corporate project!"

The Tahoe Regional Planning Agency? What? Something dripped on her cheek. It felt odd. Slimy.

"Good girl, Bella." That was Luke's voice. Awareness slowly returned. The moist feeling must have been from Bella's tongue. Rachel groggily opened her eyes and peered out into her living room. She had fallen asleep on her sofa. The room was dimly lit. Two sets of eyes—one human, one canine—stared at her from a foot away. Neither pair blinked. An image of Bugs Bunny's wide, sometimes screen-encompassing eyes from old childhood cartoons flashed through her brain. It was impossible not to laugh. Luke stared at her with a confused look on his face.

"What's so funny?"

"Your look, it's . . . nothing," she chuckled, then propped herself up on a pillow against the armrest. "Wow, I just had the weirdest dream." Rachel watched Bella prance over to her toy bin, retrieve one of her favorite chews, and circle twice before plopping down on her bed.

"Oh really?" Luke smiled, clearly hoping for something naughty.

"Not like that!" She play-punched his shoulder. "I was in this white room or something and—wait, did you say something about TRPA?"

She wondered why Luke would be talking about the government agency that regulated development in the Tahoe Basin. "I was joking. You weren't waking up, so I thought I'd say something outrageous; see if it got your attention." She laughed. "Ha, good one. They sure haven't denied a large project in a while." She smirked. "By the way, I asked the doc about whether it's true that I shouldn't go to sleep for a long time; he wasn't concerned."

"He mentioned that to me, too, so I didn't worry when you nodded off for a while." Luke grasped her hand and laid himself down next to her, sliding his warm body up close and tucking his legs against hers. He barely fit in the remaining space on her couch. Luke was always so warm to the touch. How much was a result of his body temperature versus his sexy, irresistible crooked smile, she didn't know. As he lightly massaged his fingertips up and down her arm, he said, "So, tell me about this dream."

"It's already fading. But I remember it was so bright, like trying to stare at the sun without glasses or something." She looked up at the front windows. Purple and pink shades of dusk colored the sky in the distance. "What time is it?"

"I'm guesstimating around six. I'm too comfy right now to want to move to check," he said as he clasped her hand, raised her fingers to his lips, and gently kissed her knuckles. Rachel smiled. She tried to simply enjoy the moment; however, as often happened, she couldn't shut off her brain, and it started to recount the afternoon. The accident happened hours ago. After a CT scan and other tests to confirm there were no fractures or bleeding in her brain, the emergency room doctor had sent her home. She vaguely recalled resting on the sofa, an ice pack positioned on her bruised face, while Luke went out back to retrieve firewood. He must have put the cool item back in the freezer at some point.

"Please, don't move on my account." She reached up and ran her fingertips through his tousled hair.

"Good, because I'm perfectly content right here." He leaned his head against her chin.

Rachel shifted so she could straighten out her neck. Luke scooted toward her to avoid falling off the couch. She saw him wince.

"Oh, sorry. How's your shoulder?"

"It's okay. I can move it a little better," he responded, reaching up with his free hand to rub the joint.

"PT still helping?" Rachel had encouraged him to seek physical therapy when his shoulder continued to ache months after a previous injury. At first he was stubborn, but eventually he gave it a try.

"Yep," he responded. She waited for him to elaborate, but he didn't. After a few moments of silence, Rachel positioned her head to look him in the eye. He met her gaze and held it as he released her hand to caress the side of her face. "That black eye makes you look like a badass," he said, tucking a loose strand of hair behind her ear.

"You think so, huh?" she snickered.

"Yep. It's kind of hot." He grinned as he brought his lips to hers. Heat filled her from the contact. He kissed her softly, at first. Then, his hunger grew. His body molded tight to hers. Her need for him intensified, and she craved the feel of his bare skin.

"We shouldn't do this," he whispered in her ear. The heat from his breath sent shivers down her spine. "I don't want to mess up your recovery."

Rachel couldn't stop herself. She wanted him. *Now*. She began to tug his T-shirt out of his waistband, her heart rate gaining speed as she reached underneath to massage his chest. And what a wonderful, sculpted chest it was. "I don't care," she muttered.

"Are you sure?"

"They didn't say I couldn't," she replied coyly.

"All right. I sure won't turn you down, but let's relocate. I want more room to lavish you with kisses." He disentangled from her and rolled back. A little too quickly, Rachel mused as she watched with humor while his entire form fell off the couch. There was a loud thud. "Ouch. Not the sexiest maneuver there, I must admit." He smiled, got on his feet, and reached toward her with his hand.

"I thought it was cute," Rachel said as she sat up, clasped his fingers, and let him pull her up. All at once, as if a switch was suddenly turned on, Rachel grew light-headed; her body weakened. She had to sit back down.

"Rachel? You okay?" Luke asked.

"Damn. I think you're right. We shouldn't do this yet." She sighed.

Luke sat down next to her, his hand resting on her knee. "I won't pretend I'm not disappointed, but I totally understand. Rain check?"

"Of course. And you aren't the only one who's bummed, Cowboy," she teased, using the nickname she'd given him when they first met. It hadn't been that he was a cowboy—far from it—yet he was hot, rugged, and looked good in jeans. In her mind, it fit. Rachel raised her arm and touched her fingers to his lips. Before she could lean in for another kiss, nausea rolled through her. She sat back, cursing.

"What's wrong?"

"I'm starting to feel queasy again." Rachel was seriously annoyed.

"Wow, when a guy's proposition makes a woman ill, I have to say that's a little hard on the ego." He mocked offense.

"Good one," she acknowledged. "Trust me, the thought of making love to you makes me feel something inside—all good things." Luke smiled with that cute, boyish grin that could melt her insides, which increased her irritation at having to rest and avoid a certain activity that she really, really wanted to do right now.

"I left your meds in the car; they prescribed something for nausea." He squeezed her leg and stood up. "I'll be right back." At his movement, Bella trotted over, her tail wagging. Luke bent over and massaged the pup's head before walking toward the front door. "By the way, I called Ted. He'll be over later tonight. He'll call when he's on the way."

"Thanks. I feel bad going to him first, but I'm taking your advice on this." Luke had suggested they run the situation by Ted and see what he felt she should do next.

"I like the sound of that. You should do it more often," Luke stated as he pulled the door open and walked out. Rachel laughed.

~

Luke stared at the prescription bottle, slowly rolling it back and forth in his hand. He sat in his front seat after retrieving the small bag from the console. Guilt ate away at him. They'd prescribed two items for Rachel: Zofran to manage the nausea and hydrocodone for pain. When she'd started to nod off in the ER, the nurse had handed him the two prescriptions directly. He'd known Rachel wouldn't take the pain meds; she'd adamantly refused to do so after someone had overdosed her through an IV last year. Yet Luke had allowed the pharmacy to fill it anyway.

So why did he do it? Would he really be so low as to fill it for his own use? *No, he couldn't.* He'd leave them with her. That was a line he wouldn't cross. He already felt like an asshole for the secret he had been keeping from her. And the fact was she'd never had a concussion; well, neither had he. Who knew how bad the headaches could get? She also had a nasty whiplash to boot. So she may change her stance if things got bad enough.

What kept gnawing at him was that he'd even considered taking the drugs at all. He'd fully intended to come clean with Rachel a long time ago about his escalating use of the pain pills after his shoulder pain worsened—God, was that really over a year ago now?—when fate had intervened. The night he finally got up the nerve to confess last spring, she received a call that her older brother had been involved in a car accident with multiple injuries; she'd immediately packed and driven over a thousand miles to help him recover. After that, there never seemed to be a good time.

However, at some point, Luke started wondering what the purpose of telling her would be. His doctor suggested it could be a long road before he healed and continued to write prescriptions. That meant it was medically necessary, right? Of course, he hadn't agreed when his physician reduced the dose, so he found a temporary second source. Only for a little while. At some point his shoulder would feel better, and then he'd have to deal with what was likely to be an unpleasant withdrawal period, from what he'd heard. But why go through all that now when he still needed them anyway? He continued to have pain when the dose started to wear off. That was valid, right? And really, when he thought about it, they'd merely been dating for about a year and a half. Surely she hadn't told him every single detail of her daily routine, especially someone as independent as Rachel. People spent years together and still didn't know everything about each other. He'd confess. Eventually.

Luke returned the small amber container to the paper bag and set it aside. He then reached for the package hidden under his passenger seat. He popped it open, tossed a pain pill into his mouth, and washed it down with the warm bottle of water left in his drink holder. Luke crawled out of the seat and slammed the door behind him. Damn it, he thought. This situation was tearing him up inside. He needed to fix it. To stop finding justifications to put it off.

"You're pathetic," he mumbled to himself. Luke still wondered how this had happened. When had he started taking them every day? Needing them? He'd heard about people getting addicted to these pills, but he never imagined it would happen to him. Wow, he hadn't really thought of it that way until now. *Addicted.* Either way, now was not the time to burden Rachel with his problems. It could wait until she had recovered from her concussion. Then he'd tell her.

~

Bob sat in front of his computer, recalling the image of the female skier who'd escaped him earlier. His initial assumption was the woman must be a private investigator hired to take pictures of him with Conway. He'd searched photographs of all of the PIs throughout the Tahoe area; none resembled her. Perhaps he needed to go beyond the basin; however, usually the particular Meyers sticker he'd recognized on her truck was only affixed by local residents.

"Okay, lady. Maybe you're just a hired photographer then," he speculated out loud. His younger sister had delved into the visual arts, so he'd seen a lot of quality equipment over the years. The camera slung around the woman's neck was not a cheap one. Slowly pecking at the keyboard thanks to his bandaged-up broken finger—another problem he blamed the woman for—Bob performed a comprehensive search of professional photographers. Again, no matches.

"Crap!" he complained. He had way too much to lose to let those pictures get out. He needed to find her and shut her up, quickly. *Okay, Bob, concentrate!*

Finally, a new thought presented itself. Perhaps, like his sister, she took pictures as a cash job on the side or through acquaintances. That got him thinking; his sister had come by many opportunities through advertising on social media. Maybe the woman did the same thing. Bob set about establishing several dummy accounts on Facebook and other sites, posing as a potential client. It was a long shot, but there was no harm in trying. He vowed to do everything he could before calling in the only person he could think of who could help. Because that was one favor he didn't want to owe.

Chapter 6

A few days had passed since her concussion, and Rachel was starting to feel like she could think again. At least in short spurts. The last few days were a blur of moving between her bed and the couch; the only exception had been when she'd followed Ted's advice to file a police report. Otherwise, her most intense activities had been slow, easy walks with Bella. The fresh air felt good. Otherwise, when she tried to lie still and do nothing—as was recommended after a concussion—her mind raced with everything she needed to be working on. Figuring that the brain activity from stressing over what she couldn't do was not helping her heal, she took to listening to audiobooks throughout the day. Good fictional mysteries that didn't require much concentration.

Luke started checking in on her several times each day, but she'd discouraged long visits. It taxed her to hold a conversation. Being alert, or feeling like she had to respond immediately, was exhausting. In fact, she'd been ducking phone contact when she could, letting calls from a variety of people go to voice mail. Plus, Luke was working hard to try to track down the snowmobilers. Granted his arms wrapped around her would feel nice. But Luke lying around with her listening to audiobooks all day wasn't going to help her brain mend any faster.

Rachel relaxed, sank deeper into her sofa, and tucked her feet under Bella's warm body. The dog stirred, looked up her way, and then dropped her head back down. Rachel sensed the pup was as bored as she was. The phone rang and she looked at the display. It was a call she should definitely answer since her friend was working hard to help out Rachel following her accident.

"Kris, hey, girl. What's up?" she asked, attempting to sound more cheerful than she felt.

"Checking in on my pain-in-the-ass friend," Kris laughed.

"Ha ha. You know you miss me."

"Sure, just tell yourself whatever makes you feel better."

Rachel welcomed her friend's sarcasm. She also appreciated Kris's quick wit; however, over the last few days it had been difficult for her bruised brain to follow.

"Any news?" Kris continued.

Silence filled the line as Rachel took a few moments to concentrate on what the question was in reference to—likely the snowmobilers. "No, and I'm not holding out much hope." She sighed, then tried to perk up her voice and change the subject to something positive. "Well, which color did you decide on?" Rachel queried.

While Kris was a few years her senior, no one would ever know by looking at her. Or by spending time around her. The girl had a youthful enthusiasm that made it difficult for anyone not to like her on the spot. In fact, she could get away with direct, and sometimes intense, commentary without people getting too upset or taking offense, which came in handy in their shared line of work as environmental "consultants-slash-advocates." Kris also had a thing about her hair; she loved to switch up the colors of small bunches of streaks in the otherwise solid black strands. Rachel had always thought it would be fun to try, though it would probably look utterly ridiculous on her. Kris pulled it off with style.

"Had to go with the blue streaks this time," Kris responded. Rachel imagined various shades of blue mixed in with her friend's dark hair.

"Light or dark?"

"Light. Makes me think of our clear skies around here."

"I like it." Rachel glanced out her window. It was overcast and the clouds were depressing. *Focus on the conversation*, she reminded herself. "Hey, how did the meeting in Truckee go?"

Kris had been able to attend a Placer County planning commission hearing to ask about the environmental impacts of a large housing project being proposed just north of the Tahoe Basin. Rachel still couldn't believe that a new subdivision was even being considered there. It was an open forest. All the local land-use plans were supposedly focused on building new structures only in places that already had infrastructure. Like roads and utility lines. In this case, current zoning laws limited the construction of new homes to places lower on the mountainside. In fact, the county would have to amend its own regulations to be able to approve what the developer wanted. The new gated residential subdivision, termed "Tahoe-Truckee Pines," would ruin views from Lake Tahoe that were supposed to be protected by law. And there would be even more traffic on California State Route 267, a highway that already experienced gridlock during weekends and summers.

"The usual. A whole bunch of people showed up; most were against it. About sixty people spoke during public comment, including yours truly. They ignored us." Kris sighed, annoyed.

"Sorry I wasn't there to share the pain."

"Yeah, I'm not sure what's worse—suffering a concussion or having to sit through their deliberations?" Kris joked. Listening to certain politicians wax poetic about how great this massive subdivision would be drove them both nuts. Of course, most of the public's representatives who would vote on it didn't live in the area. "Anyhow," Kris continued, "I started looking through some new info I've recently obtained and found something kind of weird. I e-mailed Anthony to ask about it. I'll let you know if anything comes of it."

"That poor guy. Sure glad I don't work for the county. He gets chewed out by all sides for just doing his job. He's certainly not the one making the big decisions. Adding to that, he's been there, what, all of two months? Poor guy has to be hating life right now." Rachel felt sympathy for the new environmental planner assigned to deal with the massive application for the controversial project. It was a big role to step into.

"Still think there's more to Sharon's quick departure than anyone is saying?" Kris asked. They had both been surprised when the last employee had vacated the position after almost ten years on her job; even more suspicious was the lack of any notice.

"Have you talked to Thomas yet?" Rachel asked. It had been a surprise to learn that Thomas Palinski, a local real estate agent now planning to run for election to the Truckee Town Council, was adamantly opposed to the project. Most of his past opinions aligned with the desires of the large corporations looking to exploit the area for profit.

"Not yet. He's just so darn awkward to talk to. Still, you're right; I'd better check in. He'll probably want another face-to-face meeting. It's a sacrifice, but he does have influence, and we need all the help we can get on this," Kris sighed.

"Let me know if you set one up. I can come along if you'd like," Rachel offered, although it was the last thing she wanted to do. A sudden craving for chocolate hit her, and she walked into her kitchen, putting the phone on speaker and raiding her sweets drawer as Kris continued.

"Thanks, but you're still not feeling well. And frankly, girl, you aren't exactly on your game yet. I feel like we've been having horrible cell service these last few days because there's always a delay before you speak! But you've been on your landline," she teased. "Seriously, don't push it, or you'll be out of commission that much longer."

"But—"

"No buts. Frankly, I don't want to deal with your grouchy personality right now anyway."

Rachel knew there was some truth to the statement. Her frustration since the accident hadn't made her the best company to be around. Her frazzled mood wasn't solely an aftereffect of the concussion, but it also resulted from her irritation with failing to identify the men who attacked her. Several officers and Luke, himself an ex-cop, had spent the last few days trying to locate any clues about the riders' identities to no avail. At best, Rachel hoped the men realized she hadn't taken any pictures of them and would simply leave her alone. She loved adventure; hell, she craved it. Too much, at times. Though not the kind that involved being shot at.

"Okay, you're probably right," she admitted as she sifted through various snack bags in search of white chocolate.

"Girl, I'm always right."

"I'm going to stay away from that one," Rachel chuckled. "How soon would you be able to meet with him?"

"I'll check with his assistant; I think he usually comes to South Shore the latter half of the week. That said, I'll suggest this Thursday afternoon or Friday morning."

"All right. Let me know how it goes and if I can help." Rachel closed the drawer, more pissed off than she should be about being out of her favorite chocolate.

"Okay. Oh, by the way, you wanted me to remind you to send those pictures off from the other day," Kris added.

"Thanks, girl. By some miracle, I remembered to e-mail them out yesterday. Actually, to be honest, remembered isn't quite the word. I wrote a note on a bright orange pad and stuck it on my coffeemaker so I couldn't forget. I swear I should buy stock in Post-its."

Someone knocked on her front door, startling Rachel so much that her entire body jumped. Bella raised her head before dashing off the couch and rushing toward the source. Her tail wagged ferociously as she stared forward, anxious to greet the new visitor.

"What was that?" Kris asked.

"Someone's at the door," Rachel whispered.

"Got your gun?"

"Are you kidding? That's the first thing that comes to mind for you?" Rachel queried as she paced across the room.

"Um, Rachel, have you met *you*? You attract danger like ski bums to the slopes on powder days."

"Cute," she stated blandly as she rose on her toes to peer above the curtains of her front window. "Whoa."

"Who is it? Everything okay?" Kris sounded concerned.

"It's Derek." Rachel fell back on her heels. She felt surprised, happy, and annoyed at the same time. It was just like her brother to drop by unannounced.

"The infamous older sibling has shown himself? I'll have to come meet this boy sometime," Kris chuckled. "You two have fun catching up, and I'll be in touch. Remember—don't overthink. You have the perfect excuse to act like a complete idiot right now. Enjoy it."

The call ended. Rachel laughed under her breath before turning the door handle. She'd barely managed a hello before Bella rushed at Derek, rubbed against his legs, lowered her front paws, and stuck her butt end up to encourage rubs—one of her signature moves.

"Sis, hey," he said as if showing up on her doorstep after six months of being across the globe and out of touch was nothing unusual. He looked down. "Hello, Miss Bella."

Rachel stared up at her brother. Between the extra half foot of height and the two years of age he had on her, he laid claim to a variety of battles during their childhood. And their adulthood too, she thought. Rachel noticed his dark brown hair had grown a little longer since she'd last seen him. It now fell loosely around his head in a retro seventies style. She was well aware that the combination of his soft, silky hair, intense blue eyes, and boyish grin had caught the eyes of many females over the years. Derek had never had any trouble getting women; he just didn't seem interested in keeping them once he had them. A true modern-day bachelor, she thought. The kind she warned her friends away from.

"D-Derek . . . ," she stuttered. "What are you doing here?"

"Mom told me about your accident, so I thought I'd come check up on ya." He leaned in to hug her. She didn't respond right away, her mind still grappling with his sudden appearance. He stepped back, withdrawing his arms and staring at her. "You okay? I heard you hit your head pretty hard, although I hadn't heard you'd lost your ability to communicate." He raised an eyebrow and grinned, then reached toward her cheek. "Dang, that's quite a shiner you have there." Without touching it, he let his hand drop.

"I'm fine. Didn't expect you, that's all," she responded as she stepped back. "Come on in." Derek leaned over to rub Bella again. Her tail brushed back and forth across the floor. He turned around, gripped a large suitcase that had been propped against the side of the house, stepped inside, and shut the door behind him.

Rachel eyed the luggage. "What's that?"

"What do you think it is? You really did smack yourself a good one, didn't you?"

"I'm aware it's a suitcase; the question is *why* do you have it?" She didn't move. Yep, it was exactly like her brother to impose on her without any warning at the worst possible time. She needed a quiet, empty, relaxing house. She did not need a sarcastic, cocky, loudmouthed older brother demanding her attention throughout the day. Rachel may have given in to Derek in the past, but not this time.

"I thought I'd stick around for a few days, help you out." Derek walked past her, pretending he didn't notice her annoyance as he looked around the house. "I was hoping to meet the famous Luke. Where is he?"

~

Numerous men and women had responded to Bob's Facebook post seeking out photographers, yet his friend's search of DMV records revealed none of them drove a blue Tacoma. Sure, the woman could have been driving someone else's vehicle, but he sensed it was hers.

Besides that, the dog hadn't hesitated to jump into the passenger seat—a sign it was clearly used to doing so. Also, none of the local female photography candidates on social media had brown hair that long. Sure, she could have cut it over the past few days and updated her profile picture, although the chances of that were slim. He slammed his palm against the desk in frustration.

"Holy shit!" he cried out, realizing too late the hand that slapped the desk was the one with the broken finger. He clenched his jaw, breathing deep as the pain subsided to a dull, throbbing ache. *Focus on the problem at hand,* he reminded himself, although he felt it was justifiable to feel even more anger as she was technically responsible for the injury.

Bob was going to have to take some more extreme measures to deal with this woman.

~

The dumb dog huddled in the corner, whimpering and pawing at her ears. Or what was left of them. Oliver looked at her in disgust.

"You'd better toughen up or you won't make it through your first fight," he spat as he tossed the scissors on a nearby table. The stupid animal had tried to bite him when he began to cut. If he hadn't thought to buy a muzzle, he'd no doubt have holes in his arms. Why had it been so difficult? People cropped dog's ears all the time; it didn't kill them. He looked back at her form. Her mostly white fur was smeared with red. The whining continued. He stared at her, thinking of how the large fist-sized black circles outlining her eyes reminded him of the Joker in *The Dark Knight*. The one played by Heath Ledger. In fact, it was kind of creepy to think about. Someone at the pet store said she looked like she was part Border collie because of how her white coat was spotted with black circles. Not that he cared.

Her loud muffled cry brought him out of his reverie. The bitch shook her head as if trying to shed excess water, although it was blood that splattered around her.

Damn. He should have done this outside. Once again, he hadn't really thought this through. He assumed he could do something so basic on his own, and he'd been anxious. In hindsight, it would probably have been a better idea to talk to Russ. His buddy regularly lopped off ears of all of his canines to reduce the chances that they could be grabbed by their opponent during a fight.

"Screw it," he mumbled. He didn't need help. Oliver had learned a lot of things by simply doing them himself. Unfortunately, this time his naivety left him with one hell of a mess to clean up. Not only was there a trail of crimson spots highlighting her route to the corner, but she'd also peed when he first gripped her head and sliced through her ear. Her lack of control worried him. Maybe this one wouldn't be strong enough—not even make it through the first fight. Wouldn't that be great, after having to beg to be allowed to participate, if his debut competitor didn't survive? He'd be a laughingstock.

"Get over here!" Oliver demanded, his irritation growing. She shivered, cowering as if she could make herself smaller. He reached down, retrieved the scissors, and began walking in long strides toward her. Her body shifted, like she was debating whether to act submissive or aggressive. "Show me what you got," he ordered and then stood tall a few feet in front of her. As if understanding, she restored her posture and stood to face him. He wasn't worried; she still wore the muzzle. Oliver could now see how crooked his work had been. One ear was trimmed down almost to her head while the other still bore another half inch or so. Well, he wasn't entering her into any dog shows. But a little trim could improve it some. Oliver took a few more steps in her direction. She growled with her hackles raised. He smiled. It was about time she showed the kind of aggression he'd wanted to see.

"Maybe you'll be fine after all," he said. He would leave her ears be for the time being. It's not like it would matter anyway. For now, he needed to get her outside so he could clean up. How long would it take for the bleeding to stop? *Couldn't be too long*, he thought. He cracked the back door open and then approached her from the other side.

The animal made no attempt to escape; rather, her growling intensified as he neared. "That's a good girl," he said. "You need to go outside now." He pointed. No response. Oliver kicked at her. She remained standing, still showing hostility but otherwise remaining still. Instead, she only stared at him with those dark, shadowed eyes. After the third assault, he felt the smack of her cloaked mouth against his leg. Good, she'd tried to bite him after all. At least she would attack when provoked. That's an instinct he needed to nurture.

Oliver scanned the room, his eyes connecting with the iron fireplace tools. *Perfect*. He grabbed the poker and swung it at her as he screamed, "Get out!" The animal shrieked as the weapon connected with her rib cage. She regained her footing and lunged at him. He immediately jumped to the side, swinging the rod to push her in the right direction. Another blow. With her tail tucked underneath her belly, she scurried through the open back door and ran through the snow in the direction of the fence. While she could try to jump over it, the snow in the yard was only about five or six inches deep. No way could the canine get out of a six-foot enclosure. He observed her for a few more seconds as she dashed around the yard, presumably looking for a way to escape while periodically pausing to rub frantically at her ears.

Oliver grinned, pleased at how this was now going.

Chapter 7

Rachel wasn't sure what to say yet. Derek was making himself at home in her kitchen. She watched with part amusement and part annoyance as he stacked several layers of lunch meat—the more expensive organic chicken that she only bought when her bank account was up—along with lettuce, tomatoes, raw onions, and various dressings on a small bun after dousing it with mayonnaise. Bella stood nearby, hoping her famous "puppy stare" would score her a piece of the poultry. Rachel knew deep down her brother meant well. However, this was so typical of his MO: drop in for however long suited him, help himself to everything, and then leave until the next time. Worse yet, she needed to be alone—to not have to talk to anyone, hold a conversation, or do anything other than rest with the shades drawn and Bella nearby in her nice, quiet house. Thankfully CiCi came and took Bella on some snowshoe hikes every day or so, too.

"So, how's work been going?" Derek asked, oblivious to her building irritation.

"Fine. Although it may not be 'going' much for a while yet. It's been hard to concentrate. I see why people with concussions can't function as well until they heal. Kris is stepping in and helping out with a few things thankfully." She leaned back on her sofa.

"She's the one that was with you with when that guy chased you at the college in Reno way back when, right?"

Rachel was surprised he remembered. She'd told him about the hooded gunman following them off the university campus—of course, long after the danger was over so he wouldn't turn into the overbearing big brother that he was prone to be and barge in on her. As he was now doing.

"That's her. I don't think you two have met." Rachel looked over at her coffee table where a *Ski* magazine rested on top. She didn't know why she still subscribed; there were more ads and stories about luxury ski accommodations than there were about gear and other articles. Usually she couldn't afford the skiing equipment in the publication anyway. It was a bittersweet kind of torture to read about advances in technology that made skiing much more fun only to never be able to buy them. She tried to read the cover, but her vision started to blur. She needed to close her eyes and rest before it got worse.

"I saw some pics of you two on Facebook. She's hot," Derek said as he sat in the recliner across from her, a plate containing his culinary masterpiece held loosely in one hand and a soda can in the other. Bella followed closely at his heels.

"She's not your type. She has brains, independence, and doesn't take shit from men."

"Ouch, Sis. Is that really what you think of me?"

"Am I wrong?"

He paused, then grinned as he set his drink nearby. "Okay. I'll admit I haven't been in any rush to find Ms. Right. Nothing wrong with finding a few Ms. Right Nows." As he took a huge bite of his food, mayonnaise dripped down his chin and onto his T-shirt.

"You're a slob," Rachel quipped.

"You want a bite?" he asked, still chewing, her critique not phasing him in the least.

She rolled her eyes. "No thanks."

"Oops, sorry, would you like a sandwich?"

She was taken aback that he'd actually thought to ask, even if it was after the fact. She shook her head, reminding herself to stay calm and be honest. He was a big boy; he could handle her being truthful. "Look, Derek, I appreciate you coming by and wanting to help out, but I seriously need to be alone—in a dark room, with no noise and no distractions. In case you haven't noticed, even my boyfriend isn't here. I'm sorry. I just can't have you—or anyone—around right now. It requires too much brain energy."

Derek didn't live in the area and traveled frequently. His job involved marketing or sales of some kind; he never talked about it much. In any case, moving around from place to place was nothing to him. Plus, Rachel lived in a tourism-dependent town; accommodations were likely in ample supply. "Wow, I . . . sorry," Derek said. He paused, grabbed his soda, took several big gulps, and then belched loudly as he set it down.

"It's amazing you're still single." Rachel's voice dripped with sarcasm.

Derek ignored the dig. "Whew, I feel better now," he said as he rose. "All right, I get it. I'm not wanted. I'll just—"

"Derek, don't pretend to be so sensitive. I know you better than that."

"You're right. Just needed to give you a hard time." He laughed. "It's what I do."

With a smile, she added, "Actually, you *always* require too much brain energy." He winced in mock demonstration. Rachel threw a small pillow at him.

"All right, in all seriousness, I get it. I did some reading up on head injuries on the flight out here, so, yes, I know not to take it personally." He tossed the soft item back at her. Of the three kids in her family, Derek was the one who was most able to let things roll off his shoulders and go with the flow. "However, I have a break from work right now and wouldn't mind catching some turns at Kirkwood while I'm here— that is, if the skiing is good?" He waited while Rachel nodded and then continued. "Know any good places to stay that won't empty my bank account?" He crammed another large bite into his mouth as he strolled back into the kitchen. Rachel pondered how he could possibly chew so much at once without choking. A few moments passed before she remembered he'd asked about a hotel.

"Not offhand." Rachel stood and walked toward the refrigerator. As she breezed past him, the strong scent of onions invaded her senses. Her stomached rolled. She had to air out the kitchen. Rachel reached up to the window above her sink and slid it open. "It's South Lake Tahoe; there's got to be some small motel rooms available, at least during the week. Weekends, on the other hand, have been busy now that we are finally getting some snow. Stupid climate change . . . can't get decent skiing until flippin' January." Rachel muttered as she sucked in one more gulp of fresh air before opening the freezer and grabbing three large ice packs.

"No prob. I'll do some checking around—that is, if you can handle my company for a bit longer." Derek rummaged through her cabinets.

"It's a sacrifice, but I'll do my best," she joked as she walked back to the couch and placed the frozen packs down flat. She lay down on top of them, her stomach facing upward, positioning herself so they matched up with where the whiplash had thrown her back and neck out of whack.

"Don't you have any potato chips? Or at least something edible?" he complained, reaching below her counter to search through more drawers.

"A few apples in that basket next to the toaster. Mixed nuts in that green container on the counter." She heard him moan in protest. "As I have a normal human metabolism, I can't cram the junk food down like you." Rachel reached for the cloth resting on the end table and placed it over her eyes to shut out the light.

"Hey, maybe I could crash with that friend of yours," Derek suggested as a small pop echoed through the room. He must have peeled the sealed foil lid off the can of mixed nuts.

"One, she'd never agree to that. Heck, she might kill you within ten minutes if you act like, well, yourself," Rachel stated. "Two, she has a cat."

"Enough said." Derek hated cats. Which is why they tended to flock around him whenever he was near one. "I could get around the first issue with my overwhelming charm, but I draw the line at those creatures." She heard him plop back down in the chair, followed by a brief shifting nearby. "I assume you have Wi-Fi."

Without uncovering her eyes, Rachel pointed toward the modem in her kitchen. "Password over there." A moment passed before she heard him walk across the floor.

Rachel's cell phone chirped. She reached over to her coffee table, her fingers feeling around a few times before coming into contact with the device. She raised it in front of her face as she peeked from underneath the material, being careful not to let too much light reach her eyes. It was a text from Luke.

"*On the way over. Need anything?*" That was sweet of him to ask, she thought. While she wanted to see him, at the same time she had hoped for some peace and quiet after Derek found somewhere else to go. Now, it could be a while before that happened. She might as well take advantage of Luke's offer.

Rachel typed in a reply. "*White chocolate. If u r going to Grass Roots. FYI brother Derek is here.*" She pressed the send key. She doubted he'd intended to go to the locals' favorite natural food store; however, on the off chance he did, she was still craving chocolate. A second later the phone chimed again. Another text message.

"*I take it no call in advance?*" Rachel had talked about her brothers to Luke on a few occasions, confessing her wonder at how she and her siblings turned out so different. He hadn't met either of them yet.

"*Nope,*" she wrote back.

"*I'll grab your choc and b there in 15.*"

Nice! He was going to get her the sweets after all. "Well, looks like you'll finally get to meet Luke," Rachel stated as she set the phone back down and repositioned the material draped across her eyes.

"'Bout time," he mumbled.

"Be nice," she warned.

"When am I ever anything else?"

"Where to start . . . ," she teased, then enjoyed the brief respite from conversation as he focused on his tablet.

Chapter 8

Thomas peeled off the address label on a nearby magazine while reading the local newspaper now spread out on his desk. For years his name had been spelled wrong in the company's computer system. Oddly, it was his first name, erroneously listed as "Tham," and not his last name. Palinski is usually what people got wrong. Realizing he was becoming lost in thought, he tossed the label and refocused on the issue at hand. Another article regarding that damn housing project had been published. How many times had they printed something related to the Tahoe-Truckee Pines over the last six months? It was as if the media was out to taunt him. The large subdivision being proposed wasn't a completely new idea. The concept of the zoning changes to accommodate the project had been discussed often over the past ten years, although he hadn't been concerned until he'd seen the actual building layout almost two years ago. He'd never dreamed they'd attempt that particular arrangement, let alone that Placer County would even consider approving it. Yet here it was, swiftly moving forward through the permitting process and drawing a lot of attention. He had to be careful. Strategic. There was too much at stake to mess this up.

After one more glimpse at the article, Thomas looked out his window and stared at the snow-crested peak of Mount Rose to the southeast. His eyes scanned along the ridgeline to the west for several miles before settling on the bare white swaths that represented ski trails at Northstar California Resort. His gaze snapped back east. Like a short video clip, his mind replayed the moment years ago when he'd first heard the news about where they wanted to build. That was when his heartburn really started acting up, and it hadn't improved since. And now, the proposed layout of buildings on the ridge only made it worse. As he clumsily reached into his drawer to retrieve the familiar chalky antacids, his vision focused on the aged picture displayed on the corner of his desk. His wife, Corene, gone now for over twenty-five years, looked directly into the camera. Her stare had always been penetrating. She could make a man feel like nothing else in the world mattered except him. How he missed getting lost in those sweet brown eyes. In the image, her smile was crooked. He recalled how their baby son, Oliver, had reached up toward her chin, surprising her at the exact moment the picture was taken. He still remembered her playfully nipping at the boy's fingers moments later as she bounced him up and down on her lap. God, they'd been so happy. Of course, they had no idea back then what fate had in store for them. And it had recently become a whole lot worse.

Loud ringing broke Thomas's reverie. A glance at his cell display revealed a picture of Oliver he'd taken years ago. It was the most recent one he had. His mouth went dry. Talking to his son was never easy. The kid had a fast temper and could act irrationally without any warning.

"Dad?" The voice on the other end of the line asked. Thomas realized he'd answered the call but failed to speak.

"Sorry, Oliver. I'm here. What can I do for—"

"I just read the *Sierra Sun*. I thought you were going to stop this thing!"

"As I have told you before, it takes time. I'm working on it; have some patience."

"You've been saying that for months," his son accused.

"Because it's true. And bugging me about it every day isn't going to expedite anything." Thomas rubbed his hand across his face, feeling the sandpaper-like feel of the stubble on his chin. He had grown tired of repeating himself to his son; the boy seemed to need reassurance every few days like clockwork. "Please, hold tight. Trust me, it will all work out." The line remained silent. Thomas waited, wondering what the reaction would be. Anger? Resignation? Apology? He never knew on any given day. He heard a calm sigh and felt himself relax.

"I know. I'm sorry, Dad."

"Don't worry about it. I know you're stressed. I am, too." Thomas needed to get off this call. The burning sensation in his chest was growing. "Look, I've got a lunch meeting I can't be late for. Let's talk later." After a quick "uh-huh," the call was disconnected.

~

The speaker system in Ted's SUV alerted him to an incoming call. How he hated the odd melody that spewed through the speakers. Every time it rang he swore to himself he'd change it soon, yet he always failed to follow through. Maybe because he was always rushing around and had bigger problems to deal with. At least, that was his excuse.

The sun's glare made it difficult to read the display on his vehicle's dashboard. Once he was able to discern the numbers, he recognized a local area code, but that was it. He answered.

"Hello?"

"Detective Benson?" a deep feminine voice asked.

"Yes," he responded, hesitating as he wondered who it was.

"My name's Maureen. Rick Keller asked me to follow up with you regarding the report Ms. Winters filed about an incident with two men on an oversnow vehicle last Friday?" Ted had to think about what she'd said. Oh, the snowmobile. *Why not just say that?*

"Yes, thanks. Give me a minute," he requested as he pulled off the road so he could concentrate on the conversation. He'd advised Rachel to file a report with the US Forest Service as well as Alpine County, where the incident had occurred. Three days had passed. In fact, he'd been about to call his friend Rick at the county to see if he'd heard anything. "Yes, thank you. Any luck?"

"Sorry to say no. Given that last storm dumped a good foot or two up there, any potential tracks in the snow were gone. I'm trying to locate traffic cams along routes that could be used to get there, but it's like finding a needle in a haystack. I mean, you've got Highways 88, 89, 50, 395—"

"Understood," he cut in, wondering if she intended to cite every highway in the Carson/Tahoe region. He heard papers shifting in the background.

"We'll keep trying. Her description of the snowmobile may be helpful, presuming the owner returns to the area. There aren't usually many snomos—I mean snowmobiles—with the bright colors she mentioned. Then again, it could have been rented," she mused. "Unfortunately, unlike her recollection of the snomo, her details about the men were lacking. I realize that can happen with head trauma. It certainly doesn't help."

"Yeah, she mentioned her memory was fuzzy. A result of the concussion, apparently. Something about a sense of recognition, but she couldn't explain where it came from."

"That's in the report as well; unfortunately, that doesn't provide anything to go on."

"Yeah, it's too bad," he sighed.

"I've got a few guys who'll go out and canvas the area over the next couple of weeks. See if we notice any machines that fit the description she provided. I'll admit, though, it's a long shot."

"I know." Ted rubbed the bridge of his nose. "Anything I can do?"

"No, other than to keep an eye out for your friend in case they come looking for her," the woman responded sympathetically.

"We've been trying." Ted exhaled, then waited as a loud motorcycle whizzed by him—a strange sight to see during the winter around here. Once the engine's rumbling noise had subsided, Ted continued. "Well, Maureen, thanks for the update. Would you like me to let Miss Winters know?"

"No, I'm going to call her next. Wanted to give you a heads-up."

"Thanks," Ted said as the line clicked off. He hadn't held out much hope they'd find anything, but it never hurt to try.

~

Rachel wasn't sure how she felt about the fact that her brother and Luke were laughing. Maybe a little too much. That should be a good thing, right? The problem was the display of male bonding was happening at her expense.

"So, there she was, covered in mud, with those little Princess Leia buns she begged our mom to style almost every day sticking out the sides of her head, screaming at the top of her lungs." Derek laughed as he recounted a time when Rachel, barely eight years old, had slid into a small creek that lined their property. They'd been building dirt "steps" in a moist embankment when the wet ground gave way, causing her to slide into the mucky water below. She remembered being scared, cold, and worried that there would be leeches all over her, even though they didn't have such parasites around her house. That latter fear came from her brothers having recently encouraged her to watch a horror flick without her parents' approval. The main story line centered around large banana-slug-sized worms feeding on people's brains. She'd had nightmares for weeks after watching it; of course, both brothers laughed every time she woke up screaming. Her parents, on the other hand, didn't think it was all that funny.

"Well, she still likes to play in mud," Luke chuckled as he reached for her hand. His palms were sweaty. That was unusual. Was he really that nervous about meeting her brother?

"Yes, all that girly stuff aside, she's a tomboy through and through." Derek laughed, then turned his gaze toward Rachel.

"Wow, an actual 'kind-of' compliment from my brother? I must have hit my head harder than I'd realized." Rachel reached over to retrieve the half-eaten white chocolate bar that lay on her coffee table. "Thanks again for picking this up," she told Luke as she broke off another piece.

He leaned in and whispered in her ear so that only she could hear. "I'd much prefer it if we could enjoy it together like last time. But with your concussion and, well, your brother here, I guess we'll have to save that for later." Rachel's face flushed. He was referring to a rather fresh memory involving melted chocolate and a lot of bare skin. That had been one hell of a night.

"Get a room, you two," Derek said through clenched teeth.

"*My* room's right over there," she said as she pointed. "I'm not the one who needs to find a room."

"Touché," Derek conceded. Rachel's phone rang. She recognized the prefix—Alpine County. It had to be about her incident report. She stood up. "I'll take this in the other room." Rachel leaned over to set the chocolate bar down and then changed her mind. If she didn't take it with her, it might disappear.

~

"All right, dude. She's gone, so let's be straight. You mess with my sister, I'll hunt you down." Derek looked pointedly at Luke, then sighed. "So far, you seem like a decent guy. Keep it that way." Caught off guard by the sudden change in tone, Luke shifted his gaze before meeting the man's eyes. When he didn't respond right away, Derek continued. "She's been through a lot."

Luke finally found his voice. "Fair enough. Appreciate you being direct." At first, Luke felt annoyed. Then he realized he wished he could have this kind of conversation with someone dating his own sister; however, that wasn't going to happen. Ever. He also doubted the man was being totally serious; he didn't look like the type who'd been trained to fight, as Luke had. While the guy was a few inches taller than Luke, height didn't matter so much as knowing what you're doing. Regardless, he'd play along. He figured the man was only messing with him. Or so he hoped.

"Good to know where we stand," Derek said as he leaned back in the chair and rested his hands on his knees.

Luke nodded and stood. It had been a while since he'd taken his last dose of painkillers; a dull ache rose in his shoulder, and his body temperature seemed to be all over the board. He had to focus. Now was not the time to run out to his car for another dose. "Beer?" he asked, in part to stop his mind from racing through his other problems and in part to reduce his pain.

"Sure," Derek replied. After Luke retrieved two amber bottles from the refrigerator, he came back and set them on the table. "So, Luke, are you one of those tree huggers like Rachel?" he asked, reaching for one of the drinks. It hadn't sounded offensive—more like a direct inquiry.

"Not necessarily, at least not until I met her and started learning more about it all. She definitely makes me more conscious of what I do and the effort involved in trying to keep Lake Tahoe looking as awesome as it does." Luke sipped on his beer. "The politics around here are ferocious. Takes a thick skin to get involved in all that." Despite Rachel's occasional gripes over her brother's "insensitivity to the environment," Luke still asked, "How about you?"

"No, I've never been very politically inclined, so to speak. Drove Rachel nuts, really," he chuckled. "Me, I went the business-degree route. I've actually been very lucky; I do marketing and sales for a company that went global a few years ago, which means that I get to travel a lot. It's a pretty sweet deal. There are times I have to work my ass off, but then there are times I get to play for a while, too. Like now." He leaned back and folded his arms behind his head. Luke noticed that Bella had quietly positioned herself nearby and sat, staring at Rachel's brother. Luke knew how hard it was to resist that look.

"So, how long you here for?" Luke focused his attention back on Derek.

"Depends. Work's slow right now, so I don't have to hurry back. However, since my dear sweet sister is kicking me out, I guess I'll have to see how long I want to stick around the area. I think I might head out to the Wood tomorrow; I hear they have a relatively decent base right now compared to other ski resorts." Derek sipped as Bella continued her pointed gaze. Luke noticed the man drop his hand and begin to rub her neck, probably without even thinking about it. He hadn't yet seen anyone who didn't fall under the canine's spell.

"Good idea. Kirkwood does get the best snow around here," Luke affirmed, entertained by Derek's use of local nickname for the ski resort. The guy rarely spent time here now. Rachel mentioned once that he lived in Tahoe quite a few years ago. It would probably be a good day on the mountain, come to think of it. Luke had gone snowboarding the previous week, though local reports claimed the recent storm had dropped another eighteen or twenty inches of fresh powder. Rachel was almost brought to tears when she read the snow reports the day before. Luke had feared she'd still take the risk of skiing with her concussion. So far, she'd been smart and played it safe. Of course, that didn't prevent him from worrying when she simply drove around town. What if someone ran into her and caused her head to bounce against the seat or something? Or she tripped over some benign item and whacked her head again?

"Ski or board?" Derek asked. It took Luke a second to reengage his mind in the conversation and respond.

"Board. Rachel's been working on me to try skiing. I'm just not interested."

"She'll do that. Ask her to consider snowboarding—it will shut her right down." Derek looked down as if he suddenly realized he'd fallen for Bella's ploy.

"Already tried that, and you are right; it ended the conversation pretty fast." Luke laughed.

"No, I chose to let the topic go because I didn't think you had the coordination for it," Rachel teased from behind him as she reentered the room. He turned. "Didn't want you slowing me down either." She smiled coyly. Luke was happy to see she was still joking after what he guessed had been a disappointing phone call.

"Hey now, you two. Break it up," Derek interjected. "Or save it for later, when I'm outta here."

Luke moved over to provide more room on the sofa. "So, what did they have to report?" he asked as he held out his hand, encouraging Rachel to sit next to him.

"Nothing. It kills me that those jerks may get away with it."

"Wait, what jerks?" Derek sat up. Luke looked questioningly at Rachel.

"I haven't told him yet," she confessed.

"Told me what?"

Luke saw that Derek had stopped stroking Bella. The canine turned her head toward him, gently nudging his arm to reposition his hand. To her dismay, it remained firmly gripped to the armrest.

"Okay, I didn't tell Mom and Dad the whole story either because I didn't want them to worry."

"Oh no, those words are never followed by anything good. I'm afraid to ask. What was it this time?" Derek sighed as he reached for his beverage.

"I didn't just ski into a tree. I was being chased."

Derek choked on the liquid he'd just swallowed. Luke watched as Derek's eyes bore into his sister's, obviously waiting for an explanation. Clearly giving up on the man, Bella stepped back, turned, and refocused her attention on Rachel, brushing her snout against the side of her hand. Rachel massaged the pup's ears as she launched into her story.

Chapter 9

Bob whipped his car out onto Highway 50, driving west on the main thoroughfare of South Lake Tahoe. The fresh scent of his sweet latte filled his nostrils. The break from his office and a good cup of joe were exactly what he needed. Failing to track down the photographer had put his nerves on edge. He took a small careful sip. *Thunk.* His vehicle shook, and the hot brown liquid spilled down his shirt.

"Shit!" he muttered. Since he didn't drive down on the southern end of the lake regularly, he wasn't familiar with where the potholes were located. Tahoe was infamous for the large pits in the highway going unfilled for weeks or more, ruining tires and messing up alignments. Bob slowed as he glanced down to wipe off his shirt. Then he quickly looked back up as he approached the stoplight at the intersection with State Route 89. A blue pickup whirred by on the right. He did a double take. *No way—it was her!* There was no mistaking that truck and the array of bumper stickers on the back. He barely noticed the light changing to red as he pressed on the accelerator. He had to catch up. He drove through the intersection, filled with excitement and relief. Eyes transfixed on her license plate, he could make out most of the letters. Bob recited them out loud in an effort to burn them into his memory until he could write them down.

A loud siren suddenly blared from behind him. He looked in his rearview mirror and saw a highway patrol vehicle, its lights flashing. *Son of a bitch.* He coasted to the side of the highway, anxiously watching her truck drive away. The blue Toyota eventually disappeared in the distance. Bob scrambled around for a pen and paper. Anything he could write on. He located an old highlighter in his console and scrawled the numbers he could recall onto the paper coffee cup. He managed to remember six of them before he noticed the officer standing next to his car door.

Less than an hour later, Bob was home. It didn't take long to contact an old friend of his that worked for the DMV. Within minutes, he had a name.

"Rachel Winters," he recited. Apparently, the skier had been a longtime local in the area. With this new information in hand, he initiated an Internet search. Curiously, her name popped up in a variety of websites, from government documents and nonprofit group pages to news articles involving local area crimes and political discussions. She was certainly no photographer. *I knew it!* Conway was wrong—again. Obviously, someone had hired her to follow him. As he continued his exploration through the Web, he slowly accumulated more details, including where she lived, her relatives, and her friends listed on Facebook. He soon had what he needed to locate Ms. Winters and make sure she didn't expose his secret. Whatever it took, he had to keep her silent. Too excited now to worry about what the favor would cost him later, Bob knew exactly who to call to help him do it.

~

Nola glanced at the stacked piles of paper lying on her desk as she leaned back in the soft leather chair, twisting her short curly locks around her fingers. It had been a month since she'd had her hairdresser cut off over a foot of hair, and yet she still wasn't used to it being shoulder-length. All these years she'd kept it in a tight bun for work. Women with long curly blond hair that cascaded freely weren't taken as seriously. She needed to eliminate anything that could work against her at this point. She was so close. After more than fifteen years slowly making her way up the company ladder, she was finally being considered for a promotion. The big one. It was all she wanted. She had no husband. No kids. And didn't want either, frankly. She grew up dirt poor and at ten years old swore one day she'd pull herself out of that life. Everything she had done as an adult had been about achieving power. Making money. Never having to apologize to anyone, anymore.

The meeting on Monday brought her dream one step closer. The new residential project near Northstar, the Tahoe-Truckee Pines, that had recently been presented to the planning commission, was her baby. While she had felt encouraged by their vote to recommend it be approved, what really mattered was the vote by the board of supervisors. They made the final call, and Nola knew them all. She'd been working as the consulting firm's main lead on the project for over five years. All she had to do was get this one project approved and the advancement was hers. Nothing could get in the way before the final vote by the supervisors. So when that new county planner, Anthony, forwarded her the e-mail from one of those environmental nutjobs asking some questions that were too close for comfort, Nola's heart almost stopped. Some tree hugger had apparently found the special arrangements they were burying in the final permitting documents. It wasn't the product of inadvertent procrastination; they'd intended it to be changed at the last minute, concealed by three levels of references where no one would notice them until much later, when it was too late to change it. She wasn't about to let one snooty little NIMBY—to her, those "Not-In-My-Back-Yard" types were hypocrites anyway—mess this all up.

~

"Hey girl!" Kris's excitement beamed through the phone line. Rachel rubbed her eyes. She had drifted off again.

"Kris, hey. What's up?" she mumbled.

"I just got back from that meeting."

"Wait . . . what meet—oh, it's Thursday. The one with Thomas Palinski?" Rachel propped herself up on some pillows as she tried to clear the cobwebs from her brain. Luckily, most people had been patient with what she called her slow "central processing" since the accident. Normally a huge fan of sarcasm and quick wit, she'd had to discourage it after she struggled to keep up with what people were saying.

"Yes, I was actually pleasantly surprised," Kris replied, drawing Rachel's attention back to the conversation. "He's encouraged a lot of homeowners and businesses to put more pressure on the board members." They both expected the eight-hundred-unit new housing project to be agendized for a final vote in front of the Placer County Board of Supervisors at their next meeting. "Some of them are big players in the Truckee area who may actually have some influence. I think there were also a few in Kings Beach and Incline Village that were willing to speak up." Kris was talking fast. Too fast. Her friend must be amped up on one cup of coffee too many.

"That's great," Rachel said, running her hands through her hair. "Um, Kris, I'm having a bad brain moment; mind slowing down?" She sat all the way up and swung her legs around, placing her feet on the expected ground, but instead she felt a warm, furry body underfoot.

"Oops, sorry," Kris apologized. "Thomas would like to touch base with us next week, if you're up for it. In the meantime, I'll get back to reviewing more files and figuring out what else we need. Sound good?"

"Sure, let me know when. My schedule is pretty wide open at the moment. Well, for the most part."

"Brother still around?" Kris asked.

"Yes, he's actually been decent enough. I think he's been out skiing the last few days. He's stopped by each night to check in but hasn't stayed too long. I'm actually kind of impressed. I think he went out with Luke last night for a beer and game of pool. I also suspect those idiots were playing some serious billiards. Derek was complaining about losing some bets."

"Hey, male bonding. All good, right?"

"Yes, but something's still off with Luke. I can't quite place it. I think something is going on that he's not telling me about." Rachel sighed. Luke was attentive and loving yet occasionally seemed to go inward, emotionally. It often felt like his mind was somewhere else and he was simply going through the motions with her. While she knew part of his distance was to give her the quiet space to rest and heal, his odd behavior had started well before the tree incident.

"Just ask him about it. Sure, last week your concussion was so fresh—it made sense to wait. Now that you're feeling better and you can, like, actually maintain a regular conversation, I think you should bring it up. It's been eating at you for a while. That and, well, you're depressing me. And ruining my fantasy that there may still be some good guys out there."

"Oh, definitely can't do that, now can I?" Rachel laughed. That was Kris—always finding a way to cheer her up.

"Gotta go. I'll be in touch!" Kris uttered before suddenly ending the call. It had taken Rachel some time to get used to Kris's quirks, like abrupt hang-ups. Rachel set her phone down and reached over to pet Bella.

~

Luke skimmed his files, doing his best to recall what he'd learned a few days ago from his new clients. Two young sisters had hired him to attempt to locate their mother, Nancy Parsons, who had gone missing roughly two decades ago. The local detectives had never solved the case. Mrs. Parsons was last seen walking home along the two-mile route from her job at the small local community college. She never made it to her neighbor's house where her six-month-old and two-year-old daughters were staying. Losing their mother was bad enough; the girls' father had been killed by a drunk driver months before the birth of the youngest, so after Nancy went missing, they were raised by their grandmother.

It was an interesting case. Cold cases could be difficult to solve, but he was intrigued. The two women sought him out after discovering an old newspaper article as they sorted through their recently deceased grandmother's belongings. The yellowed print paper contained a picture of their mother in deep conversation with an unknown man just a week before she went missing. The image was not in the original police file. The young women hoped locating the stranger could generate a new lead. Although the photograph was blurry, technology was far more advanced now, so he agreed to give it a try. The phone rang, distracting him from his thoughts.

"Yeah?" he answered, more curtly than intended.

"Yo, Luke." It took a moment to realize who was calling.

"Derek, what's up?"

"The manager of this fine little establishment has just informed me that they are booked full this weekend due to all of the skiers." There was a shifting sound, and then he continued. "Why this friendly little manager didn't tell me this, say, days ago when I could have used the notice is beyond me. In any case, would it be possible to crash at your place? Only for the weekend? Apparently there are vacancies again starting Sunday night." Derek paused as if taking a breath to continue. "I can try to look around for some other areas; however, it's already Friday. Given how crazy busy it was last weekend, I'm not feeling too confident about that plan."

Luke hesitated. Could he handle Rachel's brother for two full days? The guy was full of energy and attitude, and he didn't seem concerned with things like other people's personal space. But there were two extra rooms in his house; Luke couldn't really turn him down.

"Sure, man," Luke replied, hoping Derek didn't notice the inflection in his voice.

Chapter 10

"Seven to ten days, my ass," Rachel complained as she sprayed cleanser on her coffee table. As she wiped across the surface, she cursed at the dull ache in her head. It had been about two weeks since her painful encounter with the pine tree. Though she felt more like herself again, she still experienced regular headaches and nausea. And then there were those weird and annoying symptoms, like sudden, heavy fatigue that came on with little notice. Concentrating had been difficult, and forget about any serious multitasking. She kept telling herself to take it easy; it would get better. Finally, for the last two days, it had. Yet she still couldn't retrieve the mental image of the man who had chased her on the snowmobile; the complete blank not only bothered her to no end, but she was scared he might try to come after her again. What if he tracked her down somewhere and she didn't even recognize him?

"Think of something else. Anything," she whispered to herself as she looked around the room for Bella—because that's who she was talking to, of course. Bella had opened one eye at her words but otherwise remained tucked in her bed. Luke. She could think about Luke. At least he seemed to be getting along with her brother, even allowing Derek to bunk at his place over the previous week. Rachel could only imagine what kind of stories Derek was telling him. Her brother would no doubt dredge up every embarrassing childhood memory he could recall.

Stop thinking. She was supposed to be resting her brain. Not concentrating on anything. Doctor's orders. *Yeah, right.* When she tried, not only did her unfinished work continue to weigh on her mind, but Luke's odd behavior did, too. Something had been off now for months. Heck, it seems they had barely ten good months together—albeit, damn, those were good months—before something started causing a strange rift between them. She couldn't figure out what it was. While her growing need for an adrenaline fix had caused some arguments, there was something going on with him.

Rachel had pondered her own role in their growing distance. When she looked back, she could see that her continued need for adventure seemed to start right after the summer she'd met Luke. Then again, she did live in Lake Tahoe. Seriously, who around here *wasn't* seeking outdoor euphoria?

Snow sports entered her chain of thought, and Rachel looked out the window. The forecasters had been right for a change; it was dumping snow. The gentle drift of the huge shimmering flakes falling to the ground was mesmerizing. Countless little white wonders, none of which matched any other. She smiled, the snow quickly boosting her mood as it had done her whole life. On that note, she was feeling better. Maybe she could get some runs in tomorrow at Kirkwood. The phone rang; she looked at the caller ID.

"Hey, Kris," she answered.

"How's it going?"

"Doing well enough, all things considered." There was a brief pause.

"Stop stressing over Luke and go talk to him!" Kris advised.

"I know, I know," she sighed. "Problem is Derek's still staying there, and they seem to be getting along well, which surprises me; I never imagined anyone I'd date could actually get along with my brother. In fact, it frankly concerns me they have hit it off so well."

"Yes, I see your point. But seriously, next time he comes over, you need to just ask him. I have to admit I'm a bit tired of hearing you pine over him."

"I'm not pining over him!"

"Chill out!" Kris groaned. "I was joking."

"Sorry. I'm just so frustrated. With everything right now."

"No worries. Just remember it next time you catch me in a bad mood."

"Girl, you're never in a bad mood. In fact, it's a bit creepy." Rachel laughed.

"Well, I—Nemo, ouch!"

"Get scratched?"

"Yep. Can't blame him; he's in a playful mood, and I've been on the phone for the last two hours. So I'll be brief. By the way, thanks again for coming by tomorrow night to feed him." Kris had plans to visit her family down in Folsom for a couple of days. While her tabby, Nemo, often acted like a dog, he traveled like a cat. Meaning, not very well. He didn't tolerate the ninety-minute drive to the Sacramento Valley.

"No problem. And like before, I'll play with him a little when I'm there." Rachel glimpsed the peaceful winter scene in her backyard. "What time? I'm thinking of hitting the slopes, but I don't want to get there too late."

"Uh, are you sure you're ready to go skiing again?"

"I've been feeling better the last couple of days. The doctors said it usually takes a week or two. I think I'm good." More hopeful than confident, she spoke the truth. Rachel was going nuts after being so inactive for the last two weeks.

"I don't think it's smart. I hear horror stories about football players and—"

"Kris, I'm going crazy lying around here. Plus, we're on our fourth year of drought; I'm at a powder-day deficit," she cut in, expressing more annoyance than she intended. "I'm sorry. I just . . . I need it."

"It's okay. I'm sure I sound like your mother. I'm just worried. However, I can tell you've made up your mind already. Please don't hit any more trees."

"So long as there aren't any homicidal maniacs with guns chasing after me, I'll be fine." Rachel chuckled.

"All right, lecture over. I'm still getting through some of the information for Thomas. How about we go over the maps and some other stuff in a few days? I found a couple of strange things, too; one relates to county documents. In fact, I e-mailed Anthony about it but haven't heard back. The other is something I'll need to ask Thomas about. He's my next call."

"What did you find?" Rachel didn't want to wait until Kris returned.

"It's about Tahoe-Truckee Pines; I'll show you later. But get this—I was looking through the older plans for the area and found Thomas listed as one of the people who commented on the county's 1994 General Plan at several meetings." Rachel was familiar with the land-use plan; it laid out the zoning for what kind of building was allowed throughout Placer County. The General Plan hadn't been updated since; however, revisions had been made to some smaller plans that regulated individual communities.

"Well, sure, it's interesting he didn't say anything, but why is that a big deal?" Rachel wondered.

"One, he was advocating *for* them to construct the condos and stuff right up on the ridgeline—a total one-eighty from what he's telling us now. And two, his wife—you may recall she passed away from cancer back in the early nineties—worked for the lumber company that owned the land. That same company is now involved in the arrangement to construct the new subdivision with almost the exact same layout."

"Whoa, now that *is* interesting," Rachel mused. "Let me know if you hear back in the meantime. I'm extremely curious."

"Me too. Hey, how about we plan for Sunday, say noonish? That will give me an even better excuse to leave the family homestead Saturday night. I expect they'll pressure me to stay until Sunday."

Rachel knew Kris loved her family. The problem was her dad smoked cigarettes in the house. Granted he wouldn't do it in front of Kris, but the smoke that clung to the furniture and walls from years of exposure was enough to aggravate her asthma. Visiting during the winter was worse because she had to keep the doors and windows closed.

"It's a plan. See you in a couple of days."

~

Bob closed his office door before answering the phone call. Holding the small device up to his ear with his fingers taped together was a nuisance.

"Yeah?"

"Can you speak freely?" the man asked. His mild Southern accent grated on Bob's nerves. It sounded fake.

"Yes."

"Darnedest thing. Miss Winters ain't left the house for more than a few short trips. And when she did, that damn dog went right along with her. I mean, that lady's been home almost the entire time I've been watching her. Lazy-ass bitch," he muttered.

Bob cleared his throat. "I think—"

"Bobby, I say it's time for plan B; I don't see the gal leaving that ol' mutt of hers there alone."

Bob's grip tightened. He hated being called Bobby. And his cohort knew it. He took a deep, calming breath, biting off the retort that balanced precariously on the tip of his tongue. They'd been lucky; a vacant rental home across the street sat empty, providing the perfect place to scope out the woman's house. It was obvious she really cared about that canine. So they'd devised a plan to nab the pet and trade it back for all of the copies of the photos she'd taken of him with Conway. It was an easy, no muss, no fuss plan.

"Unless you got time to wait a few more days. See if she leaves," he continued. "Otherwise, we need to dial things up."

"I don't have a few more days!" Bob thought of the looming deadline. He couldn't afford to risk it. "Do what you have to do then."

"I'll get right on it, yes sirree." The call ended without another word.

Bob wanted to hit something, in part over the situation with Miss Winters and in part because he still seethed at having to reach out to this jerk for help.

~

Thomas felt better after his meeting with that woman, Kris, yesterday. In spite of his first impression of her last year failing to instill confidence when she'd arrived to their meeting with a big pink stripe in her dark hair, flip-flops clanking on her feet, and jean shorts, her intelligence became obvious as they conversed. The written materials she'd developed along with that other chick, Rachel Winters, had been detailed and thorough. And there was another person he'd been ready to write off right along with Kris—though it was because of the stick up her ass. All he'd done was compliment them and she'd gotten her panties in a bunch. What was wrong with saying they were both too beautiful to be so intelligent?

The women had soon proven themselves competent and, over the past six months, had identified numerous violations of California's environmental laws in the project's reports. So far, they'd helped delay its approval, giving him time to encourage the applicants to rework their layout. It was ironic to be working *with* the environmentalists; usually they were on opposite sides. In this case, they didn't want buildings constructed in the forest on top of the mountain because it would change the views from Lake Tahoe, or some bullshit like that. He didn't give a damn about views, traffic, the "poor deer herd" unable to migrate anymore, or other such nonsense. Those houses simply needed to be lower on the mountain.

Now, after the message from Kris, he wasn't feeling as confident. She found something he hadn't wanted discovered and would expect some answers. The only good news was she revealed she was meeting with Rachel—who he'd known was still recovering from some kind of accident—on Sunday to update her and coordinate on the next steps. If Kris was going to catch her up in two days, there was a good chance she hadn't shared everything with her friend yet. He had a little time. And a few options on how to both keep Kris quiet and still work to stop the approval.

Thomas also worried his son would do something stupid in the meantime if he believed it was going to be permitted. That's probably why his eye had started to twitch again. A symptom of stress. He tried to ignore it.

Thomas had learned long ago it was best to keep Oliver updated with positive news. However, he had no intention of telling his offspring about Kris's message today; responding to her inquiry required a careful, strategic response, something the boy had never been able to do. Mostly, he reacted without thinking—which got them both into this mess in the first place. He dialed Oliver's number. There were five rings before the call was answered.

"What?" snapped an annoyed voice.

"Hi there to you, too," Thomas said.

"I'm in the middle of something, Dad."

Thomas could hear an odd shuffle in the background. He was afraid to ask what it could be, so as usual, he didn't.

"I wanted you to know I think we're on a positive trajectory now. I met with one of the environmental consultants again yesterday. She feels very confident we can make the case for denial. Or at least a change in those buildings up top."

"I don't understand your trust in those cu—*women*. How come they haven't stopped this already?"

"You have to work within the system, son. It's not that easy to change these kinds of things."

"There's got to be more they could do. That's what you get for hiring women!"

Thomas bit his lip. Arguing with his son about his political views went nowhere fast. There was another noise in the background. This time, it sounded like something falling off a table or countertop. Thomas clenched his teeth to avoid saying anything, instead waiting for Oliver. Eventually, his son continued. "When, exactly, will the final vote happen?"

"At their next meeting. Look, we'll be fine," he assured him. "Just, well, please lie low, Oliver." Thomas was getting the sense his son was already involved in something new; something bad. His voice was unusual, like all of the previous times when the boy was hiding what inevitably turned out to be a poor decision.

"I'm not a goddamn fifteen-year-old, Dad!" Oliver spat.

"All I'm saying is be careful and don't stir any pots for a while. We need this to all run smoothly, and it won't if you . . . if one of us were to get caught up in anything." Thomas glanced out his window, his eyes following the path of a blue Steller's jay hopping along the gate in the backyard. His focus on the bird was instantly severed by a loud smack, followed by a high-pitched cry. "What was that?"

"Nothing. Gotta go." The call ended.

Thomas leaned back, rubbing the bridge of his nose in an attempt to stave off a headache. God, how he sometimes wished he hadn't made the promise to his wife. He'd heard of parents distancing themselves from problem children who, as adults, kept pushing them away or had gone so far over the edge that they refused to listen to their own family. If not for Corine's dying wish to always be there for her son, he might have already taken that route.

Thomas looked down at his desk, at the stacks of paper resting in front of him, and drew his mind back into the present. He had to do something, and he had to do it soon.

He stood and walked over to one of the framed pictures hanging in his office. He pulled the corner away from the wall and felt along the inside edge until his fingertips found the small key. Thomas walked back to his desk and unlocked a small storage compartment hidden behind one of the drawers. He reached in and retrieved the disposable cell phone he kept on hand for emergencies such as this. After double-checking his office door was locked, Thomas made the call.

~

Damn mutt. Of course the bitch had been perfectly quiet until Oliver got on the phone. No way would his dad approve of his latest activity, so of course he had no intention of telling him.

Just as the phone rang, the dog had tried to hide herself in the corner, her tail tucked underneath her belly. Irritation flooded him because she wasn't trying to fight back. It required a lot more prodding to incite the anger in her that he wanted to foster. But it had taken too long. As he started talking to his father, she suddenly dashed past him, running toward the back door that had been open earlier. When she realized it was closed, she turned frantically and attempted to jump up on the countertop—as if she thought she could get out the kitchen window. In her scramble, she knocked the dinner plate off the granite surface. It made enough noise for his father to hear, although at least it hadn't broken. The commotion had brought his annoyance to full throttle. He'd lashed out at the animal, smacking her snout so hard that his old high school ring sliced through the skin next to her nose. He didn't care. How she looked didn't matter. His slap agitated her more, and she'd started to run through the house— most likely looking for a way out. He'd quickly ended the call so he could catch her before the fleabag destroyed something.

The canine was certainly agile; she easily ducked his advances and swerved around his body. He caught hold of her collar and tugged so hard she began to choke. Her body went limp. Oliver was growing concerned that she wasn't going to be strong enough to pass their first fight test. *Crap.* Now he had two things to worry about.

Sure, his father constantly reassured him everything was going to work out—that it was all under control. But how many times had he said that over the last year? Last month? And yet that project had still made it this far such that a final vote was being held in just weeks. His father was far too concerned with image and political correctness to actually get stuff done. Perhaps it was time to take matters into his own hands. Oliver hadn't met face to face the two consultants his dad had hired. In fact, his attendance had been discouraged at previous meetings. Another example of how he was always treated like a child!

He'd seen them at previous meetings from across the room. They were around his age. Maybe they could be persuaded to work harder. He was an attractive guy; why not? In his experience, women were easily manipulated. Those that weren't, well, there was always a way. Go after something they care about and they'd always react on emotion. It's why only men should be responsible for tough decisions. After locking the dog in the small crate in his laundry room to keep it out of sight for a while, Oliver opened his laptop, determined to learn what he could about the two women. Looks like it was up to him to make sure they did what they were supposed to.

Chapter 11

It had been years since Luke had a hangover; he'd sure earned this one last night. After playing several games of pool, Derek convinced him to go to Stateline and spend some time in the casinos. Like many locals, Luke typically avoided the tall structures at South Lake Tahoe's California/Nevada border. To Luke, the smoky indoor air, constant machine noise, and large crowds did not meet his definition of a good time. How naïve to think he could simply let loose for a few hours. What he hadn't counted on was Derek's seemingly endless ability to keep drinking with little effect and ease at attracting a lot of female attention. A few of the admirers had put the moves on Luke as well. He awkwardly repeated that he had a girlfriend several times over. Some of them hadn't seemed to care. It was close to two o'clock in the morning when they walked outside and hailed a cab, stumbling and slurring. After they'd been dropped off in front of his house, Luke barely managed to unlock the door before they both practically crawled inside. His world spinning, Luke downed two glasses of water and went straight to bed. It hadn't taken long for him to fall asleep. Pass out was more like it.

When he woke up hours later, his mouth was dry, his head throbbed, and he reeked of cigarette smoke. After a lengthy shower and relief brought by hydrocodone, Luke emerged from his bedroom feeling refreshed. Overnight guests always caused him to appreciate a private bathroom straight out of the master bedroom. He'd hate to have to communicate with anyone pre-shower. He stepped out into the family room and was surprised to find it empty. Odd, Derek seemed too energetic to ever sleep in. Maybe he hadn't handled the booze so well after all.

The rich smell of brewed coffee penetrated his senses despite the fact he hadn't prepped any grinds the night before. Luke also detected a light odor reminiscent of sausage and eggs. He trudged into the kitchen and discovered the carafe held about two cups of beautiful, thick morning fuel. A saucepan sat soaking in the sink. Where was Derek? He checked the guest room; it was empty. When he walked back into the kitchen, he noticed a sheet of paper on the windowsill. In a very straight-edged font, the note stated that Derek had left around 7:30 a.m. to pick up Rachel and head to Kirkwood. He was "sorry again" that Luke couldn't go. *Again? Wait, why is Rachel going skiing? Why hadn't she mentioned it? What if she hits her head again?* Anger coursed through his body. This damn craziness of hers had gone way too far. She probably hadn't said anything because she knew exactly what he'd think. And she was right.

Luke glanced around the room searching for his cell phone. Calling would do no good; Rachel usually had a poor cell signal at the resort. But he could text. And he was pissed. Luke unlocked the screen and noticed the most recent app he'd used. Texting. His last message was from Rachel. The time stamp revealed it had been sent not long after midnight the night before. Luke didn't remember any of this. He'd been pretty wasted by that time. Scrolling back to earlier messages, he felt his stomach tighten as the exchanges read like a bad movie script of what not to do when dating someone. She had initially asked him if he wanted to hit the slopes; she'd learned that over a foot and a half of fresh snow had fallen so far at Kirkwood. He'd said no, then proceeded to chew her out for going, using some choice words he'd never say to her sober. She'd responded by ignoring his swearing—a worse sign than if she'd cursed right back—and simply stated that Derek had just texted that he'd go and if Luke changed his mind, he was welcome to come along. Luke had retorted with another harsh phrase. Rachel's final message read, "Let's talk when you are sober." *Not good.* He'd screwed up. Big time. Luke set the phone back down and rubbed his hands down his face. A glance out the window confirmed a good amount of new snow had fallen with this most recent storm. It would have no doubt been one heck of a powder day. Yet, what if Rachel made her postconcussion stuff worse? And how the heck did Derek get up after only a few hours of alcohol-laden sleep and go skiing?

Luke decided he needed to just take one step at a time. First, coffee. A lot. Then, a nice greasy breakfast. After that, he had to get to work. He would have to deal with apologizing to Rachel later.

~

Little white flakes of happiness swirled around Rachel as her skis glided through the light, fluffy snow. Her face had been plastered with a semipermanent grin since their first ski run of the morning. It was Friday, which meant the lift lines at Kirkwood were relatively short. Tomorrow was apt to be crazy. But who cared? Derek and she had today. One of the first sets of passengers up the lift that morning, they'd started the day making their own fresh tracks. No words could rightfully describe the feeling of sliding through untouched snow. On the ride over that morning, she'd worried that her nerves might kick in once she got out there, especially around the trees. Strangely, they hadn't. Instead, she felt the usual euphoria, but she was also slightly disconnected, or at least that's the best word she could assign to it. Maybe her brain's attempt to shut off her anxiety had tampered with something else, too. However, that didn't stop her from remaining on high alert skiing through the trees. It hadn't taken long for the mental boost she always felt while skiing to begin pumping through her system.

"Yeah, baby!" she heard Derek yell out from somewhere in the distance. It was fun skiing with her brother again; it had been years since they'd gone together. They often thanked their parents for starting them out so young. Back when they were more flexible, fearless, and less apt to break body parts. Being adults and completely comfortable on their skis, they could simply enjoy the ride.

"Wahoo!" Her voice echo through the small chute as she carved the snow from side to side, the crisp air brushing past her cheeks. In recognition of the skier's code, "there are no friends on powder days," they split up and met near the lift chair at the bottom of the run. Rachel arrived seconds before Derek. As he approached, he dug his skis into the cold surface, angling them to purposely throw snow up against her. "Jerk," she laughed.

"You got me first, dear sister," he chuckled, then advanced forward. The lift lines were starting to fill up now, probably with people who hadn't planned to ski today but had been drawn by reports of fresh powder. Thanks to climate change and drought, days like this had been few and far between. Rachel moved forward another few feet. "You feeling okay?" he asked.

"Yes, like I said, I'm fine. I was a little tired yesterday, but no headache, no nausea for a couple of days now."

"Doesn't seem like much time for a brain injury to heal. That said, who am I to judge? Today is too good to miss. I get it."

"Says the guy who got, what, four hours of alcohol-induced slumber?"

"Four and a half," he smiled, then nudged her elbow. "Gatorade, sausage, and eggs. I tell ya, it works every time." They both drifted forward as an employee instructed the people in front of them to move toward the lift.

"Oh, I'm well aware. I used that remedy a few times in college, you know. Throw in greasy fresh-grated hash browns and it really soaked things up."

"That's right! I forgot about that," Derek said as he grinned. "Well, glad your boyfriend had adequate food supplies on hand. Speaking of which, I know I mentioned this earlier, but he was pretty worked up last night with those texts. He ended up reading—or attempting to read—each one to me out loud. Very loud. I can tell you the people around us weren't impressed. That was a pretty nasty exchange you two had. I don't suppose you've heard from him since?"

"Not a word. And that's fine with me. I don't want anything to ruin today. I need a break from all of the crap right now." She skated forward as they were directed to merge with two other people to fill up the four-person chair.

"I can tell he loves you. Yet you two don't seem very happy."

"I know," Rachel sighed. "We've had some issues for a while, not all of which I understand. Regardless, can we focus on skiing for now?" Rachel inched forward, and then all four of them were swept up by the moving lift.

"Got it," Derek said as he tucked his poles on the seat under his leg to free up his hands. Rachel felt a mixture of sadness and anger when she thought about Luke. She didn't know what to do, yet something had to change. Or . . . well, she couldn't let her mind go there right now.

Focus on the beautiful winter scene around you. Trees loaded with countless white crystals shimmering on the snow's surface. Bluebird sky above. Just feel it, she told herself. Listening to her own advice, Rachel tipped her face into the sun and let the mild breeze brush against her cheeks.

~

"Do it," Nola instructed. She'd spent the last week in constant contact with one of the county's attorneys who'd helped push the Tahoe-Truckee Pines project deal forward. They'd done their best to answer e-mails from opponents of the project, carefully crafting messages to sidestep the issues they needed to avoid. Yet now one of those damn tree huggers had found it—the one thing they couldn't easily explain away. She'd had it buried deep in multiple layers of documents. Once approved by the board of supervisors, there was little they could do if no one had raised the issue beforehand. It had been bad enough when she'd learned some new homeowners in the area were contacting the county, apparently spurred by Thomas Palinski. She still didn't understand what his problem was. He assured her he supported the new subdivision; he'd merely expressed some concerns with how it was arranged. Well, she wasn't as worried about him. He only had so much influence, and she knew that enough of the right people wanted this thing approved.

Nola had to get this promotion. *Had to.* Between her associates and their insiders at the county, they had this permit approval about sewn up. The only other threat had been when that last planner, Sharon, had noticed some discrepancies. Luckily, she brought her concerns to one of the county's attorneys—thankfully, the right one—and she was able to ensure the swift removal of the woman. It hadn't been very difficult; the lawyer had easily devised a way to guarantee immediate dismissal along with a strategically created blow to her credibility, in case she had already figured out too much and attempted to notify her superiors.

"Are you sure?" the voice on the phone line questioned.

"Yes!" she snapped. "That bitch won't leave it alone. Fix it. *Today*," Nola commanded. She ended the call and threw her phone as she let out a frustrated groan. Her eyes roamed across the room, settling on the miniature tabletop model of what the project would look like when completed. Tiny luxury homes—little items about the same size as the hospital pieces in the Monopoly board game—lined small gray roads while fake little people played with their kids in the yards; it reminded her of the small Christmas villages her mom used to display each year, with people the size of her thumb going about their business among miniscule homes and retail shops. The project

71

representation in front of her even included a portion of Northstar. She'd gotten a real kick out of the little ski lift they'd included off to the side.

"You're not going to screw this up for me," she whispered, her words directed at an empty room while her mind pictured the clear image of the woman as if she'd been standing five feet away.

Chapter 12

Derek appreciated Luke's hospitality, even more so when the weekend ended and Luke had offered to let him stay. He seemed like an all right guy, though Derek had a hard time picturing him with his little sister. She was outspoken, stubborn, and very much used to doing things on her own. *Too much.* Whereas Luke seemed a bit introverted. Derek also sensed that the poor guy struggled to handle Rachel's independence. In fact, that little exchange of theirs the night before indicated some notable trouble in paradise. Then again, who was he to question his sister's choices? At least the dude had some taste, what with an extravagant TV and stereo system in his living room. Of course, that's another thing that surprised him about the pair; Rachel didn't watch much television and couldn't care less about things like surround sound.

After skiing all day, he'd planned on a couple of hours of relaxation before heading back over to Rachel's for a tasty barbecued rib dinner. She hadn't meant to invite him; she'd made a comment about forgetting to defrost the meat, which he immediately picked up on and easily wrangled an invitation. Derek wasn't going to let a good dinner pass him by. But before kicking back with a movie, he needed a shower. He noticed a scrawled note from Luke on the coffee table, inviting Derek to help himself to anything in the house.

He walked into the guest bathroom where his toiletries were strewn about on the sink. He picked up his shaving cream to place it in the shower. The lightness reminded him he'd emptied it yesterday and had forgotten to buy more. Luke probably had some. Derek walked into the master bedroom and saw a doorway leading to another bathroom. He checked in the shower stall; no luck. There were also no bottles—of anything—on the sink. Frankly, the man's house was far too clean and organized. If he cared about that sort of thing, he'd be afraid to touch anything for fear of leaving a smudge.

Maybe there was some cream under the sink. He peered inside the cabinet—nothing. In the third drawer he skimmed through, he sifted through what appeared to be a type of bathroom "junk drawer," with various odds and ends like toothpaste, razors, and other items. Several amber bottles at the bottom caught his eye. He twisted the container to read the label and saw it was a brand of hydrocodone, the narcotic painkiller. He recalled Rachel complaining the other day about Luke having shoulder pain yet being stubborn about getting massage therapy, something that had been helping her enormously since she skied into the tree. Odd it still hurt that much over a year after his surgery. Or maybe the pills were just extras left over from that time. He read the label in greater detail. It was a high dose prescribed for several times per day, and the last refill date was barely a week ago. He picked up one of the other bottles; same thing, only it was prescribed by a different doctor with a different strength. Similar time period. His stomach clenched.

It looked like Luke suffered from an opiate addiction, and chances were Rachel had no idea. "Damnit, Luke. And I was starting to think you might be good enough for my sister," he muttered in disgust. While she'd likely not hold an addiction against someone—she often preached about not judging others unless you've walked in their shoes and all that liberal BS—she *would* be upset if she'd been lied to about it. Derek placed the contents back where he found them, slammed the drawers shut, and rushed out of the bathroom, wondering whether to tell Rachel or confront Luke. One thing he could not do was leave it alone.

~

As he pulled up to his house, Luke noticed Derek's SUV parked in the driveway. Rachel's older brother was nice enough—a little cocky, full of the kind of potty-mouthed humor that drove Rachel nuts, and way too chatty for a roommate—but in general, not a bad guy.

Luke stepped inside his house and closed the door behind him. It was strangely quiet. Perhaps Derek had gone out on foot. Or maybe he was napping to catch up on sleep after an early morning. Luke turned and tossed his keys on a small table. He was startled when he looked up and realized Derek was sitting on his couch—pointedly staring at him.

"Whoa, you scared me there, bro," he uttered.

"Sorry 'bout that," Derek said. Something wasn't right. The man seemed angry.

"Everything all right?" Luke asked as he looked around the room. Nothing looked out of place.

"Why don't you sit down." Derek gestured to the chair across from where he sat. Luke got a bad feeling. He was also annoyed; it appeared he was about to be interrogated about something in his own house. How could that happen?

"I think I'll stand. What the hell is going on?" Luke snapped.

"You've got a problem, and I don't want you dragging my sister down with you."

"Huh?" Luke deflected. He had only one secret he could think of that might upset Rachel's brother like this. He glanced at his bedroom door and remembered he'd forgotten to close it that morning. *Ah, shit.*

"How long have you been hooked on painkillers?" Derek asked bluntly as he leaned forward. Luke felt the blood drain from his face. His deer-in-the-headlights feeling was quickly replaced with anger. *Did this guy go digging around in my stuff?*

"Why were you searching through my things?" he countered.

"I was looking for some shaving cream. You said to help myself to anything. Now stop sidestepping."

Luke paused, debated, and decided there was nothing to be gained by arguing now. He slowly sat down, resigned. This was horrifying—to have his most embarrassing weakness discovered by Rachel's brother, of all people. He'd always planned to tell her about it. Eventually. Maybe when he didn't need the medicine anymore.

"A while." Luke sat back. "I . . . I've never had an addictive personality. It just sort of happened."

"I take it Rachel doesn't know?" Derek asked pointedly. Luke shook his head. "Were you planning to tell her?"

"Yes. First time I thought I would was after that attack at her house last year; then there was never a good time. I didn't really think it was a problem at first. Then I needed more, wanted more. And I didn't know how to stop." He paused, then added, "I *don't* know how to stop."

"Look, I've seen addictions affect friends before, although I've been lucky enough not to be plagued by one myself. I've watched people I know struggle to kick things like this. It's not easy. All that said, you need to come clean with my sister. She deserves better than being lied to."

"I haven't lied to her . . . I just didn't tell her." Luke's guilt was making him react defensively. Derek looked at him accusingly.

"Think about this. Every single day you take those pills, you are thinking about them throughout the day then, right? And every day you don't tell her, you are lying about something that is a regular part of your life. You think that's okay?"

"Look, I was going to fess up. I know this is bad. Really bad. But . . . are you going to tell her?"

"No." Derek stood. "*You* are. Whatever your demons are, get some help. See a professional. Find a Narcotics Anonymous group. And while my sister may not judge you for getting hooked on the pills, I sure as hell hope she gives some serious thought to how you've been lying to her for God knows how long. Or whatever you want to call it." He walked to the line of coats hanging on the wall in the entryway and grabbed his black jacket. "I'm going over to Rachel's now. I won't say anything tonight." He slipped his arm into the coat. "My suitcase is already in my car. I appreciate you letting me stay here, I really do. But I think it's best that I find somewhere else now. And by the way, if you don't tell her by tomorrow night, I will."

Luke still didn't know what to say, so he remained silent.

"Or better yet, break it off with her and spare her the pain of realizing she's been lied to all this time."

After the door closed, Luke dropped his head into his hands and rubbed his face. Then he picked up a vase from a nearby table, jumped to his feet, and threw it against his mantle. Initially, satisfaction flashed through him at the sound of breaking glass. Seconds later it was quickly replaced with sorrow. How had this all gone so wrong? Derek was right: Rachel did deserve better. He had no right to ask her to stick around with someone who'd only drag her down. It was probably best for her if they ended things. Let her move on with her life and not be pulled back by someone as screwed up as he'd become.

It wasn't the first time he'd wondered about their relationship. Something had been affecting them from her end, too. Before her concussion, she'd been taking more risks. From dangerous hikes and climbs last summer to more jumps and other tricky maneuvers on her skis. It was like she was trying to seek out new ways to hurt herself, though when asked about it, she kept saying she sought the adrenaline high. Come to think of it, Luke may not be the only one with an addiction. Was her drive for constant euphoria an unconscious substitute for an emotional high she wasn't getting from their relationship anymore?

Maybe he was trying to find ways to justify letting her go. To tell himself he was doing it for her own good, even if she didn't realize it. God, how messed up was he?

~

Kris's head swirled with pain. Attempting to open her eyes only made it worse, so she quickly closed them again, aware that the only thing she'd seen was darkness. A mildew-like odor invaded her senses, and a strange hum reverberated around her. She was tucked in the fetal position on some kind of hard, cold surface. Her fingers and toes were partially frozen. She tried to stretch out, but her feet met resistance. More awareness dawned: her ankles and wrists were bound. *What the hell?* Fear set in, chilling the parts of her that weren't already numb with cold. She opened her eyes as if she could peer at her limbs, but panic gripped her as her vision was once again filled only by blackness. *Stay calm.*

If she could figure out where she was, that would be a start. She focused only on the environment around her and then realized she must be in the trunk of a moving car. *Relax. Think. Don't these spaces have some kind of internal release lever?* She frantically felt around, thankful her hands were tied in front of her and not behind. *Small favors.* Her fingers didn't encounter anything that felt like a handle. *What else?* In movies and books, abductees often kicked through the taillights and stuck their hand out to signal to nearby drivers. She felt around the corners but found nothing. Sweat beaded on her forehead even though her body shivered. Kris closed her eyes hard, willing herself to maintain her composure. Having a freak-out session would not help her out of this situation. How had she gotten here? After a few deep breaths, the memory slowly returned, albeit the details were fuzzy.

Kris had been driving through her neighborhood, taking less-traveled residential streets around to North Upper Truckee Road. A few miles in she remembered leaving her inhaler on the kitchen table.

Crap, she had thought. Thankfully, she only had to go up one more street to the next stop sign before she could swing a U-turn and head back to her house. She had just stopped before flipping her car around when someone slammed into her from behind. After the surprise wore off, frustration set in. The last thing she needed was to have to pay for car repairs; her insurance came with a high deductible. This person better have some decent coverage.

Kris released her seat belt and grabbed her phone before jumping out of the driver's seat. She held her hand over her eyes as she went to inspect the damage.

"Can you please turn off your high beams?" she called out. A figure began walking toward her. All she could see was a generic outline.

"Oh my goodness! I'm so sorry." It was a man's voice. Gravelly, like her dad's. "I'll lower them right now." He appeared to be muttering to himself as he slid into the driver's seat of his pickup. The lights dimmed and he'd climbed back out. "Better?"

"Yes, thank you." Now that she wasn't being blinded, she turned to inspect the damage, noting there was barely a dent on his truck but expensive cosmetic damage to her car. The man continued to utter apologies as he neared. And at that moment it dawned on her how stupid she'd been. She was a sitting duck. Before her brain's alarms could signal her body to move, the stranger grabbed her, twisted her around, and wrapped his arm around her throat. She remembered struggling to breathe, her arms flailing in a helpless attempt to pry his grip loose. His hold on her had been firm, and she had quickly grown weak. Dizziness fell over her, then . . . nothing.

The next thing she could remember was waking up in the enclosed space, her head throbbing. Why had someone taken her?

Chapter 13

"Hey, Sis." Derek walked in the front door without knocking, as usual. Rachel had grown accustomed to his nightly intrusions. Having wiggled an invite to dinner out of her earlier today, at least this time she knew when he'd be coming over since he'd stop in either way.

He strolled into the main living area and plopped down on her stuffed chair. His smile didn't quite reach his eyes.

"You okay?" she asked, sitting up from another session of ice therapy on her spine.

"I'm fine."

"Bull."

"Just some work frustrations that came up. It's all good." He fidgeted with his wristwatch—a clear sign he was bothered—but she knew better than to push. If he wanted to talk, he would. He nodded his chin toward the chilled gel packs she gathered up from the sofa. "What's with the ice?"

"I decided to be extra cautious, in case skiing aggravated anything." She wasn't about to tell anyone how much her headache had started up again after their day at Kirkwood. She knew what they'd say, so she changed the subject. "When do you have to go back home?"

"Probably next Tuesday or Wednesday. Why? Are you counting the minutes until I leave?"

"Um . . . let's see, that would be about four days, which means ninety-six hours, at thirty-six hundred seconds per hour." She stopped. Her brain couldn't handle any more math, but her point had been made.

"Nice one." He picked up one of Bella's squeaky toys and tossed it at Rachel. Not understanding, of course, that it was directed at her human, Bella jumped up on Rachel's lap to retrieve the toy.

"Oh, Bella! Right in the gut!" Rachel stammered, holding her stomach with one hand while throwing the toy across the room with the other.

"Oops, my mistake." Derek attempted to keep a straight face. He managed only a few seconds before he laughed. Rachel joined in.

"It's okay. Women can handle more pain than men, you know."

"You don't say. Based on what scientific data?" he played along, throwing one of her typical questions back at her.

"Childbirth," she stated succinctly. "According to other women I know," she added. Rachel was starting to enjoy these fun exchanges with her older brother again. They hadn't spent much time together in years, and usually he was so preoccupied with work that it was rare to get his full attention—which made her wonder if something had happened with his job that he wasn't sharing. Perhaps there was more to his current "vacation" than he'd told her.

"Well, yes, you got me on that one," he conceded. Rachel's cell phone interrupted with a soft upbeat tune. She glanced at the time, then back at Derek. He raised one eyebrow.

"It's an alarm. I need to go take care of Kris's cat." Rachel noticed Derek glance into the kitchen and then back at her. "After dinner," she confirmed. "The alarm was my own personal 'heads-up.' Hey, want to join me?" Rachel stood up and walked into the kitchen.

"You serious?"

"You afraid?" she baited.

"Not at all. I can handle a freakin' cat," he muttered. "It's dark outside. I just don't think you should go alone."

"Uh-huh." Rachel rolled her eyes. Sometimes the male ego knew no bounds.

About an hour later, she twisted the knob of her friend's house as she placed the key in the deadbolt. It met no resistance. A distant bark indicated Bella wasn't happy to be left in the truck. On the drive over, Rachel had decided to just keep the pets separated, otherwise they'd get too worked up playing, and she was anxious to get this done and go back home to relax.

"I think Kris left it unlocked again. Not the first time. She's always a bit scatterbrained when she has to head to her parents' house," she explained while nudging the door open. She barely heard the patter of footsteps as they stepped inside. Nemo always entered into stealth mode when people first arrived, as if he had to warm up to them for five or ten minutes before greeting them. Derek made an exaggerated sniffing noise as they walked inside the house.

"What's that about?" Rachel asked.

"That horrible smell. What the heck is that?" He clasped his nose, looking around the room.

"What are you? Twelve?" she teased, staring at him pinching his nostrils. "It's called incense, and it's actually not that bad."

"Whatever," he remarked and started snooping around Kris's living room. Rachel checked the cabinet next to the kitchen sink where the cat food was usually placed. It wasn't there. She walked around searching for the bag of kibble.

"She must have moved it or something," she mumbled as she headed into the small laundry area in back of the house. A light sliding sound came from the living room. She suspected Derek was snooping into every storage space he could find; it was so typical of him. She wondered if he'd already scoped out all of Luke's storage areas already.

Rachel saw a fresh bag of kibble on the shelf above Kris's washing machine. She quickly scooped a container of the dry food and carried it back out into the kitchen where the cat's dish sat in a corner. As expected, the sound of food being dropped into the bowl attracted Nemo from his hiding place. He rushed by her and began chowing down.

"That's a rather large cat," Derek said, staring from his position near a small hutch. Rachel had the feeling he'd been poking around inside the cabinets underneath.

"Don't worry. He doesn't bite. Well, not hard, anyway." She loved teasing her brother; he surely gave her enough trouble to warrant getting some in return. "I told her I'd play with him a little, too, so you might as well sit down—unless you need to inspect the rest of her house, too?" She watched as he opened the drawer on a small side table and peered inside.

"Just curious, that's all." He shut the drawer and sat on a nearby love seat. "So, we sit here?"

"You're welcome to stand," she chuckled. "He eats quickly. Hey, hand me that rod thingy over there." She pointed to a cat toy with a fake mouse attached to a string; it looked like a pint-sized fishing rod. As he picked it up, Nemo unexpectedly jumped up on his lap, his front paw reaching out for the item. Derek shrieked, and Rachel burst out laughing. "Oh my God, I wish I'd gotten that on video."

"Shut up," he snapped, his eyes focused on the feline and his hands raised as if debating how best to remove the unwanted animal with the least possible amount of touching. "You're right. He does eat fast," he said through clenched teeth.

"Psst!" Rachel got Nemo's attention, encouraging him to come to her. As soon as the cat bounded off his lap, Derek let out a huge breath and tossed the small toy to Rachel. She ran her hand along the feline's soft, fluffy orange and white fur, then dangled the pink-and-green-colored mouse in front of her. Nemo pawed at it, his tail twitching. Derek stood back up and strolled into a far corner. Rachel played with the pet for a little while longer as Derek browsed Kris's various pictures hanging on the wall. Rachel decided it was time to put her brother out of his misery.

"Ready to head out?" she asked.

"I'll meet you in the truck," he said hastily and then slipped out the front door.

"See you later, little guy." She rubbed the cat for another minute before following her brother outside.

~

After a lengthy internal debate, Derek had decided not to tell Rachel about Luke. He'd honor his word to the man and give him the chance to own up. As much as he wasn't fond of cats, riding along to Kris's had been better than sitting with his sister at her house trying to avoid the subject without giving away his anxiety. After they pulled into Rachel's driveway and stopped, Derek climbed out of the passenger seat and stepped down, his foot sliding a few inches on the icy surface before finding traction.

"Do you want me to put Bella's bed and stuff back in here?" he asked. Rachel had a special setup to fill in the foot space on the passenger side and prop up a dog bed so Bella could easily ride shotgun. When someone else rode along, the special structure was easily removed, and then Bella hung out in the back seat of the cab.

"Nah, it's fine." Rachel opened the small access door on the back of her truck's cab and motioned for Bella to jump down. "Come on, girl."

They walked up to her front door and let themselves inside. Derek noticed Rachel glance toward her answering machine. Most people used voice mail nowadays; however, with poor cell service in areas of the Lake Tahoe Basin, a lot of people kept landlines. There were no messages. She probably hoped for a call from Luke.

He removed his coat as Rachel walked to the freezer and retrieved some ice packs.

"Neck bugging you again?" he asked.

"Not too bad. I just want to keep up regular icing for a while yet, to be safe." She placed the packs on the sofa and then positioned her back on top. "It's a little cold. Mind tossing some more wood on the fire?"

"Am I your servant now?" he joked.

"Consider it payment for the ribs."

"All right, only because I loved that sauce you made." Derek strolled toward her back door.

"I think it's supposed to get down to twenty tonight," she called out as he stepped outside. "Nice and cool, so I should sleep well at least."

Her statement flipped a switch in Derek's brain; he stopped and then cursed under his breath.

"What?" she asked, sitting back up.

He sighed in annoyance. "I remembered when we were at Kris's I opened up her window trying to get some fresh air because of that incense stuff. I forgot to close it."

"Oops. Well, the good news is she has screens, so no worries about Nemo getting out. But, given the cold temps . . ." She started to stand up.

"Hey, I can run back over there and shut it. That is, if you trust me with her key." He smirked.

"Hmm, you clearly can't help yourself from nosing around, but I suspect your desire to avoid Nemo is stronger than your invasive curiosity."

"I'm hurt!" Derek held his hands to his heart in mock response. "Let me grab the wood, and then I'll head back over there."

After adding more logs to the wood stove, Derek took the key Rachel proffered.

"How about I plan to bring this back by tomorrow? That way you can relax for the rest of tonight and not have to entertain your awesome brother?" Part of his suggestion was born from self-preservation—he didn't want to keep avoiding the subject of Luke.

"That's fine. Call me in the morning, and I can swing by Luke's and get it from you."

"Uh, sure," he stuttered, not wanting her to know he wasn't staying there because then he'd have to explain why. He could at least buy himself one more day and hope Luke manned up enough to tell her tomorrow.

"Actually, why don't you leave it at her house? There's a small birdhouse that she keeps outside year-round. It's a little brown and white deal nailed to the railing on her front porch. Drop it in there when you're done. That way neither of us has to worry about losing it."

"Got it," Derek replied, relieved. He opened the door. "See ya tomorrow."

~

Of all the luck. Grabbing the woman had been easy enough. The rear-end ploy usually was. But Jerry's new female "guest" now needed her asthma medication. He was being paid to take her and keep her hidden away for a while. There hadn't been any advance notice to do the usual research on his subject; as much as he hated to go in blind, the payment was worth the extra risk. It's not like he hadn't done this before. In his mind, it was tantamount to babysitting: don't hurt her, and merely stash her away. Besides, he drew the line at killing people. So here he was, driving to the girl's house after what had already been a long, exhausting day. He parked one block over and carefully walked up the street, trying to avoid the black ice that had caused his tires to slip on the way over. The desire of Tahoe neighborhoods to be free of excess lighting worked in his favor; most of his trek was in the dark.

When he reached her house—the small one-story structure engulfed on both sides by massively sized vacation rentals, easily recognized after scoping it out earlier that afternoon—he looked around, seeing no one nearby. He casually walked to the side gate and into the fenced yard. Desperate to have her inhaler, Miss Drew had readily given him her key and begged him to close the doors when he left so her cat wouldn't escape. At least it spared him from having to break inside. He slid the key into the lock and opened the back door.

Once inside, he found himself standing in a short hallway. He followed it toward the front of the house where he assumed the kitchen was; that's where she thought her medication would most likely be. With a few more steps, he entered a moderately sized living room. A light was already on in the corner. Two windows lined the front room; one appeared to be partially open, so he remained to the side to avoid detection by anyone who might glance inside.

A small wooden kitchen table was tucked against the wall on his right. He looked but didn't see the small device anywhere. She'd mentioned her cat sometimes knocked it to the floor. Jerry kneeled down on the cold tile and began visually scouring the area when a car door slammed out front. *Crap. Please let it be a neighbor.* He didn't need more trouble tonight.

He straightened and walked to the front window, peering through the narrow gap between the drawn shades. A man was walking up the driveway. He cursed under his breath as he spun around and sprinted into the hallway. To the left was a small bathroom. To the right, a bedroom. He ducked inside the bedroom and hid behind the open door as he heard a click from the front of the house. He reached up to tug his ski mask down, and a horrifying realization seized him. He wasn't wearing it. It had to be in his pocket, but he couldn't risk moving and making any noise.

Jerry gripped the weapon stowed in his coat pocket, hoping he wouldn't have to use it. He remained frozen in place, listening. More light blasted the hallway. There was a quick sound as if a window were sliding closed, followed by footsteps and then the high-pitched squeak of door hinges that needed some WD-40. That had to be the front door opening—the person was leaving. *Good.* He relaxed. Suddenly, there was a loud sound a few feet away from his hiding spot. Filtered moonlight coming through the window allowed him to make out the shape of a large cat that darted underneath the bed.

"Nemo?" a male voice called out. Jerry wanted to shoot the damn feline for drawing the stranger back in. The front door slammed shut, and footsteps drew near. He held his breath, hoping the man wouldn't come into the room. There would be no way to completely hide; he'd be forced to take action.

"Nemo?" the man repeated, this time from the open entry. "I'm not a cat person, so show me you're fine and I'll—"

There was only a split second to react. Before the unwelcome visitor could turn on the bedroom light, he flung himself into the door, slamming it against the man. There was a quick grunt as the figure fell back into the hallway. The guy managed to correct his balance and advance toward him.

85

Jerry swung his leg forward and pounded his foot into the man's lower abdomen. He heard a whoosh sound. Before his enemy could fully recover, he brought his right arm back, tightened his fist, and threw a punch forward. His knuckles connected with a cheekbone. His rival's head flew back. For a split second it appeared the man might collapse, but he managed to remain upright.

Jerry barely had time to process the swift movement when a sudden intense pain ripped into his side. The man had thrown a kidney punch. Before Jerry could regain his breath, the man struck again, this time slamming a heavy boot into his shin. The maneuver caused the man to lose his own balance. They both fell, bodies slamming hard against the wooden floor. Pain shot through him as his head bounced off the unforgiving surface. Another blow struck hard against his chin. Instinctively, he reached into his jacket and retrieved his weapon.

"Don't mo—" His words were halted when something suddenly covered his face. Surprised, his hand jerked and his gun fired. As the deafening sound of the shot echoed through the house, a realization hit—the cat had jumped on him. The feline immediately disappeared back into the bedroom. Jerry realized the man on top of him was groaning. *Shit!* He must have taken a bullet. Jerry pushed the injured figure off of him and quickly scrambled up, hoping the wound wasn't life-threatening.

He located a light switch, ready to flip it on, then paused. The light had thus far been dim; there was a good chance he hadn't been seen with any detail. Jerry reached inside his back pocket and, as expected, located his ski mask. Only after the material fully covered his face did he flick the light switch. The man held both hands against his leg; blood oozed out around his fingers.

"Please, don't kill me. Whatever you want, take it," he pleaded, his voice tight and his expression pained. Jerry focused on where the bullet had struck. It didn't appear life-threatening, so long as pressure was kept on it and the bullet had exited the other side.

He couldn't let him go. At least, not until the job was done and he could get far away from this place. Where no one could track him down and it wouldn't matter if this man had seen him.

"Do what I say and I won't. But you're going to have to come with me," he replied, annoyed. He did not need this extra work! Jerry inched toward the front room, his eyes searching. He noticed scarves hanging on a coatrack near the front door. "Don't do anything stupid.

I'm going to get something to wrap that up." The man nodded, his face pale and his forehead dotted with beads of sweat. Yes, those gunshots wounds could be a bitch; he sure knew all about that.

After yanking one of the scarves free, Jerry walked into the bathroom and searched through the medicine cabinet. Nothing. He checked underneath the sink and found a small first aid kit. After retrieving the container, he retraced his steps and kneeled down, careful not to slip in the fresh blood. "Is the bullet still inside?"

"I don't think so," the man replied through clenched teeth.

"Good. Now, wipe your leg with this." He held out a small package. "Then smear on this ointment, cover it with a bandage, and tie that scarf across as tight as you can." He set the items down and rose back on to his feet, gun at the ready. The man fumbled with the first aid kit with one hand while the other remained pressed into his leg. After reaching for a large bandage, he used his teeth to rip the package open.

Before he placed it on the wound, Jerry interjected. "I strongly recommend that salve I set next to you; you'll pay for it later if you don't."

The man looked at him as if momentarily confused, then he picked up the small packet, tore the corner, and squeezed out the substance.

Once the scarf was securely tied around the man's leg, he asked, "What's your name?"

"Derek."

"All right, Derek. Like I said, I won't kill you so long as you do what I say. Try anything and it's lights out. Got it?"

"Yes."

Jerry watched the man double-knot the makeshift wrap, and then he walked to the front door and twisted the deadbolt to lock it. He turned off the bright lamp near the doorway and turned back to Derek. "Come here. I need you to locate an inhaler. I think it's somewhere on this kitchen floor," he said without emotion. Better to keep an eye on the guy rather than search for it himself.

"A what?" Derek asked as he slowly rose up on his feet, leaning against the wall for support.

"You deaf? An inhaler! For asthma. I think the cat knocked it off this table." He waited.

After a few moments of uncertainty, Derek asked, "For Kris?"

"Just get it!" he barked.

Derek stepped, faltered, regained his footing, and advanced a few more feet into the kitchen. His eyes met Jerry's and then moved to the gun still aimed in his direction. He dropped to the floor, looking from one side to the other. A few seconds later he crawled toward the refrigerator, smearing blood as he went.

"I see it." Derek reached behind the large appliance. He appeared to feel around for a few seconds before he sat back up with a small inhaler in his palm. Jerry grabbed it and stuffed it into his pocket.

"Get up. We're going for a ride." He saw his hostage's gaze darting around the room as he slowly rose. "Don't try anything. And by the way, I'm the only one who knows where the girl is," Jerry warned. Derek nodded, comprehending the underlying meaning of his words.

~

Luke couldn't bring himself to do it tonight. His emotions were too raw from their argument, followed by Derek's discovery. However, if he didn't get in touch with Rachel, she might wonder what was going on, given how they'd left things last night. He merely wanted to delay the conversation to tomorrow. Luke picked up his cell phone and typed a short note.

"*Sorry about last night. I was worried and wasted. Bad combo. Do u want 2 talk tonight? Hope you had a good day skiing.*" It was a lame text, but what else could he say? Luke pressed the send button, hoping the answer would be no. Juvenile, yes, but once she got started on something, she wouldn't let it go. A minute later, there was a response.

"*Thx. Let's talk tomorrow. Long day. Good snow.*"

Luke was relieved. He texted back, "*Okay. Sleep well.*"

Luke set the phone down and paced to the refrigerator, planning to grab a cold beer. He paused and reached for a can of soda instead. Getting drunk again wouldn't help. He carried the beverage back to his couch and turned on the TV. Maybe he could simply zone out tonight and focus on this all tomorrow with a fresh outlook.

One bad action flick later, Luke's mind quickly returned to thoughts of Rachel. Maybe it was for the best. They'd started off hot and heavy, yet when things died down, what did they really have in common, anyway? In fact, he felt like he had to keep compromising his beliefs to suit her views more than the other way around. What he'd seen as her making him a more understanding person was now starting to look more like something else. She'd molded him and reshaped him into something he wasn't—manipulated his feelings, even if she hadn't consciously intended to do so. Noticing his shoulder pain returning, Luke paced into his bathroom and swallowed another pill. On the way back into his living room, his mind raced. The more Luke thought about it, the angrier he got. He started picking apart every conversation they'd ever had about ideals and beliefs. Sure, they'd both listened to each other and, in some cases, changed how they viewed something or found a middle ground. But he was pretty sure he accommodated her views more than she did his. Hadn't he? Yes, they were physically compatible, by far. But were they otherwise compatible?

His emotions were all over the board, bouncing between irrational anger at Rachel, love, attraction, then back to despair and the feeling that he wasn't good enough for her. Maybe the best thing would be to break it off right now. Rip off the Band-Aid, so they could both move on. With his mind made up, he threw on his coat, grabbed his keys, and rushed out the front door. Better to do this now before he lost his nerve.

Chapter 14

Rachel's eyes strained to read the detailed notes on the screen, taken from meetings where Thomas Palinski had spoken in favor of the Tahoe-Truckee Pines project. How odd he had completely changed his tune. His previous stances on other projects dictated that there had to be political motivation behind the change. So long as it lent support to protect the land, though, she shouldn't complain. The screen was starting to blur, an indicator her brain needed another rest. This postconcussion stuff was the pits. Rachel set the computer down and looked at Bella, who was curled up asleep by her front door where she suspected the cool tiles felt good to Bella's furry form.

"You should go outside in the snow, girl." Rachel smiled and then rubbed her eyes as if that would help clear up her vision. Two silky black ears perked up.

"You don't need to wait for me to let you out. That's why I got you the doggie door." She laughed, pointing at it as if Bella understood. Then again, sometimes Rachel wondered if Bella did actually know what humans said and simply played dumb to make her feel better. It was amazing what the pup seemed to comprehend. A knock on the door startled her. She glanced at the clock. 9:06 p.m. People didn't usually drop by this late unannounced. Well, except for her brother, but he'd just walk right in. Rachel stood and called out as she stepped to the front door.

"Who is it?"

"Luke."

She was a little surprised; based on his text she hadn't expected to hear from him until tomorrow. She was tired and not in the mood for another fight. Why had he come? Sighing, Rachel opened the door. He stood in front of her with a strange look on his face. His hair was tousled as if he'd just woken up. Damn him; the simplest things on him were sexy as hell.

"Hey. Did you come by to argue?" she asked, trying not to sound too defensive or annoyed. Why push it.

"I, uh, no. Can I come in?" he asked, resting one arm overhead against the wooden frame. She stepped backward, and he walked past her.

"What's up?" Rachel was doing her best to keep her tone light.

"I needed to see you. First, I'm so sorry about last night." He stood in the entryway. The lights in her house were dim; too much illumination still bothered her sometimes. She noticed he hadn't shaved today.

"Me too," she responded. With some reflection, she understood he had only been concerned; they'd both done a poor job of communicating—again. She could admit it wasn't likely the smartest idea to have gone skiing today, so she really couldn't blame him for calling her out on it. "It probably was too soon to go, although I didn't hit any more trees," she said and smiled. "I shouldn't have been so annoyed; you were just worried."

"Thanks, but you shouldn't apologize. I was the one being an asshole." He reached up and tucked a loose strand of hair behind her ear.

"Can I make a request?" she said, letting her face rest against his palm. He nodded. "Can we table the bigger picture discussion we need to have? Just for tonight." A strange look passed over his expression before quickly disappearing.

"Yes," he said as his eyes dropped to her mouth. "Just for tonight," he repeated as if reminding himself. "Did you have a good day on the slopes today?" He moved closer to her.

"Total euphoria. Soft, fluffy powder. No Sierra cement with this storm." Warmer winter temperatures in the Sierra Nevada often dropped warmer moist snow, known by locals as "Sierra cement" due to its weight and aptitude to grip skis. She dropped her gaze to his neck. His skin was partially exposed by the shape of his shirt.

"That's great." His other hand reached up behind her head and caressed it softly.

"And you know how a good day on the slopes makes me feel, right?" she teased. His lips inched closer. She could feel the warmth of his breath on her skin. The sweet scent of cinnamon mints penetrated her senses.

"Yes, and I am forever thankful to the snow gods for that." Luke gently pulled her head closer. Soft, moist lips brushed against hers. Chills ran down her spine.

"My turn," she stated seductively, then traced his jawline, his throat, and then his neck with small kisses. He tilted his head and moaned. The primal sound revved up her senses even more. Rachel slid his jacket off his shoulders and tossed it on the sofa. Then she reached for his waist and frantically tugged at his shirt.

"Wait a minute," he said.

"Huh?" Rachel paused, confused.

"You worked hard today. Let me pull the weight tonight." He traced his fingertip along her jaw. She looked up at him. His ocean-blue eyes bore into hers. Talk about a smoldering gaze. She was on fire.

"Then get to work, cowboy, because I can't wait much longer." Rachel reached behind and cupped his bottom, pulling him against her center. He groaned.

"Bedroom. Now!" he instructed. She happily obeyed.

As they stood in front of the bed, he carefully removed her sweater and pressed his lips to her neckline. Rachel sighed. Luke traced an imaginary line to her shoulders, up her neck, across her mouth, and down the other side.

"You're killing me!" she whispered, desire burning inside of her.

"Patience, mountaingirl. I want to savor every minute." He chuckled. She couldn't resist; she pushed her hands up underneath his shirt and swept her fingers across his chest. The definition of his muscles indicated a man who engaged in a lot of bike riding. *And the things he could do with that upper body strength.*

"This needs to come off. You're not being fair," she complained, pulling up on the fabric. He conceded, backing away and holding up his arms. Rachel ripped off the material, tossed it away, and quickly positioned him against her. His body radiated heat.

"Okay, now it's my turn again." Luke stepped back and loosely clasped his hands around her wrists. "Lie down." Once she complied, Luke took his time unbuttoning her jeans and slid them off one leg at a time. He proceeded to explore every part of her body with his mouth. Rachel surrendered to the physical sensations, letting complete bliss envelope her.

Chapter 15

The rich vanilla-scented aroma of the coffee helped awaken Rachel's senses. She sipped from her mug while browsing the morning's news. It was important to keep apprised of what was going on around her, both locally and nationally, but damn, it could be frustrating. So many depressing stories. Maybe it all just seemed worse because information now spread farther and faster on social media. Luke didn't have a Facebook or Twitter account; in fact, he still had a couple of newspapers delivered to his doorstep. She envied that.

Rachel had been disappointed when Luke left in the middle of the night. He said he needed to wake up early to run an errand and she should rest to help her brain keep healing. That, she understood. What really bothered her was the strange way he acted when they'd lain together after making love, and then as he dressed and said goodbye. Several times she caught him staring at her, a sorrowful look on his face despite his attempts to hide it. Like he was storing every detail to memory. *Stop overanalyzing, Rachel.* It wasn't the first time she'd caught herself doing it.

Rachel looked at the clock and decided it was time to bundle up and go check on Nemo again. Kris was either coming home very late tonight or she would be talked into staying until tomorrow. Either way, it wasn't that far to drive. She could go back again later tonight if need be. She composed a quick text.

"Going over 2 check up on Nemo. Let me know if u plan to stay another night. Have fun." She pressed send. It took about ten minutes to change into jeans and load Bella in her truck. Still no response, which

was odd, but Kris could easily be in the middle of something with her family. Rachel never assumed someone would immediately reply. People knew if it was urgent, she'd call.

Bella remained in the pickup as Rachel approached the front of Kris's house. The canine had copped an attitude because Rachel wasn't letting her out to play with Nemo. Rachel carefully stepped around patches of ice as she ascended the steps to Kris's front deck, then turned to reach inside the small birdhouse. No key. Derek must have forgotten. *Why am I not surprised?* Thankfully, Kris regularly hid a spare key in her backyard. After retrieving what Kris had once called her "backup to her backup key," Rachel unlocked the deadbolt and swung the door open.

"Hey, Nemo, it's only me," she called out as she stepped inside the dark interior. Rachel closed the door behind her, turned, and opened the curtains in the living room to allow natural light inside. When she swung back around, her heart jumped. Red smears covered the kitchen floor. Rachel dashed to examine it. Upon closer inspection, she knew it was blood. Her insides tightened. Had the cat injured himself? Although it seemed to be a lot of blood. Regardless, something was seriously wrong. "Nemo?" No response. Rachel stood and followed the crimson trail into the hallway. Another larger patch of red. Small feline prints had tracked through it, yet there also appeared to be several large shoe prints.

"Oh my God," she whispered. Then she frantically yelled, "Derek? Kris?" The house remained quiet as she ran through all of the rooms, searching and calling out. Nothing. Her hands were shaking as Rachel slid her phone from her pocket and dialed her brother's line. A moment later, the faint sound of "Highway to Hell" played from somewhere in the room.

"No . . . no," she cried as she followed the music. Tucked underneath a bunched-up throw rug a few feet down the hallway was his cell. Like the floor, it was caked with the rusty substance, none of which was fresh. Whatever had happened had played out last night—when Derek had come back to close the window. Her hands trembling, she managed to dial Ted.

"Rachel, what's up?" He answered in his usual upbeat tone.

"Ted, I think something's happened to Derek. Or Kris! Or *both*," she blurted as she looked around. "I don't know. I'm at her house right now. There's blood everywhere. Derek came back last night to close the window and—" She choked on her words. The dam let loose and tears streamed down her cheeks. "No one's here."

"I'm coming right over," he said, his tone all business. "Call 9-1-1."

"That's my next call," she said.

The emergency dispatcher asked her to stay on the line until the police arrived. Rachel kept the phone at her ear as she peered around for the cat. Did he escape last night? Although large for his species, he'd still be coyote bait in Tahoe. Then she remembered the small paw prints she'd seen in the hallway. She followed them, careful to step around the red areas. The trail led under the bed. Rachel kneeled as she lifted the comforter's edge and looked underneath. Nemo stared back at her from the other side. She reached toward him with her free hand, and he scooted farther back. He didn't act like he was hurt. Rachel straightened up, shut the door to keep him inside, and paced back into the kitchen.

After confirming the emergency operator was still on the line, Rachel used her cell phone to snap photos for herself. As she maneuvered to capture a full image of the kitchen floor, she noticed a small trail of red drops leading to the side of the refrigerator. Balanced on her toes to avoid the red evidence, she leaned over and peered around the corner. On the side of the appliance a message was written in blood.

"*have kris iNhlr masked ma*—" The final "*a*" was smeared down to the right a few inches. The capital "N" caught her attention. This was definitely her brother's writing. For some strange reason, he always capitalized that one letter, simply making it smaller when it was used as lowercase.

Her nerves going haywire, Rachel tried to concentrate on what the note could represent. First, it was clearly Derek's message, and most likely his blood. Second, if she read it straightaway, it meant he had Kris's inhaler. But what did that mean?

Rachel immediately reached for the landline phone on the countertop and dialed Kris's cell again, despite knowing deep down her friend wasn't going to answer. It rolled immediately to voice mail. Rachel examined the blinking red light on the girl's answering machine.

"Are you still with me?" The distant voice penetrated her thoughts. The 9-1-1 operator. She'd almost forgotten. She put her cell back to her ear.

"Yes."

"Don't touch anything," the woman warned.

"I know. I'm . . . dealing with my friend's cat." It was the only fib that came to mind. Rachel selected mute so the operator couldn't hear, grabbed a tissue from her pocket, and covered her fingertip as she pressed the play button. A soft woman's voice issued from the device. It was Kris's mother, wondering where her daughter was. The automated voice announced the message had been left at 10:12 p.m. last night. Another recording followed. Again, her mother, this time sounding more worried, stating she'd tried Kris's cell again. Her message rambled on.

"I must have an old number for your friend Rachel. I tried her, too; I keep getting one of those damn recordings. So please, call us when you get this, sweetheart."

The third and final message had been left about an hour ago. Her mother said she had called the cops, but they wouldn't do anything unless twenty-four hours had passed. She begged Kris to call her. Rachel suspected their daughter had never made it out of town. Now Derek had disappeared. And was injured; who knew how badly? Were they both wounded? Or worse? Rachel's stomach flared with nausea, and she quickly sank into the nearest chair. Pain slammed through her head, and her vision in her left eye blurred.

"Ma'am, the officers have arrived at your location." The female voice intruded into Rachel's thoughts. She depressed the mute button. Fatigue set in, and it took all the effort she had to walk toward the front door when the first officers knocked. Rachel opened it and immediately explained, "I'm the one who called."

A young policeman stood there, stone-faced yet unthreatening. His sunglasses engulfed half of his face. It would have been comical if not for the situation. Behind him a tall female officer, her face stoic, eyed her. "Can you please step outside and tell us what's going on?" the one with sunglasses asked.

"Yes, but I need to sit down." She moved forward and dropped into the bright pink Adirondack chair Kris kept clear of snow all winter long.

"Are you hurt?" The woman officer asked. Was her headache that obvious? Oh, that's right. The big shiner around her eye hadn't fully healed.

"This isn't fresh," she waved at her face, although she'd expect that to be obvious given the faded coloring. "I recently had a skiing accident and can't keep standing right now," she mumbled. Rachel leaned her head back and tried to concentrate. It was becoming more difficult by the minute. Seconds after relaying her story, Rachel felt her phone vibrate. She hadn't realized she was still holding it. The display indicated that Luke was calling. Why hadn't she thought to call him herself?

"Sit tight. Do you need an ambulance?" the female officer inquired. Rachel shook her head, which magnified her headache. She winced. "Not necessary. I'm recovering from a concussion." Luke's call had gone to voice mail. Seconds later, her phone alerted her to a new text.

"*Need 2 talk 2 u. Would now b a good time?*" What an odd message. And why hadn't Luke already called about Derek? Wouldn't he wonder why he hadn't shown up last night, let alone this morning? Worried about her brother and friend, and weeks—no, make that months—of annoyance with Luke's behavior suddenly overcoming her, she texted back an abrupt reply. "*No.*" *Let him ponder that one.* Right now, she didn't care.

"Rachel?" She looked up at the sound of Ted's voice and breathed a sigh of relief as he kneeled in front of her. "What happened?"

Rachel began.

~

After being yanked out of the trunk, almost falling on her cramped legs, an armed man wearing a ski mask instructed her to sit on a waiting snowmobile. Before he sat in front of her, he placed a handkerchief over her eyes and fit a helmet on her head. That gave her hope; protective gear suggested he wasn't looking to harm her; then again, being stowed in the trunk of a car hadn't been all that safe. Either way, it would be irrelevant if she had an asthma attack in the meantime.

"I need my inhaler," she said anxiously. The man paused.

"You need what?"

"I have asthma." Kris figured she had nothing to lose by pressing the issue. She heard the man swear under his breath. He remained quiet, and she got the sense he was internally debating.

"Tell me where. I'll go get it later." Once she relayed the information, he warned her that attempting to escape would mean a bullet hole. Or getting lost in subfreezing temperatures overnight with nowhere to go. He sat in front of her, pulled her arms around his sides, and handcuffed her wrists together in front of him. She couldn't think of what to do. Her mind raced while he guided the machine across the snow. Her body was chilled; the only warmth she felt came from where she was forced to huddle against the man's back. Kris tried to catalogue the area with her senses. Were there any distinct smells? How much time had passed? Her arms became stiff from being held in the same position for too long. She wasn't sure whether to be relieved or not when their speed dropped and they came to a stop.

A small click preceded the removal of the handcuffs. Her arms dropped, and she alternatively stretched and shook them in an attempt to regain the feeling. The man moved, and the sudden chill of the night air combined with the shifting of the machine indicated he'd dismounted. Instinctively she reached up to pull the helmet off, but he grabbed her arm and pulled her toward him. "Come," he commanded. She carefully stepped as he tugged her forward on what felt like hard-packed snow. There was a clicking sound followed by the squeak of a door's hinges. "Step up." Kris obeyed, raising her foot as she moved forward. She felt warmth in front of her as her feet touched a carpeted surface. She was nudged forward another step before a door slammed behind her. He ripped her helmet off and removed the cloth over her eyes. She opened them, her vision blurred from her eyes having been covered. She couldn't see much, but it was enough to guess he was wearing a ski mask. The man spoke. "As I told you before, do as I say and you'll be home before you know it. There's food and water in the kitchen. And by the way, you can scream to your heart's content; no one will hear you. Even if you did get out—which I guarantee you won't—you'd find yourself roaming in the snow for miles. I've run snowmobile tracks in every direction; there's no obvious path to follow. Point is, you'd get real cold, real fast. There's a full tank of propane out back; you'll be warm inside here. By the way, don't get any ideas about trying to burn your way out; this place is sealed up tight. You'd die from breathing the smoke before you'd make any headway." He reached for the handle. "Finally, remember that I'm the only one who knows where you are, so don't try anything stupid." The door opened and he slipped outside. There was a click. She'd been locked inside.

Her eyesight grew clearer. She advanced forward, pounding against the door in frustration. Finally, she let her arms drop and turned to examine the room. Several large water bottles and wrapped food items rested on a two-person dining table. The butterflies in her stomach shifted from lightly fluttering to banging around her gut as she considered her situation. Would he really come back with her medication?

Trying to remain calm—after all, getting worked up could spur an asthma attack—she carefully spent what felt like hours checking every part of the cabin for any way out. It had a small kitchen that didn't appear to have been updated since the 1970s. Scratched and warped drawers and cupboards contained plastic silverware, a few paper plates, and plastic cups. A tiny bathroom had been squeezed into one corner, yet there appeared to be no door. An old-fashioned gas wall heater kept the chill down while, across the room, a long-ago abandoned fireplace was masked with black char. A twin bed was pushed against the wall, and seventies-style stuffed chairs and a love seat were tucked throughout the remaining space. More important, however, were the steel bars attached to the outside of the windows. All she could see was a dense thicket of pine trees; there were no distinguishing features to help her figure out where she was. Her calm but swift search had caused her to break out in a sweat. She gave in and opened the bottle of water set on the table. Minutes later a heavy fog settled over her.

Now here she was, spread out on the old mattress. How long had she been asleep? Was he here? She surveyed the small cabin and did not see him. Thank God. Her queasy stomach suggested whatever the water had been spiked with must have been strong. Kris gazed around the room, hoping to see something new in the daylight that she'd missed in her haste the night before.

Had something moved?

The worn love seat covered with dirty blankets was positioned against the wall; her view of it was mostly blocked by the stuffed chair in the middle of the room. She stood up and stared in horror. Someone was sleeping on it, feet hanging out to the side. Was that her kidnapper? Kris's mind shot into overdrive. If he was inside, maybe the door was unlocked. She tiptoed to the front door, slowly twisted the knob, and pulled. Nothing. *Damn.*

The figure shifted, and she heard a light moan. Adrenaline coursed through her veins. Could she find a way to immobilize him before he woke up? She scanned the room. There had to be something she could use as a weapon. Two compact wooden chairs framed the kitchen table. If she could swing one of them with enough force, perhaps she could knock him down long enough to . . . to what? The door required a key. Unless she could find it, she was stuck. All such an attack might do is serve to piss off the guy. And he'd warned her: do what he said or die. That she was still alive gave her hope that he hadn't lied.

The person stirred, drawing her attention back. There appeared to be cloth wrapped around his leg, and it was coated in something dark. She dared a closer look. A black-and-white zebra scarf—*wait, isn't that my scarf?*—was smeared by a dark red-brown substance. If he was already injured, maybe she could do some damage with that chair after all. She quietly inched backward, edging toward it. Kris suddenly stepped on something and slipped, falling against the small table. It tipped, scattering the packaged food across the floor. Relief swept through her as she noticed her inhaler among the array of items. Behind her, the man groaned again. She whipped her head around. He hadn't moved. *Curious.* Maybe he was too injured to fight back. Could she be so lucky? Concentrating on staying calm, she cautiously stepped toward him. When she was a foot away, she leaned over to peer at his face, expecting to see the black mask from last night. A small throw pillow rested on his eyes, but she could see his chin. She reached out to peer underneath when a hand shot out and gripped her wrist. Hard.

"Ouch!" she gasped, surprised by the movement. The man turned to look at her as panic set in. She got a look at his face. After a moment of confusion, she pieced her thoughts together. "Oh my God. Derek Winters?" He looked perplexed at her question, but didn't relax his hold. "I've seen your picture. I'm Kris, Rachel's friend." Tense silence filled the space around her, and she wondered if he was going to release her. His fingers loosened, and she pulled her hand back.

"Sorry about that," he said, staring at her. As he struggled to sit up a pained expression settled across his features. Black wavy hair clung to his head; he was sweating.

"It's okay. How are you here? And what happened to you? Your leg?" She waved at his injury.

"Got shot," he said simply. Before she could respond, he continued. "Are you okay? Did he hurt you?"

"No, he hasn't. I think he drugged the water last night, though. I haven't slept that sound in years." She laughed, trying to lighten the tug on her nerves.

"Now that you mention it, I think he may have done the same to me." He rubbed his eyes. "I remember someone placing a bottle to my lips, although it's a little fuzzy. Where are we? He tied a scarf over my eyes." Rachel's brother looked around, his gaze resting on her makeshift bed. "Actually, now that I think about it, I remember trying to wake you right after he left, but you were out. Then I got tired and collapsed on the nearest thing I could find." He moved his legs and leaned back, resting his head against the arm of the furniture. "Holy crap, this hurts. Wish I had some of Luke's pills," he murmured.

"What?" Had she heard him right?

"Nothing. I was thinking of how he got shot a while back."

Kris sensed something was off; she had watched politicians and developers sidestep questions all of the time. Before she could press, he drew in a deep breath. Exhaling, he admitted, "It burns like something awful."

"It looks like you're bleeding again. I don't suppose he'd have any first aid stuff around here." Her eyes scanned the small cabin.

"I think he brought your first aid kit. Oh, and your inhaler. To be honest, I don't think he meant to shoot me. He seemed interested in me not dying. Granted, clearly not enough to take me to a goddamn hospital." He looked around and pointed to one side. "There, I see something in the corner over there. Down on the floor." Kris squinted in the direction he'd indicated. A small square container sat among the food she'd knocked off the table.

"Well, I'll be . . . I hope you're right about this guy." Kris retrieved the kit. Derek slowly untied the scarf and pulled it aside. She flinched; the wound looked bad to her. Not that she was a nurse; however, it seemed like a lot of blood. And there was debris around the inflamed area, too. She knew enough about injuries to understand his wound needed to be cleaned. "We need to get these pants off."

"I love it when a woman says that to me," he teased. She stopped and looked at him pointedly.

"Oh, that's right. Rachel has told me about you."

"Told you what?"

"Nothing," she chuckled, examining the material. "I think if I can get a good grip on these jeans where they are frayed, I can tear them apart enough to peel them away from your injury."

"That doesn't sound as appealing," he replied.

"I think you may want to keep pressure on this. It's bleeding again."

She grabbed his hand and placed it on the hole without thought. He grimaced, and she realized it probably hurt. A few seconds passed before his expression relaxed and he spoke.

"I also like a woman who puts my hands exactly where she wants them."

"Do you ever quit?"

"Just getting started, sweetheart."

"Don't call me sweetheart," she snapped as she tightened her grip on the material, preparing to split it apart—although a little smile formed at the corner of her mouth. "Ready?" she asked. Before he could answer, she pulled the material to the side and heard a satisfying rip. Her hands inadvertently grazed his skin, and he moaned, then sucked air between his teeth as he closed his eyes. "Sorry," she apologized. "The good news is it worked well enough to give us access to the bullet hole. How about you tell me what happened while I bandage this?"

She went to work as Derek recounted the attack.

"So Nemo's okay then?" she inquired.

"Should be. He closed the door when we left."

Kris nodded, relieved. "By the way, I read somewhere that you should elevate it. Something about helping with swelling."

"That isn't the only thing that can be elevated," he smirked.

"My God! If someone hadn't already used you for target practice, I'd shoot you myself." She finished rewrapping his leg.

"Geez, tough crowd." Derek scooted himself down so his torso lay flat on the love seat while he propped his leg on the armrest. Kris rolled her eyes and straightened, watching sympathetically as Derek wiped at the moisture beading his brow. Kris couldn't imagine how much he was hurting. Too bad her kidnapper didn't grab her pot stash, too. That would help ease his pain, with the side benefit of making him more tolerable. Hungry yet afraid of more laced refreshments, she turned toward the kitchen. "Think they've figured out we're missing yet?"

"I think so," Derek responded. "If anything, Rachel is very attentive to your cat. She didn't want him to get lonely. Mentioned she was planning to go back again this morning. I expect my blood should clue her in."

"I imagine so," she agreed. Good—that he felt well enough to flirt and use sarcasm might be a good sign. "Hey, weren't you staying at

Luke's? If you didn't come back last night, maybe they discovered it then?" she asked, hopefully.

"I wasn't staying there last night. And Rachel had no reason to look for me either after I headed back to your place."

"Why n—"

"Please don't ask me to go into that right now," he interjected, sounding sad. Or annoyed. Or both. Kris nodded in agreement. It wasn't any of her business anyway.

"So, you said you left her some kind of message?"

He recounted his blood-smeared note.

~

"No?" Luke stared at his phone. *That was it?* Such a short, curt response was not like Rachel. Did Derek already tell her about his pills? Probably. So much for the twenty-four-hour window to confess to her himself. Well, now what? Even if she never wanted to see him again, he didn't want it to end this way. They should at least see each other face to face and talk. Regardless, there would never be a good time to share how much he'd messed up. Maybe he should force the conversation now and get it over with. He stood up and reached for his keys.

~

Chase was still surprised he'd been asked to do this favor. Although left with little time to prepare, he had known he'd have no trouble following through on the request. Sure enough, so far, so good. And even better—it would be good to be owed a favor in return from his caller. Reaching out for help to anyone, let alone to him, was a rarity.

After driving by Miss Winter's home repeatedly and watching people in the only two other occupied households drive away earlier that morning, not long before the woman herself also left, he felt certain no one was around to see him. He'd rented a standard white SUV—one that matched hundreds, if not thousands, of other vehicles around the area. His own rusty old Ford truck would certainly stand out.

Following one more scan of his surroundings, he parked a few feet away from the black mailbox. He quickly slipped the sealed envelope inside, tucking it into the stack of letters the mail carrier had already left. He was confident she'd receive the note today; who didn't check their mailbox when they got home? Time was of the essence, and this letter, combined with his other actions, would provide her the proper motivation to follow their directions, and to do so quickly. Sure, things had become more complex than originally anticipated, but he always figured out a plan B, and this time was no different. He casually strolled back to his vehicle, climbed inside, and drove down the street to park and observe her house from a distance.

Chapter 16

In the privacy of her own vehicle, tears flowed freely down Rachel's face as she drove away from the police station after giving her statement. She didn't know what to do. Her brother and best friend were missing. According to Ted's observations, one or both of them had been shot. They found one bullet so far; it had apparently exited its target and become lodged in the wall. But that didn't mean only one shot had been fired. She couldn't consider that right now. While the lab was running a DNA screening on the blood samples, it would take some time to get results—likely weeks or longer—but preliminary testing indicated the blood type didn't match Kris's, which Rachel had remembered from the times they'd donated blood together. At the moment, it appeared most likely to be Derek's. Where were they? Who did this? Could this be related to the snowmobilers? Her mind wouldn't stop playing through a collection of worst-case scenarios. Rachel was about to launch into another round of crying, even though it accentuated her headache, when Bella intervened by leaning across the console and resting her snout on Rachel's thigh. Bella didn't like it when Rachel was upset. She reached up and rubbed the canine's head.

"Thank you, sweet girl." Rachel calmed down. There was nothing she could do, other than wait for Ted and his crime scene investigators to process the scene. That and try harder to remember the image of her attackers, but two weeks had passed and it remained fuzzy in her brain. In fact, she'd lost hope of ever recalling what they looked like.

Calling Kris's parents had not been easy. They'd already been notified by the police and were in the process of packing their car.

In response to their stated intention to drive to South Shore as soon as possible, Rachel repeated Ted's suggestion they wait until he had more information. They hadn't listened, citing the need to take care of Nemo even though Kris's neighbor had been happy to take him in for a few days. Rachel cautioned them Kris's house might still be a crime scene, but they were determined to come. She couldn't blame them.

Unable to relax, Rachel's head throbbed. Her stomach still remained ill at ease, but the mild prescription they'd given her after the concussion helped knock the sick feeling down a notch. The only other thing she could do was rest, although doing so wouldn't be easy. But if she could, she'd be better able to help when Ted did have something. When she saw Luke's Subaru parked in front of her house, Rachel let out a long frustrated sigh. *Not now.* Her nerves couldn't take much more.

Rachel wiped her tears but then quickly gave up caring how she looked as she let Bella out of the pickup. She retrieved the stack of letters in her mailbox before walking to the front door. The top one was another medical bill. *Screw them.* It could wait. When she entered, she tossed the mail onto a small nearby table. Rachel was surprised to look up and see Luke quietly sitting in a chair—staring at her. Bright light penetrated the large windows. He looked agonized. She sniffled.

"What are—?"

"Can we talk now? I mean, last night was great. Hell, it's always great. But we've put some of this stuff off for too long." It wasn't like him to talk so fast. Rachel stood, confused, then slowly walked over and sat on her sofa.

"Do I have a choice?" she answered, unable and unconcerned about hiding her anxiety. He looked at the floor and then directly into her eyes.

"There's never been a good time. I meant to tell you last night. Then . . . well, I'm so sorry you had to find out this way. Regardless of that, I think it's clear to both of us that this hasn't been working for a while."

Find out what? Before she could ask, Bella jumped up next to her and curled up on her lap. "Bella, girl, not right now," she said, gently nudging the dog to the side.

"Maybe we should take a break. Or something." He glanced down at the floor. His knee started to bounce up and down—a clear sign he was nervous. However, she had no sympathy to give at the moment, so she told herself she didn't care what he was referring to right now. Fueled by anger, frustration, and worry, her annoyance with Luke's amazingly bad timing grew to new heights, and she spoke without thinking.

"Seriously? You're going to do this *now*?" she snapped back. How could all of this be happening? She'd barely processed the danger her brother and Kris were in, assuming they were still alive. Her head felt like it was going to explode, and she was finding it hard to concentrate. Now Luke was going to dump this crap on her, too? Rip out the heart that was already breaking for Derek and Kris?

"I think it's better than leaving this hanging between us. Maybe it will give us each a chance to figure out what we want. Why we've both been struggling with some issues lately." Rachel stared at him, too shocked to speak at first. "And for me to get cl—"

"You know what? You're right. Let's end this now," she lashed out as anger replaced sorrow. "Call it good and move on." Rachel smacked the table. "And on that note, I really need to rest now. So leave. Please." She stood up, fighting the moisture blurring her already reddened eyes.

"Wait. I . . . uh, think we should take some time. That's all," he stuttered. He actually appeared surprised at her reaction. What had he expected?

"Why? Sometimes it's easiest to rip off the Band-Aid all at once, right?" Rachel did her best to stave off more tears until after he was gone. She stiffly walked to the front door, and Bella followed her as she swung it open. "Bella, sit," she commanded and then turned back toward Luke. He seemed glued in place. She needed him gone before she let herself process everything.

She waited. The only sound in the room came from the soft clicking of an old-fashioned clock on her mantle, the third hand moving with each passing second. *One. Two. Three. Four.*

He rose and looked at her. She could see he, too, was holding back tears. She held her chin up, urging her heart to hold on a bit longer. "I'll gather up your things and get them to you when I can," she stated matter-of-factly.

"Rachel, I love you. Know that I'm going to figure this out," he said as he walked toward her. She stepped back, fearing he would attempt to kiss her goodbye. She couldn't bear that right now—knowing what it meant—feeling his lips on hers for the last time.

Luke looked hurt when she stepped away from him. *Good.* Because that's how she felt right now. She didn't move. He stepped out onto her front porch and then turned back around.

"By the way, Derek left one of his bags at my house. Please let him know when you talk to him." At Luke's comment, Rachel froze. She felt the blood drain from her face. That was the final straw.

"You have got to be kidding me!" she yelled. "If you'd taken just one moment to pull yourself out of this pity party you've been in lately, maybe you would have noticed that I was a bit upset when I got home—*before* you dumped your crap on me. Kris and my brother are missing for God's sake. Derek's been shot, and I have no idea what condition he's in or where either of them might be. So please, go somewhere else and feel sorry for yourself. I've got bigger things to worry about right now!"

Rachel noticed Luke's expression morph from miserable to utterly horrified as she spoke. She didn't care. She couldn't afford to. Before he had the chance to respond, Rachel stepped back and slammed the door shut as hard as she could. A scraping sound broke the momentary silence as a framed picture swung back and forth before resting in place again. She turned around and pressed her back against the door, letting the floodgates open up as she slid down the surface until her body was resting on the cold tile floor.

"Rachel?" She heard him call out from the other side, sounding as if he were mere inches away from the door.

"Just go!" she shrieked.

Several silent seconds passed before she heard the soft sounds of footsteps exiting her porch. Rachel leaned her head back and glanced at the ceiling. Her vision blurred—whether from her emotions or her concussion, she didn't know. What was she going to do now? Her gaze dropped and she saw that Bella had remained in place, anxiously wagging her tail but waiting for permission to come nuzzle her. "Aw, girl, come here," Rachel sighed and reached out. Bella tumbled into her and rubbed up against her. Rachel's head dropped as another wave of emotion hit. A wet nose touched her cheek. Once again, the canine didn't want to see her cry. She wrapped her arms around the squirming figure and sighed. "I can't help it, Miss B," she whispered and then let the tears fall.

~

Luke replayed the conversation in his head, debating about whether or not to demand she let him back in once she'd told him about Derek and Kris. No, it was best to give her time. She wouldn't respond well to any insistence on his part. Right now, he would just contact Ted and see what he could do to help. He opened the door to his Subaru and drove away.

As he gained speed and the conversation replayed in his mind, Luke realized—clearly far too late—that Derek hadn't told her anything. Her red eyes weren't from crying over learning about Luke's problem. Instead, she'd had one of the worst days of her life, and he'd made it even worse. All because he was too focused on his own misery to see how upset she had been when she arrived home. Yes, she was far too good for him. He was doing her a favor by letting her go. No sense in dragging her down with him. However, he still wanted—no, needed—to help find the missing people she loved. Once he had full cell service, Luke slowed to the side of the road and took a moment to calm his insides before dialing Ted. It went to voice mail, so he left a short message.

"Ted, it's Luke. I heard about Derek and Kris. Call me." After hanging up, he steered back onto the road and debated where to go. He didn't know. For now, his only choice was to head home and wait to hear more.

~

As he paced down the hall toward his desk, Ted looked around at the flurry of activity among the other officers. Two missing people, taken in what appeared to be a violent way, had everyone working overtime this weekend. Ted's phone beeped, alerting him to a new message. There were some places in the office that didn't get reception, including the small conference room where he'd spent the last forty-five minutes. Yet move ten feet and most phones had full strength. It annoyed them all.

The number on the display indicated the last caller had been Luke. Ted assumed he would be with Rachel now—she'd gone home over an hour ago; he dialed her number as he sat down in his office chair. As usual, the old parts squeaked as he leaned back. An exhausted-sounding Rachel answered.

"Ted? Did you find them?" she asked.

"Not yet, Rachel. I'm sorry. I'm returning Luke's call. Is he there?"

There was a momentary silence before she responded. "No. And he won't be."

Uh-oh, Ted thought. *Trouble in paradise.* He waited; she didn't elaborate. "I'll call him directly then." He shifted in his seat and nudged his mouse to begin the slow process of waking up his computer.

"I've been thinking," Rachel said. "We know someone took both of them. If Derek's point was that he has Kris's inhaler, that's good, right? His way of telling us they're still alive, so it matters that she'll have it?"

He heard the hope in her voice. "That would make sense," he reassured, wanting to give her something to hold on to. In his own mind, he knew never to assume anything. Criminals didn't always think like everyone else. He reached up and rubbed the stubble on his chin. "I know you went over this in your report, but have you given more thought to anyone who would have wanted to harm either of them? My first inclination would be that because it happened at Kris's house, she was the initial target. Unless someone had a reason to think your brother would be there."

"They've never even met." Rachel blew her nose.

"I didn't think so," Ted continued. "Which lends more support to the idea that Kris was the original target. Your brother hadn't planned to go over there, right? You mentioned he went to close a window?"

"Correct."

"So maybe he caught someone there in the act. Still . . . Kris's car isn't there. I put out an alert to look for it. We know she left her house because she texted her parents. Given she never made it to her destination, coupled with the attack on your brother at her place, perhaps she returned for some reason and found Derek there. Then someone overtook them both?"

"But if she came home, where's her car?" Rachel wondered.

"Maybe her abductor—or abductors—drove it away to make it look like she had still made her weekend trip," Ted brainstormed. "Look, let's focus on the good news. All evidence suggests they're both alive. If someone were out to kill them, they could have easily done so and left them there." Ted's computer booted out of hibernation and asked for his password. After typing it in, his inbox appeared. There was a new e-mail from one of their patrol officers. According to the time stamp, it had arrived only minutes ago. He scanned through it and then spoke.

"You still there?" he asked after the line remained silent.

"Uh-huh," she responded, her voice congested, likely from crying.

"They found her car. It has some rear-end damage," he said, squinting to read the small font in the report included with the message.

"It was fine yesterday," Rachel stated.

"I figured that was the case, especially if she planned to drive it down the hill."

"Where was it?"

"Looks like it was parked a couple of streets over in that small industrial area behind Raley's. The one at the Y." Ted skimmed through the additional page. "I'll get someone looking through security camera feeds around the area." Ted scrawled another note on his pad. An idea occurred to him. Rachel could start exploring potential scenarios; plus, it wouldn't hurt to give her something to do. He cared for her like the sister he never had, and he hurt at the despair in her voice. Keeping her occupied would help. And maybe she'd find something useful. "If you're up to it, how would you feel about checking out what Kris was working on?"

"Of course," she replied immediately. "Does that mean you found her laptop?" Before Rachel had left Kris's house to file her report at the police station, Ted and the other officers had searched for her computer.

"No, and they didn't say they found it in her car either. I was hoping she used one of those cloud service things and you could figure out how to access her files?"

"She does, although I don't know the password. But we do share most of our work files on a web server when we are both involved with the same project. I can easily access those, but not any solo tasks." Rachel sighed, although Ted also heard a flicker of hope in her tone. Rachel continued, "I might be able to see her calendar, too; maybe it will show something useful."

"It's a start," he replied. Ted tapped his finger on the down arrow, looking for anything else that might be helpful. He found a list of items discovered along with the car. "Her cell phone was found inside. It's smashed. There was also one large suitcase, an ice chest, a pillow, and a few other loose items, including her wallet. Weird . . . no purse."

"Someone abducts her yet allows her to keep her purse while leaving everything else behind?" Rachel queried.

"That's strange. Or we merely haven't found it yet. But—let's assume she has it for the moment. In fact, you mentioned earlier that she uses an inhaler. I imagine she'd carry that in her purse? Which would be a good sign and may confirm the potential translation of Derek's message." Ted turned in his chair and then winced at the noise.

"She often swaps it out between her purse and backpack. I think she was waiting on a refill, so she'd have two units: one for her purse, one for her car. One had expired. I remember because she was complaining the other day about how long it took for the doctor's office to refill it, and she worried she'd forget to take it with her everywhere. What a pain in the butt to have to deal with that regul—"

"Rachel, you're a genius!" Ted cut in. Her tendency to babble when nervous or anxious may have paid off.

"What?" she uttered.

"What if she left it at home? And the abductor came back to her house to get it?" Ted continued his train of thought, gaining excitement as he formed his theory. "There was no glass out front, so the perp didn't rear-end her when she arrived home. He must have nabbed her somewhere else, which means he came back after he had her, maybe to get her medicine, and found your brother."

"That would mean that one, they aren't planning to kill her—at least not immediately—and two, maybe for Derek it was simply the wrong place, wrong time," Rachel added to Ted's brainstorm.

"Exactly."

"If that's the case, then Kris probably was the original target as you surmised," Rachel concluded.

"Which means, my friend, that you need to start looking through those files and tell me if anything she was working on was contentious or could have upset the wrong people." He heard a small choking sound escape her.

"Ted, our work involves large development projects, government regulations, and environmental policy; everything we work on is generally contentious and likely to upset people," she stated flatly.

"Good point."

The line grew silent. Then Rachel spoke up with renewed excitement in her voice. "Hey, if the person who took her plans to keep her alive, then there's a reason they're holding her captive. I'm wondering if I should focus on projects that may have approaching deadlines? Of course, this all could be entirely unrelated, but you never know. What do you think?"

Initially, his suggestion for Rachel was more of a way to occupy her attention. Instead, their conversation had increased his suspicions that it actually could be a premeditated kidnapping related to Kris's job.

"That makes sense," he agreed. The line went silent for a few seconds.

"Ted?" Rachel's tone had quieted.

"Yeah?"

"In your experience, the amount of blood that was on her floor... is that enough for someone to bleed out?" Rachel's inquiry sounded tentative as if she was afraid if she spoke too loudly the answer would be yes.

"According to the crime scene techs, no. It's a bad wound, but not likely a fatal amount of blood loss on its own," he assured her and hoped he wasn't providing false hope.

"OK, thanks. I'll be in touch if I find anything."

Chapter 17

Luke stared at his computer screen. He'd attempted to focus on work as a way to avoid thinking about his breakup with Rachel. He still couldn't believe it. Even though he'd gone over there telling himself it was best for them both to end it, deep down he hoped for something more like a temporary reprieve. Hell, he wasn't sure what he intended. Either way, the prospect of a final goodbye, of never holding her again in his arms or teasing her when she sang along out of tune with her favorite songs . . . or kissing her. It was agony.

Beep.

The noise drew him out of wallowing in self-pity. He had a new e-mail. He focused on the monitor, trying to see through the moisture in his eyes. The message was from one of the girls who'd hired him yesterday to search for Nancy Parsons. The younger daughter was clearly anxious to hear whether he'd tracked down any police department files associated with the disappearance. The woman's mother—the grandmother who had eventually raised them—had filed a missing person report at the time; unfortunately, it had never amounted to anything. The sisters obviously didn't understand how slowly the wheels could turn for cold cases. But he couldn't blame them either. He remembered the angst after years of searching for his younger sister. Like their grandmother, he'd eventually given up. Unlike the two ladies, he finally had answers. Luke composed a short response to let them know he'd made the official request for files.

As soon as he sent the reply, he found himself thinking of Rachel. And those damn pills. And Derek and Kris. Could their disappearance really be a case of foul play? God, he hoped it was something benign, like maybe they met up and decided to get away and have some crazy weekend sex or something. People did that sometimes. He didn't know either of them very well. He'd met Kris over a year ago and seen her several times with Rachel. Although, based on the impression he'd formed, he wasn't sure she'd fall for Derek's game. Too intelligent. And too serious. Of course, who's to say women don't occasionally go looking solely for a good time? Before he could ponder the possibilities, his phone rang. He glanced at the screen.

"Ted, hey, what's going on with Derek and Kris?"

"I'm working on it." Ted's tone bordered hesitant.

"What's wrong?" Luke asked.

"I'm busy. Plus, so you know, I'm aware something happened between you and Rachel. I don't know what, and frankly I don't want to know. However, I also don't want to be a go-between among the two of you," he stated.

"Understood," Luke said, caught off guard by the man's abruptness.

"Good. That said, she's looking over her and Kris's files to see if there're any red flags." A voice called Ted's name in the background. "Hold on," he instructed. Luke ran his fingers through his hair as he heard someone talking to Ted. A moment later, his friend's voice returned with full volume. "Thanks for waiting." Ted gave him a quick rundown of what Rachel had found.

"What can I do to help?" Luke asked, agitated.

"Just . . . be available if we need anything. We're still processing the scene. We did locate Kris's car. Looks like a smash-and-grab," Ted stated, using the common lingo for setups when someone rear-ends someone else and then kidnaps them when they step out to swap insurance information.

"Crap. What about Derek's car?"

"It was sitting out in front of Kris's. Nothing helpful inside."

"All right. Call me if there's anything I can do. Seriously."

"I'll be in touch," Ted said before he hung up. Though the man was distracted by his case, Luke also got the sense that Ted was more sympathetic to Rachel's heartbreak than his own.

~

"Well, I think it's safe to assume they've got to be looking for us by now," Kris muttered as she fingered through the wrapped food items. She heard a pained grunt from behind her and turned around to face Derek. He was half standing, partially balanced on one leg, his hand tightly gripping the armrest for support. She glanced down at his leg. "I don't think you should be moving," she said and then turned her gaze back to the various plastic and foil packages. He was a big boy; if he was dumb enough to make his injury worse, well, that was his choice.

"I gotta pee," he responded.

"Oh." She turned. "Well, in that case, need some help?"

"You going to hold it for me?"

Kris just stared at him. He raised a brow.

"You really are a pig," she said.

"That's what my sister says." He grinned. "I'm assuming that opening in the corner over there is some kind of bathroom?"

"Yes, and FYI: there's no door." Kris resumed her search, deciding on a chocolate peanut butter protein bar.

"Somehow I don't think I need to worry about offending your womanly sensibilities," he said as he began dragging himself toward the bathroom. The scuffing on the floor reminded Kris of a zombie-themed Halloween party from a few years ago when a group of her friends took to walking around town, playing up their costumes to the hilt. Kris smiled and bit into the snack, watching his progress while expecting him to lose his balance and fall to the floor. It would serve him right, maybe knock that ego down a peg or two. It only took a few steps before he faltered. She tossed the food aside and rushed over to him, but not before he'd fully collapsed on the ground.

"Stubborn much?" She helped raise him back up on his good leg. "I was wondering if you were ever going to ask for help." They began walking at a slow pace.

"I could've gotten there without you, you know," he said as they reached the opening.

"Trust me, I was definitely tempted to simply watch, but I don't need any bad karma . . . from ignoring someone in need and all." She released him as he grabbed the doorframe for support and leaned against it.

"You believe in that crap?"

"What goes around comes around. Don't tell me you've never experienced it," Kris responded as she walked across the room and picked up her discarded half-eaten bar, peeled the wrapper off, and took another bite.

"You trust what's on this floor?" he asked.

"Five-second rule. Plus, it was still mostly wrapped." She smiled. "Oh, here, I'll turn away. Don't want to offend your manly sensibilities," she said as she laughed, pivoting around so her back faced him.

"Cute," he muttered. A minute later the toilet flushed. At least they had running water in this place. Wherever it was. And heat from an old wall heater. In fact, if not for the circumstances, she could almost visualize this cabin as a nice place to get away from people for a while. "Okay, Miss Kris. What's our plan here?"

She looked his way and watched with amusement as he half walked, half hopped his way back to the love seat. He grimaced a couple of times, and she thought he might topple over again, but he eventually made it without incident.

"I think we can both agree that this guy isn't planning to kill us." Kris did her best to remain calm and assured as she peered at their food and water supply, then back at Derek. "At least right away." With her attention once again solely focused on their dilemma, the idea of being kidnapped by someone who could easily decide to murder her at any time twisted up her nerves.

"Says the girl to the guy with a gunshot wound," he responded sarcastically. She caught his gaze and noticed a slight curve in the corners of his mouth. It was a sexy look.

Wait, what? Where had that last thought come from? She quickly responded, "Well, it wasn't through your heart, right?"

"Yeah, that would have really sucked. Death and all." He chuckled and then grew quiet. Kris walked over to him.

"How's it feeling?"

"Like I wish I had some narcotics. Or alcohol. Or even some weed. How about all of the above?"

"Are you ever serious?"

"Life's too short to be so serious," he said as he leaned his head back. "Then again, I hope life isn't *this* short," he mumbled. "And I think I *am* being serious; I'd take any one of those options at the moment."

"We're going to get out of here. I mean, really, like, think about it. There's two of us. So far, one of him. We can do this. We need to have a strategy. Unless we believe him—that he won't hurt us if we do what he says." She mumbled the last sentence as she looked around the cabin. "Not sure I want to believe someone who's kidnapped me. Either way, I didn't find any way out of here last night or figure out any way to attack him." Her wordy brainstorm continued. "But with two of us . . . if I can find a makeshift weapon of some kind, maybe you could distract him. Give me the chance to hit him with something."

"Let's slow down and give this some thought," he said, putting his palm out as if signaling her to stop. "First, can you grab me some water?"

"Sure." She walked into the kitchen area and retrieved a bottle from the twelve-pack bound with shrink wrap in the refrigerator. Although the drugged bottle from last night had been set by itself on the table and not packaged, she still looked for small holes or anything else that could indicate the rest of the water had been laced with something. She recalled seeing that on one of the *CSI* shows on TV. Probably the Vegas one. Kris tipped it upside down. Nothing dripped. As best as she could tell, it hadn't been tampered with, but there were no guarantees. She handed it to him, noticing fresh blood on his makeshift bandage. He caught her gaze and followed it as she nodded toward his leg. "Should we change that again?"

"Let's give it a little time. That first aid kit is small; not sure how often we'll be able to change it before running out."

"When do you think he'll come back?" she asked, not expecting an answer. She was more just dealing with nervous energy.

"Hopefully we have a little time. Given the luxurious food and water supply, I think we're holed up in here for at least another day, maybe two. Yet who's to say he won't return sooner?"

Kris didn't respond, pondering what he'd said.

Suddenly, there was a loud creak on the outside of the front door. Kris looked up anxiously. Was he out there?

Chapter 18

Rachel groggily opened her eyes to see Bella staring at her; the dog's entire body shook as her tail swished back and forth. She smiled just before the recollection of Kris and Derek's situation rushed to the surface of her sleepy mind. Sitting up, Rachel realized she had fallen asleep on her couch. *Crap!* Frantic, she scanned the room and spotted her cell phone on the floor. After reaching down to retrieve it, she viewed the display. Vision in her left eye was blurry again, and she squinted. How long would this concussion affect her? Rachel's heart sank when she noticed it was now 8:03 a.m. on Sunday. Derek and Kris had been missing for a day and a half. Her nerves rattled with the realization she had lost a whole night of looking through Kris's files.

She jumped up so fast she tripped over Bella. "Shit!" The sudden movement shot pain through her head. She dropped back down, taking a deep breath as she reached over and massaged Bella's head. She had to work through the throbbing. There was no other option. This time, Rachel rose with more care, then walked into the kitchen, flipping on the coffeemaker before realizing she had to put the ground coffee in first. She swore as she prepared the contents. After a quick shower and some caffeine, she'd get back to her search.

~

After tossing and turning for hours, Kris gave up on any hope of falling back to sleep at four a.m., according to her watch. She remained in bed, not wanting to disturb Derek. She figured rest was especially important for his wound. Plus, what would she have done if she'd gotten up anyway? It was now almost nine a.m. It had to be Sunday—which meant she'd been in the cabin for two nights. After they determined the noise on the front steps last night was most likely a bear and not an eavesdropping kidnapper, they resolved to search the room again for any kind of weapon. Kris double-checked every nook and cranny while Derek had gone about dismantling two of the wooden chairs. Not the most ideal ammunition, but there was nothing else. While both were apt to believe the man's warning about their disconnected location and that no one else knew where they were, there was still the chance he was a skilled liar. Or that he planned to kill them eventually even though he claimed otherwise.

Kris stretched her arms, stood up, and looked toward the love seat. She'd suggested Derek take the bed, but there was no way to prop up his leg. Though neither of them knew whether elevating it would actually matter, they agreed it made sense that it might help reduce swelling or bleeding. Kris did a double take; Derek wasn't there. She walked around the furniture to investigate. He was lying nearby on the floor, his face flushed. He looked bad. His shirt was tossed nearby and he was on his side, hugging himself as if he'd become cold in the night. She knelt down and touched his forehead. It was hot. Too hot.

"Derek?" she said, sorry to wake him up yet unwilling to leave him on the floor. He groaned. She called out again.

"Yeah?" he responded. His eyes remained closed.

"Wake up. It's Kris." She waited patiently. He shifted, untucked his arms, and rolled on his back. His eyes opened.

"I'd hoped this was all a dream," he whispered.

"Why are you on the floor?"

"I think something was dripping on me." He sounded confused but looked up. Kris followed his gaze. A dark spot spread out on the wooden beams lining the ceiling.

"A leaky roof? Just what we need," she complained and turned back to him. "You're burning up. I think your wound might be infected. Can I look at it?"

"That would explain why everything hurts and I feel like I partied all night. Go ahead," he said, wincing as she untied the scarf, which was matted with more dried blood. She did her best to peel off the bandages without making anything worse. Kris inhaled a sharp breath when she saw the red inflamed skin underneath.

"Shit," she whispered.

"That doesn't sound promising." Derek tried to lift up his upper body, presumably to look, but he made a pained sound and relaxed back against the cold floor.

"Let's get you onto the bed, and then I'll try to wash it as best as I can."

He nodded. "Bathroom first," he said as she helped raise him up. "Guess I'll need your help after all. You know you've wanted a peek at it anyway," he teased.

"You wish," she replied, then helped him into the small washroom. Once he was able to grab the small sink for balance, she gave him some privacy. A few minutes later he exhaled a long breath as they reached the bed. He rolled face up onto the mattress. "I think there may be one more antiseptic cloth in here." Kris fingered through the small kit.

"This is not how I like to spend my mornings with beautiful women."

"You really are a playboy, aren't ya?" she said as she smirked. She found the tiny package she'd been looking for and carefully read the directions. "Maybe I should find something you can put in your mouth while I do this; it might hurt."

Derek laughed. "Maybe there's still hope for this morning after all. I'm happy to make a recommendation."

"You just don't quit, do you?"

He chucked, but then his tone grew serious. "Go ahead. Get it over with. I'll live." She nodded, grabbed a nearby water bottle, and flushed the inflamed area. His entire body tensed as she pressed the medicinal cloth against his skin. To his credit, he didn't make a sound the entire time. She wasn't sure he let out a breath either. After fixing up the bandage and tying the scarf again, she handed him the water and then looked back at the small pile of refreshments.

"You think he'll come back today?" she asked, noting that while they had extra water, the food wouldn't last as long. There was a good chance the man only planned on having one captive and hadn't run to the grocery store when he'd ended up with two. Which meant it could be a while before he returned.

"I don't know. Do you?" He unscrewed the top of the bottle and chugged down the remaining water. Several drops slid down the side of his mouth.

"Don't waste any of that. You never know. And based on the lovely shade of copper in that sink, I don't think we'll want to drink from the faucet." Before he could respond, she heard a hum in the distance. As it grew louder, she recognized what it was. A snowmobile. She looked at Derek; he'd heard it, too.

~

"I was wondering when I'd hear from you," Ted said after he answered the call.

"My brain failed me last night."

He heard the frustration in Rachel's voice. "You can only do what you can do, and you're still healing from a TBI." After his cousin had banged his head in a car accident, he'd learned that traumatic brain injuries like hers could plague people for months, even years. Now wasn't the time to mention that.

"Thanks, but I can't just sit around and wait." Her voice cracked, and then she continued, changing the topic. "So far, I found a few projects involving especially profitable ventures. The more they stand to make, the more they might be ticked off with efforts to challenge the permits. Then again, very few large projects *don't* upset someone. Anyhow, I'm looking through them again with emphasis on the timing. Have you found anything new?"

"Nothing. No unique phone calls to or from either of them. No one noticed any unfamiliar cars or noises. Unfortunately, the few full-timers in the area weren't home." Ted had barely slept for more than a few hours after spending most of the night scouring Kris's home, yard, and neighborhood in search of clues. So far, he had nothing.

"Okay, I'll keep looking."

"Sounds good. And Rachel—don't overdo it. Take breaks. You won't be able to help at all if you wear yourself out. Remember what my cousin said: don't forget 'brain naps.'"

"I'll try," she responded before ending the call. He didn't have much confidence she'd listen. He'd probably be just as stubborn in her shoes.

~

Oliver had been watching Miss Winter's house since the sun rose that morning. The SUV he'd stolen in Tahoe City was parked about half a block away. No one had come or gone from her home. The few neighbors in the area had already left, probably for church or skiing. Which meant she was there alone. It was the perfect opportunity for him. A whimper escaped from behind him. He thumped his hand against the small steel grid on the front of the dog crate. The canine shifted around inside for a few seconds and then grew quiet—not what he wanted. The bitch needed to be agitated and ready to attack the woman's mutt to keep it occupied while Oliver pursued his plan.

Yesterday he'd tested her reaction, using a black dog he'd seen fighting another stray while in Carson City. It was his luck the new creature was already aggressive toward her. Within seconds he had started growling, anxious to get to White—Oliver realized he now thought of them as "White" and "Black." Black had ferociously snapped in her direction. In response, White had tucked her tail underneath her belly, sunk down, rolled over, and bared her stomach in a submissive gesture. He released Black, hoping he would attack. He was right, and after a couple of bites, she started to defend herself. They'd tussled around his yard for several minutes. Oliver considered switching them for Tuesday's fight, but the black dog's long ears and thick tail made him too easy of a target for other contestants, as he thought of them, to grip onto. He still needed to break the animal down so it understood who the master was. As a result, he'd only chosen to bring White along for this excursion.

Oliver cruised forward and parked his vehicle in the vacant driveway next to the woman's house. After pulling the ski mask over his head—a disguise that could be easily justified by the cold temperatures if he encountered anyone—he climbed out, turned around, and opened the back door to retrieve White. She cowered in the back of the crate. He grabbed her collar and yanked. Once she was on the ground and leashed, he slapped her head so hard it swung off to the side. She didn't shrink away this time. But she didn't attack either; she just stood there, hackles raised and her uneven ears lowered. He was obviously going to have to work more to stir her aggression. He whipped her backside with the end of the leash. It took a few swings for her to finally lash out, biting down on his gloved hand.

"Good girl. Now turn some of that anger on the other dog, and you'll make your master very happy." He jerked her across the layer of snow that coated the ground between where he'd parked and the corner of the woman's house. His feet sank almost six inches in the fresh snow with each step. Good thing he'd brought a shovel along to stamp out any boot prints when he was done; he wasn't sure the cops could get any useful information from them, but why risk it? A wooden six-foot fence encircled the backyard. He wasn't worried; he was strong enough to lift White over the top. With the creature still jumping around and yanking on the leash, he grabbed her muzzle and held it closed, and then he clicked open her collar and removed it. He lifted her squirming body and dropped her over the fence. There was a small cry, some shuffling, and then the thwacking sound of her shaking her head. A second later, the jingle of tags indicated the woman's dog was approaching. *Perfect.* The chiming stopped. A low growling sound emerged from White. He waited and watched the scene over the top of the fence with growing anticipation. The woman's mostly black dog stood in place, staring at White. Its tail projected straight out with the slightest hint of a curve at the end. There was no wagging. *So far, so good.* He looked back at White. She remained still as if preparing to attack her prey. The black one took a step closer, sniffing the air between them. White crouched down getting ready to lunge.

"Get 'er!" he whispered, egging them on. Both canines ignored him, maintaining intense eye contact with each other. Oliver waited, anxious for the scuffle to begin.

The black dog's bushy tail started to wag, and the animal whimpered lightly. He looked back at White. She was still bent in a bowed position. He held his breath. Waiting.

Oliver watched in complete shock and horror as White's tail started to wag. She leapt toward the other canine. Two tails shook in unison as they playfully began to wrestle. *No! This wasn't supposed to happen!* He debated his options. *Okay, think.* Without White keeping the other one occupied, Oliver's best chance was to get to the woman before she heard the commotion in the yard. If it wasn't already too late. At this point, he had nothing to lose.

He pivoted and jumped through the snowdrifts toward the front door. When he reached it, he grasped the handle. Sometimes people left doors unlocked while at home. No luck here. He stepped back and reached into his pocket. Oliver brandished his gun, pulled the trigger, and shot out the deadbolt. He may not have been at the top of his class when it came to academics, but he had been a natural when it came to hitting his target. He kicked the door open and bounded inside.

Chapter 19

Rachel leaned back and reviewed the files for the larger projects to determine which ones had timelines involved. A couple of proposals were still in the draft environmental report stage, which meant there would be months before any final approvals. She marked those off her list of recent actions. Two large resort and housing developments with recently released final environmental studies were close to being voted on. One was a project on the West Shore of Lake Tahoe. Misleadingly masked as a *"re*development" project because it built a portion of the new five-hundred unit, four-story condominiums on an existing parking lot, it had garnered support from the Tahoe Regional Planning Agency, often referred to as TRPA. How removing a 2,500-square-foot parking lot and replacing it with an eighty-thousand-square-foot multibuilding condo development was not considered "new" development was beyond her comprehension; however, use the words "redevelopment" and "recreation" and voila!—pesky details, like worsening traffic jams, were overlooked by land-use agencies to accommodate the developers. It didn't seem to matter that the highways around Tahoe were mostly two-lane roads that couldn't be expanded. That was another reason there were supposed to be limits to how much new development there could be in the basin, if anyone ever cared to fully enforce them. Rachel realized her mind had drifted again, and she worked to focus her attention back on the task at hand.

"When is this monstrosity up for a vote?" Rachel asked as she downed the remnants of lukewarm coffee. One more click and she confirmed it was scheduled for a final public hearing at the next TRPA governing board meeting. Now *that* could fall within the time frame Ted suggested.

Rachel scrolled the mouse over the next file folder for the Tahoe-Truckee Pines project. It was the new subdivision off State Route 267 between Kings Beach and Truckee that had been recommended by the Placer County Planning Commission earlier that week. In fact, she'd been talking to Kris about it a few days ago; the recent meeting had been extremely contentious. It was likely going to be put forward for a final vote by the county's board of supervisors soon. That was another one to keep on the list of potential suspects, so to speak.

Rachel scrawled more notes as she continued reviewing documents and web pages. So focused was her attention on the computer that when Bella dashed outside through the doggie door, causing the entire inserted door to shake, she jumped a little from the rattling noise. It was rare for Bella to run out like that. It usually meant she'd seen something in the yard, like a squirrel or, even once, a raccoon. Not that she ever caught them.

Another few minutes passed without any new revelations. Rachel yawned as she eyed her empty coffee mug. This situation definitely warranted a second cup. She stood and walked toward the kitchen. A sudden, resounding crash came from her back door as Bella dove back into the house through the small opening. A second later, she was followed by a white-and-black dog. *Huh?* The two bodies ran in circles, playfully nipping at each other. Rachel found herself temporarily mesmerized by the special canine dance. She eventually focused on the white one and noticed there was something wrong with its ears. One more circle around the room and they dashed back out to the yard. Recovering from the shock of spying the extra canine, she placed the ceramic mug down and opened her mouth to call out to Bella.

A loud sound exploded at the front of her house. *Holy crap—a gunshot?* On instinct, she dropped to her knees behind the kitchen counter. She heard the front door burst open. Rachel carefully peered around the corner, attempting to get a glimpse of the intruder without being seen.

A bulky man stood in the doorway, his eyes scanning the room. He held a small weapon in his left hand and wore a dark blue ski mask. So far, she didn't think he had looked in the kitchen, let alone at floor level. If he had, she'd likely already be dead. She slowly moved back so she was entirely hidden from his line of sight. What should her next move be? And who the hell was this? He looked tall, maybe a few inches taller than Derek. She remained crouched, her body frozen in place while her mind tried to process her options. She didn't have a gun, and she'd make an easy target if she tried to run. Her eyes surveyed her kitchen, hoping for an idea. No way could she get to her knife drawer without being seen. Same for the house phone. Where was her cell? She heard him step inside, and her adrenaline spiked.

Footsteps were closing the gap between her and freedom. He was getting close. The lone advantage she had was that he didn't seem to know where she was. The downside was that she was a sitting duck if she didn't take action. Doing her best to keep the butterflies in her stomach at bay, Rachel prepared to jump against him when he rounded the corner. Perhaps she could catch him off guard and knock his hands free.

Another step.

Rachel tensed. One more and he'd no doubt see her. She had to act. *Now!* Rachel slammed into him, throwing all her weight into the movement. At the same time, she slashed her arms downward where she'd seen him holding the gun. Fate was on her side. Her forearms smacked hard against flesh. The weapon fell and clattered on the floor. He stepped backward, grabbing her arm and yanking her against him. The awful stench of body odor and stale beer filled her nostrils. Rachel fought the urge to vomit. She had to think fast.

Rachel swung her knee up, aiming for the man's groin. Her leg connected with its target. He grunted, his fingers loosening their grip. She jerked away from his clasp, but he was able to reach out and grab her again. They both tumbled to the floor. She struggled to break free, but he was too strong. It didn't take long for him to straddle her, pinning her down. Bile rose in her throat. She couldn't move. Both of her arms strained in an attempt to hold him at bay. He wore the sick grin of a crazy person. Rachel screamed. The man started to laugh. Tears blurred her vision.

Suddenly he cried out. His body shifted as his torso was wrenched sideways. With the lightening of his weight, Rachel twisted and slid out from under him. A deep guttural growl erupted nearby. She continued to drag herself, palms gaining traction on the floor. *Almost there.* Finally, she cleared him. Only then did Rachel turn her head and see that the white dog had the man's right arm in its jaws, tugging.

Her gaze shifted. Bella had joined the defense, a mirror image of the other animal, except she pulled on his leg instead. Rachel watched, horrified, as the man slammed his clenched fist into the white dog's face. It blinked but didn't let go. In fact, if anything, the canine seemed even more determined to cause him damage.

Her mind kicked into gear. *Where's his gun?* She frantically looked around the room, not seeing it anywhere. Had it slid under the couch when they'd fallen? No time to look. She needed to find something else to defend herself.

Rachel jumped to her feet and ran a wide berth around the struggling intruder. Like practiced partners in a dance routine, the canines kept him pinned in place. He alternated between hitting with his free fist and kicking with the untethered leg. They held their ground. She'd never heard Bella growl like that. Ever.

It only took a few seconds to yank the door of her coat closet open and reach inside. Her fingers touched the cool surface of a canister of bear spray. She pulled it out and aimed but then hesitated. If she let it stream out now, it would get into the dogs' eyes and ears, too. Forcing her nerves to remain calm, Rachel stepped forward, considering their position. His attention still on the pups, he hadn't yet seen her. Rachel swallowed and then spoke.

"It's over," she said, aiming the sprayer his way. The intruder paused and turned, looking up at her. Then he smiled—that horrifying, creepy grin he'd had when he first pinned her down. The strange dog maintained its grip on his wrist. Rachel noticed red smears on his fingers. *Please let it be him, not a dog.* He didn't attempt to move, but his expression became pained.

"Don't," he begged. Sweat beaded on the exposed skin near his eyes. She imagined the dogs' teeth were causing him some serious discomfort.

"Stay right there," she instructed, keeping the nozzle aimed at him as she inched her way toward her house phone on the kitchen counter—not only to call 9-1-1, but because from that side she could release the hot liquid and reduce the risk of splashing the dogs. Only a few more feet to go.

Rachel's foot landed on something round—Bella's Kong toy—and her ankle twisted. She lost her balance and tripped. Instinctively her arm swung to her side to break her fall, and she dropped the bear spray. Before she could stabilize, the man swung his raised arm in a large arc, landing his knuckles squarely on the white dog's mangled ear. The canine screeched and dropped his wrist. Rachel's eyes darted around the floor. Where was the spray?

Then she saw it. A mere foot or two away. The man followed her gaze, but Bella maintained her tight grip on his leg. *Please hold on a bit longer, my sweet girl.* Rachel dove toward the can. Her fingers wrapped around it. Lying on her back, she turned to face him. Anger surged as she watched him pound his free heel against Bella's face. The dog released him and pawed at her nose. Rachel had one chance.

She aimed and pulled the release. The fiery substance hit its mark, and he began to yell and claw at his eyes. As Rachel scooted back, the white dog attacked him again, this time burying her jowls into flesh right below his rib. He jabbed his elbow into the creature's eye socket. It let go, whimpering. Rachel scrambled to her knees, preparing to douse him with more. Her attacker, his eyes red and irritated, looked behind her toward the front of the house. He quickly jumped up and ran past her. Was he leaving? She jumped up intending to tuck herself behind the kitchen counter for cover and get in position to spray him again if he returned. In her peripheral vision she saw the stranger bend over for something on the other side of her couch. Then she realized it had to be the gun. He instantly held up the weapon and turned her way as Bella lunged at him. Rachel screamed as he pulled the trigger. Nothing happened. His face scrunched in confusion right before Bella seized his shin. He kicked her off and bolted out the front door. Both dogs followed.

"Bella!" she cried out, fearing he'd try shooting again and this time it would fire. Rachel grabbed the phone, pressed talk, and dialed 9 as she stuffed her feet into an old pair of boots. The phone slipped from her hand. There was no time to mess with it. She couldn't let the dogs go after the man. Just after she jumped through the busted doorway, Bella bounded into her. Rachel looked around her yard. The man had disappeared. Bella's new "friend" stood in the driveway as if contemplating whether to follow Bella or the human. A few heartbeats passed before it crept in Rachel's direction, its head bowed. Rachel waved toward the animal.

"Come here!" she encouraged as she stepped back into her house. Bella followed, and her new friend tagged along behind her. Once inside, Rachel slammed the door shut and slid down to the floor against it. Both canines leaned into her legs. They had just possibly saved her life.

~

Luke pondered the decades-old missing person case involving Nancy Parsons. He needed something to keep his mind occupied—to prevent the sick feeling he got every time he thought about what had gone down with Rachel. And what could have happened to her brother and Kris. Ted was a smart guy; until he called Luke with something for him to help with, there wasn't much more he could do. Had things been normal, he'd be over at Rachel's, diving in to assist her file search. Or he would at least be there to comfort her.

"Focus," he said to himself, frustrated his thoughts had wandered again. He looked back at the records he'd located so far. There had been no response from the cops on his request for the MP folder. However, it was still the weekend, so that was no surprise. And with it being such an old case, he'd probably have to keep contacting them to follow up. It could take time. In the meantime, an intensive online search produced an old picture of the woman from her high school yearbook and a couple of references to her first year both attending and working for the community college. That had to be tough—earning your degree while raising a family.

He was surprised how much the young Nancy resembled the oldest daughter. Or rather, how much her daughter had grown up to look like her. The odds were that their mother was dead. He didn't get the sense it was one of those situations where the parent willingly abandoned the kids. Skimming through other sections of the high school yearbook, he learned Nancy had been a cheerleader and class president. Clearly not a shy person. She'd gone missing two summers after her high school graduation, about eighteen months after she'd been married. Her husband, the girls' father, had raised them for several years on his own before he was killed by a drunk driver. After that, their grandmother had taken custody of them. Luke sincerely hoped he could provide some answers for them; they'd lost both parents at far too young of an age, and now their only remaining family member. All they had left was each other.

When his phone rang, he was so entrenched in thought that he jumped at the sound. Luke picked it up off the desk and saw that it was Ted.

"Yo," he said by way of answering.

"Luke, I realize you may not be in touch with Rachel but thought I'd ask if you'd heard from her recently?" Ted sounded worried.

"No, I haven't."

"I've been trying her for the last hour or so, and she hasn't answered. Her landline is busy, which almost never happens with call waiting, and she's not responding to my texts. I'm pretty sure she had no plans other than to try to go through Kris's files. I'd go check on her myself, but I'm stuck at the station."

"I'll head over there right now." Luke jumped to his feet.

"Keep me updated," Ted responded.

Luke grabbed his coat and keys and dashed out the door. He barely noticed the six inches of fresh snow on the ground.

~

"What should we do?" Kris asked Derek, her eyes wide.

"Grab those legs." He pointed his chin toward the dismantled chair pieces. Kris hurriedly plucked them up, handing two to him and then placing one in each hand. "Get behind the door. Wait until he walks inside, then slam it against him as hard as you can. You have more strength than I do right now. I'll try to get his attention focused in my direction." He leaned his weight on the small kitchen table.

Kris hesitated. "Do we really want to piss off this guy?" she inquired as she walked over and stood against the wall next to the door.

"I don't know. Let's just feel it out." There was a loud click. The deadbolt had been unlocked.

"*Are you kidding me?*" Kris mouthed her response at Derek. What kind of plan is that?

"Remember what I said: do anything to me and you're stuck here," the man called out before opening the door. Kris looked at the slow twist of the doorknob and then back at Derek. His eyes drooped like a child fighting sleep. He'd clearly be of no help. "I told you, I won't hurt you so long as you follow my directions."

Kris sagged, her arms dropping to her sides. Whether or not it was a good idea to try to overtake him didn't matter; she couldn't do it on her own. She leaned over and set the makeshift weapons down. Glancing at Derek, she saw that he had also released his grip. Kris stepped into the kitchen where she could face the doorway, positioned between an ailing Derek and their approaching captor.

"Okay. We heard you," Kris proclaimed loudly. Derek began to lightly cough. He was going downhill—fast. The door creaked open, refocusing her attention on the entryway. The first thing she saw was the barrel of the gun. It moved toward her as if floating through the air—or maybe it only appeared that way because nothing else around it mattered. A moment later the man lowered the weapon and stepped inside. Once again a black ski mask hid his face. Several flakes of snow swirled into the room around him. She raised her hands to show they were empty.

"Good," he said and nodded. Once fully inside the cabin, he looked around as if searching for anything out of the ordinary. His eyes paused on the broken chair parts, and then he looked back up. "I'm going to bring in some more supplies. Don't try anything stupid." He looked from Derek to Kris. She nodded. He stepped back outside and knelt on the small front step. He reached for something outside of the entryway with his free hand, stood up, and tossed a brightly colored bag into the room before turning and pulling the door shut.

"Wait!" Kris cried out. The man paused but didn't face her. "His wound is infected. He needs a hospital or he'll die." No response. "Please, if you really don't want to kill us as you've said, you need to get him help. Just . . . keep me. Wasn't that the original plan anyway?" she rambled, feeling the need to fill the silence.

"No, Kris," Derek pleaded from behind her. His words sounded slurred. The stranger stepped back inside and peered in Derek's direction. There were several seconds of silence. Kris waited, afraid to move for fear it would cause him to run.

"I can't," he stated.

"But—"

"I'll get you some antibiotics. It may take some time with this storm."

"What if something happens and you don't come back?" Kris contemplated.

"You die: I don't get paid. Consider me motivated," he stated plainly as he stepped back and banged the door closed. *Click*. "There are some first aid supplies in that bag," he hollered through the wood. Kris stood for a moment, unsure of what to do next. A motor roared to life. Kris spun to face Derek.

"Should we have still tried some—" She stopped at the sight of him. He leaned to his side, his hands wrapped around his stomach.

A distressed expression fell across his bright red face. "Derek?" she questioned, walking toward him.

"I'm . . . okay," he stuttered before collapsing on the mattress.

~

Of all the goddamn things, Jerry thought as he carefully steered the snowmobile through the trees. This job had been a pain in the ass from the very beginning. First, the girl almost spotted him when she'd unexpectedly whipped a U-turn before he planned to retrieve her. Second, the inhaler. Third, the guy at her house. Now, this. What was supposed to be an easy, well-paid job had become a huge mess. Jerry would definitely be renegotiating the terms of the arrangement with his client. The price had now gone up. He ducked as his machine passed under a low-hanging tree branch. If he'd had sufficient time to prepare, he could have become more familiar with the area. Although he felt confident he could find his way, especially with his GPS app, he'd have to be careful to avoid running into anything else unexpected.

~

"What the fuck?" Oliver stared at the useless weapon in his hand. After stashing it in his pocket upon leaving the woman's house, he hadn't removed it until he got home. He now sat at the small kitchen table, inspecting the damn thing. He couldn't find anything wrong with it. There were enough bullets in it. When was the last time he'd cleaned it? He slammed it down on the table, frustrated. A strangled cry burst from the other room. The black dog. He still couldn't believe that white bitch had started playing with the woman's mutt. *Playing* with it! Now what was he going to do?

Oliver stood and walked into the other room where a crate contained the one dog he now had left. There was no other option; this was the only fighter he had to enter the game. He'd just have to work harder. As for that slut, Rachel Winters, he'd go back and deal with her later. This time, he'd just shoot the animals first. In fact, the memory of her body writhing underneath him increased the anticipation. Yes, she had to be eliminated, but first he intended to have some fun with her. A lot of fun.

Chapter 20

As the adrenaline wore off, the throbbing in Rachel's head increased. She watched, transfixed, as the strange dog reached over and touched its muzzle to Bella's. After a brief pause, it turned back toward Rachel. A red scratch oozed blood along the side of its nose. It stood and gently nudged at her hand. Rachel's eyes were drawn to the mangled ears. It looked like someone had recently cut them off. Anger coursed through her veins.

"You poor thing," she whispered. The animal lay down and rolled over, exposing its belly. "Oh, so you're a girl," she spoke gently as she rubbed. Bella plopped down at her side, her eyes looking up at Rachel as if waiting for instructions. As much as she wanted to stay here and cuddle with these two sweet beings, Rachel needed to get up—and call 9-1-1. How long had she been sitting here petting them? Her brain seemed to have slowed down as if it couldn't process everything that had happened, like a computer working over its capacity. She needed to focus and act quickly. What if he came back to finish the job?

Rachel took a deep breath, then rolled and propped herself up on her knees. She felt a little nauseous but, otherwise, not too bad. Dizziness washed over her as she positioned herself closer to the couch and used the back to boost up to a standing position. She heard a vehicle drive up outside, and she tensed. Her eyes searched for the canister of bear spray. It rested on its side just a few feet away. Without removing her hand from the sofa, Rachel reached down and clenched it in her other fist, her eyes staring at her entryway.

"Rachel?"

Relief swept through her, and she leaned against the side of her sofa. It was Luke. Footsteps hammered on her front deck. After a brief pause, he pushed the door open. "What happened to your—" He caught sight of her. "Oh my God! Rachel, are you okay?" He ran toward her, his eyes scanning her body.

"This guy. He, uh . . ." Her voice faded as she struggled to form the words. Her fingers relaxed. The bear spray dropped.

"Let's get closer to the fire. It's freezing in here! Wait, are you hurt?"

"Nothing major, just feeling a little woozy," she said, struggling to stand up straight.

"Whoa, here, let me get you." She felt his arms wrap around her. She let herself lean into him while he slowly walked her over to the soft chair positioned next to her wood stove. "I'm going to add some wood. Be right back."

She noticed that both dogs had followed her and now sat quietly side by side a foot away. Bella's tail swung back and forth against the carpet, her eyes following Luke's movements. Remaining still, the other dog appeared hesitant around the new human in the room, although her body language didn't suggest she felt threatened or was poised to attack.

Luke placed more wood into the stove. Rachel leaned back as he walked over to the kitchen and filled a glass of water.

"Where's your phone?" He looked around.

"Oh, on the floor somewhere, I think," she replied. "And my cell. Maybe it's in my bedroom?" she wondered aloud.

Luke searched, spotted the landline phone in the entryway, and picked it up as he walked back toward her. He handed her the water before sitting across from her on the couch.

"It's on. Guess that's why it was busy," he mumbled as he pressed a button and then looked over at her. "I can call 9-1-1 for you, but I don't know what happened." He held out the handset.

"Thanks." Rachel took it, contemplating. With the danger temporarily dissuaded, she feared filing a police report could eat up precious time that could be better spent trying to locate any new leads on Kris and Derek.

"What's wrong?"

"I'm just so worried about Kris and Derek," she admitted. "I'm afraid to take downtime. Even to report this." She gestured around the room. "And what if it takes officers away from looking for them?"

"If you don't get checked out, and you have a brain bleed or something, you'll really be no help," he pointed out. "You look dazed. You can barely stand," he said as if explaining a basic concept to a child.

"My head is fine. I didn't hit it against anything. No ER," she asserted. "But I will file a police report and let them dust for prints. Only . . . not this minute. Look, I had just figured out some leads before that man burst in here, and if I don't make note of them now, they'll probably get lost in here." She pointed toward her head. "Ten minutes, then we'll call. I need to lay this stuff out for Ted."

Luke exhaled and looked around the room in an obvious attempt to avoid direct eye contact with Rachel. He did a double take when his gaze caught the dogs. He looked back at Rachel.

"The white one. I think he brought her, or she somehow got into my backyard at the perfect time. She helped Bella save me."

"Why am I not surprised?" Luke sighed, but then he corrected himself. "That she helped, I mean. Having her appear out of nowhere, now that doesn't happen every day." He reached out to let her sniff. Before her nose touched his fingers, Bella pushed her head underneath, moving the new dog out of the way and positioning herself for a rub instead. The other animal nudged Bella back. "No collar, I see," he said, petting their muzzles. "What happened to her ears?"

"A despicable human, I think," Rachel replied in disgust as she reached for the laptop on the coffee table. "Maybe the same one who attacked me. Wish I could slice his ears off and let him see how it feels," she griped but then refocused. "Let me get this message ready for Ted. Then I'll see if we can stay at CiCi's while the crime scene techs are here."

"Are you going to take her to animal control when they're open tomorrow?" Luke asked as he continued to stroke both of the animals.

Rachel was so taken aback by the question that she stared in silence. He finally looked at her.

"Dumb question," he acknowledged.

"I'll call to see if anyone's reported her missing, for sure," she stated.

"Of course," he said. "Look, I'd really feel better if you were checked out by a doctor."

"I'm sure you would," Rachel snapped, then regretted her harsh tone. He only worried because he cared. But why did that annoy her so much? She raised her hand and continued, "Look, if I start to feel worse, I promise I'll get checked out, okay?" She could tell he didn't like it, but he knew she wasn't going to budge. He nodded.

Reminding herself several times to concentrate, Rachel finally managed to type a message to Ted, listing information and contact names for the two projects she'd found earlier that were up for approvals soon. She couldn't imagine there was any connection. Then again, some people did awful things for money. She certainly had personal experience with that.

"Okay, it's sent. Now how about I call CiCi and you call Ted? Let him know to check his inbox ASAP."

"You can stay at my pl—"

"Luke, I know you mean well. But we broke up, remember? Your idea, though I'm thinking you did us both a favor. We haven't been doing so hot for a while now," she admitted. He didn't respond. Instead, he reached into his pocket for his cell phone.

"If the cops don't post a patrol at CiCi's, or wherever you go, let me know. I've got some people who could keep an eye out for you." He stood. Rachel watched as he walked toward the back door to where his cell service worked best. She wanted to argue but decided it best to pick her battles. Deep down, she had to admit she'd feel better having some security until they caught this creep.

~

"Derek, stay with me." Kris gripped both sides of his face. He was burning up. She ran over to the bag of items the man had left, dumped the contents onto the floor, and knelt to sift through them. Besides more packaged food and water, there was a box of large bandages, Neosporin ointment, hydrogen peroxide, cotton balls, and Tylenol. At least this guy was thorough. She reached for the bottle of pills; those should help with pain and fever. Kris swiped another bottle of water. As she hopped up on her feet, she inspected the lid for any signs of tampering. Nothing looked out of the ordinary, and the seal hadn't been broken. The water was nice and cold from being outside.

"I need you to wake up and take these pills," she pleaded as she emptied two into her hand. He moaned, but his eyes remained closed. She lightly slapped his cheek. He winced. "Come on!" she cried, continuing to tap at his skin. Finally, his eyes opened. Only halfway, but at least it was something. After twisting the cap off the water, she reached behind his head and propped it up a few inches. "Swallow these."

He nodded. His hand reached up to hers and lightly grasped it. She pressed the two round shapes into his palm. After he tossed them in his mouth, she tipped the water to his lips. He gulped a few times and began to cough. "I—can—do—that," he choked out as he reached for the bottle. "Sure, laugh at me all you want." More hacking. "You're enjoying this. I know it." His last few words came out as if spoken by a drunk person.

"Of course. I'm big on torturing cute guys."

"So you think I'm cute, huh?" The corners of his mouth turned up briefly but then relaxed, and he appeared to fall asleep. She reminded herself to calm down and give the fever reducer time to work. She also should clean the wound with hydrogen peroxide. The half-ass job they'd done earlier with the cleansing wipes was exactly that—half-ass.

Kris gathered the supplies before kneeling on the floor next to the small bed. She unwrapped the scarf and slowly peeled off the bandage underneath. The sore was red and filled with pus. She almost heaved. After glancing away for a minute to settle her stomach, she soaked a cotton ball with the liquid. *Pretend you are tending to a wound on Nemo.* Her cat had managed to develop a few disgusting sores over the years that required her attention. Puking right now wouldn't do either of them any good. When she squeezed the chemical on the bullet wound, white foam appeared. It reminded her of when she poured bath soap into the tub and watched the bubbles multiply. Derek jerked, moaned, and sucked in a deep breath. But he didn't completely wake up. Good, because this had to hurt. She continued to intermittently rinse with water and add more peroxide until it stopped fizzing. She smeared it with ointment and applied a fresh bandage.

After sorting through the supplies and anxiously pacing back and forth for what felt like hours, exhaustion tugged at Kris. The lack of sleep and stress of the last two days must have caught up with her. Based on what she could see out the window, it was getting close to dusk.

She couldn't leave Derek unattended. What if he woke up and needed something? She glanced at the far side of the bed tucked up against the wall. About a foot of space remained on one side of

Derek's body. She could lie down there and rest for a little while. If he needed something, she'd be right there to hear him. If she didn't sleep soon, she wasn't going to be able to take care of either one of them. As she carefully crawled across him and lay down, she wondered, yet again, why they'd been abducted. Should they keep following the man's instructions, or was he stringing them along for some sick game, all the while planning to kill them both after playing with them? Her mind started imagining all sorts of horrible scenarios, and she chastised herself for watching *Criminal Minds*. What a horrible TV show it could be for the imagination, as every episode featured some new level of depravity about what people did to other people.

~

Ted sent two officers to Rachel's house. There was no evidence to suggest the attack on Rachel was related to the disappearance of Kris and Derek, so he felt it best to continue his investigation while other officers dealt with the crime at her place. Rachel had provided him background information and two contact lists for upcoming controversial projects. He had no other leads. Had Kris not been taken first, he'd be diving into Derek's life with more depth.

Kris's parents knew of no one who'd want to hurt their daughter. Friends, including Rachel, all described her as someone who could charm almost anyone without trying. Ted had met her on several occasions, and those descriptions about summed it up. Yet people usually didn't know everything about their loved ones. We all had secrets, things we didn't readily share with others.

Ted had barely slept over the past twenty-four hours. He'd been too busy working with others on the force, sorting through the details of Kris's life. They hadn't found anything, past or present, that raised any red flags. Even ex-boyfriends had nothing bad to say about her. While many described her as "too energetic" or "too liberal," no one used any words suggesting anger or malice. That a stranger would return to gather her inhaler seemed odd but possible. It still felt more calculated. Strategic. Whoever held her captive had something more in mind. They wanted her alive in the meantime. He hoped they'd do the same for Derek Winters.

With his mind focused on the present, Ted stared at the e-mail from Rachel. While unlikely, he still had to consider that her attack today could be related to Kris's initial abduction. Rachel said the intruder had attempted to shoot her, but his gun jammed. Why would anyone kidnap one woman and return to retrieve lifesaving medicine for her yet kill the other? He picked up the phone and contacted one of the officers who had been processing the scene at Kris's home.

"Carina, it's Ted."

"Hey, boss. What can I do for you?" she asked, her voice chipper as always.

"I'm going to send you some names. I need you to find out all you can and report back to me ASAP," he instructed as he pushed the send button on his tablet.

"Will do, sir. Anything else?"

"No, that's it. Call me when you have some info," he replied. "And thanks." After hanging up, he dialed Luke. He needed to get more information on these people, and to do so quickly and without red tape. The call was answered on the fourth ring.

"Ted, what's up, man?" Luke sounded anxious.

"I need you to do some digging on a few people for me. On the QT."

"I'm with Rachel now."

"I know. I wouldn't ask if it wasn't important. She'll understand." Luke hesitated. Ted was preparing to chew him out when he finally responded.

"I'll need to do it at my office. Send me what you need. I'll let Rachel know, and then I'll go straight there and get started."

"Sounds good." Ted hung up.

Chapter 21

"I'm going to CiCi's for the night," Rachel told Luke after he'd returned from another conversation with Ted.

"I still think you should go get checked out at the ER." She stopped and glared at him with her "Are you serious?" expression. He continued, "If you're worried about the medical bills, I can—"

"Don't." She knew he was going to offer to pay. The money issue had certainly crossed her mind. She'd actually wondered whether, presuming they located the jerks involved in the snowmobile incident, the two riders could be forced to pay her medical bills. Luke remained quiet, visibly annoyed yet patiently waiting for her to say more. "Look, I know you're doing this because you care. And I appreciate that you helped me out this afternoon. Even if we were still together, you know I wouldn't let you pick up my bills. Either way, I need to focus my energy on finding out more to help Kris and Derek. Not on the crap between us," she blurted. The room was silent.

"Crap?"

"You know what I meant," she said, calming her voice. If she gave her broken heart any more thought, she'd lose it. And she couldn't afford to go there right now. The emotional fallout would have to wait until later. Rachel quickly changed the subject. "What did Ted need?"

"Oh." Luke almost looked as if he'd forgotten he had his phone in his hand. "He asked me to look up some people. I suppose the ones you e-mailed him about."

"Good. So go do it, please." She reached over and squeezed his hand. Their eyes met. A car door slammed out front, interrupting the

141

awkward silence. The cops, or possibly CiCi, had arrived. Luke let go and walked toward the front door. Bella leapt in front of him, likely hoping for a walk. He reached down and massaged her ears. The other dog came up next to them and prodded his hand. She let him stroke her back, but Rachel could see her shy away when his hand moved toward her face.

Luke straightened, opened the door, and walked out without another word. Rachel's heart sank as she watched him go. She saw CiCi's bright red car parked out front. The woman was running toward Rachel's porch. Movement to her side caused Rachel to pull her gaze away from the scene out front. Inside, the two dogs trotted past her, the white one close on Bella's heels as they casually exited onto the back deck, their tails wagging. Once outside, they began to tumble around, play fighting.

CiCi knocked, drawing Rachel's attention again. She'd barely greeted CiCi when the woman charged into the room.

"Yo, chickie. How ya doing?" she asked as she brushed past Rachel, carefully studying the living room as if the investigators were hiding in the walls.

"Still sane, I think."

"Where are the cops?" CiCi asked.

"On the way. I told them the guy was gone. I suppose it wasn't an emergency anymore." She looked out front once more. The distant image of Luke's Subaru driving away almost took her breath away. Rachel shifted her gaze back into the room. "You sure rushed over here."

"I was worried after your call." CiCi plopped down on a kitchen stool. "Hey, I passed your man leaving. He didn't look too happy."

"He's not my man anymore, for starters." Rachel almost choked on her words.

CiCi stared at her for a moment before speaking. "What?" she asked.

"How about I catch you up on that once we all get settled in at your place? First, how about meeting this new dog?" Rachel called the pups inside. She waited for a moment, watching them chase each other around in the fresh snow. Bella was so happy.

Boom! Several windows vibrated, and both dogs ran toward the house before Rachel said anything.

"Avi control," Rachel said as she chuckled. Given the topography and relatively short distance between her home and Echo Summit, when the state's transportation department performed avalanche control on Highway 50—called "avi control" by locals—the blasts impacted the homes in her neighborhood. Normally she preferred quiet, natural sounds, but to Rachel the avalanche bombs represented fresh snow; like the noise of snowblowers, it was a welcome sound.

"She helped save my life," Rachel called out as the canines came crashing inside, so much so that they slipped on the floor and bounded into Rachel's legs.

"Speaking of avalanches." CiCi laughed. Bella ran right up to CiCi with her tail ferociously wagging. The other dog followed her lead. CiCi reached down to pet both of them. "Well, aren't you a sweetheart!" She rubbed her ears, examining the mutilated nubs. "Whoever did this to you should be shot. After having their own ears cut off first," she said in disgust. "You think she belonged to the guy that attacked you?"

"It seems too much of a coincidence that she somehow got over my fence moments before he blew the lock off and charged in. Actually, I remember him saying something like 'get her' at one point. I'd forgotten about that."

"I'd guess he brought her along, maybe expecting her to attack Bella so he could have a clear shot at you?" CiCi surmised.

"That makes sense in a twisted sort of way. So he either owned her or possibly stole her from someone. She didn't seem to like him very much." She suddenly realized the dog might be hungry. Not only was the poor creature thin, but if she'd spent much time with her attacker—and chances were high he's the one who had lopped her ears like that—nutrition was probably not of much concern. "Let me see if she'll eat." Another car door shut out front.

"Cops are here," CiCi said as Rachel walked into the kitchen, retrieved a spare dish from the cupboard, and poured kibble inside. The animal howled with excitement. Or that's the closest word that came to mind. It was a friendly, happy sound. Rachel smiled as she set the bowl down. The dog devoured the food. The poor thing had definitely been starving. Rachel raised her head to look back at CiCi.

"I hope they don't keep me too long. I need to be helping Ted." Before they could knock, CiCi slid off her stool, signaling for Rachel to stay put.

"Like I said on the phone, I can take the pups with me now in your truck, leave you to give your statement, and then when you're done, just drive my car over. I'll have the table cleared off so you can keep working. And put me to work, too. I search files well enough."

"You're awesome. Thanks, girl!"

~

Bob raised the phone to his ear. Part of him was happy to receive the call; the other part was annoyed because the silence had stretched for weeks. They hadn't spoken since the day the snowmobile had broken down.

"Conway," he stated.

"How are you doing?" Conway's voice was quiet as if tentatively feeling out the situation. Good, he should be wondering.

"I'm fine. And you?" Bob sensed this was not going to be an easy conversation. They were both tense and tiptoeing around their words.

"Doing okay. I just wanted to check in on you. How's your finger?"

"Why thank you for your concern." Bob couldn't hold back his sarcasm. How dare Conway not return his calls this entire time, and then he, what, wants to check up on him all of a sudden? Really?

"It's healing. And in case you're wondering, I've dealt with the photographer; you don't need to worry about it." Silence.

"What do you mean you dealt with her?" Conway asked.

"Why do you care?" Bob countered.

"Because I care about you. That hasn't changed. I don't want you to get into any kind of trouble."

"Well, I appreciate your belated interest," he said flatly. "Like I said, I took care of it. That's all you need to know." Bob started to wonder if Conway had called simply to check up on what he had done about the pictures. He tilted his neck from side to side, trying to stretch out the tense muscles.

"But what did you—"

Bob ended the call before Conway could finish his question. Without thought, he tossed the device across the room. It slammed into the wall and clattered to the floor.

~

The snow was falling again. Weren't they in a drought? Go figure! The one job Jerry had taken on the West Coast happened during the only big storm of the winter. That was another reason his client was going to pay a lot more than they originally agreed to.

He didn't think he was too far off his snowmobile's previous tracks, which were now indiscernible underneath the new snow, yet somehow he'd veered in the wrong direction. He stopped, slipped off his gloves, and removed his helmet. Something caught on his ski mask, so he carefully peeled the material over his head and placed it inside the helmet, which he positioned on his lap. The fresh air and wet flakes felt good on his skin. High winds were causing horizontal snowdrifts. Jerry retrieved his cell phone from his coat pocket, accidentally brushing his elbow against the helmet and knocking it off his lap. It only took a minute or two of using his phone to figure out which direction he needed to go to get back on track. He set his foot down on one side to stand and stretch, almost losing his balance as his foot seeped down low and slushy snow squished around his boot. He hopped and caught himself, managing to swing his other leg over and regain his posture. With his balance restored, he tucked his phone away and bent over to retrieve his helmet and gear. Aside from his gloves inside, the helmet was empty. Jerry looked around for the mask and saw nothing. He reached down to the side, figuring it had fallen in the snow. He dug several inches below the surface where his feet had sunk down. No luck. Jerry weighed his options. What were the chances that his disguise would be found before snowmelt at this point? Dismal. No one was out here. If someone eventually came across it, any trace evidence would be gone from exposure to the elements. Annoyed, he positioned himself back on the machine, secured his helmet, and accelerated.

~

Derek felt warm. Too warm. He kept his eyes closed. He felt groggy, like he was drifting in and out of sleep. His thigh throbbed. And there was an odd pressure on his chest. As he began to regain awareness, his mind recalled his situation—the cabin. Were they still there? What about Kris?

The strange weight atop his rib cage shifted. *Huh?* He reached his right arm around to brush it off. It felt like hair. Derek struggled to open his eyes and lift his head enough to see what was there. It required far too much effort for such a brief move. He lifted a strand of hair so he could see it. Black hair with streaks of purple fanned out below his chin. Now he remembered; he'd fallen asleep on that small bed. Kris must have joined him. He heard a slight wheezing sound coming from where she lay. Oh no—she had asthma. Was she okay?

"Kris?" He shook her gently. Nothing. That sound again. "Kris, wake up!" he stated with more force. He heard a sniff.

"What? Where am I?" she mumbled. Derek let his head drop back. She sounded fine. Not out of breath. Then it occurred to him—she had been snoring. Not suffering from respiratory distress. With no need to worry, at least about her bronchial tube, he almost laughed. But the first muscle contraction hurt. Actually, his entire body hurt.

"I see you couldn't keep your hands off of me any longer," he teased, then coughed. A chill settled on the spot where her head had been resting. He continued, "I know, I can be hard to resist."

"Just keep telling yourself that," she quipped. The bed moved next to him as she pushed herself into a sitting position, twisting so her back was propped against the cabin's wall. She rubbed her eyes and yawned. "I guess I dozed off. I didn't want to be too far in case you needed something."

"Oh, I do need something, but I'm afraid my performance wouldn't be up to par at the moment."

"You ever get sued for sexual harassment? You seem far too comfortable with these cheesy lines." Kris scooted toward the end of the bed, stood, and stretched her arms above her head.

"Are they working?"

"That would be a no." She walked around to his side, leaned over, and placed the back of her fingers to his forehead. "How are you feeling?"

"Like I slid down The Wall." She looked perplexed. "You know, The Wall at Kirkwood? Every time it's icy, a whole bunch of people who ignore the skull-and-crossbones 'Experts Only' sign at the bottom of the chairlift end up falling and then sliding down the entire top half of the run."

"I don't ski."

He paused, waiting for her to say, "Just kidding." It never came.

"Seriously? Why not?" He was surprised. Who lived in Tahoe and didn't ski or snowboard? She ignored his question.

"You're still feverish, though I think the Tylenol helped." She stood. "I'll grab you some water. And I think you should eat something." He heard her rummaging through their food stash. "It's almost dark outside. So unless we slept for over a day, I'd venture a guess that it's just been a few hours and we're approaching Sunday night." She returned and held out a protein bar and bottle of water.

"I can't." He brushed away the food, feeling queasy at the thought.

"You need some calories," she complained, opening up the foil wrapper.

"Don't they say starve a fever, feed a cold?" Another coughing fit struck. It caused his entire body to shake. Intense pain shot through his leg, causing him to hold his breath.

"I better check that wound again. Here, drink this first."

He reached out, took the container she offered, and chugged down half the bottle. Apparently, he was thirsty after all. A muffled hum developed outside, and their eyes met.

"He's back!" Kris said excitedly. He hoped their captor was telling them the truth and had brought medication. Derek wanted to get up and assist Kris. To be next to her in case the guy tried anything. Yet he could barely move. He'd be useless. He lay there helplessly watching as she paced toward the front door. Finally, they heard the click of the lock.

"I've got some medicine. Step away from the door," the man instructed. Kris backed up and waited. The door creeped open. Derek saw an arm emerge and toss a bag into the room. Kris dashed over to it, picked it up, and emptied the contents on the table.

"Penicillin. NyQuil. Vitamin C?" she questioned, opening one of the bottles. She didn't seem to expect a response. She didn't get one. The door immediately shut, and they were once again bolted inside. After twisting the cap off one of the containers, Kris rushed over and tapped out two pills. "Antibiotics. Take them."

Derek struggled to hold up his head. Was it always this heavy? Damn, he was exhausted. Kris reached around behind him and gently held him. He took the two white pills and gulped more water.

"I think you should take more Tylenol now, too." She picked up the bottle. He saw Kris look at her watch as he swallowed them. He was already too tired to hold his eyes open. He let himself lean back and rest. There were several shuffling noises around the small cabin. At one point, the faint sound of water running broke into his dreamy state. It took a moment to realize that Kris was taking a shower. As out of it as he felt, he took comfort in the imagined visual of her standing naked under the shower. Streaming lines of water caressing her soft skin. *Where had that come from?* She was so far from his type it wasn't even funny. Yet she was kind of growing on him. And not in a sisterly way. His body relaxed as his mind grew foggy. The intense pain he'd been feeling for what seemed like forever dimmed, and he let sleep take him away once again.

~

Luke rested his head on the back of his chair. His office was quiet. It was dark outside. He stood up, stretched his arms and legs, walked to the front windows, and dropped the heavy curtains. At night he felt like a fish in an aquarium, as if anyone could peer inside his office from outside unseen. Based on the stuff that had been going on in his life the last two years, caution was warranted. Luke grabbed a soda from the refrigerator and sat back down. As he leaned forward, he reread the document on the computer screen.

Rachel's list included information on two development companies and three county employees. About five years ago, developer number one, the PHC Corporation, had purchased a large property near West Shore Pizza in the small community of Tahoma. It included lakefront property—normally an astronomical cost in Lake Tahoe—but it had been quite a deal to purchase at the time, given the downed economy and death of the previous owner. The existing land contained a small bed-and-breakfast. The business had been operated by the same family since the late 1960s; however, the oldest family member, a ninety-two-year-old woman, had passed away over six years ago. She was barely in the ground when her grandchildren put the property up for sale.

Upon purchase, the PHC Corporation launched a multiyear effort to promote a major five-hundred-unit resort hotel, touting it as beneficial "redevelopment," notwithstanding the fact it added 496 more tourist units to an area where nothing of that size currently existed. Given what he'd learned through Rachel, he easily identified the various steps of manipulation the corporation had pulled. There were articles touting local community benefits while mislabeling anyone who spoke against the project as against "all" development—a viewpoint generally looked upon as negative. These misrepresentations often divided a community by creating a situation where people were classified as either for or against it, thereby making it difficult to discuss what other versions of a proposed project people could collectively support.

Fast-forward to the present, and project approval was recommended by the Tahoe Regional Planning Agency's Advisory Planning Commission a few weeks ago. It hadn't mattered enough that almost a hundred people attended the meeting, including Rachel, Kris, and others they worked with, stating major concerns and asking to scale it down in size. The two women had also identified several potential legal questions and miscalculations. Rachel had suspected that's one reason the hearing for the final vote was delayed until March rather than in late January, as originally intended.

Luke searched for information on the PHC representatives. When so much money was at stake, you never knew who might be willing to take things too far. In the end, he learned that two of their people lived in Colorado—no surprise there with so many resort corporations based out of Colorado—and the other in San Francisco. The company did have a record involving several shady deals, including smaller infractions like broken promises to communities and larger offenses such as stiffing local businesses on payments they were due for work through the employment of various legal loopholes. It appeared they'd gambled a substantial chunk of their corporation's success on the Tahoma property. As he reviewed the names associated with the company, he was able to remove one person from the list. The guy, also noted as the "project lead," had perished over eight months ago in a strange boating accident involving a fire.

Luke raised the soda to his lips. The can was empty; somehow he'd already finished the entire drink. He retrieved another and sat back down, his fingers on the keyboard. More searching showed the executive officer from San Francisco, a woman, had recently resigned. A reason was not disclosed. *Now that is someone worth further investigation.* The third name was unique: Anson Matheson. He made a note next to that one as well. He also had to find out if someone else had been assigned the lead role given the death of the original project manager. Was it the remaining Colorado Matheson or someone else? The ringing phone interrupted his mental musings. He looked at the display.

"Hey, Ted," Luke said after he answered.

"Learn anything?" Ted's voice still seemed strained. Was it because of his breakup with Rachel, or something else? Luke had noticed Ted growing somewhat protective of her over time, like a self-appointed brother. That thought reminded him to focus on what was most important—finding Derek and Kris.

"In progress." Luke gave Ted a rundown of what he'd learned about PHC.

"My God, would something that big actually be approved?" Ted was exasperated.

"People are calling TRPA the Tahoe *Resort* Planning Agency for a reason." Luke couldn't help but smile, thinking of Rachel's occasional rants.

"That's too bad," Ted sighed. "Anything else?"

"I was just pulling it up. Let me call you back in a few." Luke ended the call and continued his search. About fifteen minutes later, he dialed Ted back.

"Developer number two is called Mountain SBC Inc. They are the ones who want to build that big subdivision of homes off of Highway 267 near Brockway Summit. Have you heard of that? Rachel's been griping about it for over a year."

"Yes, it has a lot of people pretty pissed off," Ted responded. Then he mumbled, "Rightly so, in my opinion."

"I agree. But in any event the idea of it has been around for a long time. It was only in the last year or two they started getting more specific about it. Looks like controversy was minimal until they proposed the specific layout of the new homes and commercial stuff. They want to locate several high-rise buildings right on top of the ridge up there."

Luke could understand why so many people were upset about it; there was nothing there now except trees. He had grown up in Southern California; too much light pollution made it impossible to see the starry night sky. One had to travel well out of the city to get a decent view. How anyone could consider ruining Tahoe like that was still beyond him. Well, no, it wasn't—*greed*.

"Clearly another moneymaker surrounded by controversy." Ted stated the obvious. "I take it Kris was also doing most of the work on that one due to Rachel's concussion?"

"Yeah, although they were both coordinating on it for a long time before that." Luke could hear Ted scribbling notes. The man still put pen to paper rather than finger to touchscreen. His eyes fixed back on the screen, Luke scrolled down. "Time-wise, it's scheduled for a final vote soon. At the next regular board of supervisors meeting. The project lead is a 'Nola Swenson.' Lives in Truckee somewhere now.

She's been working for Mountain SBC for at least ten years, maybe more. That's all I've got right now."

"All right, thanks for the info. Keep looking and keep in touch."

"Will do." Luke took down one more name and then, without thinking, placed his pen in his mouth and typed. It took a few moments to realize he was biting down. Another bad habit when he was anxious. He spit out the pen and continued to tap the keys, searching the meeting summaries, agendas, media articles, and other items—all stuff he'd learned through Rachel—which could provide information about people involved in a plan or project. It was part of how they'd determined who was trying to kill them after they first met. *Was that really more than eighteen months ago?*

Chapter 22

"Rachel?" Ted's voice was distant.

"Huh?" she mumbled as she reached to brush hair from her eyes.

"Wake up," he instructed patiently.

Rachel realized she was holding her phone to her ear. She pulled the device away to view the time. 6:54 a.m. She lay on her side on the open futon CiCi had made up for her the night before. Her entire body felt like it weighed four times as much as normal, and her head ached. Yep, she'd overdone it. Yet what else could she do given the last two days?

"Rachel?" Ted called out again.

"I'm here," she muttered, forcing her body to sit up. She couldn't move her legs. The dim sunlight peeking in from the narrow sides of thick window shades outlined two furry bundles on the bed. When she shifted, Bella's eyes opened and she gently nudged Rachel's fingertips. This woke up the other dog, who immediately jumped up and began walking back and forth across Rachel's body.

"Too much!" She gently swiped them away as she slid her body out from underneath the covers and jumped out of the bed. "I'm up! I'm up!" she chanted.

"I get that." Ted sounded confused.

"Oh, sorry." She'd forgotten he was on the phone, even though she still held it to her ear. She was going to blame this one on her concussion, too. "I've got this extra dog with me, and she's apparently livelier than Bella in the mornings." Rachel walked across the room, keeping her voice low so as to not wake CiCi in the adjacent room. Both canines jumped down and followed her.

"I wanted to let you know what we've found so far."

"Okay." She waited.

"The techs worked all night again. They said they've figured out a few things about the scene at Kris's house." Rachel perked up. "One: there was only one blood type found. O neg. Do you know Derek's—"

"That's it." She cut him off anxiously.

"Okay, good."

Rachel heard him type something on his keyboard. Ted wasn't the fastest when it came to transcription on his computer, but he sure was loud. It was as if he stabbed the keys rather than pressed them.

"Two: the amount of blood on the floor is not enough to suggest someone bled to death."

Rachel relaxed slightly. "Go on," she said eagerly.

"They can't be sure. However, based on the location and angle of the bullet in the wall, they estimated the height and location it was likely fired from. Your brother is, what, six-three, six-four?"

"Sounds about right."

"Assuming he was standing at the time and assuming a few other caveats I won't get into right now, the likely trajectory suggests the shot probably entered and exited somewhere in his upper leg."

"That's good news, right?" Rachel blurted, too excited to whisper.

"It could be. Again, remember this all comes with a whole host of disclaimers. And not to say where he could have been hit wasn't serious, nor do we know if he was in a standing position. But if he was, then it could potentially exclude some areas that would be more severe. Like his heart or head."

Rachel didn't like to consider those two other options, but she appreciated Ted wasn't tiptoeing around the situation either. She heard him sip something. Tea, she figured. "So now what? I tried to dig up more on our work stuff last night. Nothing else involves the timelines you suggested."

"We keep looking. Between the note about the inhaler and because your brother likely wasn't killed, my gut tells me they are both being kept alive. If that's the case, then it's possible the kidnapper had to purchase some medical supplies. We didn't locate a first aid kit at Kris's. You mentioned she kept one in her bathroom?"

"Yes. Then again, she moved the cat food, so it's possible she moved other things, too." Rachel's eyes had adjusted to the partial light in the room, so she opened the shades a few inches to peer outside. Another foot of snow had fallen overnight.

"I'm going to call around to local pharmacies to see if anyone recalls someone buying the types of supplies needed over the weekend. It's a long shot, and they could have picked something up in Reno or Carson where we'd never be able to narrow it down. Still can't hurt to try."

"Can I help make calls?" Rachel dropped her hand, letting the shades close. The room grew partially dark again.

"No, let us handle it. I'm going to have Carina make a list and get going on the phones."

Rachel heard more typing. While she'd only met the other officer he referred to once or twice, it was easy to put a face to the name. The woman attended a dinner party at Ted's and arrived carrying a small dog with a large pink ribbon on its head. The image contrasted hers as a tough female cop who could easily kick the crap out of any criminal without breaking a sweat.

"Okay," she sighed. As much as her brain was warning her to rest, she couldn't fathom simply waiting around and doing nothing. "Would you happen to know if I can go back to my house today?" Rachel plopped back down on the bed.

"Oh, thanks for reminding me. Another reason I called. Yes, they are done. Unfortunately, we didn't find any prints; admittedly we didn't expect to since you said he was wearing gloves."

"Too bad." She wasn't surprised, but she was disappointed. The bed sagged as both animals jumped back up next to her. Bella rubbed against her, which seemed to start a competition as the other dog joined in. Bella finally relinquished her position, sat back, and stared at Rachel with one of her saddest expressions. The white dog moved in, and Rachel grabbed the collar to hold her back. She blinked. "Ted, I just had an idea." He didn't respond, which she knew meant that she should continue. "Can your people get prints, or maybe DNA, off of a dog collar? It looks like there are some metal parts on this one, if that matters."

"Hmm, we can definitely give it a shot. Bring it on over." He didn't sound hopeful, but it couldn't hurt to try. After all, Ted had managed to retrieve fingerprints from a rock when Rachel and Luke ran into some trouble over a year ago. "Also, Luke's been digging into the names you provided. I'm touching base with him next." The mention of Luke's name caused a prick of pain to her heart; she set it aside.

"Great. Let me know if I can follow up on anything, too. And Ted...thanks for the update."

"No problem. I have one more thing to mention. Normally we'd contact your parents directly, but you said you'd let them know. Have you talked to them yet?"

"They are on a cruise right now, and the ship is out to sea until Tuesday. They couldn't do anything regardless, so my other brother and I agreed to wait. I hate the idea, but they'd just spend the next few days going crazy." Rachel had struggled with what to tell her parents. In the end, she went with her younger brother's recommendation.

"Is your brother coming here?" Ted asked.

Rachel could sense he hoped the answer was no. "He's got pneumonia, so you are spared from dealing with another Winters sibling." Rachel tried to keep her words lighthearted, although she felt anything but.

"We'll find Derek. And Kris. Hang in there," he assured her.

"I'll do my best," she promised.

After a quick shower, Rachel poured steaming coffee into an insulated mug she'd found in the cabinet. CiCi emerged from her bedroom wrapped in a bright red robe. Both dogs dashed from their positions by Rachel to greet her. As Bella rubbed against one leg, her new counterpart lowered her head and licked at CiCi's bare feet.

"Hey, that tickles!" she exclaimed, scooting her feet back.

"I've noticed she has a toe fetish," Rachel said as she set down her coffee. CiCi laughed for a moment, then her expression grew serious. "Any word?"

"I talked to Ted. The CSIs think they are both alive." Rachel explained the details.

"That's great! See, I told you to stay positive." Her friend strolled into the kitchen, her eyes intently focused on the brown liquid in the large carafe. She was obviously amused when Bella began to walk backward in front of her path—one of the canine's favorite tricks. The white dog, appearing confused at Bella's behavior, trailed behind CiCi. As CiCi poured the coffee into her own mug, both animals dashed back over to Rachel, presumably because her hands were free and therefore ripe for massaging them.

"I'm trying not to get too attached. Not sure I'll be successful at that. I keep thinking what if she was stolen from someone who's been looking for her or something? Yet I can't keep calling her 'dog.'" Rachel looked down at the animal. "Know what? I think— for now—I'll call her Avi. She kind of burst into our lives like an avalanche, you know?"

"That's fitting. Works with her coloring, too." CiCi took a sip before continuing. "I agree about not getting too attached, as impossible as that will be." She walked toward Rachel. "You going to the vet this morning?" They'd talked about getting a checkup and scanning for a microchip.

"Yes, after I drop something off with Ted. It occurred to me this morning that the guy who brought her may have left prints if he handled her collar without gloves before coming to my house." Rachel glanced down, her eyes following Avi's path back to CiCi.

"Wow, your brain *has* been healing! That's a good idea." CiCi suddenly laughed, and Rachel saw that the dog—Avi, for now—had quickly turned and licked her other foot.

"Thanks. By the way, I noticed the conditions outside aren't conducive for a two-wheel-drive car. Before I take off, you need a ride anywhere?" Rachel waved toward the front door, knowing her friend's chains were "lost" somewhere in the garage.

"Not now. I called in sick, so I'm flexible." CiCi turned to her. "Should you be out driving alone? I mean, what if that guy is still after you? Or rather, it looks like at least two people seem to want to do you harm lately."

"Well, the idea had crossed my mind, too, but I'll be vigilant, okay?"

"Because that has worked so well for you in the past?" CiCi was pulling no punches.

"What other options do I have? For God's sake, I can't stop living!" Rachel knew she was overreacting but couldn't hide her irritation. Fear and anxiety fueled her pent-up anger.

"Whoa, chill." Her friend raised her hands in front of her. "I'm merely concerned."

Rachel sighed. "I know. I'm sorry. I guess that hit a nerve."

"Obviously," CiCi quipped and dropped her arms. "It's okay. Frankly, I'm not sure I'd have any nerves left to be hit if I were in your shoes. Just be careful. Please."

"I will," Rachel sighed. "And thank you. Not only for taking today off to help us out, but also for everything." Rachel quickly hugged her, then called to Bella to follow her out the front door. Avi schlepped along behind them as they loaded up into Rachel's Tacoma and drove away.

~

Something roused Derek. He opened his eyes and raised his hand up to shield the bright light before his eyes could adjust. A weird humming sound carried from across the room.

"Mmm."

When it went silent, Derek turned his head and tried to peer through a small space between two fingers. The noise started up again and then continued for what seemed like half a minute at least. Slowly removing his hands, his eyes adjusted and he saw that he was lying on the cabin's sole bed. He gave pause, mentally scanning the rest of his body to identify how he felt. Still foggy but better. Aches and pains like he had the flu. At least the intensity of the discomfort had lessened. His leg, unfortunately, continued to throb.

"Mmm."

What the heck? he wondered as he cautiously rolled to his side. Once he could gaze across the cabin, he noticed the back of Kris's head near the love seat he'd first woken up on . . . *how many days ago was that now?* Most of her body was blocked by one of the old stuffed chairs in the middle of the room. Curious, Derek raised himself up a few inches onto his forearms. She appeared to be sitting on the floor, facing the other direction. Her elbows poked out to her side, and her posture was straight and rigid.

"Kris?" His voice was softer than he'd expected. The dryness in his throat made it difficult to speak. Her body jerked, and she turned around.

"Oh, you scared me," she laughed, holding her hand up to her chest.

"What are you doing?"

"I was meditating," she replied matter-of-factly as she rose to her feet and walked toward him.

"Why?" He attempted to sit up but was too exhausted, so he collapsed back onto the mattress. He had to pee, big time, but didn't want to ask for her help again. He shifted his position.

"It relaxes me. What do you do to destress?" She reached out and touched his forehead.

"A few things come to mind." He winked.

She dropped her hand and scoffed. "Funny. Seriously, anything *else?*"

"I guess hanging out on a beach, having a beer, watching the sun go down. That's pretty cool."

"Relaxing in a calm environment—it's not very different if you think about it. I reduce stress through meditation. You should try it sometime."

"Uh, no thanks," he laughed. "I'm not into that mumbo jumbo stuff." Yes, he was egging her on, but he kind of enjoyed it. And she looked so cute when she got fired up. Derek moved again, stealing a glance toward the bathroom.

"Suit yourself." She turned and walked into the kitchen. "I think your temperature dropped. How do you feel?"

"Better," he answered, disappointed she hadn't taken the bait.

"Need help getting to the bathroom?" she asked as she reached for a bottle of water and twisted the top.

"No, I can do it," he retorted and then once again raised himself up onto his palms. He couldn't remember the last time he'd felt so bad. Every limb weighed a hundred pounds; his head, two hundred. She watched, the slightest grin forming on her face. She was clearly waiting for him to fail. Well, he'd show her! Derek let his feet drop to the floor and sat erect. He stretched his neck from left to right and twisted his back around to each side.

"You getting ready to run a marathon or something?" She chuckled. He ignored her, raising himself up and placing weight on his feet. After standing for a few moments, dizziness overcame him and he fell back on the bed.

"Damn!" he complained.

She took a few steps in his direction. "Done being stubborn yet?"

"Screw you," he countered, embarrassed.

"You wish you could be so lucky." She turned back around and strutted into the kitchen.

~

Luke waited patiently for the woman to answer her phone. A few weeks ago Cynthia O'Donnell had resigned from her well-paid position at the PHC Corporation and opened her own consulting firm. It hadn't been difficult to locate her new number. While Luke felt a face-to-face meeting was always preferable because body language could be revealing, time was of the essence.

"Mr. Reed, she'll be right with you," a youthful voice reiterated. He wondered if the "receptionist" was her daughter. The girl was sixteen according to the records he'd found. She sounded more like someone pretending to be an office assistant than an actual professional.

"Thanks," he replied, keeping his voice even. A moment later, he heard a loud click, followed by a deep feminine voice.

"Good morning. How can I help you, Mr. Reed?"

"Ms. O'Donnell, I appreciate—"

"Cynthia, please," she corrected.

"Cynthia," he stated. "Thank you for taking my call. I know this is out of the blue, but I'm looking for information related to the PHC Corporation and saw that you recently left the company." He paused.

She didn't speak.

Luke continued. "I'll be straight with you. Someone is after my friends in a bad way. I'm working with local law enforcement. There's a chance it may be related to a project they are trying to get approved in Lake Tahoe." Silence. "In Tahoma," he added. He heard her exhale deeply before responding.

"My, er, assistant said you were a private investigator. Is that correct?"

"Yes, ma'am."

"What's your name again?" she asked. He heard her typing as he responded. She was probably looking up background information on him. It's what he'd do. In the silence, Luke heard a faint clicking sound overhead. It took a second for him to realize it was raining. Finally, the woman spoke. "All right, this is the deal. PHC has a lot of good employees. The higher up you go, that's where the problems start. I didn't sign an antidisclosure agreement. Not that they didn't try. I have the luxury of not needing a lot of money, so I chose to refuse their proposed agreement and the severance package that went with it." She paused, and he heard a loud squeaking sound. It reminded him of his own office chair. "Although what I'll tell you is all public record; you'd simply have to dig a little deep to find it yourself."

"Okay," he said, waiting anxiously. He was intrigued.

"I won't pretend to be an angel. I was aware of some, shall we say, *extreme* practices they employed to make things happen. However, to not completely subject myself to a slander or libel lawsuit, let me confirm it was nothing illegal per se. They simply had friends in high places. Land-use planning, public and private land deals . . . things often had a way of working out in their favor."

Luke took notes as fast as he could write, but she hesitated as if waiting for his acknowledgement. "I understand," he said. He could picture it after reading one of Rachel's favorite books, called *Downhill Slide*, which documents the sometimes shady practices of large resort corporations and how they adversely affect small ski towns.

"A situation came up where there was significant opposition to a deal they were working on in Colorado. And it is my belief that they went too far in swinging the votes in their favor."

"Can you give me any specifics?" He waited, his pencil poised over paper.

"No, not without divulging secrets that could put me in a vulnerable position. I'm starting a new business and would rather move forward. Not have to worry about anyone placing more obstacles in my way."

She seemed experienced with the careful use of words, Luke thought. Perhaps because a corporation like that could sue her and take away everything she owned and then some. He sighed but remained silent.

"What, exactly, has happened to your friends?" she asked, sympathetic.

"Two have been kidnapped; another one was assaulted in her home."

"Wow! I'm very sorry to hear that." She paused. He sensed she was concentrating on how to phrase her next sentence. "Those are not the type of tactics I saw with PHC. Hypothetically speaking, members of large corporations have been known to utilize personal information about certain public officials to encourage favorable votes. In any case, with regard to PHC, admittedly there are some new people there now who I never became familiar with. Their methods could certainly have been revised since my departure."

"I see," he replied. His gut told him this woman was being sincere. Whatever the company's transgression was that had been her last straw, it was apparently something less sinister than kidnapping.

After a few more questions, he was confident she wasn't going to give him anything more. Luke thanked her and hung up. He scrolled down to the next name on his list: Anson Matheson. His call was immediately sent to voice mail, which informed him the man was in Tahoe this week and would only check messages intermittently. He didn't want to give the guy any chances to think up responses in advance, so he hung up. While the company's paperwork listed Colorado as his primary residence, he'd also discovered that Mr. Matheson owned lakefront property in Homewood, about twenty-five miles from Luke's house. Was it merely a coincidence the man was in Tahoe right now? Perhaps Luke would drop in and introduce himself. He snatched his keys from the corner of his desk, tucked them in his pocket, and pushed his chair back. Time for a drive.

Chapter 23

Oliver kicked at the crate containing "Black." Even though the white dog was gone, he'd grown accustomed to calling it by that name. It kept things simple. He smiled as it growled; now *this* one held some aggression.

"Perfect!" He might have a chance of winning tomorrow after all, presuming his competitor didn't grab hold of Black's ears. Those would have to go; granted, this time he'd ask his friend for help. Oliver stepped back from the enclosure. The mongrel huddled in the back, baring its teeth. "Be a good boy and come on out now." He held a chunk of cheap steak a few feet in front of the opening, but the creature remained crouched inside. "Get out here!" he yelled, quickly losing patience. He didn't have time for this shit. Oliver grabbed the edges of the structure and shook it. The dog alternately whimpered and snarled but still refused to come out. Just as Oliver lifted his leg for another blow, he heard sirens in the distance. It wasn't an uncommon sound; he lived a few blocks from the emergency room. Curious as always, he stood up and walked toward the front window to peer outside. An ambulance whirled by the intersection a block and a half away on a mad dash to the emergency room. Just as he started to drop his gaze, he noticed the outline of a cop car following behind, although there were no lights or sirens. But rather than continue the route behind the emergency vehicle, the car turned and drove down his street. A few seconds later, it was joined by a second. Somewhere inside, Oliver knew they were coming for *him*.

He tugged his arms into his coat, yanked open a nearby drawer, and retrieved a small handgun. Frantically, he searched the room for his keys, but they were nowhere to be found. *I have to get out of here*, he thought. *Now!* He took one last glance at the frightened animal before sprinting out the back door. The stupid thing stayed inside, even with the door wide open.

Oliver tripped as he launched himself off the dilapidated wooden deck, but he corrected his footing and aimed for the small gate in the back of his yard. The fresh rain made the snow heavy and wet. Every step sank deep, slowing him down. It seemed like hours had passed by the time he managed to pull the gate inward, pushing and sliding it across the piled-up snow in its path. Luckily, there was no house on the neighboring lot; it was managed by the US Forest Service. He crossed the empty land, mere inches away from jumping over the small zigzag wooden fence typical of forest service lots, when his leg was suddenly grabbed. Oliver yelled out as something sharp broke through his pants and lodged into his flesh. He looked down. "Black" had followed him after all. Oliver shook his leg, panic coursing through his veins at the idea he'd be caught. He swiped his hand at the growling fleabag, connecting with its skull. But it didn't let go. Instead, the dog began to shake his leg like a wild predator attacking its prey. His heavier weight kept his body in place, but the agony of the deepening wound caused him to collapse into the cold, wet snow. He moved his other leg around to kick at it. His foot connected; relief swept through him as the animal let go. Just as he turned to look at the beast, intense pain tore through his crotch. Nausea overwhelmed him. He could barely breathe. He gasped for air as the canine maintained its firm grasp. White light marred his vision.

"Oliver Palinski! Stop! Police!" A man approached from several feet away. Oliver was in too much misery to respond. He heard the officer instruct him to drop the gun. He hadn't realized he was still holding it. He attempted to focus in on the animal, but he couldn't. There was just so much pain. The weapon slipped out of his fingers.

"Get him off me!" he cried as tears filled his eyes. There was a scuffling sound and a slight tug, but the sharp teeth remained clenched. "Off!" he screamed.

"I'm trying," the officer replied, grunting. Oliver glanced at the image below his waste. The man was tugging at the mutt's neck, but it held firm.

"Meat. In the house." Oliver struggled to get the words out. The cop said something as if speaking to another person. After what felt like hours, a uniformed figure appeared, holding something in the air.

"Here, doggie," the other officer called out, shaking the meat close to the canine's nose. More agonizing minutes passed as the men attempted to lure the creature away. Black finally let go when they placed the raw meat next to his nose and relinquished their grip. The dog snatched the treat and quickly turned to run. Oliver gulped for air as if just emerging from being under water for too long, his hands cradling his crotch.

"All right, Mr. Palinski. Hands behind your head."

"Please. It hurts. So much . . ." Oliver didn't want to release his grip, fearing it would only hurt more.

"I said, hands behind your head."

Oliver reluctantly complied; he couldn't run if he tried. His dad wasn't going to be happy about this. Not one bit. As he was cuffed and placed into the back of a police unit, he wondered how that bitch had identified him. He'd worn a mask and gloves the entire time.

~

Rachel's emotions swung up and down when the device emitted a high-pitched sound as the veterinary technician positioned the microchip scanner over Avi's back. She was chipped. Rachel's breath caught while she waited for the registration information to display. The young man looked at the computer screen.

"Says here she's registered to an animal shelter down in Sacramento."

"An animal shelter?" Rachel asked, hopeful. She needed something positive right now. And that would qualify.

"Want me to give them a call, check it out?" he asked. Then he added, "Keep in mind that someone could have adopted her and not changed the owner information yet."

"Yes, please. Can you do that now?" Rachel reached down and rubbed Avi's neck. Bella nudged at her other hand.

"How about I find out what I can while the vet checks her out?"

"Deal. Thanks."

It took the vet barely ten minutes to complete her examination. She'd guessed the ears had been cut within the last couple of weeks. Other than malnutrition and the fresh scratch on her nose, the canine was in good health. She'd already been spayed, too. The technician pranced back into the room, beaming.

"Good news, Rachel." He smiled and glanced down at his notes. "No one has adopted this sweet girl. She's actually been missing. A local teen took her out for a walk one day as part of an after-school program at the shelter. He let her off the leash, and she took off. They've been looking for her for almost a month. How she made her way to Tahoe is a mystery."

"That means she's available for adoption?" she asked, perking up. As if understanding her, Avi nibbled on her fingers.

"They're e-mailing me your application form as we speak. Simply fill it out, pay the fee, and there should be no problem with you being approved." Rachel looked down at both pups. Their tails wagged in unison. Not long ago she considered looking for another dog but knew it would require a careful fit with Bella. Obviously that was not a problem with Avi. Rachel's phone alerted her to a new message.

"Bella, how do you feel about having a sister?" she asked as she glanced at the display. The last caller was Ted. She excused herself and listened to the voice mail. Relief washed over her—the man who'd come after her had been caught. She thought he said the perp's name was Oliver; she'd have to get more details later. For now, she could take a little solace in the fact that at least one threat had been extinguished.

~

Ted still couldn't believe they'd managed to pull a useful fingerprint from the dog collar. It had been found on the surface where the collar snapped into place. Thank God Rachel had thought of it. As he walked down the hallway toward the interrogation room, Carina trotted up behind him.

"Ted, glad I caught you," she said, sounding out of breath.

"What's up?" He paused, bending the small notebook in his hand back and forth.

"I called around to some pharmacies. Turns out someone broke into one of the smaller places up in Truckee over the weekend. They took penicillin."

"Well, I'll be damned," he exclaimed.

"But," she continued with a don't-get-so-excited look passing over her features, "we reviewed the video surveillance in the store. The perp was wearing a mask."

Ted's shoulders slumped. *Of course.* "Well, it's a start. Anything from nearby cams?"

"None that we found; we're still canvassing the neighborhood, looking to see if someone else may have picked up any images from other locations."

"I don't suppose we could easily check the highway cameras for anything suspicious?"

"Nope. Busy winter weekend, pent-up ski demand, and fresh snow from the last storm . . . the roads were jam-packed. It would be like searching for a needle in a haystack, but we'd have no idea what the needle even looked like." She sighed.

"Yeah, I figured." Ted rubbed his chin, realizing he hadn't shaved in a few days. "Keep on it. One of my officers is going to see what this loser Oliver can tell us about why he attacked Rachel. I'll let you know if we get anything useful."

"Do you think he's involved with the kidnapping?"

"Don't know. The timing is definitely suspect. Yet he doesn't come off as the smartest tool in the shed either. Seems it would take brains to have managed grabbing Kris, and then Derek, without leaving any witnesses behind." He made eye contact. "By the way, good work," he acknowledged before he turned and walked away with questions already starting to swirl through his mind.

~

Luke double-checked the numbers to make sure the address matched the one in his files. 3562. This was Matheson's place. The man's house was lined by a dominating wall of elaborate stonework roughly eight feet high. The open strip of land between the wall and the narrow roadway contained partially melted snow. His Subaru idled in the driveway. Rain slammed against the roof, and the wiper blades struggled to keep pace with the downpour. His headlights lit the entryway in front of him; otherwise the warm storm had given the night a dark, eerie feel.

On any other day, Rachel would be bitching about the rain ruining the snow. Pulling his thoughts back to the present, Luke noticed the snow in the driveway was entirely melted. The pavement must be heated from underneath. *Sweet deal.* Luke zeroed in on the tall, curvy iron gate that crossed in front of him. There was a boxlike structure to his left at about the same height as a drive-up ATM. It was an intercom system. Why was he not surprised? He crept his car forward, rolled his window down, and searched the display. Before he had a chance to make a selection, a loud voice radiated out of the device.

"Can we help you? Or do you plan to block our entry for a while longer?"

"Oh." Surprised at first, Luke paused. Well, at least they were direct, he thought. He touched the reply button. "Sorry, I was confirming the address. My name is Luke Reed. I was hoping to speak to Mr. Matheson."

"With regard to?"

"His proposed resort project in Tahoma." Luke waited, wondering how much he should reveal at this point. Wet spray drenched his face and the front of his clothes through his open window. He swiped at his cheek in annoyance.

"Contact our project manager. I can provide you his number—"

"Look, to be honest, this is about a missing woman. I'm happy to provide more details, but frankly this rain is blowing all over me. Please, I wouldn't be here if it wasn't urgent," he pleaded. "I assume you have a camera on me," he mumbled as he held up his PI license to where he expected it would be focused. "I'm a private investigator and could really use his help." Luke waited as he turned up the heat with his other hand. Finally, the man responded.

"Mr. Matheson can meet with you for ten minutes. Drive to the porte cochere, and someone will meet you there." Luke watched as the gate slid to the side.

The long narrow path turned a corner and passed underneath a large carport-like structure. It reminded him of the check-in areas at hotels or the casinos' valet service areas at Stateline. A man wearing a dark red coat and black pants stood nearby. Luke was tempted to hand the guy his keys, but he didn't sense the man would appreciate the humor. Everything associated with Mr. Matheson screamed formal and rich, much like the way Luke had grown up. Luke plastered on one of his best smiles. He'd barely stepped out of his vehicle when the valet look-alike spoke from a few feet away. How had the guy gotten so close, so fast?

"Mr. Reed, please follow me." Luke nodded and silently fell in step behind the man. He was led into a spacious entryway. As he wiped his shoes on a large rug immediately inside the doorway, he wondered if he was supposed to remove them instead. Bright carpet lined the hallway ahead of them. Why does anyone have white carpet in the mountains?

Luke looked up. The ceiling rose about two stories in height. Mr. Matheson must have one heck of a power bill, Luke pondered and then glanced around as they continued. Wooden floors and white walls displayed a wide collection of artistic pieces related to majestic mountain scenery.

"Mr. Matheson is waiting for you in the den." The man waved his hand forward, made a small bow, and walked back toward the front door. Luke stepped forward. As he approached the sizable room, Luke's gaze fell upon two massive walls of glass that provided an enormous panoramic view of Lake Tahoe. If not for the rain, he expected he'd be able to see clear across the lake since it was only twelve miles wide. *My God, the sunrises from this place must be absolutely breathtaking.* Luke tore his gaze from the raindrop-smeared windows and scanned the rest of the room. The flames burning in the large enclosed masonry fireplace in the corner of the living space gave off a surprising amount of heat. Luke's natural gas stove wasn't even a tenth that effective. A large black leather sectional sofa sat in the middle of the room. Luke almost overlooked the man who was seated on it and apparently staring at the storm outside.

"Please, join me," he said without turning his head. "Can I offer you a drink?" he asked as Luke stepped into the room and found a spot on the love seat nearby. He looked toward his host; the man's face was partially scarred, like he'd been severely burned in a fire. As he tipped his glass to his lips, Luke saw similar scars on his hand.

"No, thank you," Luke responded.

"Don't worry about your reaction to my burns. It happens to most people." The man's voice, as well as his expression, remained calm. "I was on a yacht that exploded last year. Some advice: don't hire your cousin's son to be your mechanic just to keep your relative happy." A smile stretched across his thin lips, though the curve on one side was partially obscured by thick scar tissue.

"I'll keep that in mind," Luke stated. "I appreciate you seeing me without an appointment."

"Don't thank me. I admit I'm simply a very curious soul," Anson said as he tipped his crystal glass to his lips. Luke nodded.

"I'm a private investigator, and a friend of mine is missing. She's in a position where she may have upset several people through her job. It's a long shot, but I'm trying to see if those involved in some of her project meetings might know some details that could help me locate her." Luke did his best to remove any implication of wrongdoing as he spoke.

"And which project led you to me?"

"Tahoma." Luke leaned back and examined the man's expression. A glimmer of something—recognition, perhaps—sparked in his eyes, which was quickly replaced by the same expression he'd worn since Luke first laid eyes on him. It was best described as amused.

"I see," he said as he pulled a small cloth from his pocket and dabbed at his cheek. "And this woman, what is her name?"

"Kristina Drew." Another flicker. But something like that could simply be from a result of seeing her at various meetings, or being aware of those who had expressed opposition to the project.

"How long has she been missing, as you said?"

"Since Friday," Luke replied.

The man appeared to ponder this for a moment. "And what led you here?"

"I'm helping my friends talk to people involved with the projects that have upcoming votes." Luke didn't want to give away all of the details. "I don't know much more than that."

"I assume law enforcement is searching for her?" Anson shifted and wiped another invisible speck from his cheek.

"Yes, but they are spread thin. And this woman is a good friend of my girlfriend." There was no need to say "ex." It was irrelevant. Anson nodded as if it all made sense now.

"I see. Your girlfriend is . . . ?"

"Rachel Winters." *Was that another flash of recognition?*

"Not ringing a bell. I rarely attend public meetings in person anymore." He took another sip and waved in front of his face. "For obvious reasons." Luke waited for him to continue. The pinging of raindrops intensified, and marble-sized balls of hail began to slam against the windows. "So what can I tell you that could possibly help?"

"Do you know anyone who might take her position on the project personally? Perhaps someone who gets overly emotional or has expressed anger toward her in the past?" Luke didn't expect a straight answer of course. His interest was mostly in how the man reacted. Something about this guy was off, but he couldn't pinpoint what it was.

"Hmm." Anson silently observed the storm outside. It felt like several minutes passed before he spoke again, yet it had most likely been less than a minute. "Besides myself of course?" He grinned. Good—the guy didn't beat around the bush. Luke merely nodded, waiting. "The last manager for that run-down bed-and-breakfast we bought out after that old lady kicked the bucket was a bit of a hothead. We had to let him go last summer."

Luke pulled out his cell phone and typed in the person's name as Anson spelled it out. Why an employee who'd been laid off months ago would take offense to someone who was challenging the new development was a mystery; yet it never hurt to check.

"On another note, Ms. Riley—I'm sorry, she's one of our environmental consultants—has a tendency to be, shall we say, too passionate about her tasks. She does wonderful work. We've just had to advise her to tone things down on occasion. But I honestly don't picture her doing such a thing. Not sure why I even mentioned it." Once again, Luke recorded the name as Anson dictated. The room grew silent.

"Anything else you can think of?" Luke asked, his finger poised over his cell.

"I'm afraid that's all that comes to mind. If you leave me your card, I'll contact you if I think of anything." The interview was clearly over. Luke stood.

"Mr. Matheson, thank you for your time." He held his hand out. The man was slow to reach out with his own, but his shake was firm. Luke retrieved his business card from his wallet and set it on a nearby table. "Here is my number; call anytime."

"Yes, of course." It was obvious Anson did not intend to stand or walk him out, so Luke retraced his steps through the hallway and exited. As he gently closed the solid wooden door behind him, he thought about the odd conversation. Yes, something was definitely off with this man. But was it related to Kris?

~

Despite Derek putting on a good show, Kris could tell he was still suffering. He had been better last night and this morning but now appeared to be going downhill again. His face was flushed, and he was no doubt in a lot of pain. He'd propped himself up in a sitting position on the bed and leaned back against the wall. Kris sat next to him with her knees to her chest and her elbows resting on top. Both of them stared out into the room as there was a momentary lapse in conversation. A loud bang on the roof above them grabbed their attention.

"The wind really picked up again," Kris said, her eyes looking up as if she could see the weather through the roof.

"That rain has to be making the top layer of fresh snow on the trees seriously heavy," he responded, then launched into a coughing fit. Kris waited until he quieted down.

"You're worse again, aren't you?"

"Maybe a little," he confessed as he let his head fall back against the wall. Kris reached up and pressed her hand to his forehead.

"Derek, you're warm again. Shit! I wondered if those antibiotics were the right kind," she mumbled.

"Aw, you're worried about me. See, I knew you'd started crushing on me. Admit it," he joked. She rolled her eyes, mostly because he expected it. Her thoughts grew serious.

"How long do you think he plans to keep us here?"

"I don't know," he sighed. They remained in silence for a moment as more loud pounding beat down on the roof.

"Should we start working on plan B here?"

"Yeah, I think that's a good idea." He leaned forward and covered his mouth as he retched again. Another big thump followed by a parade of smaller clinking sounds came from objects that seemed to be falling overhead. Kris visualized a large hand descending from high above, tapping its massive fingertips on the roof. She remained in place.

"That last one sounded more like a tree than a pinecone." She was starting to feel even more unnerved. If that was possible. They both flinched when another crash echoed. It was followed by a strange sloshing noise. She raised her eyes and noticed Derek had done the same. Kris watched in amazement as the ceiling on the other side of the room, exactly where they'd noticed a moist spot yesterday, began to cave in. Water soaked the love seat below. She remained still, mesmerized by the scene before her. Wooden beams cracked apart and a wet mix of slushy snow, pinecones, and green pine needles fell to the floor. White slop continued to flow inside for another several seconds. Kris's eyes followed its path in disbelief.

"You've got to be kidding me," Derek choked out as he stared at the scene before them.

"Ditto," she replied. Cold air seeped around them. Kris peered back up. A large Jeffrey pine had broken through the roof, causing several areas to collapse. Her spirits lifted as she observed that it left an opening adequate to fit a human through. "Mother Nature may have just done us a favor," she stated.

Chapter 24

"We've got something," Carina said as she approached Ted from behind.

"Go on," Ted encouraged.

"We found a recording taken a couple of blocks away from that pharmacy. One of the residents recently installed a motion-triggered camera to find out who was letting their dog crap in the front yard overnight. Last night it recorded a man with a truck parked partway on their property—enough for the sensors to pick up."

"Is the image useful?" Ted asked, hopeful.

"Possibly. The motion detector switched a light on. It appears our driver wasn't expecting that. The camera caught a brief clip of him standing near his truck before he slipped on a ski mask. It's a little fuzzy, but it's a start." Carina handed him an eight-by-ten picture. Ted studied it.

"To think we may end up with a lead because of some dog shit. That's one for the books," he said and grinned but then grew serious. "I've also been thinking—it's unlikely this dude's driving his own vehicle; they usually don't. Now that we have this," Ted pointed at the photograph, "do you think there's enough in the recording to identify the model of his pickup?"

"It looks like a Ford Ranger, early 2000s," Carina immediately replied.

"I see you've already given this some thought."

She glanced around the room and then whispered, "I used to date someone who was really into trucks."

Ted laughed. "All right, let's check for Ford pickups stolen in the region. And start running facial recognition on this guy, if it's enough for the scan."

"Already in progress." Carina nodded before dashing away.

~

Jerry glanced at the clock: 5:47 p.m. He'd meant to check on his two captives sooner, but he'd been stuck in traffic for the last two hours—almost the entire route from Kings Beach heading west on State Route 28. He'd barely traveled seven or eight miles and was now inching along at five miles per hour a few miles north of Tahoe City. Getting through town would probably take even longer, but there was no other way to get to West Shore from here without a long detour.

Jerry was still reeling from that damn rash on his face caused by the new ski mask the night before. Just one more incident in an already pain-in-the-ass job. He cursed and rubbed his cheek as he pondered what he was allergic to in the mask he'd purchased yesterday. It hadn't taken long to start feeling the intense itching. He'd ripped the damn thing off while driving and had stepped out of his truck before he remembered he had to put it back on. His skin was unbelievably irritated while he broke into the pharmacy for antibiotics.

Jerry had spent all morning lathering up his face and neck with calamine lotion. As much as he just wanted to stay indoors, mask-free, he had to check on the couple. The man's condition worried him. He didn't want someone's death on his conscience. That traffic might prevent him from getting there tonight was not something he had ever considered. A weekend—yes. But on a Monday? He was debating whether to turn and try the long way around, but he would have to reroute onto Highway 267 all the way to Truckee and then come back south to Tahoe via Highway 89. It would add hours. He wasn't too far from Tahoe City now. It was probably best to just bear the traffic.

~

"Well, that's interesting," Rachel muttered as she stared at the computer screen. It had been about forty-five minutes since CiCi drove her Tacoma away. While it had been raining for hours, some roads still contained slushy snow, making for a slippery drive without chains or four-wheel drive, so CiCi had borrowed her pickup again.

It had been weird for Rachel to go home after what happened yesterday. Her house seemed quiet—too quiet. Maybe her unease was the result of something other than exhaustion. Fear? Anxiety? There was at least some noise thanks to the two dogs play fighting with each other nearby. Whatever her feelings were, she didn't have time to process them now. She'd set up a new bowl for Avi, thrown together a sandwich, and logged online to see if there was anything more to learn about the projects Kris was involved in.

After searching through documents that spanned several years and countless meetings, newspaper articles, and other information, she'd finally found something. Ironically, it was buried in the most recent staff report on the Tahoe-Truckee Pines ridgeline project that was to take place near Brockway Summit. The proposed agreement with the developer had been modified since the last public hearing. The new version relinquished the developer from having to pay extensive ongoing mitigation fees to lessen the negative impacts of the project, which amounted to over a million dollars annually. The change appeared to affect future annual payments toward public transportation, water and sewer infrastructure upgrades, storm-water system maintenance, and several other things. The modification wasn't identified or called out in any meaningful way. Rather, she had only seen it by comparing the newest document to the last draft and then following the various footnotes and disclaimers to other files. This would save the developer—Mountain SBC, another large out-of-town corporation—a lot of money in the future. Of course, as roads and utility systems failed down the line, taxpayers would be stuck with the bill—well, after the company that built the project had made its profits and moved on.

"Bastards!" Rachel said aloud.

Based on what she read in text highlighted by Kris, Rachel suspected this revised agreement was one of the things her friend was going to talk to her about when they'd planned to meet yesterday. Rachel tried to recall their discussion. Kris mentioned sending an e-mail to Anthony, the environmental planner at Placer County who'd had this project dumped on him two months ago. Kris's inquiry could have made someone nervous. Chances were that Anthony had forwarded the message to the county's attorney. And from there, it would have been shared with the project applicant, no doubt. Rachel already knew who the lead manager was for Mountain SBC—Nola

Swenson. The woman's snide remarks, occasional dirty looks, and other behaviors suggested she took any opposition very personally. She was exactly the kind of person who might react negatively to an e-mail from Kris that questioned the agreement.

Rachel quickly dialed Ted. After sharing her discovery, she decided a shower might help stave off the fatigue that was overtaking her yet again. *Damn concussion.*

Rachel's cell flashed with a new text. CiCi would be bringing her truck back shortly. Rachel would then need to run her back home. Yes, she definitely needed to perk up if she was going to drive in this weather.

Chapter 25

"Bingo!" Ted stared at the alert regarding a stolen pickup truck. The theft had occurred in Reno, Nevada, only a few days ago. The vehicle's color, as well as the blurred blue image of a sticker in the corner of the windshield, made them fairly certain it was the same one they'd seen in what Ted now thought of as "the dog shit video."

"Can we track it?" he asked, looking up at Carina. She was still breathing hard after racing to him with the theft report.

"In progress. The owner said the truck doesn't have GPS. However, his girlfriend happened to leave her cell phone inside; she thinks it fell under the passenger seat. The battery likely died in the last day or two, but we can at least track its general location up until it lost its juice. I've got someone calling the cell company right now."

Ted's excitement grew. Finally, they were getting somewhere.

Carina's cell phone chimed. Contrary to her strong, almost masculine appearance, the ringtone was a Celine Dion song. Like the toy poodle he'd seen her carrying around in a purse, it was another enigma of the woman. She answered the call while Ted scrawled out more notes. He heard her thank someone before ending the call.

"Was that case-related?" Ted asked.

"Yep. The GPS data from the towers the cell phone pinged off of shows the truck located in South Lake last Friday, then in West Shore, and then again in South Shore that evening. Intermittent signals show it was frequently in the vicinity of that place in West Shore where off-highway vehicles go. McKinney something."

"McKinney/Rubicon?" Ted asked.

"That's it!" She pointed and smiled.

177

"Okay," Ted said, taking a moment to think out his instructions. "You grab a few officers and head over to that area; see if you can locate the truck. I received a call from Rachel that I want to follow up on. It's going to mean a trip to Truckee for me. After that, I'll come back and meet you along the way, presuming you found anything. Sound good?" Ted expected to arrive at Ms. Swenson's place by eight p.m. "And let's get going on this quickly, before this rain causes an avalanche and closes Emerald Bay." Avalanches were fairly common on the steep slopes where Highway 89 rounded the bay, causing temporary closures during most winters.

"On it." Carina bolted out of the room. Ted snatched up his coat, keys, and water bottle and ran out to his SUV. As he left, he radioed his captain with an update of what they'd learned along with his current plan of action. After a brief period of no cell service around Emerald Bay, his signal was once again strong enough north of Tahoma to check in with Luke. He listened intently as Luke summarized his interviews. Ted trusted the man's instincts, at least with regard to investigations. Luke's instincts with women . . . well, those were a different story. Either way, Ted knew Luke would keep digging; if there was more to learn about Anson Matheson, he'd find it. Same with Nola Swenson. Ted didn't know why, but something told him the clock they were working under might run out sooner than expected.

~

The roof had caved in between two heavy four-by-twelve-inch rafters. Kris surmised if she could only reach the beams, there was a chance she could lift herself through the space in between, thanks to those upper body workouts she'd been doing since last summer.

"I'm really wishing we hadn't disassembled those chairs," Kris confessed as she stood on the small table they'd set underneath the opening, trying to maintain her balance.

"Me too," Derek said, his voice scratchy.

Kris worried about him being exposed to the weather in his condition. After considering their circumstances, they'd decided it was best to stick together. What if she found help but couldn't find her way back to the cabin? What if he needed immediate help from her? In the end, she'd reluctantly agreed to have him come with her. She could hear him rummaging through the room.

"I'm not finding anything that we could use for makeshift snowshoes," he said, his disappointment obvious. "Or a flashlight."

Kris listened as she stacked two kitchen drawers on top of the table in an attempt to get herself closer to the hole in the roof. It was probably a very stupid idea. The stacked furniture could easily break or fall and she'd come crashing down. But she saw no other options. Not only did they need to get away from this kidnapper; they also had no assurance he'd even come back. His failure to return before the sun set had been the final impetus to putting their escape plan into action. Kris carefully placed each foot as she stepped higher, testing the stability of the stack before placing all of her weight on top. It held. She caught her breath as she gently set her other foot on the top and rose. Waiting. Nothing crashed down. She looked up, relieved she was close enough to grab the wooden rafter. She pushed the protruding pine branches away from the opening.

"Finally," she said as she rubbed her face against her sleeve in a failed effort to wipe off the fresh rain. "I'm going to see what's out there." She began to lift herself up.

"I have been waiting to see this." Derek smirked. He'd teased her about whether she could actually pull all of her weight up, saying even he couldn't do that, and he went to the gym at least a few times a week.

"Watch and learn, boy," she joked, although her voice strained with the effort. A few more inches higher and her eyes were scanning the outside of the cabin. Unfortunately all she could see was the eerie blackness of the night. No surprise there—the storm clouds blocked the moonlight. She hoisted herself up higher. Without anything to prop her foot on, she couldn't transfer weight from her hands to her elbows. She dangled for a moment, her mind racing. Something pressed against the bottom of her foot.

"I got ya. Just hurry," Derek said from below. She did as he'd instructed, quickly springing off of the palm he'd provided for support. It gave her the lift she needed to boost her upper body high enough for her head and shoulders to clear the top of the hole. Kris lay with her rib cage flat across the edge while switching the position of her arms. She gripped the ledge of wooden shingles securely and raised herself up to her waist. From there, she wiggled the rest of her body up and out.

Rain pounded her. She'd never been so thankful for a waterproof coat. Sloppy, wet snow still covered the roof; but the fresh rain would likely melt it away before the night was over. It would be slick to walk—or rather crawl—across. As her eyes adjusted to the darkness, she saw the full girth of the branch that had punched through the roof. It was about twice as wide as her waist. Kris leaned over to look inside the shack that had been their prison for the last few days.

"I'm officially eating crow," Derek said. He was standing on the edge of the table lowest to the floor.

"As you should be," she laughed. "But seriously, thanks for the lift. Not sure I could have pulled off that final rise without it."

"You getting out of here is the only way I'll escape, too. Don't read so much into it."

"Whatever," she sighed, not believing his lame excuse for a second. "I'm not sure I'll be able to get back up here once I jump off, so it's now or never. I sure wish we had a light," she complained. "You ready to come?"

She watched as Derek glanced around.

"Still think there's got to be some way to bust through that lock from the outside," he mumbled, gazing toward the front door.

"As I said, that is one hell of a quality deadbolt he has. I wouldn't count on it." She watched as he sighed, then lifted up and retrieved the pillowcase he'd filled with the remaining antibiotics, water bottles, and protein bars. His veins pulsed in his neck as he moved, slowly ascending their teetering tower of furniture.

"Here goes nothing," he said. They both waited, tense, as he maneuvered the full weight of his body up to the stacked drawers on top and then quickly reached up with one hand to grip the wood. He handed Kris the bag of supplies with his free hand before wrapping both palms around the frames and pulling, same as she'd done. Kris could see sweat on his forehead as he strained to lift his weight. That was hard enough to do without an infected gunshot wound. She was impressed; he definitely hadn't lied about working out, although it had already been obvious from first glance at his toned arms. Kris slid back, allowing him room around the busted edges. He managed to pull his head through, but, like her, he reached a point where he was stuck with his feet dangling in the air and nothing to boost himself up and out. Even worse, another coughing fit struck; Kris feared he might lose his grip and go crashing down below. She quickly grabbed under his armpits, taking on some of his weight. Her maneuver bumped the pillowcase of supplies they'd brought and it dropped back down into the cabin. She ignored it.

"Let me help," she said, straining. He continued to struggle, eventually pulling himself further out. It took several attempts before he was extended far enough above the edge to bend at the waist and hold himself on the roof. She waited as he caught his breath.

"Thanks," he whispered. "Let's keep this between us, okay?" He drew in more air, then exhaled. "I don't want to jeopardize my *man card.*"

"And what do I get in return?" The reply had rolled off her tongue before her brain had a chance to consider her flirty statement.

"Whatever you want, babe." He grinned. An image of his bare chest pressed against her own flashed through her mind. *Where did that come from?* "This is cold!" Derek's proclamation broke through her thoughts.

"Rain sucks!" Kris sat back on her heels after letting go of him. "And unfortunately, we just lost our supply bag," she continued. "Give your eyes a moment to adjust. Even though the moon's hidden, I can make out a few things with the background light barely breaking through the clouds, at least with the white backdrop of the snow." He nodded and they fell silent. A minute later Derek sat up. While she couldn't see his features, she sensed he was struggling to overcome the intense pain he no doubt was feeling.

"I think I'm ready," he said. She nodded and then realized he probably couldn't see her.

"All right. I'll go and see if I can make out any dark shapes that might show a way down. As opposed to jumping and hoping for the best," she said, wanting to keep her spirits lifted. Inside, she was a bundle of nerves, her mind questioning how they would traverse through this storm when they didn't even know where they were. She was no astronomer, but she knew enough basics that if the clouds did start to thin, the position of the stars might help her at least assess directionality. Kris maneuvered her way down to the edge in a slow controlled slide.

"Watch your step; it's slippery," Derek warned.

Once her toes felt nothing except air, she leaned back to stop her downward movement. It took some shifting around, but she was able to prop herself on all fours and look toward the ground. Her view consisted primarily of a white landscape marred by various dark outlines. *Please let there be a fence up against the house we can climb down on. Or something.*

"Still alive?" she called out over her shoulder.

"Yep. Don't celebrate quite yet."

"Too bad," she added as she peered down again. There it was; the outline of a stacked row of wood. *Score!* "I think there's a woodpile over here. I'm going to feel it out."

"Be careful," he called out. *Is that sincere concern in his voice?* Kris grunted in response as she dropped her legs over the side and slowly scooted downward, hoping her toes would soon touch something solid. Luck was on her side; she felt the top of the woodpile. A few more strategic moves and she was safely on the ground.

"Derek, can you hear me?" she shouted, hoping the blowing wind and rain weren't too loud.

"Yeah," he responded.

"I found a way. Follow the direction I went. Just be careful not to slide straight down. There's some wood stacked below the edge about ten feet over to the side I crawled to." She backed up, straining to make out his frame above her. He hacked a few more times as he traced her path. "Actually, here, I'll get back up on the woodpile. It was hard enough for me to manage with *two* functioning legs," she offered.

"I'll be fine," he muttered.

"Drop down there. It's maybe three, three and a half feet from the edge," she instructed.

"Seriously, woman, I don't need the play-by-play," he snapped. She closed her mouth. Maybe she *was* directing him too much. A second after she heard the sound of him landing on the woodpile, a string of curses penetrated the storm. He carefully slid off the side.

"Holy mother of . . . that was painful," he uttered as he leaned over, his hands propped on his knees.

"Sorry," she said. Looking around, she noticed a dark outline that resembled a small shed ten feet to her right. "Let's go see what's in there."

"In what?" He stood erect and looked at her. She pointed, though she wasn't sure if he could see her gesture.

"There's a shed. Maybe it has some supplies." She trudged over to it, her feet sinking into the snow's surface above her ankles with each step. Her hands reached out to feel for a handle or clasp. A small latch was fashioned at eye level. She didn't feel any kind of lock in it. "Here goes nothing," she said as she pulled outward, praying the inside wasn't filled with spiders, rats, or some other creatures. The hinges squeaked as the door opened. Derek arrived next to her.

"Can you see inside?" he asked.

"No, left my night-vision goggles at home," she responded.

"Dumb question, I know," he acknowledged. She laughed.

"How about you reach inside and see what you feel?"

"Hmm, is the powerful Miss Drew afraid of a little bitty spider?" he teased.

"Not at all. But hey, you need to earn that man card, don't you?"

"Cute," he said.

She could tell he wasn't thrilled about searching the inside either, but she decided not to say anything.

"There are some shelves on the left side. Let me reach in a bit further," he muttered. A squishing sound indicated he'd taken another step toward the door. "Actually, we may be able to stand inside. There's some open space here."

She waited. This time, there was a thump, like he was stomping on something hard. "All right, no rat den," he said.

"Huh?"

"Indiana Jones trilogy—the third one. You know it, right? I mean, when they end up in that tunnel below the library. Wait, don't tell me you haven't seen those. They're classics!"

"Yes, I have. It's just that old movie plots are not exactly at the forefront of my mind at this moment." She sighed. "Is there room for me in there? It would be nice to get out of this rain for a minute."

"As long as you don't mind cuddling up next to me."

"I'm not afraid of you," she said as she moved inside. His rock-hard body was pressed firmly against hers. It felt good. Once again, her mind took a nosedive into the gutter before she pulled it back out.

"I'll check the back if you want to skim those lower shelves behind you," he said. She felt his body shift as he turned away from her to reach farther into the shed. Kris managed to twist herself around and investigate what the shelves held. There were cans, like old peanut cans her dad stored nails in for fixes around the house, and some other few odds and ends—nothing she recognized. Kris started to search the lowest level when Derek called out.

"I think there's a pair of snowshoes here," he said excitedly. She could hear shuffling, and a few seconds later he turned back toward her. She reached out and touched the large objects in his hands. They reminded her of tennis rackets. Sure, they were snowshoes, but definitely the dated kind.

"I don't suppose there are two pairs?" she inquired without much hope.

"Not from what I can feel." A clanking noise told her he'd set them down. Kris refocused her pale vision on the lowest shelf and stretched out her arms. Tucked far in the back was an object. As she felt the familiar edges of a battery-operated camp light, her heart raced.

"I think it's a lantern." She pulled the object free and felt for buttons, whispering, "There's probably no juice left." She switched it on and light filled the small space. "Yes!" She jumped up in excitement, bumping her head against his arm. "Oops," she exclaimed as she positioned the light to illuminate the interior space.

"Can't recall the last time I was so happy for the lights to come *on* while in the dark with a hot woman."

"You never quit!" she snapped, even as she fought the urge to laugh.

"You've got to admit it. You kind of like me," he said, grinning.

"I'm tolerating you," she stated, doing her best to keep from smiling as she resumed investigating the supplies. They examined every shelf and bin they could find. In the farthest corner, Derek discovered an old pair of ski poles stacked among rakes, shovels, and gas cans. "I'll put the snowshoes on and check around outside now that we have light. You stay in here and keep dry. This strain and wet weather may cause your fever to get worse, so please no macho bullshit."

"Understood," he said. Wow, no sarcasm or flirty responses? Kris wasn't sure if she was disappointed or not. She strapped her boots into the bindings, then wrapped one hand around the pole and the other, the lamp.

"I'll be right back," she promised as she stepped out of their temporary shelter. The cold rain pelted her face. In her mind she drew up the picture of a warm, crackling fire. Hot cocoa and marshmallows. Her warm fuzzy slippers. *Bad idea.* Now the chill felt even worse. After trekking around the cabin and doubling back to make sure she didn't miss anything, she unstrapped her boots and quickly tucked herself back inside the shed. "Did I mention I hate rain?"

"Only a few times," Derek chuckled.

"So the bad news first: no cars or anything. Although given the guy has been using a snowmobile, I'm not surprised. Good news: while fresh snow would have made it hard to tell which tracks to follow away from the house—he warned me that first night that he'd made several paths to discourage my escape—the melting from the rain has made it easier to see where there has been more consistent compaction from snowmobile use on the other side of the yard. I think we can make out the route well enough to follow it. What do you think?"

"Let's do it."

"You wear the snowshoes. Comes with the territory of having a gunshot wound in your leg and all." She stepped back out, postholing several inches into the snow.

"That sounds logical," he answered as he bent over to strap them on. "As wounded as my pride may be." A moment later they slowly marched toward the packed path Kris had discovered. The rain felt lighter; Kris hoped the storm was diminishing. Neither of them discussed concerns about the unknown distance. She knew they both were well aware that they could be following tracks that went on for miles.

~

Nola hadn't heard back from her secret consultant. What was happening? Were things going according to plan? Especially given the mishaps that had already transpired? She did not handle being out of the loop very well. In fact, her job was based on being *inside* of the loop. It's how she got things done. She looked out the expansive windows of her home. It was such a beautiful location, tucked up against the sizable golf course. Rain and darkness now obscured the panoramic images of the Sierra Nevada ridgeline she was typically afforded from the south side of the property, with privacy provided by pine trees lining the northern and southern sides. She'd worked hard for this place and she damn well wasn't going to let two nosy hippies take it away. Nola sat back in her favorite leather recliner, propped her feet up, and reached over for her glass of wine. She had to calm herself down. Be patient. He'd check in soon. This kind of weather meant bad roads and slow travel. Cell service around the region could be poor on a good day.

The ring of her doorbell broke her reverie. Who would drop in, unannounced, on a Sunday evening? Nola didn't have a lot of friends; she was too busy working most of the time. A majority of the homes in her neighborhood belonged to people who didn't live in them full-time. She waited. About half a minute passed before it rang again. Nola stood up and strolled to the door to look out the peephole. A tall man with thick brown hair stood on her front stoop. He was handsome; she was definitely curious. She tucked her hair behind her ear and painted on one of her best smiles before opening the door.

"Can I help you?" Now able to see the man's full appearance in the dim light of her porch lamp, she noted the warehouse-quality men's sport coat and snug-fitting jeans.

"Are you Mrs. Nola Swenson?" he asked, pleasant yet reserved.

"Yes. That's *Ms.* Swenson," she clarified. "How can I help you?" *This could be interesting.*

"I'm Detective Ted Benson with the South Lake Tahoe Police Department. I was hoping I could ask you a few questions." Nola's insides twitched as the detective displayed his badge. She quickly regained her composure, feeling confident her expression hadn't given her anxiety away.

"I don't spend much time in South Shore. Not sure what I could help with, but come on in." She stepped to the side and waved him in. While she could refuse to talk to him unless he had a warrant, that would probably make her look guilty. She didn't need to give him any reasons to pay her more attention.

"Thank you." He nodded and entered, then proceeded to wipe his shoes on a mat in her entryway. By the fifth swipe, she interrupted.

"Let's go into the family room; it's far more comfortable." She led him back to where she'd been relaxing, motioning for him to sit on an overstuffed love seat. She positioned herself on the sofa directly across from him, retrieving her glass of wine. "Want anything?" she asked, tipping it in his direction.

"No thank you, ma'am."

"Please, call me Nola," she said, taking another sip. "What can I do for you, Officer Benson?" She emphasized the last two words, careful to exude a friendly, flirty tone. She found men often responded better that way.

"Are you familiar with a woman named Kristina Drew?"

Nola didn't respond right away, acting lost in thought.

"You may know her from working on that ridgeline project up

on Brockway? Tahoe Pines, Truckee Pines. Something like that?" He waited, clearly studying her for a reaction. Of course she knew the woman, and no doubt he was already well aware of that fact.

"I do recognize that name. Isn't she one of those environmental people?" She swirled the red wine before her.

"Yes. She's been missing since Friday. Were you aware of that?"

"Officer Benson, I have better things to do than follow the lives of everyone who complains about my projects," she responded, perhaps more smartly than she'd intended.

"Of course," he said as he smiled. His grin revealed dimples on both cheeks. "The reason I'm here is because Miss Drew had been in touch with Placer County staff—and presumably with you—sometime on Friday regarding a discrepancy in the draft development agreement. Does this ring any bells?" He folded his hands across his knees and leaned forward. Nola felt her face flush. For this information to have made it to the cops, someone had clearly failed her.

"I think I recall a message related to that, but I don't follow the day-to-day details of the county. I presumed whatever it was, they'd fix it." She brushed at the air, as if she were dismissing the subject without concern.

"Are you aware of anyone who might want to harm Miss Drew? Maybe an employee or contractor who would have overreacted in response to opposition to the project?"

She noticed a slight hesitation as he asked the first question. The officer obviously suspected something. She needed to be extremely careful. "Not that I'm aware. Most people I collaborate with understand this is simply business. They know not to take these things personally."

"Regarding this e-mail on Friday—Miss Drew noticed some changes to the development agreement that would save your clients a hefty sum of money over the next twenty years. It doesn't seem like something you would leave to the county to address."

His quick change of subject had almost caught her off guard. *Almost.* "As I stated before, I don't get involved in such details. Those agreements are for the attorneys to figure out. I'm not an attorney." She savored another sip of the smooth merlot.

"So, as the project lead, you wouldn't be aware of such a substantial issue?" he pressed. She stared straight into his eyes.

"As I said, I'm not an attorney." She set her glass down. "On that

note, I do have work to do. If that's all, please let me show you out."
It was time to end this.

"Of course," he said as he stood up and reached into his pocket for a business card. "If you think of anything else, please call me." He held it out for her. She quickly took it and then gave him the overly sweet smile that served her well with other men.

"Certainly," she responded and set it on the nearby table. As she walked with him toward the front door, she said, "I hope you find this woman."

"Me too," he replied.

The front door clicked shut. She let several seconds pass before she peered out the peephole. She watched him walk away until he was out of sight, then took a deep breath. This guy was way too close for comfort. Nola picked up her phone and redialed, begging for her partner to answer. It rang and rang. She tossed it into her purse, slipped her coat and boots on, and walked into her garage with her keys in hand.

Chapter 26

That woman is clearly hiding something, Ted thought as he drove away. When he'd mentioned the change to the development agreement, there had been a small crack in her otherwise practiced expression. The question was whether or not her anxiety was as simple as worry about the project being approved, or something more sinister? He got the sense it was the latter. Ted noticed Carina had left a message while he was interviewing Ms. Swenson. He played it back.

"Ted, it's Carina. Currently en route to the areas frequented by stolen truck. No vehicles fitting description so far. Rain making it hard to see. Holler when you're on the way." Ted smiled. Carina's voice messages had a tendency to sound like someone reading the script from a text. Extra words were skipped. Tangents avoided. It had taken some getting used to, but he'd grown to appreciate her getting straight to the point.

The next message was from another officer in Tahoe City who'd interviewed the county's attorney. Or rather, attempted to. The lawyer refused to answer any questions, referring them to her boss after chewing out the two officers for disrupting her evening at home. Ted made a mental note to follow up then returned Carina's call.

"I'm leaving Truckee now. Meet you in about thirty minutes, maybe a bit longer. There's major traffic heading north out of Tahoe City, but it's been clear in my direction," Ted said to Carina.

"Got it. Radio me when you get here. We'll keep looking around."

As he drove through the Truckee River canyon, Ted noticed the rain splashing against his windshield had lessened. *That should help improve the roads at least.*

189

~

Bob paced around his office as the rain beat down on the roof above, nervously rubbing his broken finger. How had it gone this far? What was supposed to be a straightforward solution to deal with the threat from Rachel Winters had gotten out of hand quickly. There had been one problem after the next. Although he didn't have to deal with most of it directly, he'd still end up paying for it in the end. Plus, the call from Conway yesterday still made Bob upset every time he thought of it. He had to put the man, and the emotional baggage that came with him, out of his mind. It was time to focus and make sure things got back on track. Bob picked up the glass of whiskey on his desk and downed it in one gulp.

~

After taking CiCi back to her house, Rachel and the dogs returned home. Her landline began to ring. Rachel dashed to the phone and glanced at the display before answering.

"Ted, have you found them?" she blurted.

"Not yet."

"Damn," she groaned, pacing across her kitchen. "What about my attacker? Oliver something?" Rachel knew she should be paying far more attention to the situation surrounding the stranger who came after her, but until her brother and friend were found, she felt like she could barely take a moment to breathe.

"We're still interviewing Mr. Palinski. He—"

Rachel stopped in her tracks. "Did you say *Palinski*?"

"Yes, I'm sorry. I guess I hadn't mentioned his full name before. I—"

"Is his father Thomas?" she cut in again, her mind reeling. It wasn't exactly a popular name around the area.

"Yeeeessss," he said, stretching out the affirmation.

"Kris and I have been working with Palinski Senior on that Tahoe-Truckee Pines project. For once, we were on the same side; he's also against putting up buildings on that ridgeline."

"Well, that's interesting." Ted pondered the news.

"Yes, but Oliver seemed less interested in kidnapping me than attacking me. You said you are outside of Tahoe City?" Rachel changed the subject, not wanting to think about the "what ifs."

"Yes, we have a potential lead on the man who stole the penicillin."

Ted gave her a rundown of the video clip, stolen truck, and his interview with Nola. It occurred to Rachel that scarcely a year ago, he'd never have confided so much in her. She had proven she knew how to keep her mouth shut when needed. Then again, part of it might also be Ted's recognition that she wouldn't sit around and wait. It was better to keep her updated than to leave her to try to find things out on her own.

"What can I do?" she asked, frustrated.

"Keep doing what you've been doing."

"But I've been through everything three times over. There's nothing new."

"Wait, is this Rachel Winters I'm talking to? A woman who never gives up, even when it drives those around her crazy?" he said and smirked.

"Message received," she said.

Ted continued, "Just be careful. I really wish someone could stay with you. What about Luke? I know you are having some issues, but—"

"No," she stated with more emphasis than she'd intended. "I'll be very watchful. Plus, I now have *two* dogs keeping an eye out around here." She looked over at the energetic pair, who were busy playing tug with a snake toy. "And I feel pretty confident they'd attack someone trying to hurt me."

"That's true. Okay, at least rest your brain. You sound exhausted," he encouraged. "I'll have a unit swing by your house every hour or two. Don't argue."

Rachel heard a loud thump, as if his wheels had collided with a pothole.

"I'm currently on 89 south of Chambers Landing. I'll be joining the others to check out the area around the off-roading McKinney/Rubicon Trail. You know, that place where snowmobilers go in the winter."

"Yes, I'm familiar. All that leaking gas, noise, trash, and—"

"I should have a signal there; call if anything else comes up." Ted cut her off. Rightly so. Now was no time for a rant.

Rachel agreed, hung up, and decided to head out back to retrieve some wood before taking off her boots. She noticed one good thing: the rain had finally stopped.

"Mr. Palinski, you are in serious trouble here. You understand that, right?" the officer repeated to Oliver. They'd placed him in a rigid, cold chair with his hands cuffed behind his back. He looked down at the scratched gray table. Two policemen stood in the room; the younger one looked like he was fresh out of high school, playing dress-up in an oversized police uniform. The other wore a wrinkled suit. It was the suit—minus the wrinkles—that, along with his clean-cut hair and pointed nose, made the guy looked like Tom Cruise in one of those *Mission: Impossible* movies. He asked the first questions. Oliver refused to speak. His father would be here as soon as he'd heard in the message he'd left with his one phone call. The man rarely went more than an hour or two without checking his phone.

"Tell us where you have them stashed away, and we'll go easier on you."

Oliver had no idea who the "they" were that the men were talking about. He wanted to ask; however, his father had always instructed him not to say a word if he was ever arrested. But deep down, he was worried. Had the cops really found them? He couldn't wait. He had to know.

"Who?" he asked.

Tom Cruise seemed surprised at the response. High school grad remained still. It unnerved him.

"You know damn well who," Cruise stated, slamming his palm against the table.

"No, I don't." Oliver alternately opened and closed his fists—a nervous habit for as long as he could recall. It was one of the things he'd frequently been teased about as a child. The more they picked on him, the more anxious he became, and the more he did it. It was a vicious circle. Oliver felt his anxiety ramp up as the cops glared at him. He waited.

Silence.

His nose itched. He raised his cuffed hands and scratched.

They stared.

He couldn't take it anymore. "Jason?" he blurted.

The officer looked confused, then asked, "Jason?"

Oliver swiftly backtracked, realizing his mistake. "Uh, you look like s . . . someone I used to know," he stuttered. He wasn't sure old Tommy boy believed him. The man nodded and then sighed, as if he were weighing his next words carefully. Which he probably was doing. As if Oliver were nothing more than a child! His insides coiled. The longer the cop waited, the more he imagined ways to kill the guy, presuming he wasn't handcuffed. If he had knife, he could swing out and slice his throat. Although his blood would probably spurt into Oliver's face. He wouldn't like that. What about an ax? Yeah, that would be fun. Just swing it nice and hard, sideways, straight into his neck. Lop his head right off. Would something like that make a popping sound? It took him a moment to realize the man had started speaking again.

"Okay, Mr. Palinski, I'll play along. We are looking for Kristina Drew and Derek Winters," Cruise disclosed. Oliver perked up. *Not Jason, or the woman for that matter.* Maybe they had believed his excuse for the slip-up. Although not what he was expecting, those two names were familiar. *Drew . . . wait, isn't she one of those bitches working with his father to combat that damn ridgeline project? Yes, that had to be her. Working with Rachel Winters. Oh, Rachel. How much fun I was going to have with you. And once Father gets me out of this joint, we'll pick up where we left off.* Oliver felt himself grow hard at the thought of resuming things with Ms. Winters. *Did the cops see it?*

"Mr. Palinski?" High school grad broke through his reverie. Oliver suddenly realized his mind had wandered again.

What had they asked? Oh, that's right. "I honestly have no idea what you're talking about," he responded and then relaxed back into the chair. For once, he didn't have to lie.

"Where were you last Friday?" Tom Cruise asked. Their tag-team approach was so obvious. As if that would work on Oliver. He was done talking.

"Mr. Palinski?" High school grad prompted. "Answer the question." Oliver's hands began to tremble. Their stares were so intense. The silence in the room went on forever. He knew better than to talk. But he couldn't stand the quiet any longer. And those glares. Well, he hadn't done anything to the couple they were asking about. So why not answer?

"I was at home."

"All day?"

Oliver nodded.

"Can anyone verify that?" Cruise asked, staring intently. Oliver felt himself shrink as the room stayed quiet. He wanted to fill the silence. But he was already talking too much. He probably should have followed his father's advice.

"I'm going to wait for my attorney before I answer any more questions." At this, Mr. *Mission: Impossible* appeared annoyed. He stared at Oliver for several seconds, then stood up and walked to the door. High school grad followed behind. Oliver wondered how long it would take for his dad to send someone. He was also confused about the interview. He'd assumed he was here because of his little visit with Rachel Winters, yet they hadn't even asked him about that. What was going on?

~

"You know what his reference to a 'Jason' could be about?" Officer Shoals asked as he slipped off his suit jacket. He noticed it was heavily wrinkled and frowned.

"No idea," his younger partner replied.

Shoals gave it some thought. "He mentioned that name in response to my question about telling us where he had *them* stashed away, right?" Posed as a question, it was in fact more a statement, and his partner had been around him long enough to know to simply wait for him to continue. "You know of any Missing Persons in the area named Jason?" He waited but received no response. "This time it's a question," he chuckled.

"No, sir."

"Call me Shoals; everyone else does." The "sir" had started to irritate him by about day two of being paired with the kid.

"Okay, sir. I mean, Shoals. I'll call the MP folks and find out."

"Good. Let me know what you hear."

Chapter 27

Ted ended the call with Rachel as he glanced at the bright headlights approaching from behind. He didn't have the emergency light attached to the top of his SUV. When it was there, people usually recognized him as law enforcement and slowed down. They rarely tailgated him. The slick roads made him nervous. Much as he wanted to ticket the jerk, he decided to pull off and let him go by instead. He could alert the highway patrol once he got going. Ted glided his SUV over to the side and watched the vehicle swerve erratically around him. Once it was in view of his own headlights, Ted noticed the Nevada license plate. Black truck, Ford Ranger, early 2000s.

"Well, I'll be damned . . ." He couldn't believe it. Could this actually be their guy? Ted radioed Carina, advising her of the vehicle's approach and instructing her to block off the highway south of Tahoma and to send someone up to block off the northbound lane as well. Ted could park across a narrow section of the highway to the north, effectively trapping the perp in between the two roadblocks. He retrieved the magnetic flashing light from his passenger seat and placed it on top of his vehicle in the "on" position. The driver immediately tapped on the brakes, as was instinctive of most people when they spotted a cop car.

After the brief slow-up, the truck accelerated. Ted examined the highway, his eyes searching for a good spot to block the road. Carina also sent another officer in his direction to assist. The assailant's truck reached the roadblock to the south. The sound of screeching tires filled the night as the vehicle skidded to a stop, whipped into reverse, and attempted what ended up being a five-point turn. It was reminiscent of one of the *Austin Powers* movies. The extended turning movement was so ridiculous that everyone appeared surprised; perhaps that's why the perp managed to turn around without interference, until Ted blocked his northward path and another law enforcement vehicle pulled up next to him. Ted jumped out of the driver's seat and yelled, "Hands in the air where I can see them!"

The guy remained still, as if he were contemplating his options, while a cadre of officers surrounded him. Finally, he opened his window and stuck out his hands. Within seconds he was cuffed, read his Miranda rights, and stashed in the back of a patrol car as officers searched the pickup. After letting the guy stew for another ten minutes, Ted slid in next to him and closed the door.

"Where are they?"

"Who?"

The guy had a good poker face. Ted would give him that. "Don't be stupid. The only way to help yourself now is to tell us where they are. Things will be easier for you if you cooperate."

"I don't know what you're talking about."

The man was a skilled liar, but Ted had seen far too many "innocent" people to count. "Look, I stole a truck. I admit that. But whatever else this is, I have no idea."

Ted waited. Sometimes people couldn't handle the silence and would inevitably talk. Unfortunately, not this one. "I'll spell it out for you. We searched that truck. We found two ski masks, a helmet, a snowmobile key, and other gear. I'd say you were getting ready to take a little evening spin somewhere, right?" He waited. No response. As much as he'd normally prefer to keep someone guessing on what they had until a proper interview, given people were missing and injured, he couldn't risk the time. Rather, he hoped that if the kidnapper realized they already had a solid case against him, he might be willing to talk if it could reduce future prison terms.

"We've also got you on camera breaking into that pharmacy on North Shore. We know one of your abductees was shot. We also know you were in South Lake Tahoe when both were kidnapped and driven back and forth to this spot here," Ted said as he waved behind them. He noticed a quick expression of surprise flicker across the man's face. It disappeared just as fast as it had come on. Headlights turned on nearby, lighting up the man's face more than the dim interior light had done. Ted noticed a flaky white substance smeared across his cheeks. Strange. Ted ignored it and continued. "I can go on and on about the evidence piled against you. There's nothing to lose now by helping us out. Seriously, man, tell us where they are and make it easier on yourself. I'll inform the district attorney that you cooperated." Ted waited.

"I want a lawyer," the man stated obstinately.

"Fine. Just know that we'll find them, with or without you. You're not doing yourself any favors by refusing to cooperate," Ted said, then crawled out of the vehicle and marched over to Carina and a handful of other uniformed officers.

"Anything?" she asked. He shook his head.

"Based on the equipment he had back there, there's got to be a snowmobile around here somewhere. It's the only thing I can think of given the location to off-road areas where people wouldn't think twice if they heard or saw one. Plus, keep in mind his repeated visits. Maybe he is holding them somewhere you can't get to in a regular vehicle?"

"Every now and then I've run into old cabins or shacks in the outskirts of the basin. Could there be something like that up there?" She waved at the rising mountains to the west.

"I'll get someone to scan old land records. In the meantime, let's start searching for tracks, equipment, anything," Ted said. The other officers nodded, and Ted left Carina to coordinate the search as he went back to his own vehicle to add more layers of outdoor apparel. It was cold and wet, but at least the storm was drying out. That would make it easier to travel, and more likely they'd see something.

~

All this trouble because of fallen trees. Thomas Palinski figured it was a major irony; he'd spent a large part of his life fighting to build projects opposed by tree huggers. His wife had worked for one of the largest private timber companies on the West Coast. In essence, they both established careers based on cutting down large trees. Yet fallen trees had, in fact, prevented him from cleaning up their mess all those years ago. Perhaps there was something to all of this talk about karma. Thomas's eye started twitching again.

As if they didn't have enough to deal with right now, his useless son had to go and get himself arrested. He hadn't immediately returned

Oliver's call. The message had been difficult to understand—something about dogs and attorneys. Instead, Thomas first contacted an old friend of his at the station to obtain more information. She explained Oliver had been picked up after his prints were found at a crime scene. An assault on Rachel Winters—of all people! His son had absolutely zero common sense. This was not going to be an easy fix this time. Frankly, he wasn't sure it was even possible. They had the boy's fingerprints. And making matters worse, another hitch had just come up in his own plans. His son would have to wait.

~

"Ms. Winters, Officer Shoals here," the man introduced himself as soon as Rachel answered her phone.

"Yes?" she asked groggily. After driving CiCi back home, Rachel lay on her couch with ice packs under her neck and back because it still helped. A glance across her small living area confirmed that the two pups were nearby. Avi's head was resting on Bella's back.

"I've been interrogating the man who assaulted you yesterday."

Now this perked her up.

"Did he confess?" She stood and carried the ice packs back to the freezer.

"No, and we've been trying to find out what he may know about your friend and brother first. He's asked for an attorney."

"I thought Ted had a line on the kidnapper . . . that it was someone else on West Shore?" she questioned after a brief pause. Her mind was having trouble following the man's information.

"He does, but we haven't ruled out Mr. Palinski's involvement. Unfortunately we now have to wait to talk to him further unless he rescinds his request for a lawyer. Based on who his father is, I don't see that happening." He sounded annoyed. Rachel understood that sentiment. "Sorry to bother you, but it would help us out if you could come down tonight and take a look at him, see if anything looks familiar?"

"My attacker was wearing a mask. I don't see how I could help. And don't you have his prints?"

"That alone may not be enough; his attorney could claim a variety of other reasons his prints would be on the collar, and we're not sure we could disprove them enough to get around reasonable doubt. I know you didn't see his face, but maybe something will jump out at you."

"What about puncture wounds? Both dogs got him good in several places."

"Yes, we've got those, too. But, look, it's frankly another check mark for the paperwork, you know?"

Oh, yes, paperwork was something she was all too familiar with. Rachel looked outside and noticed the storm had lightened. As much as she didn't want to leave home unless it involved Kris and Derek, she agreed.

"All right, give me a few moments, and I'll head on over." She looked around for her boots. "Do you really think Oliver's involved in the kidnapping, too?"

"Ted indicated it was worth exploring. Maybe you were next on the list to be taken. I'll tell you, though, he really did seem perplexed when we questioned him about the kidnapping. In fact . . ."—he paused for a few seconds and cleared his throat—"the guy mentioned another person we suspect may have been missing for some time. You ever recall someone named Jason who disappeared from around this area?"

Rachel gave it some thought. "No, doesn't ring any bells."

"Very well. I'll let you go so you can drive over here. Tell the receptionist to come get me when you arrive."

"Officer Shoals, right?" Rachel still didn't trust her brain; it had been a struggle to follow the conversation at times.

"You got it."

Rachel scrawled his name down on a nearby notepad and tucked it into her pocket. She decided to leave the dogs home so they could move around; there was no need to stuff them into the pickup for this. She threw on her coat, grabbed her purse, and headed out the door. Thankfully, Ted had made sure a locksmith came by earlier in the morning to replace the lock. Then again, based on how the new dynamic duo had protected her from the intruder, the level of security around her home had likely just experienced a significant boost.

The temperatures hadn't dropped enough for the rain-soaked roads to turn icy yet. Able to drive at a normal speed, she pulled into the police station's lot in under twenty minutes. It took less than five for Officer Shoals to greet her and walk her back to the viewing area.

Seeing the guy who most likely had come after her was weird. She remembered how it felt when he'd grabbed her, held her down. And those horrible odors that had clung to his body. If they asked her to smell him, she didn't think she could handle it. *Would scent recognition even be admissible in court?* The memory sent chills down her spine.

"I can confirm his build looks similar. That's about it. Sorry," she said apologetically.

"I understand. Had to try."

Rachel turned from the image, not wanting to stare through the one-way mirror any longer.

"I know we already have your statement," Shoals said. "Let me make sure we don't need anything else. Can you wait here for a few minutes?"

Although Rachel longed to get back home and cuddle with the girls, she nodded.

"There are some chairs right outside this room, if you'd like to grab one."

"Sure," she mumbled. Still feeling fatigued and with her headache not quite gone, she was happy to rest and lean her head back against the wall. Barely a minute after she'd positioned herself and closed her eyes, a familiar voice echoed from across the room. Rachel's eyes flew open: Luke had walked in. Without looking in her direction, he leaned against the counter, joking with the clerk sitting behind it. Rachel turned her gaze away, wanting to avoid a run-in. She considered standing and walking the other way, but that might draw his attention. Damn, though, it sure hurt her heart to see him. A side conversation in the small lunchroom down the hall caught her attention, and she gladly eavesdropped to distract herself.

"They arrested someone," said a loud female voice.

"Really? Did they find the two missing people?" another woman questioned. Rachel's heart started to race, and she strained to hear better.

"Not yet, but word is they may have an idea of where to find them," the first woman said. Rachel heard the sound of a drawer being pulled open and slid back shut. "Something about a snowmobile area off that McKinney/Rubicon Trail."

"Oh, Richard has taken me for a ride back there in the summer in that beat-up old Jeep of his," the second woman chimed in. "That's sure a lot of ground to cover."

"Yep. The guy isn't talking, so they've started a search. Just called asking for any available officers to come and assist."

"How do you know all of this?" the second woman inquired.

"A well-timed visit to the restroom."

Rachel couldn't believe it. They'd actually found him already? And arrested him? She was annoyed Ted hadn't called her; at the same time, part of her understood. He was organizing a search party. She'd rather he focus on looking for Kris and Derek than keep her updated. *Although he could have had someone else call me*, Rachel thought. *Screw it. They need more people to assist in the search. Why not me too?* Bella wasn't a trained search-and-rescue dog, but she always sensed other people well before Rachel ever saw them. And Bella knew Kris and Derek; if they were nearby, she would definitely pick up their scents. She stood anxiously. In her haste she knocked the chair backward, slamming it into the wall behind her. The crashing sound blared through the station. She looked up. Sure enough, Luke had turned and spotted her. Rachel barely noticed when Officer Shoals approached.

"Ms. Winters, you're good to go. Thanks again for coming down tonight." He held out his hand. She shook it, distracted. A moment later Rachel hurriedly headed toward the door. Had there been no people around, she'd be in full running mode. Rachel thought she may have heard Luke call out to her as she brushed by, but she ignored him and continued, pushing her way through the front door and charging into the parking lot.

"Rachel?" Luke's tense voice rang out so much it startled her, and she turned to see him running toward her. *Damn.*

"Not now, Luke," she sighed as she climbed into her pickup.

"Let me guess? You're heading to Tahoma for Ted's search?"

How did he know?

She didn't respond right away, so he continued. "I'm here because Ted told me he needed the help and asked that I check in with the station first."

"Yes, I'm going over there. But first, I'm going home to grab Bella. Not sure Avi wouldn't run away, though I guess I should take her along and just leave her in the truck." She rambled as she verbalized her thoughts.

"Abby?" He tilted his head. She rolled her window down and shut the door.

"Avi. For Avalanche. I've adopted the other dog."

He seemed to mull something over before speaking. "I'm going with you," he stated.

"No, you're not," she countered.

201

"Don't be stubborn."

"I'm not," Rachel insisted. "I'm going to have Bella and Avi with me. No room." Before he could respond, she closed the window and backed up. Luke stood in her headlights with a mixture of sadness and anger on his face. *Too bad*, she thought. *But nothing is stopping him from driving his own ass over there.* What she did not need was time alone with him right now. Her emotions were already fried from everything else that had happened.

Luke stared with obvious annoyance as Rachel drove past him.

~

Derek stopped abruptly. He needed a break. Kris was trailing behind him. Although there were compressed tracks from repeated use of a snowmobile, the rain's softening effect meant she still sank down several inches with each step. He'd made her use the one set of poles they'd found, while he carried the light. She had to be wet and cold; he was freezing—although how much was from being in the wintry conditions versus the fever he no doubt had, he didn't know. Either way, he knew if he stopped too long, the heat from the exertion that had kept them both warm would likely die off. But he'd pushed forward for as long as he could.

"You okay?" she called out. He leaned his weight against a tree. Everything ached. He definitely had a fever and his leg throbbed. He didn't want to tell her how bad he really felt; she was already worried.

"Yeah, I could use a little rest," he replied. The end to the rainfall had given him hope. But how far had they gone? Their route traveled downhill most of the way until the trail had curved up and gone over a small knoll. Now it was descending once again. Derek clicked off the light and peered overhead through the dark shapes of the pine trees. Was that a star? "I think the storm might be thinning out."

"You may be right," she said, much closer than he'd expected. "And it looks like there may be some moonlight trying to peek out from behind the clouds." She shifted and he felt her press the back of her bare hand to his forehead. "You're burning up." Her voice was calm, until a faint crack broke through her last word. Derek sensed she was scared. Then again, so was he. "Let's take five," she said, dropping her hand away and putting her glove back on. It left a cool spot on his skin. "But let's spare the battery; keep the light off."

He nodded agreement as he leaned against a tree. "You're not even breathing hard," he observed.

"Remember, I do this kind of thing for fun," she chuckled. Her features lit up in the dim light, and Derek saw her face brighten. He gazed upward again. A sliver of moonlight had broken through the clouds. "Hey, look that way," she pointed. He saw a string of lights in the distance that appeared elevated, as if from homes positioned up the side of a mountain.

"What is that?" he wondered aloud.

"Derek, I think we're still in Tahoe," she said. He looked her way and saw her scrutinizing the view. "I think that big dark area is the lake. Those lights over there, that's the top of Kingsbury Grade. The trees around us must be blocking lights between us and the lake from here."

"Well, I'll be damned," he whispered.

"If I'm right, we're somewhere on the West Shore." She removed a water bottle from her coat pocket and sipped. "Which means we head that way and we'll eventually get to a road—either a residential street or Highway 89."

"I could so kiss you right now," he exclaimed. Then, without thinking, he reached for her hand as he pushed himself from the tree. She appeared surprised and, for once, uncertain of how to respond. He laughed, staring at her mere inches from her face. For the first time ever, she looked flustered. "But I won't." He stepped back, grasping the tree again with his free hand to keep his balance. "Let's go," he said, feeling more energetic than five minutes ago. "I think there's enough moonlight to keep the camp light off."

"Agreed." She let go of his palm and reached for her poles. About ten minutes had passed when they heard the distant sound of a motor. It wasn't coming from below them; it sounded as if it were to the north and higher in elevation. Derek stopped and waited for Kris to catch up. Her steps were now sinking even deeper into the slushy snow. She was getting one heck of a workout.

"Do you think that's our guy?" She looked worried. "Would he be coming from that direction?"

"I don't think we can take that chance," he responded, looking around. The faint glow from the sky illuminated a nearby thicket of trees. He pointed. "Let's go over that way. He may see our tracks if he's looking, but at least we'll be hidden and we'll see him coming."

Kris nodded and they quickly turned south. About two hundred feet remained between them and the cover of the pines.

~

How the hell did Jerry get himself arrested? No one with a more impressive record had been available for the abduction job on such short notice. And now the couple had to be dealt with directly. Remaining unseen was still vital. Though the ski mask's fit was snug, it would work.

It had been upsetting to hear the rushed voice mail from Jerry earlier, explaining he'd been discovered by the cops and was literally sitting in his truck waiting to be handcuffed. In his message he referred to a previous e-mail containing directions to the small cabin, stating that the couple couldn't be left there without food and water. The man was also seriously injured and had required antibiotics. *Damn it all to hell, too. Why did Jerry have to take that second captive? Go figure! A hired gun with morals!*

After listening to Jerry's information, the pros and cons had to be weighed. In the end, the "if you want something done right, do it yourself" mantra prevailed. At this point, it would, indeed, be undesirable for them to die; it would cause far too much trouble. That meant food and water had to be provided for a while yet. It was doable, with very cautious strategizing.

Jerry had also warned it would be best to approach from the north side, suggesting a snowmobile route from the Barker Pass area that ran south across the ridge. Noise from this high elevation wouldn't easily resonate down into the residential neighborhoods along Highway 89, making it fairly safe to ride up this way. In fact, it was almost a little exhilarating to know the cops were down there with no idea that their missing people were so close.

The moon now fully revealed itself, lighting up the landscape and creating an almost surreal wintry scene. There were areas of thick, dense patches of forest located among more open spaces. The path to the cabin, coming in from McKinney/Rubicon Trail, lay up ahead. It would be easy cruising from here on out.

~

Luke tucked his Subaru behind a restaurant sign, planning to follow Rachel when she passed by on her way to Tahoma. By his estimate, it would take her about twenty minutes to drive home from the station and pick up the dogs. He pulled out the amber bottle from under his seat and popped two pain pills. The stress was taking its toll on his aching muscles. That had to be it. He also wasn't too keen on driving back to West Shore again today, but he had to do whatever he could to help.

Luke's thoughts returned to Rachel. He wasn't surprised in the least that she'd ended up keeping the canine. So long as Bella and the new pup got along, Rachel wouldn't think twice. Luke glanced at the clock, then back up to the road. There was not much traffic out tonight. A set of headlights approached and a vehicle cruised by. Pale streetlights cast just enough glow to confirm it was Rachel's Tacoma. He waited another half minute before pulling out to follow her. Granted, he knew exactly where she was going, but the protective side of him worried about her getting their safely given her emotional and physical state. A lot had happened to her over the past several days—and he certainly hadn't helped. Furthermore, the pained expression on her face and dark circles under her eyes suggested she was still suffering from postconcussion symptoms, too.

As usual, Rachel kept her speed fairly close to the posted limit. And tonight, he knew she'd be extra careful. The roads would turn slippery soon. Luke maintained about a quarter mile's distance between them. He only encountered one vehicle heading in the other direction.

He slowly approached the bustling area where Rachel had parked near a collection of emergency vehicles in Tahoma. Several marked and unmarked autos lined the otherwise empty lots along the highway. Luke pulled up next to her and looked over into the cab, but she'd already climbed out.

He jumped out of his seat and opened the passenger door behind him. A tailgate slammed shut nearby, and then Rachel appeared.

"Are you kidding me?" she yelled. "Think I didn't notice you behind me? The whole damn way over here?"

Oh yeah, she's pissed. "You told me to drive myself. So I did," he replied with a casualness he didn't feel as he leaned inside of his Subaru to search for a pair of gloves. She rolled her eyes, turned, and walked away. Luke watched with some amusement as she reappeared on the other side of her truck in front of the passenger door where the two dogs pressed their noses against the glass.

"Avi, I need you to hang here," she said as she opened the door and held Avi inside while instructing Bella to jump down. Two pairs of brown eyes focused solely on her, as if they understood this was no time to mess around. Although that didn't keep Bella from dashing around the truck to come greet Luke. She rubbed her body up against his legs and then fixed him with her infamous puppy stare.

"Sweet girl," he said as he massaged her ears. Rachel walked around back and grabbed the pair of snowshoes she'd leaned against her truck. She didn't look his way.

"Bella, come," Rachel instructed as she walked toward the small crowd gathered by the law enforcement vehicles. As Bella fell in step beside her, Luke glanced once more at Avi, who watched them leave as if the world were ending. He dashed forward and walked alongside Rachel as she approached one of the uniformed officers. "I'm here to help with the search. Is Officer Benson around?" she asked. Luke heard the man sigh and then reluctantly address her.

"He's over that way, but he's busy coordinating the operation. You can stand over there if you'd like." He pointed to a line of bystanders huddled behind one of the law enforcement SUVs. Before Rachel could respond, the officer looked behind her at Luke. "You here to help?" he asked. *Uh-oh. That's going to tick her off,* Luke thought.

"Excuse me," Rachel cut in. "Sorry to ruin the boys club, but as I already said, I came here to help." She held up the snowshoes clutched in her hand and looked pointedly at the officer. Luke knew the gender-based assumption had riled her, but she kept her cool.

"Seriously, she can probably out-ski and out-snowshoe most of the men here," Luke cut in. Rachel gave him an "I-can-fight-my-own-battles" look. He stepped back with his own "excuse-the-hell-out-of-me" glare aimed back at her.

"Ma'am, we—"

"I'm taking my dog and my pretty little snowshoes over there to meet Officer Benson." Rachel pointed, her voice remaining relatively calm. Luke was impressed. "I'll try not to break a nail and disrupt the search." Luke almost smiled.

"Whatever you say, ma'am." The officer moved to the side, holding his arm out. The motion was overly dramatic. The man was clearly mocking her, but Rachel didn't take the bait.

"Thank you," she said, and then she commanded Bella to heel once again. Luke smiled apologetically at the officer and followed behind her. When they reached Ted, he was busy holding up a large map and pointing to various scribbled lines as he gave directions to the group around him.

"We tried to find old records that could indicate where any structures might be up there but came up empty. Ditto on aerial photos, although the trees have been known to hide a building or two. So we need to make sure we cover all of this ground. Check anything that looks out of the ordinary or elevated. While the rain has caused some melting, there was some heavy snowfall up here in that last storm." The half-dozen or so people circling Ted nodded. He looked up, noticing Rachel. Luke saw an expression of concern fall across his face. Ted finished his instructions and then approached her as the others shuffled away.

"Rachel, what are you doing out here?"

"I came to help. I think Bella could be valuable, too. She's good at scenting people she knows from a distance. Heck, even people she doesn't."

"I get that, but your concussion . . ."

"I'm okay," she said, touching his shoulder. Luke knew it was ridiculous—Ted was like another brother to her—but a stab of jealousy shot through him at the comfortable gesture. "Which route can we cover?" she asked.

Ted paused. He glanced at the snowshoes and back at Rachel and then nodded. Like any man who knew Rachel, the guy clearly understood that once her mind was made up, changing it was virtually impossible. Luke stepped closer as Ted raised the map and pointed to a line.

"This is the one area we don't have covered yet. I didn't want anyone going out there solo. You and Luke can cover that line. It's all on foot right now. We don't have any snowmobiles yet; we've put in calls to borrow some equipment from the local emergency responders. Problem is they were all out searching for a kid who went missing while backcountry skiing with his dad," he explained, clearly frustrated. "All the radios we have on site have been claimed, so I'll coordinate with you via text. You should get a strong enough signal along most of the route. Text me every twenty minutes to check in. If I don't hear from you, I'll assume something is wrong and send someone after you. And given we are short on manpower, I don't want to have to do that, meaning I need everyone to pay strict attention to time! I'll stay here and coordinate ops until the captain arrives. I'm about to update him now. I also want another stab at that asshole." Luke and Rachel both followed Ted's intent gaze. A man, his features obscured by the shadows, was seated in the back of one of the patrol units.

"That's the kidnapper?" Luke asked.

"Yes, he refuses to cooperate. I recovered his cell phone. He made a twenty-two-second phone call to another burner phone as he was trying to escape. We can't trace it, but I'm pretty sure he was warning someone else."

"Okay, let's drive up to the starting point. First . . ." Rachel retrieved her cell and clicked a picture of the map. Then, almost as an afterthought, she turned to Luke. "I have two headlamps in my truck; I'll grab them."

"Appreciate it," Luke mumbled, thankful he left his winter gear stowed in his car, although he hadn't even used the snowshoes in months. It wasn't something he had ever done before meeting Rachel.

The memory of the first time they'd gone for a walk together with snow on the ground flashed through his mind. That was over a year ago. Rachel had teased him for failing to bring snowshoes. When he claimed he wouldn't need them, she had simply taken off and proceeded up the trail with hers on. He remembered sinking almost a foot with each step. Ten minutes into their trek he'd admitted defeat and purchased his own pair the next day, then just left them in his vehicle through the winter. *When was the last time I used them?* He couldn't recall and a thought struck him. Had he really not gone snowshoeing with Rachel even once this year? Lord knows she'd asked several times. The realization was eye-opening.

"Wake up." Rachel snapped her fingers. She was standing next to her truck, her keys in hand.

"I'm sorry," he said.

"For what?"

"For not going out snowshoeing with you this winter when you invited me." His confession had clearly caught her off guard—much like the thought of his own complacency had done to him. For a brief moment, a flicker of something—sorrow, disappointment, anger, or all of the above—fell across her features. It diminished quickly, her expression falling back into one of intense concentration. "You may want to follow me up to the end of the road where we'll launch into the forest. Unless you want two dogs on your lap." She turned and opened the door, holding Avi in place while Bella jumped back inside the truck's cab. Luke looked at the two canines; both were sitting close on the passenger seat.

"I'll follow you," he agreed, reaching into his pocket for his keys. She nodded, whipped her head around, and dashed to the driver's side. Her engine started and she zipped out of the lot.

~

"Sir, I mean, Shoals, I've found something, but I'm not sure it applies."

Shoals looked up from the paperwork on his desk at his young partner sitting nearby. His expression conveyed that he should continue speaking.

"There are no recent MP reports for anyone named Jason from South Lake. I checked North Tahoe—same deal. I was going to search records outside of the basin when I started wondering if maybe it wasn't recent." Shoals had to concentrate to hear each word. The kid talked fast and, when he got going, didn't enunciate his words well. Or maybe it was just that Shoals was over fifty and all millennials sounded that way to him.

"And?" he encouraged.

"Since Oliver was raised here, I thought I'd check our cold files before I reached out to other departments. I found a report from twenty years ago: Jason Maxwell, eighteen years old, went missing sometime in August of '95." He paused.

"Got the file?"

"I'll e-mail it right now, sir." He turned and raced to his desk across the room. Shoals smiled. He'd just have to get used to sir. A new message popped up in his inbox. He clicked it open and read through the attached report filed by the kid's parents in Kings Beach. Their son had gone out with friends after dinner and never returned home. Some people assumed that he'd run off after a huge argument with his dad.

Shoals stood up and looked over at his partner. "By the way, good work." He received a slight nod in response.

Five minutes later, he'd managed to skim through most of the file when his partner e-mailed a phone number. Shoals didn't understand how people could be all of fifteen feet apart in the same room yet still communicate electronically. Sadly, that's how it was now; he had to get used to it. He picked up his phone and dialed.

~

Kris watched anxiously as the snowmobile turned and began approaching from the direction they'd come from. How long until the driver noticed their footprints?

"What is our plan B?" she asked.

"No idea," Derek replied. He sounded out of breath. *Was that a small wheeze, too?*

"Stay with me. We're so close to getting out of this." She stuck the poles in the snow and reached for his hand. Moisture had seeped into her gloves, numbing her fingers. As she'd only been intending to visit her parents, she hadn't been wearing her best gloves when she was taken. That seemed so long ago now.

"I will," he said, sounding determined as he squeezed her hand.

"Okay, let's think this out. The one thing we have going for us is the element of surprise. Then again, if he sees our tracks and follows them, maybe not so much." She looked down. "Unless you have some serious fencing skills you can use with these poles?"

"No, I have skills wielding things, but not like that." He grinned. She raised her brow.

"That's the best you've got? I'm disappointed."

"It's the fever." He smirked and then waived around him. "What about these aspens? I had to bend around a few already and we barely walked in here, what, twenty feet?"

"Good point. It would be tough to ride a snowmobile through here," she said, examining their surroundings more closely. She handed him the poles. "Let's get farther inside this grove. I'll go in front and pull branches out of the way." He nodded, although Kris suspected it wounded his pride. *Too bad.* She estimated they'd covered another thirty feet. "He'll definitely have to slow down to get in here or do it on foot. But then what? Chances are he'll have a gun. We don't."

"Maybe he won't shoot? He's made a point to keep us alive so far," he said hopefully.

Kris looked from Derek's eyes to his injured thigh with her brow raised.

"Good point," he conceded.

"Plus, our escape attempt could change his mind. Or maybe it's someone else. Who knows? We should be ready for anything, as much as we can be." She looked around and then glanced skyward.

"I agree. But we have, what, old snowshoes and a pair of hollow ski poles between us? That's not much."

The last few words came out more like a whisper. She could see he was struggling to remain upright. There was enough light now to discern that his cheeks burned bright red. She was worried. Very worried. What if he collapsed? *Can't worry about that until and unless it happens*, she advised herself. Kris contemplated the large tree above her. "Derek, I have an idea," she articulated as she pointed. "I think I can climb that tree." She waited while Derek looked up.

"Seriously?"

"I love to climb, and old aspens like this are easier to grip than, say, pine trees." She walked over to the large trunk, feeling around to investigate a route for her ascent.

"All right, I believe that. So then what?"

"You run. Go get help. If I have a chance to drop down on him, I'll have to take it."

"Are you freakin' nuts?! What if he's armed?"

"Aw, you're worried about me," she teased, tilting her head to the side.

"Don't read too much into it. I'm simply not interested in explaining your death to Rachel; that's all," he replied.

She let go of his hand, removed her glove, and reached up to his cheek. She could feel the rough stubble from several days' growth. He was hot to the touch. Kris lightly boosted herself up on the front of the snowshoes and gently kissed his lips. "I'm sure that's all it is," she whispered, enjoying the feel of his mouth against hers for a brief moment before falling back down and stepping off of the snowshoes. Derek took a long, deep breath and then released it, never removing his eyes from hers.

"I like your style, Kristina Drew." He smiled. "If I weren't hacking like a pig, and we weren't in imminent danger of losing our lives, that maneuver would have cost you." His gaze moved to her mouth.

Focus! Kris tore herself from their connection, turned to reach up, and quickly pulled herself into the tree. Her arms already ached from climbing out of the hole in the roof. She pushed through the strain, hearing Derek speak below her.

"You're a mountain goat. Or maybe more like a brown bear; those buggers can climb, although you're far sexier."

"Since when are bears sexy?" she played along as she raised herself another few feet.

"Since . . . wow, I can't think of a witty response," he admitted.

She laughed. "That might be the first time you've sounded like your sister." She brushed another limb from her face. "And stop staring at my ass." It sounded like he partially choked.

"How'd you know that—"

"Easy deduction. Now, are you ready to make a run for it if he follows our tracks?"

"I still think you could run with me and keep up. You're in great shape," Derek suggested.

"No way. I'm sinking far too much. Look, did it ever occur to you to climb a tree out here?"

"No, can't say it did."

"Then maybe it wouldn't occur to that guy either." *Right*, she thought. That was one big maybe.

"That's true. But wouldn't he notice if your footprints just ended?" Her stomach sank at his insightful question.

"Shit. I suppose, but maybe not as easily in the poor light." The problem was no other ideas came to mind. "I guess we'll have to do our best to get the drop on him first. Literally." She resumed climbing with the pole straps wrapped around her wrists. Her boots scraped against the bark. After several more feet, Kris realized she hadn't heard any follow-up comments from below. "Derek? You still with me?"

"Oh, sorry, a little moment of lightheadedness; that's all."

Crap. He may not have the strength to walk out of the forest, whether chased or otherwise.

The distant hum of the machine returned, growing louder.

Chapter 28

Rachel wasn't happy to be paired with Luke; it brought a whole slew of emotional baggage into the mix. Yet what else could she do? In the few minutes it had taken to drive through the residential streets to where they'd begin their search, she'd done her best to mentally prepare for being close to him. Had it really only been two days ago that they'd broken up?

After parking near the entry, she focused on strapping into her snowshoes and getting Bella ready. No canine booties were needed; the dog thrived in cold temperatures. Avi sat in the truck seat glaring at them with a sad expression.

"I'm sorry, girl, but word on the street is you like to run away off-leash. You'll be fine here." Next to her, Bella dropped down, rolled on her back, and moaned in the snow, wiggling like a kid making a snow angel. If it were any other time, Rachel would have laughed.

Once Luke was by her side and ready to go, they set out. "Let's go straight up here for a ways. Once we get to that first elevated knoll, we'll want to start heading diagonally to the south. That way we don't cover any of the same ground as the other people," she instructed, then ripped her glove off and grabbed her phone, double-checking the image of the map to be sure. No way would Rachel trust her brain right now.

"I'll follow your lead," he said. As they walked, they both began to breathe harder. It was always a workout snowshoeing uphill. They'd been ascending for almost an hour, with short breaks to text Ted, when Luke called out behind her, "I need a few minutes." She paused and turned, fearful that if she stopped too long, her bruised brain might catch on and start trying to drag her down again. With the moonlight beaming through the clouds, she could see Luke's form. His shoulders rose and fell several times.

"See, if you'd gone snowshoeing with me . . ." Rachel teased him in an attempt to lighten the mood. It occurred to her only after the words left her mouth that it might be a sensitive topic for him given his recent apology. His regret had been sincere. It wasn't right to cause him to feel worse. "Sorry, bad joke. I wasn't trying to make you feel bad."

"It's okay," he said in between gulps of air. "I deserve it." The setting grew silent, with one exception—the bear bell attached to Bella's collar. Bears weren't a big concern; Tahoe's bears tended to care little about humans so long as no one threatened their babies. Rachel attached the bell primarily for the ease of detecting the canine's location audibly. Something rumbled in the distance.

"Bella, sit," she commanded. The chiming stopped. The wind that had thrashed around all day had died down. The night was perfectly quiet. Eerily so.

"What?" Luke inquired, taking a few steps until he stood right next to her.

"Shh! I thought I heard something," she whispered as she placed her finger to her lips. He nodded. They stood in silence for at least a minute, maybe longer. There it was again. The soft purring of an engine. "Do you hear that?" she asked, and then she clicked off her headlamp. Luke followed suit.

"Yes, do you think it's a snowmobile?"

"Probably. It couldn't be the kidnapper since Ted has him, but it's curious. Plus, I'm not even sure if it's legal to ride after dark." She crooked her head as if it could improve the acoustics. The sound grew louder. It was still some distance away, yet she could discern between the acceleration and deceleration of the motor. Rachel felt Bella growing anxious next to her. Bella didn't like the loud roar of such engines.

"We should hide," Luke suggested as he started to look around. Rachel's gaze traveled up the mountain in the direction of the noise.

"There," she pointed to a dense patch of trees. Luke turned, glanced where she indicated, and nodded.

Rachel directed Bella to heel and set out with a fast pace. The snowmobile still had to be a good half mile away. Or so she thought; Rachel wasn't good at estimating distances. Once they both penetrated the thicket, they slowed. "Now what?" she asked, her heart pounding. "Let's text Ted to let him know what's going on. Then I guess we wait and see if the rider comes through this area." Luke pulled off one of his gloves and retrieved his cell phone from a pocket.

"You got your gun with you?" As much as Rachel hated them, she'd feel a lot safer if Luke were armed.

"Definitely," he said as he typed on the small touchpad.

"Good. Just don't shoot Bella. She isn't easy to see out here."

"I know." He glanced up at her, clearly annoyed, then looked at his phone again. "Luckily the message went through. We have one bar," he said, pocketing the device. The noise grew softer.

"I think it turned. I wonder . . . any chance it's someone helping with the search?"

"Ted would have let us know if that were the case," Luke responded, and then he looked around again.

"All right, I'll let Bella get back into wander mode. You never know." She looked down at the canine. "Okay, run!" The dog jumped into high gear. Postholing never deterred her, but it did make running difficult. Bella tripped in the heavy snow and fell to her side, but then she quickly recovered and trudged upward. Slushy-sounding steps indicated Luke wasn't far behind Rachel. She concentrated on making sure to follow the search line they'd agreed on with Ted. Bella stopped and sniffed.

"Bella? Did you find something, girl?" Rachel queried. Bella's muzzle rose, and she continued to scent the air. Her tail started to wag. Rachel looked at Luke and smiled. "I think that's a good sign!" she said excitedly. "Bella, show me the way!" Bella traipsed up the sloped mountainside, periodically stopping to turn and confirm the humans were still following her. Suddenly, the pup dashed forward, making a deep-throated sound that Rachel knew represented major excitement. The distant echo of an engine returned. Whoever it was must have turned around.

"I think . . ." Rachel pondered and then decided to call out, "Derek? Kris?" She leapt forward, trying to keep within sight distance of Bella as the animal sprinted. A sneeze behind her told her Luke was doing a decent job of keeping up. Rachel called out again. This time, she heard something—quiet but distinct.

"Rach?" Kris's response had come from somewhere up the mountain.

215

"Kris?" she asked, her eyes darting around to distinguish features in the limited moonlight. So long as the snowmobile was in the vicinity, they'd kept their lights off to avoid drawing attention.

"We're over here!" Kris yelled. Rachel glimpsed Bella in the distance. She followed the dog's tracks, her heart racing. Another ten feet and she heard Derek's voice greeting Bella. He sounded so weak. She stepped around a large tree and saw a tall figure leaning against an old pine, one hand resting on a knee, the other petting Bella.

"Derek!" she shouted, making her way toward him.

"Hey, Sis," he greeted hoarsely, then collapsed against the tree, sliding down several inches. Bella nosed at him.

"Derek?" Fear gripped her insides as she rushed to him and slipped her shoulder underneath his to help support his weight before he ended up on the ground. She reached out to his cheek. It was burning up.

"Sorry, I just—"

"It's fine. You're fine," she repeated, as if saying it enough would make it so. "What's wrong? Are you okay?" Her eyes scanned his body for a wound, even though she didn't expect to see details in the dim night's glow. "They thought you had been shot," she cried.

"It's merely a flesh wound," he whispered, attempting to recite one of his favorite lines from an old satire-laced *Monty Python* movie. "Went through my leg," he answered before she could form the question.

"Where's Kris?" She looked to the side and behind her brother.

"Up here," said her friend's voice. Rachel looked around but didn't see anything. Derek pointed toward the tops of the trees. Rachel lifted her gaze and saw her friend.

"What the heck are you doing up there?"

"Long story."

"I think the snowmobile's coming back," Luke finally spoke. Rachel saw Derek peer in Luke's direction. Curiously, he didn't greet him right away.

"Luke," Derek acknowledged.

"Derek," Luke said calmly. He then turned to Rachel and warned, "We need to be prepared in case that's not a friendly search and rescue."

"You guys armed?" Kris inquired as she slowly inched down the tree.

"Luke has his gun," Rachel answered. "So you don't know who that is on the snowmobile?" She looked back at Derek.

"We're assuming it's the guy who took us," Kris stated.

Rachel turned her way. "He's been arrested."

"What?" Derek and Kris exclaimed in unison.

"So who the hell is that?" Kris looked toward the distant snowmobile.

"No idea," Luke chimed in. "Look, there are about six other cops out here so far and more on the way. But they're covering a large area. I don't think any of them are close enough to get here before that rider does, presuming we could even get a text to Ted in time." Luke stepped next to Rachel. "We have to be ready. Ted is pretty sure this guy was working with someone else."

"And the kidnapper's not talking," Rachel finished. She saw Luke pull out his phone, check the screen, and then shake his head.

"Nothing new. Just an 'OK' from Ted after our last message."

Kris jumped down onto the packed surface. Rachel stepped over and embraced her. The distant hum grew louder. She stepped back and looked at the group.

"Whoever is driving that thing followed the tracks back to where we were kept. It seemed deliberate," Kris said, and then she turned to Rachel. "Did the perp get his one phone call?"

"Don't know, but Ted mentioned something about the guy making a short call to a burner phone just before he was arrested." They all grew quiet and glanced up the mountain. The snowmobile was closing in quickly.

"What should we do?" Rachel wondered.

"You said Luke is armed," Kris began. "What if I let myself be seen to draw them in. You all hide nearby, and then I can pretend to surrender while you come up from behind."

"Or you could just shoot them," Derek cut in. He then winced as he attempted to take his weight off Rachel. "Ask questions later and all."

"There are two big problems with that, dear Brother. One, what if they aren't associated with your kidnapping? And two, it makes Kris an easy target if they are. They could take her down before Luke could—"

"Do you have a better plan, Rachel?" Kris cut in before shifting her gaze. "Luke, how about you?" He had no answer. "Let me do it," Kris pleaded.

"I can't let you—" Derek started to argue, but Kris cut him off.

"I thought we were past this macho BS thing?"

"She's right," Luke interrupted. "Much as I hate it, too, I don't see what other choice we have."

"Whatever we do, we need to do it now!" Kris yelled. The machine was close. Too close. The motor's rhythm suggested it was already weaving through trees. Seconds later, beams of light emerged in front of them. Before Rachel had a chance to react, Kris darted out into the likely path.

"Down!" Luke called. Derek let go of the tree and fell sideways to the ground, his stance awkward because the snowshoes were still attached. Rachel lunged next to him, reaching out to help. Luke kneeled in front of them both. All three crouched low to the ground. Bella joined them, rubbing her belly against the snow's surface.

Rachel turned her attention back toward Kris but couldn't see much through the trees. Occasional glimpses revealed her friend waving her arms and running right at the snowmobile.

"I need to get closer to get a clear shot," Luke said as he stood back up and moved in Kris's direction. Rachel watched him struggle to hide behind the narrow trees, slowly moving from one to the next as he closed the distance. The snowmobile abruptly stopped. Rachel tried to keep her hands steady as she retrieved her cell phone to text Ted. Bella waited patiently at her side.

~

Ted had already received the third round of texts or radio calls from all searching pairs. No one had located the couple or found any relevant evidence. However, Luke's text about another snowmobiler in the vicinity had Ted on edge.

Six more officers and four civilians had arrived to assist over the last half hour. He'd tracked down two snowmobiles that were nearby and available for immediate use. Both belonged to residents in Homewood a few miles away and were being brought over as quickly as possible. He was frustrated that the storm had thus far prevented helicopters from flying. His phone buzzed in his pocket. Ted quickly grabbed it, instantly recognizing Rachel's number. The text message read, *Kris & Derek with us now. Snomo approaching, bad feeling. Luke armed.* While Rachel had her moments, one thing he'd learned was that her instincts tended to be right in situations like this. He grabbed his radio and asked how soon the borrowed machines would arrive. Another officer informed him they were two miles away. Ted looked toward the highway as if he could will them to show up faster. His captain, Ron Taylor, drove up and parked.

Ted ran over to update him.

"Cap," he said and nodded.

Ron, about twenty years Ted's senior, climbed out of his Lexus, immediately ready to engage. "Any new information since we last spoke?"

"Just received a message from Rachel. They've found the couple. All four are together now, but an unknown subject is approaching them on a snowmobile, and there are concerns it may be our guy's partner." He waved toward the police car that still held the obstinate man.

"Okay, how long until we can send someone up there on a machine?"

"Should be here anytime," Ted said as he motioned for Ron to follow him back to where he'd been coordinating the operation. "Here's the map and search routes. It's been about five minutes since the last round of check-ins." Ron nodded. Ted saw headlights approach from the north and sprinted to their source. As he'd hoped, it was a large truck towing a trailer—the kind that held snowmobiles. "Cap, can you take over the op? I'm pretty familiar with that area up there." He pointed up the mountain.

"Yes, but take someone with you."

"Of course." While Carina would be his first choice, she was already covering the southernmost area. He glanced around and saw a uniformed patrol officer standing next to one of the roadblocks. "You ever drive a snowmobile?" Ted called out. The man didn't hesitate, even though Ted's brisk approach had likely surprised him. *Good*, Ted thought.

"Yes, sir, in fact, quite regularly." The young recruit was about Ted's height and carried another twenty pounds or so.

"Perfect. I'll explain on the way to that trailer." He summoned the man to follow.

~

Kris's heart was beating so hard she feared it would leap out of her chest. It would be so easy for this person, whoever it was, to simply shoot her if that was the intent. But she had to risk it. Otherwise they were all sitting ducks. On the off chance it was merely an innocent moonlight-seeking rider, she would start with the "lost backcountry hiker" story. It wouldn't take long to know if this person was friend or foe. The small vehicle had begun to slowly weave in and out of the spindly pines. It stopped again, this time mere feet away. The driver remained still. It was impossible to make out any features. Kris stood, frozen in place. Waiting. Finally, the figure motioned for her to sit on the back.

Perplexed, Kris shouted in an attempt to be heard over the clamor of the machine. "You want me to get on that?" The driver nodded and looked around. The message was clear: where was Derek? Obviously not an innocent bystander. Kris backed up a step. "Who are you?" she demanded. No response. It was creepy how the driver just stared, motionless. Kris moved another foot away. The figure motioned again. She shook her head, waiting, uncertain of what to do. *Where the hell is Luke?* The engine suddenly revved, and the snowmobile lurched forward, aiming right at her. She panicked and spun around to run, but her feet sank too deep, and she struggled with each step. Just as she blinked and prepared for the collision, a huge weight fell against her, knocking her to the side. She fell into the snow, her body fully covered by Luke's. The machine sped by inches away.

"Kris, you okay?"

"I think so," she replied, turning her head toward the snowmobile. The rider was trying to turn around but the thickness of the trees made it challenging. Luke's body rose. She felt his hand on her arm, urging her up. Somehow she managed to stand.

A piece of bark flew off of a nearby tree. *What the—?*

"Gun! Get down!" Luke shouted as he pushed her back to the ground and jumped on top of her, shielding her body.

That was a bullet? My God! Time blurred. The snowmobile remained idle. Luke's body suddenly twitched, and she heard a moan escape his lips. *Oh no.*

"I'm okay," he muttered as he twisted, raising an arm and returning fire. Nothing indicated he'd hit his target. But no bullets flew overhead either. Her breath caught in her throat as she waited. The hum of the engine began to recede. Their attacker was leaving.

~

Damn it! How did they get a gun? It had been a shock to arrive at the cabin to find the captors gone. A large tree branch fell through the roof—*what were the chances?* The haphazardly stacked furniture revealed how they'd managed to climb up and escape. A quick inspection of footprints documented their discovery of the nearby supply shed. Eventually the tracks had veered off into the trees. *The idiots probably thought they could hide in there; it shouldn't be that difficult to track them down.*

As expected, they hadn't been hard to locate. But how did they get a weapon? Unfortunately, maneuvering the machine through the trees had become challenging, even more so while dodging bullets. The only option may be to take them out—here and now.

~

"Who is Jason?" Shoals asked casually as he walked into the interrogation room. Oliver's father hadn't shown up. Instead, he sent a defense attorney who was now sitting next to the man. Oliver didn't respond. Shoals remained standing as he directed his gaze at the lawyer. She surely fit the stereotype of a high-priced female attorney, from her expensive dress suit to her shiny black high-heeled shoes. He wondered how she'd made it through the slushy parking lot out front without going belly-up. "I recommend you instruct your client to cooperate," he stated. He then pulled his chair back from the table and sat down, once again staring at Oliver. "We know about Jason Maxwell."

A look of surprise, then fear, passed through Oliver's features. They'd clearly hit on something with that name, although the room remained silent.

Shoals continued, "Turns out this kid, Jason, has been missing for twenty years. Funny thing, he attended North Tahoe High School— like you. He went missing right before your senior year. Ring any bells yet?"

Oliver's gaze faltered, and he looked over at his lawyer. She either had an amazing poker face or no knowledge about the missing person. Shoals probed further.

"We dug a little deeper. Found a few old classmates that remembered Jason picking on you a few times. They sure told us some memorable tales; guess that's why they hadn't forgotten even after all of these years. I have to say, Jason had some clever ideas." Still no reply, but Oliver shifted in his seat. "In fact, the records show *you* were interviewed when he first went missing. Apparently someone spotted you two having heated words in a parking lot earlier that night." Shoals waited and tapped his finger. Finally, Oliver leaned over and whispered something to the woman. She nodded.

"I need more time with my client."

"Suit yourself. And advise your client that it will help him if he comes clean. We've already got him on the breaking and entering, assault, illegal firearms, to name a few charges." Shoals tapped the edge of the manila folder in his hand against the table, stood up, and left the room.

~

"You really okay?" Kris asked after the machine noise ebbed.

"Yeah, just grazed my arm," Luke responded as he climbed off of her. It had occurred to him that either the guy was a really bad shot, or the shots were intended to scare them but not kill them.

"Thanks for the save." Kris stood up next to him.

"Kris? Luke?" Rachel anxiously approached.

"We're fine," he said, brushing snow off of his coat. The movement caused more pain, but he felt the need to occupy his hands.

"Where's Derek?" Kris asked as she stretched her neck to look past Rachel.

"I told him to stay there. He's pretty weak," Rachel replied.

Luke knew that tone of voice. Rachel was worried about her brother—big time.

"I didn't hear any gunshots, but I suppose they could've had a silencer. Or would the snowmobile's noise drown it out?" Rachel rambled.

"Actually, the asshole *did* shoot at us," Kris stated. "I'm fine. Luke got hit, but it's not—"

"Are you okay?" Rachel cut her off, focusing intently on Luke.

"I'm honestly fine," he assured her quietly, although his mind briefly flashed to the pill bottle in his pocket; he could use another one right about now. "I don't think they were aiming to kill, if that's any consolation." The jingle of a bear bell approached, indicating Bella had joined them. Luke looked back at Kris before he spoke. "I suspect our mysterious traveler is going to return. Unfortunately, the fact that we have a weapon is no longer a secret; he may have also figured out I'm not Derek."

"He?" Rachel asked. "Did you see something?"

Her question made him pause. "No, guess I just figured as much," he mumbled.

"Who cares?" Kris interjected. "The bigger issue here is that we can't outrun a snowmobile. So now what?"

"You both go," Luke said to the two women. "Get Derek down that mountain. I'll stay here and try to hold the asshole back."

"It's suicide!" Rachel argued.

"I knew you still liked me," he teased, hoping to lighten the situation.

"Just because we broke up doesn't mean I don't care about you," she admitted.

"Broke up?" Kris stuttered.

"Later," Luke said. "Look, we don't have time to argue about it. Go! Now!"

"I'm staying. He expects one man and woman, right? If he doesn't see that here, he might start looking elsewhere. Derek needs help." Rachel pleaded. "And you just said he wasn't trying to kill you, right?"

"I don't *think* so. Not the same as knowing for sure." Luke sighed. *She's being stubborn as usual*, Luke thought. But damn if she wasn't right, too.

"Kris, here's a leash." Rachel clasped one end to Bella's collar. "Don't let go. You may have to tug her at first; Bella won't like leaving me here." She handed the nylon tether to Kris.

"But—"

"Get Ted," Luke urged. "The cops might have their own snowmobiles to drive up here by now. You can follow our tracks back down."

"We should switch coats now that they've seen you. And . . . oh, right, no snowshoes. Here." Rachel unstrapped the bindings and stepped back, sinking several inches in the snow. Kris nodded and then bound them to her boots. They hastily exchanged outerwear.

After Kris and Bella left, Luke refocused his attention on Rachel. "Should we head north?" She looked down, appearing to study the prints in the snow. "Try to leave a trail in the opposite direction of Kris and Derek?"

"Maybe, but no matter what, we won't get far. I think the only option we have is, well, better aim." Luke held up his weapon. She nodded. Her eyes sparked, determination evident on her face.

"All right, let's get going," she said. "How's your arm?"

"Aches a bit, but I can still use it just fine," he responded. Luke hiked maybe twenty or thirty feet up the mountainside when the engine noise grew nearer again. Slower without the snowshoes, Rachel had fallen behind. Luke took the opportunity provided by the temporary privacy to reach into his pocket and retrieve a pain pill. He swallowed it dry and then grabbed some snow to help wash it down. Rachel came up and stood next to him.

"The trees are too narrow here to fit that machine through. He'll be forced to get off to follow our tracks," he speculated as they both looked for trees wide enough to hide behind, at least partially. He watched Rachel position herself against a pine tree ten feet downslope.

"I'm good," she called up.

"Got it." Luke leaned down to the cold surface, knowing there was no way to fully conceal his entire frame. The snowmobile engine waned and then sat idle. Their trail had just been discovered. Luke tightened his hold on the trigger.

Chapter 29

Kris found Derek sitting on the ground, his back propped against a tree. It looked like he'd given up and just stretched out his legs, sitting directly on the snow. The old snowshoes were still attached to his feet and stuck up vertically out of the snow. She was going to say something about how getting his pants wet would harm his fever, but then she realized they were both already soaked through from rain. He tilted his head to look up at her. Although a faint smile crossed his face, she could sense he was fading fast.

"We need to get down and find help," she said as she reached out.

"Where's Rachel?" He gripped her hand. With her assistance and a good push against the tree, he rose up.

"They stayed behind to distract the guy," Kris answered before he could ask. "We need to get the cops. And to get you medical help. Let's follow their tracks."

"I can't leave my sister to—"

"Yes, you can. She's a big girl, and you aren't in any condition to help, but we've got to move," she urged. "Can you handle it?" Although he nodded, his pained expression worried her. They took a few steps with Bella following at her side, no longer pulling against her restraint. Derek suddenly lost his balance and tumbled against her. She held steady as she managed to hold him up. "You okay?"

"Yes, uneven step, I guess," he mumbled as he stood straight and continued forward. The distant echo of the snowmobile evoked a sick feeling in the pit of her stomach. *Please let Rachel and Luke be okay.*

"So they apparently broke up," she said, in part to distract herself from dwelling on her current anxiety. Derek didn't respond right away. Perhaps he was too focused on moving, given how bad he must be feeling.

"I'm not surprised. Did she say why?"

That's odd. Why is Derek not surprised? Kris thought. "No time. It slipped out when they were discussing the plan back there."

"Yeah, about that, I still don't like this plan—"

"Wait!" she cut him off. There was a sound coming from somewhere below them. "Derek! Someone's coming up the trail!" she blurted.

"Oh no, more of them?"

"I think it's the police. Rachel and Luke mentioned Ted was trying to locate snowmobiles for them to use, and that's the way they would come up to search."

"Let's move over behind those trees, just in case," Derek recommended, pointing to their right.

"Good idea." Kris turned to Bella. "This way, girl." As they pivoted, Derek again tripped and stumbled into her. He moaned but managed to straighten. "Put some weight on my shoulder. Just be careful so we don't tangle up our snowshoes." With only a few missteps, they finally reached their intended hiding place.

"Thanks," Derek said as he removed his arm and then stared in the direction of the approaching machine. Butterflies fluttered in Kris's stomach as they waited; she hoped this was the rescue they desperately needed. The driver slowly cruised by where they stood. Kris read the print on the back of the driver's coat—a welcome acronym. Thank God, it was a cop. But how could she get the officer's attention now that he'd passed them by? She couldn't yell loud enough to be heard above the engine. Kris looked down at Bella. Rachel had trained the canine to avoid running in front of moving vehicles and equipment. Instead, she followed alongside them. *Maybe* . . . Kris unhooked the leash and shouted, "Go get 'em!" Bella enthusiastically dashed forward, quickly catching up and trotting out to the side of the machine as she barked in excitement. Kris watched anxiously; the driver's head turned and the snowmobile cruised to a stop.

"Bella?"

"Ted!" Kris yelled as she ran toward him. Bella nuzzled his gloves. Ted's gaze fixed on her, his eyes squinting.

"Rachel?"

"No, it's Kris. We swapped jackets," she explained, closing the distance quickly.

"Where are the others?" Ted asked as he rubbed Bella's ears. Kris explained what she knew. Ted tugged on the lanyard around his neck, pulling a radio up from inside of his coat and pushing the button to speak. He explained what he'd found and instructed another officer to come and take Derek down to an ambulance.

"Wait here, and flag the other cop down when he comes; he won't be more than another couple of minutes. You two," he said but then paused with a quick glance at Bella, "you *three*, get down ASAP, and then send the officer back up here."

Kris nodded, reaching out to grab hold of Bella's collar.

~

Rachel stared intently at the approaching headlight. The snowmobile edged forward; there was no way could they outrun it now. Adrenaline coursed through her veins, and she sucked in her breath, as if she could make herself fit behind the tree better. Luke stood nearby, his gun firmly grasped in his hand. The machine stopped ten or fifteen feet away. It idled through a dozen beats of her heart before silence filled the night air. The single headlight remained on, making it impossible for Rachel or Luke to move without likely being seen by the driver. The crunching sound of footsteps cut through the still air. The cold temperatures had started refreezing the snow's surface. Rachel's breath formed mist in front of her. The stranger didn't say anything.

Thump!

Rachel froze. What the hell? Then it dawned on her—a heavy chunk of snow had fallen off the tree above her.

Illuminated from behind, the man—or was it a woman?—proceeded toward them. Was there a weapon aimed at her and Luke? Should she run? Or stay put and give Luke a chance to do something? Rachel couldn't think fast enough.

Thud! The branches above assaulted her once again. This time, the tree's bomb landed right on top of her. Without forethought she swiped at it.

Crack! It felt like something breezed by above her. Bark flew off a tree barely a foot above her head. *Holy shit! A bullet!*

She wanted to run. Yet nothing would provide protection if she did. All she could do was hope the person really wasn't aiming to kill them and try to distract him or her so Luke could get a clear shot.

Overcome by that disconnected-from-reality feeling, like she'd had skiing with Derek, Rachel found herself walking toward their enemy. With her head tucked downward to continue to appear as Kris, she raised both gloved hands in the air. The driver stepped closer. She could now see the outline of the arm holding the weapon; it was aimed at Luke. Rachel shifted, and the weapon swung back in her direction. She stilled herself again; it moved back toward Luke.

"Don't move." Luke calmly articulated his words. The figure stopped as if debating. Luke must have made the same hopeful deduction as Rachel: since Derek and Kris were kept alive, hopefully this person would not rush to kill them. It's probably the only explanation for why they were still breathing. "Obviously you don't want to kill us. Let's just resolve this now," he asserted. No response.

Thwack. A huge wad of snow smashed their attacker's head. Surprised, the aggressor backed up a step and reached out with both arms. Something told Rachel to move. *Now.* She leapt to the side, seeking partial cover. Gunfire pierced the darkness.

Rachel's cheek slammed into the packed snow. Pain shot through her head. As she worked to catch her breath, the sounds of a struggle penetrated her senses. Rachel saw Luke poised on top of the offender, his fingers attempting to pry the gun away. The barrel swung back and forth, aimed in her general direction. Time to move. Rachel jumped to her feet and dashed around to the other side of the scuffling bodies. She watched helplessly as Luke's chin took a hard punch, snapping his head back. Although the snowshoes limited his mobility, he managed not to fall; instead, he raised his elbow and slammed it down into the assailant's rib cage. Rachel's mind, noticing that the two were fighting with their fists, raced for a way to help. Where was the gun? Rachel's eyes scanned the scene around her. There it was, scarcely a foot away from the sprawling shapes. She kneeled to retrieve it, having barely touched it before Luke crashed against her. The motion flipped her on her back, and his weight landed on top of her. Cold steel prodded her back.

Oh please, don't let that damn thing go off. As Luke struggled to untangle himself from her, the rider quickly rose. Luke jumped up, precariously balanced on his snowshoes. Rachel rolled over and reached into the impression left by her back. It was empty. *Where did the gun go?* The rider slammed a leg into Luke's side. Luke lost his balance and fell backward.

Rachel turned to face the ground, ripped off her gloves, and plunged her hands into the snow. She thought she heard the sound of a motor approaching. Hope flooded her that it might be the police. She glanced at the fighting duo. Luke was kneeling with his arm tightly wrapped around the jerk's throat from behind. Luke appeared to have the upper hand, although the attacker was trying to slam his helmet against Luke's face. The roar of an engine grew louder. Despite losing some feeling in her extremities from the cold, Rachel kept digging. Finally, it paid off. She grabbed the cool firearm and whipped her arm around to aim. But they were too close together to fire.

"Police! Don't move!" Ted's voice shouted over the sound of a nearby machine left idling. The rustling figures suddenly stopped. Rachel was unable to tear her eyes from the scene before her. Luke maintained the chokehold; she knew his maneuver would cut off air supply and make his opponent pass out. The assailant appeared to be weakening. "Luke, I've got him. You can let go," Ted instructed. Rachel saw Luke hesitate. She understood his reluctance. After all, what's the harm in letting him finish until the criminal was down for the count? "Luke!" Ted repeated.

"Fine," Luke complained, releasing his grip. The driver slumped down as Luke scooted back. Suddenly an elbow slammed into Luke's neck, and the figure jumped at Rachel in an attempt to rip the weapon from her hands. Rachel dropped backward. A shot rang out from behind her, and the stranger collapsed in a heap. Rachel remained still, stunned by what had transpired. She was unaware she still held a gun until she heard Ted.

"Rachel, it's over. Put the gun down," he instructed calmly. She looked at the metallic object in her palm as if it were foreign, and then she slowly set it down and backed away. Reality set in again. Luke, half bent over, was propped against a tree.

"Luke!" she cried, giving a cursory glance at the prone figure before running over to him.

"Damn, that hurt," he croaked as he rubbed his neck.

"You okay?" Her eyes sought his. Their gazes locked; something flickered between them before Ted interrupted.

"Let's see who this is."

Rachel had almost forgotten Ted was there. With her visual connection with Luke broken, she glanced to the side and saw Ted checking for a pulse. He shook his head. The shot had obviously been fatal. Ted unfastened the chin strap and removed the helmet, revealing a dark ski mask underneath.

From her sideways vantage point, Rachel couldn't see much detail, but it looked like a man with short brown hair. She leaned forward, forcing herself to take a closer look under the beam of Ted's flashlight. The man's face was disfigured, as if it had been burned in the past. He looked familiar, although she couldn't say where she'd seen him before. Luke shuffled over next to her.

"That's Anson Matheson," he stated flatly.

"Wait, with the PHC Corporation?" Rachel was surprised her brain had made the connection so fast.

"Yep," Luke whispered, still massaging his skin.

"I know his name, but I don't think I've ever met him," Rachel stated. "I've probably seen a picture somewhere. Always thought it was kind of odd that he never came to any meetings for his own project." Rachel's pulse was slowly returning to normal.

"You two injured?" Ted asked as he stood up.

"I'm fine," Rachel said.

"I'll live," Luke replied.

"Did you see Kris and Derek?" she asked Ted anxiously.

"Yes. Hold on a minute so I can check in with my team." Ted turned, walked over and shut off his snowmobile, and then spoke into his radio.

"How did you know who this was?" Rachel asked as she turned toward Luke.

"I just interviewed the guy. I knew something was off about him," he mused.

"Was this really all about that damn project in Tahoma?" she wondered aloud.

"Greed knows no bounds," Luke sighed.

Ted's conversation ended, and he returned to them. "My guys found them. They're hauling them both down right now."

Rachel exhaled. The stress of the last several days threatened to overwhelm her; she forced it down. *Later.*

"As soon as my crew returns, I'm sending you two down to get checked out as well," Ted stated. "Not a suggestion—an order."

~

"Ouch!" Derek protested as the medic slid the needle into his vein.

"Lightweight," Kris teased, standing nearby. He hadn't seen her

SIERRA NEVADA DANGEROUS DEVELOPMENTS

since they'd arrived at the law enforcement's staging area and been whisked away to separate ambulances. Several minutes ago he'd been informed his sister and Luke were safe. After that, he relaxed, as all of the tension from the last few days left him drained. The banter with Kris had been one of the few bright spots. He lifted his head to peer over to her from his seated position and saw that Bella still clung to her side.

"I hate needles. That's not a bad thing, I'd say." He played along. She stepped up next to him, watching as an IV bag was set up.

"So, no tats then, I take it?" She tipped her head. The light from inside the ambulance fell across her face. She was grinning.

"No. Why? You got tattoos?"

"A few."

He looked her up and down. She was bundled up, of course, though his mind began to fantasize about her bare skin underneath. Derek felt the first flash of warmth since they'd climbed out of the cabin. "Sexy as hell. What kind of art?"

"That's reserved for special audiences only." She smiled coyly.

"I'll be right back," the EMT mumbled before abruptly walking toward the other medical vehicle.

"How are you feeling?" She moved closer.

Screw it—he was going for it. With his untethered arm, Derek reached out to the nape of her neck and gently pulled her mouth to his. She didn't resist. Derek's lips touched hers. They were soft, even after the exposure they'd endured. Warm and inviting. He kissed her tentatively at first. Then their mutual hunger grew. Her fingers lightly caressed his cheek and brushed down the side of his jaw. It stoked his desire even more. He intensified the kiss. She moaned, returning his kiss with matching fervor.

Chapter 30

As she reached the staging area, Rachel saw red and blue lights in every direction, so she asked a uniformed officer where Derek and Kris were. He pointed across the parking lot. "Ambulances are on the other side of those trailers."

She took off in a slow run toward where he'd indicated, pain shooting through her head with each jarring step. She slowed to weave through a collection of law enforcement vehicles. When she rounded the corner of a tall van, she stopped short. A couple embraced in the back of an open ambulance. No, they were not just embracing. Kissing! It took a second to notice the woman's blue-streaked hair in the faint light. *Is that Kris? And Derek?* Rachel wondered. She wasn't sure how she felt about that. *Weird? Maybe a little.* Bella looked her way and immediately pulled, tugging free of Kris's grip on the leash. She dashed to Rachel with her tail madly swinging from side to side. Derek and Kris stopped and looked her way. Kris's cheeks flushed.

"Sorry, I was going to leave, but Bella . . ." Rachel stuttered, embarrassed and still a little surprised.

"It's okay, Sis," Derek said, although she could hear mild annoyance in his tone. No surprise there. "Come here," he called. Bella bounced happily at her side as she walked over.

"Is Luke okay?" Kris asked, looking around behind her.

"For the most part. He got banged up a bit. They are checking him out now."

"And you?" Derek asked.

"A few bruises," she said, brushing off his concern. "I hear they expect you to recover. Too bad they couldn't fix your brain, too, dear Brother."

"There she is!" Derek laughed. "It's official; my sister is feeling better. Let the insults roll." He reached out and pulled her to him for a tight hug. Rachel worked to keep tears from welling up in her eyes when she thought how easily she could have lost them both.

"Love you, Rachel. Even if you are a pain in the ass," he said as he released his grip.

"Love you, too. Even with all of your faults. As long as that list may be."

"Cut it out!" Kris chimed in. Rachel laughed.

"Oh, I have some news for you two. I'll be right back!" Rachel ran to her truck. Now untethered, Bella followed excitedly at her side. She opened the door and greeted Avi, snapped on the leash, and encouraged her to jump out. The two animals playfully tousled as they walked. When she came around the corner, Bella sprinted over to her brother and Kris and then back again to Avi.

"Meet Avi, short for Avalanche," she said, massaging the mutilated ears. Kris was the first to reach her hand out for the dog to sniff. Derek let his hand drop to his side. The canine nuzzled his fingertips.

"What? You were so worried about us that you had time to go and adopt a new dog?" Derek asked, mocking hurt in his voice.

"Long story. I'll tell you once we get out of here."

~

They'd taken a cell phone off Anson's body, and now it rang as it lay in the evidence bag on the passenger seat. Curious, Ted pulled on a pair of gloves, unsealed the plastic, and retrieved the device. The prefix was easily recognizable as a local mobile number. He debated and then decided to go ahead and answer. The timing was certainly intriguing.

"Yes?" he asked briskly.

"Uh, Anson?" a familiar female voice said.

"Who am I speaking to?" he asked. There was a brief pause before the call ended. But Ted knew exactly who had been on the other end of the line. He quickly contacted one of their techs back in the office to trace the number. In the meantime, Ted began to think about why Nola Swenson would be calling Anson Matheson.

~

Shoals returned to the interrogation room at Oliver's request. He sat down to face the attorney and her client. The woman did not look pleased.

"I'm going to record this," he advised as he laid a small device out on the table and pressed a button. Oliver nodded.

"I'm ready to talk. About Jason." He tipped his head toward the woman. "She's fired. I told her to go. She's not listening. Can you make her leave?"

"Oliver, I urge you to reconsider. I'm only here to help you," the attorney explained, clearly frustrated. This wasn't the first time Shoals had seen this kind of disagreement between a criminal and their legal representative.

"No, you represent *him*." Oliver spit out the last word, then looked directly at Shoals. "If I tell you what I know, can I get a deal?"

"I can't guarantee it, but I will let the district attorney know you cooperated." Oliver seemed to mull this over for another minute before addressing the lawyer. "Leave." She sighed and picked up her briefcase. After the door shut behind her, Oliver faced him again.

"I didn't kill Jason, but I know who did."

Shoals remained silent, scratching a note on the pad in front of him, waiting.

"My dad. To protect me. Jason attacked me at school. It wasn't the first time; Jason picked on me all of the time. It was . . ." He stopped as if waiting for a reaction from Shoals.

But Shoals's insides had clenched at those meaningful two little words: my dad. *Thomas Palinski? This is way above my pay grade.* For now, Shoals was stuck. He eyed the recorder. Once word got out, there'd be a shitstorm for sure. At least it was all on tape, though. The kid fired his attorney and consented to being interviewed without one. So Shoals's ass was covered.

"Look, I can tell you where they are buried."

Wait, did the kid say they? "Are you saying there is more than one body?"

"Yes, at least I'm pretty sure. There were other people who messed with me who also just up and disappeared. I suspected, but I never asked my father about it. I was afraid of what he'd do to me. I expect you'll find more than one body up there." He sniffed. "I think Nancy's up there, too," he continued.

"Nancy?"

"Parsons. She worked in admissions at the college. I think my dad tried to get her to change my grades; I almost flunked out that first year. One day, she was just gone." Shoals did his best not to let the pettiness of humankind pull him down. A woman had been murdered over a bad grade?

"And where is this . . . are these bodies buried?" he asked, clearing his throat. The air had suddenly become very dry.

"On a ridgeline above the Fibreboard Freeway. You know, that old Forest Service road west of Highway 267 between Kings Beach and Truckee." He leaned over and wiped his mouth against his cuffed hands. "They're still there—somewhere."

"You don't know exactly where?" Shoals asked, exasperated.

Oliver shook his head. "About fifteen years ago a huge windstorm knocked several massive trees down along that ridgeline. Dad complained he couldn't figure out where he'd buried them because everything looked different afterward. He's gone out every summer, looking for signs. Guess he buried them too deep; go figure."

"He never found them?" Shoals was surprised. Whether or not he believed this perp was blaming his father for his own sins didn't matter right now; he wanted to recover the bodies and give closure to the families.

"No, and then that project came along and proposed to build some homes and stuff right in that area. He's been fighting the development ever since."

Chapter 31

Rachel felt two warm bodies tucked against her—one near her shoulder and one by her feet—Bella and her new sister, Avi. Though she'd just met the pup, it was like she'd been part of their family for ages. After multiple belly rubs and averted face licks, Rachel sat up and pulled on her robe. Mornings were bad enough as it was; after the activity of the last few days, the relapse of her postconcussion symptoms made her grogginess far worse. Rachel trudged out of her bedroom and made a beeline for the coffeemaker. Damn Luke for getting her hooked on the stuff.

Rachel let the dogs out into the yard while the percolator cycled through its daily ritual. By the time she finished her shower, the hot liquid was ready and waiting. She watched the steam rise as she poured the scalding coffee into a mug. After adding a tablespoon—or two or three—of creamer, she walked to the front of her house and parted the curtains. Sunlight beamed into the entryway. She followed its dust-laden path, noticing the pile of mail she'd tossed on an entry table a few days ago. It had completely slipped her mind.

"Wonderful. I'm sure there will be more medical bills," she complained before looking around and realizing the pups were still outside. Oops, without them nearby, she was technically talking to herself.

Her eyes focused again on the discarded stack; she prepared herself for bad news. The first two envelopes contained the anticipated bills. Not only was she stuck with the expenses from her injury, but it frustrated her to no end that they hadn't yet found the men who chased her. While several officers had suggested the snowmobilers had most likely decided to leave her alone after all this time, she wasn't going to let her guard down. One never knew what made sense in the minds of crazy people. She also worried about her failure to ever recall what the men looked like, or why she remembered a familiar feeling about the one toting the firearm.

She continued sorting through the correspondence. There were some utility bills, a few ads and flyers, and several nonprofits seeking additional funding. "Join the club," she muttered. Toward the bottom she found a folded piece of white paper that had simply been stapled shut. No address, no stamp. She opened it. Typed in black ink in the center of the page were the words:

Give us the pictures and we'll give you back your dog unharmed.
Keep copies and know that we'll come back for her.
Wait for further instructions. No cops.

"What the hell?" she wondered aloud. Her gut twisted at the thought that someone was threatening Bella. Yet the letter read as if they'd successfully dognapped her. She glanced again at Avi. Maybe they'd tried and been thwarted by Avi? Rachel tried to concentrate on timing. That didn't sound right. The letter had to be from Saturday at the latest—*before* she was attacked by the man who'd brought Avi. Tears blurred her vision as she picked up her phone to call Ted and tell him about the note.

"Okay, Rachel, hold on to that letter! Any idea when someone could have slipped it into your box?" He sounded exhausted. She couldn't blame him. She'd been able to return home last night with the promise to come into the station today and give her statement. Ted didn't have that luxury, and who knows how late he was stuck working again tonight.

"I remember setting the letters down . . . on Saturday, I think, after I'd reported the scene at Kris's house. When I got here, Luke was here, and well, I'd forgotten about them until this morning."

"All right, good. Now, I don't suppose you have any nosy neighbors? Or the kind who might have security cams?" he asked, clearly not expecting such an easy break. Rachel thought a moment and then beamed.

"Rod and Joy, across the street. They got a camera about a year back. I know because they showed me how it was angled to assure me it didn't record my house. As I recall, I think it did catch the end of my driveway."

"Have their number?" Ted asked enthusiastically. Rachel scrolled through her contacts and recited the information.

"I'll be in touch." Ted ended the call. Rachel sighed, walking toward her recycle bin as she scanned through the colored ads and brochures one more time before tossing them in. A political flyer caused her to do a double take. The main picture was of a middle-aged man standing with his family. It was the typical "look-how-happy-we-are" family picture often used by politicians and attorneys for public relations. Why did this particular image bother her? She skimmed over the text. The brochure was meant to advertise a Mr. Robert McDonnel. The politician was running in an upcoming special election to fill a state senate seat after the previous representative was killed in a car accident. The ad was clearly meant to portray Robert as a family man. Come to think of it, she'd read a featured interview with him a few weeks ago in the local paper. She remembered only because it had stirred sadness in her at the memory of hearing about the car accident. She'd liked the senator who'd been killed.

"Ugh, always such BS," Rachel murmured, ready to toss the item. But something caused her to look at it again. She found herself staring at his eyes; they bothered her. She couldn't tear her gaze away. Then it clicked.

"Holy shit!" she exclaimed, so loud that Bella came rushing into the house. *This is him.* The guy on the snowmobile who tried to shoot her and skied after her down the mountain. That's why he'd stirred a sense of familiarity. She looked at his wife and the pieces all fell into place. She'd caught him with his male lover—a camera in her hand. That's why he came after her.

Rachel reached for her phone. Before she could dial, it rang, displaying Ted's name. He started to speak the moment she answered the call.

"Got a hold of Rod. He scanned the footage and found a guy sticking something in your mailbox early Saturday morning. They are sending me the clip right now. Wait, wow, that was fast," he said as if talking to himself. "Hold on, it just popped up in my inbox." She heard Ted pecking at his keys. "Let me rewind that again," he mumbled. She waited on the line anxious to tell him what she'd just remembered but afraid to interrupt his thought process. "Rachel, I think we've caught a break! He's bundled up, but when he reached inside your box, he exposed part of his arm. And lucky for us, he's got a unique tattoo. Dang, this is a surprisingly good quality video. Glad your neighbors forked out the extra bucks for high resolution. Let me get someone on this, and I'll call you back. If the perp's been arrested before around here, it won't take long to ID—"

"Ted, I remembered," she said, cutting him off.

"Huh?" he asked.

"The guy who chased me out by Forestdale. I recalled who it was."

"Well, why didn't you say so?"

Rachel rolled her eyes. As if Ted had given her a moment to speak.

"Who?" he urged.

"Robert McDonnel. Goes by Bob." She was greeted with silence. "Ted? You still there?"

"Yes, just please don't tell me that is the same Robert McDonnel who is running in the special election later this month?" Ted pleaded.

"One and the same, I'm afraid."

She heard a long sigh, followed by his exasperated tone. "My God, you sure know how to pick 'em, don't you?"

~

Chase still couldn't believe he'd been arrested. Again. And all because of the damn letter. Hell, all this trouble and he hadn't even been able to get the gal's mutt. A fact he hadn't wanted to tell his cousin Bobby, knowing there would be ramifications. He'd assumed even if he failed to obtain the woman's pet, the threat to her dog was clear, and she would have listened either way. Sure, the police could have been brought into the situation, but it's not like they'd assign officers to protect a pet. It had seemed like a win-win situation—low risk and high payoff. Now some pansy-ass pretty-boy cop was threatening him with his last strike? What the hell did they even have to charge him with? He had been so careful.

"I have to tell you Mr. McDonnel. Chase. Can I call you Chase? Anyway . . . two previous drug deals on your record. I'm afraid you'll be sent away for a long time now," the detective said. Benson or something like that.

"What exactly do you think you can charge me with?" Chase asked.

"Tampering with federal mail, for starters."

Chase waited for the punch line. There wasn't one.

"You've got to be kidding," he said and attempted a self-assured laugh. How did they even track him down? No one had been around. He'd worn gloves, so no fingerprints.

"Let me show you something," the officer said. He pushed a button on his phone and a video played. Chase watched, a pit forming inside his stomach. *The neighbors recorded it? How could this happen?* The video ended, and the officer sat back in his chair, staring at Chase.

It was time to use his get-out-of-jail-free card: his cousin Bobby. Frankly, Bobby owed him anyway since he'd done all this at the request of his dear cousin. He'd get out of this mess somehow.

"I'd like to make a call," he said.

The officer chuckled. "Of course you would." He turned to another officer and arranged for a phone.

Minutes later, Chase fumed when his call to Bobby went to voice mail. Chase wouldn't snitch on his relative; he was simply going to ask him to send an attorney. Family was family, even if he was in this mess because of his cousin. He hung up the phone after leaving a brief message that simply said where he was and why. A few minutes later, he sat back down and stared at the cop who seemed to be smirking. *Cocky bastard.* He'd be waiting for a while; Chase wasn't going to say anything until he spoke to Bobby.

"So, your good ol' cousin Bob didn't answer the phone, huh?" the officer asked. Chase froze. How did they know? Chase hadn't said anything. The cop continued. "Well, that's okay. Because we already talked to him. To be frank, your cousin says he hasn't talked to you in years. That he separated himself from the, and I quote, 'lowlifes in the family' years ago." His interrogator sat back, waiting for a response. His resolve to stay quiet fell away.

"You're bluffing."

"Am I? Would I make that up?" He raised his hands in an innocent gesture. "Bob said you two grew up a few houses apart. He was saddened to see that you'd thrown your life away dealing drugs."

Chase cringed. That sounded like something Bobby would say. And the information about their childhood was true. So that was how Bobby was going to repay him for all of this? Throw him under the bus? A lifetime of frustration all rose to the surface. All those times he'd covered for Bobby, took the blame for things because Bobby was the one who "had a chance to be someone," but he'd always look out for his little cousin. Always. Well, clearly that was a lie. Chase couldn't stop himself.

"Son of a . . . *he's* going to judge *me*? Really? Mr. High and Mighty is just as bad as I am. Hell, maybe worse. He's convinced everyone he's this wonderful, family-loving angel when that's about as far from the truth as you can get. In fact, he is *worse* than me. At least I own up to what I do. Who I am. Bobby's a full-on hypocrite!" he blurted. "All right, I'll tell you what I know. But I want a deal first."

"I'll tell you what. You give me something worth knowing, and I'll tell the DA you cooperated. That's the deal. Fact is we've already got you. We don't need your cousin to make anything stick here. Got it?" The officer waited with his brow raised. Chase sighed in frustration.

"I put the damn letter in there for him. It all started because of something about photos. I don't know the details," he said and then launched into a full recounting of his cousin's recent activities.

~

"That was impressive." Shoals complimented Ted after he stepped out of the interrogation room and followed him down the hall. "I have to ask—was *any* of what you told him true?"

Ted stopped and grinned. "It wasn't hard to track down their history and figure some things out. I just built on that. And it worked."

"I wonder how he'll feel when he learns that we really only had him for tampering with mail until he started to fess up to all the other stuff, which is also going to give us what we need to tie Robert to the shooting incident with Rachel."

"Yeah, and tie Chase back to an attempted murder plot because of what his cousin had done in the first place. Guess it's clear why Bobby was the one with the more advanced career. Too bad he ended up being a bad seed." Ted started to turn to the right when they entered a large room, but then he paused to speak to Shoals again. "Thanks for putting in so much extra time on this. And getting all of that information out of Oliver."

Shoals nodded and headed the other way, appearing embarrassed by the praise. Ted laughed under his breath because he could be the same way.

~

Nola sipped her coffee as she stared out her bay windows at the bright wintery scene around her. It had been a day since she'd received the news, but she still couldn't believe Anson was dead. While their relationship had started off as more of a business arrangement, somewhere along the way she developed real feelings for him. Then there was that one night—a few glasses of wine, the moonlight creating a shimmering path on Lake Tahoe as if leading right up to where they stood on Anson's pier. Nola wasn't big on romance, but that night had sure put her in the mood. The sex had been mind-blowing. Well, she didn't have the luxury of dwelling on that right now.

"That bitch!" she cursed, her thoughts on Kristina Drew and that other fucking tree hugger. She had just days to do what she could to make sure those women didn't completely mess up the final vote for the Tahoe-Truckee Pines project at the upcoming board meeting. It would have been so much better if they'd both been kept out of the way a bit longer, as originally planned. Unfortunately, with the discovery of those last-minute changes, her clients were going to have to give up a little profit in order to move the bigger picture forward. They could afford it; in fact, money had never been the primary issue. They'd simply wanted to increase their profits, and she was going to be the one getting the kudos. Now, her additional reward was in jeopardy as well as her promotion.

No matter what it took, those women would pay. Somewhere, somehow. Nola could be very patient.

Anson's face flashed through her memory again. Ironically, it had originally been her idea to work with Anson after they'd met several years ago. They both realized if they spread the public's attention thin by pursuing their large projects at the same time, and did so while Placer County was also updating the twenty-year land-use plan, they were more likely to get approval for the Tahoe-Truckee Pines project. Nonprofits and other members of the public don't have the financial resources her clients do nor the staff to scour through layers upon layers of environmental and legal documents. It had been imperative for both of them, once Anson had invested in it personally, to ensure the ridgeline project was approved. Getting a permit for the large resort in Tahoma was going to be a bonus, but it was also expendable; if something had to be compromised for the greater good, the Tahoma project was it. Not that Anson's partners knew that or about his connections to Nola.

He'd offered once to tell her how he'd planned to resolve the poorly timed questions from Miss Drew. She hadn't wanted to know. When one of them went missing, it wasn't difficult to figure out who was involved. A small part of her had wondered if the woman had been killed or simply held somewhere. Either way, she had plausible deniability if he got caught. Just another woman who didn't fully know the man she was dating. A blow to her pride, yes, but nothing that could land her in jail.

Her ringing phone broke her reverie. Caller ID indicated it was her friend at the county attorney's office. Not all was lost. She smiled as she answered.

Chapter 32

Two Days Later

Kris walked into Derek's hospital room. Butterflies fluttered in her stomach. Why was she so nervous? He looked up from his tablet and smiled. Those dimples of his could really catch a girl off guard.

"Hey." He set the device aside.

"Hey. How ya feeling?"

"Better. Guess I'm getting released today."

"Going to Rachel's?" Kris asked as she sat in the chair next to his bed.

"Yep. I know she's dealing with a slight postconcussion relapse, so I promised to be quiet and watch movies all day. She's being far more accommodating; I think I've gotten more mileage out of this whole 'brother almost died' thing than I anticipated." He laughed.

"For how long?"

"Few days, maybe."

"Then what?" She wasn't sure what she wanted to hear as his answer. Kris wasn't looking for a relationship. Sure, she'd been attracted to him, but it couldn't work; it wasn't meant to. So why did her mind even go down that road?

"I'll head home. I need to get back to work. I've already missed a business trip to France this week; hopefully I can still make it there for a few days. We have a very promising client." He wrung his hands. Perhaps he wasn't the only one feeling the discomfort in the room.

"Good. Honestly, I hope it works out," she said. "Is she coming to pick you up?"

"Yes, I'll text her when they are ready to release me." He looked around the room, clearly anxious to leave.

"Heard from Luke?" Kris was still surprised Rachel and Luke broke up last weekend. It was difficult to imagine them apart. It was just another reason she assumed it best to avoid entanglements. Nothing other than pain came of them.

"No, but to be honest, I know more about that than I've told you or Rachel. But there's no point in my getting involved now. I'll just say that Luke and I aren't exactly on each other's friends list at the moment. Not that I don't respect the hell out of what he did for us Monday night. But there are some things I can't overlook when it comes to my sister."

So Kris had been right after all. Deep down she sensed Derek was holding back, though she hadn't pressed the issue. He was correct; it was up to Rachel and Luke to deal with it, if they wanted to. The room grew silent. Kris sighed.

"Okay, let's stop beating around the bush." She finally got the words out. Kris disliked awkward conversations. She almost laughed when Derek's expression changed to a deer-in-the-headlights look. It lasted for a mere second or two before transforming to unreadable.

"I agree. Look, I—"

"I'm not looking for a relationship," she said, cutting him off. His reaction surprised her. Was he annoyed?

"Well, n . . . neither am I," he stuttered. "Not sure why you'd have thought otherwise." He looked down and began studying his knuckles intently.

Awareness dawned inside Kris. "Oh my gosh, you thought I'd be coming in here and begging you to stay, didn't you?"

"Of course not." The speed of his response only solidified her suspicion. He had expected to be the one breaking *her* heart!

"Liar." She smirked.

"I'm not—"

"It's okay. If that's what you need to think to sustain that delicate ego of yours, feel free," she said. "I've got to get back to work; just wanted to see how you're doing." She smiled and turned to leave.

"Hey, Kris," he called out. She pivoted back to face him. "Thanks for saving my life." It was the first time Kris had seen such a serious look on his face.

"You're welcome," she said with a smile and turned again to leave. As she walked out, she spoke over her shoulder, "You owe me one, Derek Winters, and I always collect."

She heard him laugh and call out from inside the room, "I'm counting on it, Kristina Drew."

~

Rachel closed the heavy wooden door behind her and turned. Bella and Avi rushed to greet her. As usual upon her arrival home, Bella clasped a toy in her mouth as if presenting a gift to Rachel. Avi's muzzle went for her toes, but upon discovering boots, she switched to sniffing fingers instead.

"You girls are so sweet," Rachel commented as she placed the day's mail on the small table before kneeling down to pet them both. She thought again of the threatening letter she'd found days ago in a similar stack. Both men were behind bars now: Robert McDonnel, for shooting at her from the snowmobile, and his cousin Chase, the apparent mastermind behind the thankfully unsuccessful dognapping plan. Her phone rang, pulling her out of her reverie. She looked at the display.

"Hi, Ted," she answered while slipping out of her boots.

"Rachel, how ya doing?"

"Hanging in there." Rachel carefully balanced the phone on her shoulder as she removed her coat, her eyes glancing longingly at the couch. Her body felt like she'd just run a marathon, not made a simple trip to the store. She almost forgot about Ted until he spoke again.

"Good. I wanted to let you know we had to let Nola go."

Rachel wasn't surprised. The woman had been questioned extensively by the police but had adamantly claimed to simply be dating Anson and been clueless about his illegal activities. Ted confessed to Rachel he believed she was involved in some way, but Nola was a smart woman. She'd covered her tracks well. Every call and visit could easily be explained by a relationship.

When the cops learned Anson had previously been involved in a suspicious fire in Colorado that had caused the death of one of his partners—one that had disagreed with the direction he was taking the company—Nola's contention that he acted alone had been considered much more plausible by the district attorney.

"I figured she'd find a way to slither out of this one," Rachel sighed as she plopped down on her sofa. The girls climbed up next to her, competing for attention from her free arm. "Convincing people of half-truths and misleading facts is what she's paid to do."

"Unfortunately, there's no definitive proof at this time. That doesn't mean we won't be keeping an eye on her," Ted assured. "Did you get in touch with the county about what Kris found in those permitting files?"

"Yeah, they revised the permit language. It will cost the developer more money, but compared to the billions in profits they stand to make, I don't think they'll care much. I suspect Nola was so intent on getting it approved just to make herself look good for saving them millions. It doesn't seem like something large enough to have hinged the entire project on. I still think there's more to the story, especially given Anson's investment in it. I guess we can only do what we can." She exhaled and lay back on her couch. Avi started to crawl on top of Rachel's stomach, inching her muzzle closer to her face. Over the last few days she'd quickly learned that if she didn't stop the pup's advance, she'd be subjected to a string of wet dog kisses by a creature reluctant to move off of her. Rachel gently nudged the canine from her belly. "What's the word on the Palinskis?" She knew search crews had uncovered two sets of remains the day before.

"Both under arrest. The son claims his father killed those people and he was too afraid to ever say anything for fear of reprisal. Thomas also paid his bills, so I doubt he wanted to threaten that luxurious arrangement. Of course, Thomas claims it was Oliver and he only helped cover it up to protect his son."

"Thomas actually admitted to knowing about both of the murder victims?"

"Sure did. I don't think he intended to. My guess is he slipped up and mentioned bodies in the plural sense, then tried to think fast of how to take the least amount of blame. He probably banked on people's tendency to forgive parents for doing extreme things to protect their children."

She heard someone call Ted's name in the background. "I've got to go. Catch you later." The call abruptly ended, and Rachel tossed the phone onto her coffee table. The excitement of her arrival home had waned, and the two dogs jumped off the couch and bounded out back. Rachel smiled as she stood and walked toward the kitchen. The girls were running in circles, playing chase. She thought of the other dog they'd found at Oliver's house and was grateful a local animal welfare group had taken it in.

She heard a knock on her door. Rachel walked across the room and opened it. Luke stood on her front porch. A sense of déjà vu fell over her. Same spot, same sexy mussed hair as the night before they'd called things off. The lone difference was that he hadn't shaved in days. Damn that scruffy beard; it was hot as hell. A large bruise covered his left cheek from his fight with Anson.

"You're not here for another booty call, are you?" she joked, a strategy she tended to take when she was nervous.

Luke grinned. "No, not that I don't want one whenever I look at you." His expression grew serious. "I just wanted to see how you were doing." He leaned against the doorframe. He didn't ask to come in, nor did she invite him.

"I'm fine. Tuesday was a bit of a crash; thankfully, I'm starting to feel better again now." She'd spent most of the day in bed or on the couch when the heavy "concussion fatigue" had slammed into her again after Monday's events.

"Good," he said.

"I heard you solved a cold case?"

"Yeah, in fact, I had been trying to identify a young man in an old picture with the victim. Now I know it was Oliver Palinski. Small world." Rachel nodded, and then the room grew silent. "So, where do we go from here?" he finally asked.

"I don't know. I think we definitely need some space," she admitted, shifting her weight from one foot to the other. She vowed she would not let him see her cry over this.

"I agree. I have some stuff I need to work on for myself, ya know?" He tipped his head and averted her gaze. "And there are some things I haven't told you, but I'm not ready to yet."

"Yeah, I've got some issues of my own, I think." She nodded as the ache in her heart tightened.

"Stay in touch?" he asked tentatively, his voice hoarse, cracking like hers did when she was struggling to hold back emotion. He looked over her shoulder, the dogs in back likely having caught his eye.

"Yes, let's do that," she replied.

He refocused on her. "I, uh . . ." He slowly closed the few inches between them. She didn't move. He raised his hands and cupped her cheeks, gently drawing their faces together. At first, his lips merely brushed hers, and then heat burst through her as he strengthened the kiss. Without thinking, she reached behind him and wrapped her arms around his back. She wasn't sure how long their bodies stood there intertwined before a heavy weight crashed into the back of her legs, breaking the connection. Rachel stepped back and looked down. Bella and Avi stood next to her expectantly, shifting their attention between her and Luke. He bent down and rubbed both sets of ears, and then he straightened and backed out of the doorway with regret and sorrow in his expression.

"Goodbye, Rachel," he whispered as moisture filled his eyes.

"Goodbye, Luke," she said and then slowly closed the door. Rachel barely managed to walk the short distance to her living area before tears overwhelmed her. She dropped down on her sofa and hung her head down, too tired to hold off her inner turmoil any longer. Her brain understood that they needed space, but her heart was breaking inside. Two cold, wet noses pressed against her cheek. She looked up, her vision blurred. Bella and Avi were at her side with somber looks on their faces. Bella nudged her arm and then moved into a full cuddle against Rachel. Avi mimicked Bella's behavior, rubbing against Rachel's other leg.

"My sweet girls, come here," she said, patting the couch. They jumped up on either side of her. She closed her eyes and encased them both in a tight embrace.

If you loved the book and have a minute to spare, a short review on the page or site where you bought the book would be greatly appreciated. In addition, your feedback helps guide the future adventures of Rachel, Bella, and Avi.

For updates, newsletters, previews, and other information, visit www.mountaingirlmysteries.com and the *Mountaingirl Mysteries* Facebook page. And don't forget to sign up for the *Mountaingirl Mysteries* newsletter (via the website)!

ACKNOWLEDGMENTS

I am deeply thankful to the following people, without whom I would not have been able to write this book:

My parents, Carol and Terry, who are always there to help me get through the tough times and celebrate the good ones, and who once again reviewed the (choppy) first draft of the manuscript to give me the initial thumps up or down determination. On another note, I am also extremely thankful to them for putting me on snow skis when I was four years old.

My sister, Shelley, who always finds a way to be there for me when I need her (and even better, tends to bring a bottle of Bonterra with her).

My Aunt Linda, fellow "mountaingirl" and avid skier, key manuscript reviewer, and dear friend.

My amazing and supportive friends. I honestly couldn't do this without them.

Richard Bodisco, JoAnn Conner, and Gayle Wedgwood, who took the time to carefully read the draft manuscript and provide invaluable feedback, and then patiently waited to see it come to fruition after I delayed the original release.

The talented and dedicated Tahoe Writers Works authors for their ongoing encouragement, moral support, honest commentary, and astute editing skills.

Mary Cook, an amazing copy editor, whose time and expertise helped polish all three *Mountaingirl Mysteries*.

Kristen Schwartz, a talented cover designer, who created a beautiful book cover and visually appealing interior.

And of course, last but not least, my canine "girls," Bella and Avi, who make my life exceptionally better every single day.

AUTHOR'S NOTES

Sierra Nevada Dangerous Developments was in large part delayed by the long recovery associated with a concussion I sustained after an unfortunate encounter with a tree while skiing (which bears a slight resemblance to Rachel's accident in this book). I am so appreciative to my readers for their understanding, patience, and encouragement during these past two years.

Of course, Bella and Avi have been here to help me, too. Avi came into our lives in the spring of 2016, and I could not ask for a better "sister" for Bella. Unfortunately, Avi's life appears to have been rough before she made her way into our hearts and home. But she's here now, and we are all better for it.

On that note, for those who are looking for the amazing companionship a dog can provide, I encourage you to do some research into breed characteristics with your lifestyle in mind. After that, if you decide to add a dog to your family, please first consider adoption/rescue. It won't be long before you find yourself asking exactly who rescued whom.

Jennifer Quashnick holds a master's degree in environmental science and health and has spent over twenty years advocating for scientifically supported policy making to protect Lake Tahoe's environment and rural communities. She also makes a point to spend regular time hiking with her dogs, Bella and Avi, refreshed by the beauty of the Sierra Nevada and the joy of being outdoors.

Jennifer's creative side emerged when she adopted Bella and became inspired by the dog's antics. The *Mountaingirl Mysteries* series is a result of regular time outdoors; years of hard work in environmental science, planning, and politics; and two dogs named Bella and Avi.

Raised on a small ranch in Northern California, Jennifer's childhood revolved around an outdoor lifestyle with weekends and summers spent in the mountains. Jennifer loves all that the Sierra Nevada has to offer, although she is most fond of hiking, snowshoeing, and downhill skiing, and is typically accompanied by Bella and Avi—the true stars of her books.

Made in the USA
Columbia, SC
13 April 2018